Georgina Newbery grew up in Cambridge. She went to a convent school despite the fact that she wasn't and still isn't a Catholic, and where she shocked her mother into saying that she hadn't s[illegible] Georgina away to become a clothes snob. An abiding passion for fashion was [illegible] Polytechnic she lived and worked i[illegible] department in Europe [illegible] current company. She now di[illegible]

Catwalk

GEORGINA NEWBERY

A *Warner* Book

First published in Great Britain in 1997
by Warner Books

A CIP catalogue record for this book
is available from the British Library.

ISBN 0 7515 1940 5

Typeset in Perpetua by M Rules
Printed and bound in Great Britain by
Clays Ltd, St Ives plc

Warner Books
A Division of
Little, Brown and Company (UK)
Brettenham House
Lancaster Place
London WC2E 7EN

Emily has been working for Nina for a little under six weeks. Everything besides the Nick part of this diary makes her feel sick.

To my godchildren, Sasha and Mia

Acknowledgements

I WOULD like to thank Serena Cullen, Susan Train, Alex Tarn, David Tusa, Gill Coleridge and, most importantly, Geoff Richards and Mike Pohling for not cutting me off without a penny.

Prologue

Thursday 13 July, Emily Carlton-Jones, assistant to Nina Charles, editor-in-chief of the biggest fashion magazine in the UK, has a diary that looks like this:

Friday 14 July

Confirm hotels for couture. Superior Queen for Rory at the Crillon. Usual suite for Nina. What's the usual suite?

9.30	Nina hair – confirm colour	*Get couture schedule started!!!!!!!!*
11.00	Meeting – features. Budget cut	
1 p.m.	Nina to lunch with publisher – where? SF's? Ivy? SL's?	Ring Morgan *PERSONAL* – for once!
4 p.m.	Get NYC – confirm Don Elson plans	Check Rory's shows for couture and fax houses
	Party meeting with Nina. Get list out. Finally	

Try and check that Nick and Morgan managed to get it together with Pandora and Max for lifts down.

MY TWENTY FIRST BIRTHDAY PARTY

5 p.m. *Leave early for PARTY – fat chance!* Max is coming Max is coming

Max Max Max Max Max Max Max Max Max Max Max Max Max Max Max Max Max Max Max

SATURDAY 15 JULY

Gloria in New York – overcoat story. Staying Royalton. Film to be in office Tuesday a.m.

WEEKEND THANK GOD – RECOVER

SUNDAY 16 JULY

RECOVER MORE AND DREAD MONDAY

MONDAY 17 JULY

9 a.m.	Nina hair	*Confirm flowers*
10.30	Couture shoot meeting	*Champagne*
12.30	Nina lunch Gloria – ask where to book	*Food, tent, check everything again*
2 p.m.	Management meeting – rough up November book	
4 p.m.	OK September for printing – make sure OK for couture	
5.30	Conference call Knowle McLulack – 555 447 6341	
7 p.m.	Nina dinner Saul – at Saul's house Order car	

Tuesday 18 July

Don't forget to bring your party dress
Gloria's film in
Get the Rolodeks on computer – likely
Go over Pandora's shows with Nina – why can't her agent do it? Stupid
Nina out of office nearly all day – fab
6.30 Nina's party – HELP

Wednesday 19 July

8.30 Breakfast Chanel for the advertising department – Claridges
10.00 Budget meeting – 12th floor. Get out forecasts till end March next yr – if you can work out how to print the spreadsheets
Nothing else – yet

Thursday 20 July

Finalise plans for couture – make Nina OK runway list to be shot. Fax Sly in Paris. Get him to confirm his price. $? £? FF?
1 p.m. Lunch Nina's mother at Nina's house. Tell Mrs Davies to order in.

Friday 21 July

9 a.m. Features Jan. Remind Nina about food in Florence piece – decided but not commissioned. Ulster peace story? Get Alan the dangerous missions man in. Where from? At least he's Jewish!

11.30	Final pre-couture meeting

SATURDAY 22 JULY

11.30	Train to Paris NC, RW and me. Wow, first-class too.
3 p.m.	Hair and make-up – Hotel Crillon TBC Who does she want? Korin Van Der Donk
6.30	Versace, Ritz Hotel, Place Vendôme
8.30	Versace party, Ritz Hotel, Place Vendôme

SUNDAY 23 JULY

9 a.m.	Hair and make-up – Hotel Crillon TBC	Max in Paris
11.30	Lacroix – Hotel Scribe	Fax????
1 p.m.	Lunch Gianfranco – TBC	
4 p.m.	Givenchy – address to be confirmed by carrier pigeon the morning of the show. They can't be serious surely?	
8.30	Dinner Karl TBC – not the night before his show, surely?	

MONDAY 24 JULY

9 a.m.	Hair and make-up Hotel Crillon – TBC
10.30	Dior – Caroussel du Louvre
12.00	Chanel – Caroussel du Louvre
5.30	Valentino – Hotel Ritz

TUESDAY 25 JULY

9.30	Hair and make-up – TBC
11 a.m.	Yves Saint Laurent – Caroussel du Louvre

4 p.m. Train home – everyone. TBC

WEDNESDAY 26 JULY

Can't stay empty for long – maybe I'll get some time off. Fat chance!

THURSDAY 27 JULY

I expect it'll be a nightmare
Mum's birthday – Flowers DON'T FORGET!!!!!!!!

FRIDAY 28 JULY

9.30 Mark Bozo w.book
10 a.m. Daisy F – look see
Otherwise . . . empty

SATURDAY 29 JULY

Couture shoot???????? TBC Where?
Who with?
Which girls to be shot?
What to shoot?
Fuck if I care. I hope nobody ever reads this.

SUNDAY 30 JULY

Home at last????????

Emily has been working for Nina for a little over three weeks. This diary makes her feel sick.

Chapter 1

Friday 14 July

Nina Charles swept through the editorial offices of the largest and most glossy British fashion magazine like a sudden gust of wind, leaving files upended, stories binned, layouts rehashed. She smiled sweetly at her exhausted staff and sat down behind her desk, carefully appointed so that she had a birds-eye view over every member of her team. Who cared if the weather was like something out of the first chapter of *Jane Eyre*? Nina Charles was editor-in-chief of this wonderful little world, and everything in it was perfect today. She called for her new assistant, Emily, carefully pointed out the faults in the layout of her desk and asked for some sushimi to be ordered in for her working lunch with the publisher; not sushi, too much rise, so heavy. Emily, short and chic, dressed from head to foot in Jigsaw as she couldn't yet afford Joseph, religiously wrote down everything, trying not to look too frantic as she scribbled notes on her block. Finally Nina reached for her mail file and found, to her great surprise, a message from her old friend Andreï Fyodov. Would she call him at his London flat? Curious, she gave the number to Emily and asked her to get him on the line for her. What could the old devil want?

'Right, Nina. Oh, one more thing. Gay Smith wants to confirm the couture backstage. She wants two assistants. She says someone must carry a light for her or she absolutely can't shoot anything. I tried to tell her nobody would ever give her three backstage passes but she was very insistent. She wants to speak to you.'

'Emily, be firmer. As far as Gay's concerned I'm out of the office until Christmas. Just fob her off. She'll be all right. She always tries this one. She's lucky if she gets one pass for herself, let alone one for an assistant. You just tell her in the nicest possible way to go and jump in the nearest lake.'

Emily sighed. 'I'll try. Oh, and Nina, you said I could leave early today. For my birthday party. Is that still all right?'

'You've only been here three weeks and you're already taking liberties.' Nina smiled. 'Of course you can go early. Remind me, though, or I'm liable to pile work on you at the last minute.'

'Thanks, Nina. I'll go and get Mr Fyodov on the phone for you.'

While she waited for the call to come through, Nina flipped through the rest of the mail and found a fax from her editorial director. To her horror, Don Elson was coming to London and naturally wanted to lunch with her. Her fantastic good mood was ruined. She hated having to behave like an employee when she was used to being the boss. And Don was such a slimeball, expecting ass-licking whether he deserved it or not. Another staff reshuffle, Nina thought as she picked up the phone, a smile in her voice, and welcomed Andreï Fyodov to London before asking him what on earth he wanted from her.

Only on such a filthy English summer day could Sam McAllistair have returned to the UK. As Concorde came in to land over the vulgar green of the fields surrounding south-west London, the rain set in. Resigned to a typical English summer, he put on his sweater and prepared to suffer the horrors of Heathrow at the beginning of the tourist season.

In a daze of disgust he queued for passport control and tried to find a sign for the Underground. No such thing – all his fellow passengers seemed to have drivers waiting for them. He kicked himself for being stupid enough to turn down Andreï Fyodov's offer of a chauffeur-driven car, and headed off blindly into the maze of Terminal 4.

'Mr McAllistair! Mr McAllistair! Stop, please!' Sam turned to find himself being chased by a young man who could have been classed as a tramp if it weren't for his unmistakable public-school accent and an air of such self-confidence that begging or mugging would have been done with much more style. 'Thank God I found you. Please don't tell my father I was late. His driver's on holiday and he said I absolutely had to collect you or he'd cut off my allowance for terms to come – sorry to sound so mercenary, but he's like that. He's probably serious. He told me specially to be on time or I'd miss you . . . Sorry.' The boy held out his hand. 'Max Fyodov, I'm Andreï's son.'

'No kidding!'

Sam could well believe it. Before him was the spitting image of his friend Andreï, the likeness remarkable right down to the different-coloured eyes and the shock of white-blond hair. All the boy lacked was the scar.

'Well, nice to meet you. I didn't think anyone was going to be here and I had every intention of taking the tube into London, but as you took the trouble . . .'

'Right, come on then, the car's just out here. Where am I taking you?' Before Sam had time to answer, Max had grabbed one of his cases and was off into the crowd. Sam hurried after the ancient flying jacket, ripped jeans and grimy baseball cap to an equally battered open-topped car which Max, stroking the bonnet lovingly, introduced as 'my *danseuse*'.

'Shove your bags behind.' Sam nervously packed his luggage into the joke of a back seat, wondering how much of it would still be there by the time they reached London. Max laughed and jumped into the car. 'I'd put it all in the boot for you, but there's so much shit in there already that there really isn't room.'

For a second Sam couldn't work out why Max was staring at him with his eyebrows raised. Then he realised that he hadn't told the boy where he was going. Gingerly trying the handle of the passenger door he grinned. 'Sorry,' he apologised. 'I'm a bit disorientated. I'm going to the Savoy, if it's not too far out of your way.'

'Let's go then!' Max roared into the nose-to-tail Heathrow traffic. Sam hung on, trying not to flinch too openly.

Max ignored his passenger, turned up the Pearl Jam CD and glowered at the road.

Emily sat and chewed her fingernails, staring distractedly at the pile of work Nina had left for her on her desk. It was her twenty-first birthday party that night, and she was even more nervous than she'd been before she started working for Nina. All those people, in her house, with her mother. She groaned.

'Emily!'

She looked up, blushing guiltily as Nina called from her office.

'What on earth's the matter? You've been sitting there for hours looking as if the weight of the world's problems is on your shoulders and not dealing with the Paris schedule at all.'

'Sorry, Nina. I'll finish it right now.'

'Finish it! We're a week away. It'll change every day. Just make sure that the people I told you I wanted to meet with are going to be available, and tell them we'll confirm dates and times when we get there.'

Emily nodded.

'Well, you'd better get your block so you can tell me where you've got to, hadn't you?'

Emily blushed again. She hated being told she wasn't doing something right, and ever since she'd started working for Nina Charles she hadn't seen a day go past without a stream of imperfections in her work being pointed out to her. She'd thought a fashion magazine would be fun! Well, so far it was just a grind of lunch appointments and people shouting at her because they didn't dare shout at her boss. She grabbed her block from her desk and went over to Nina, who barely looked up from the layouts in front of her.

'Lacroix.'

'Done, dinner after his show.'

'Galliano.'

'Done, lunch late in the week. He'll confirm back.'

'Ferré.'

'Don't know yet.'

What did his assistant say?'

'I left a message. She hasn't called back yet.'

'Well, call again. You can't expect other people to do your work for you.'

'Yes, Nina . . . Except . . . um . . . I can't today. It's a bank holiday in France.'

'I know the French like to give their employees incredible benefits, but I doubt the fax machines have the day off as well. You could always try that avenue, don't you think?'

'Yes. Of course. Sorry, I didn't think.'

Nina sniffed. 'And Karl?'

'You said you'd do that yourself.'

'Right. OK. And when did Don's office say he'd be back?'

'They said he'd call you when he'd firmed up his schedule and knew when he'd have time to see you.'

Nina swallowed hard. How dare Don make her look like a little nobody, especially in front of a new assistant.

'All right, Emily. Send him a fax, will you? Tell him I'm free for lunch the day after my party, make sure he's got a copy of the party invitation and tell him I'll meet him at the Groucho Club at one. Let me check it, but you can sign it.'

'Right, Nina.'

'And tell Gloria I'm free any time after five if she wants to drop by and talk about the New York shoot before she leaves for the airport.'

'OK. She came in and said she'd like to see you some time. You were on the phone, otherwise I would have told you.'

'All right.'

'Gay rang again.'

'I told you, Emily, I don't want to hear her name again until after the collections.'

'Yes, Nina.'

'Right. And now you could nip down to the art department and get me those pages of September they promised I'd have before the end of the afternoon. At the rate we're going, the book's going to be half-empty.'

'The book?'

'The magazine, dear. Learn your vocab or you'll never understand a word anyone says round here.'

'Sorry.'

'Stop apologising, Emily! Go on, get me the pages.' Emily didn't move fast enough. 'Now!'

'Right.' Emily, flustered, hurried down the corridor. She prayed that Nina would never see her block, which, after a list of instructions, was always a mess of scribbles that she found hard to decipher herself. When she was out of Nina's line of sight she stopped and went through the list so that she would have some idea of what it said when she returned to her desk. She sighed. At least she wouldn't have time to feel nervous about her party until she left the office.

Nina smiled to herself. Poor Emily. She would learn. She picked up her phone to call Rory. Now here was someone who should know better. She hadn't seen him in the office for nearly a week!

Morgan James jumped at her mother's voice calling from the kitchen.

'Aren't you supposed to be catching the two o'clock to London?'

Shit, she'd forgotten that it was Emily's party and she'd promised to go to Pandora's so they could all get a lift down to Surrey with Max. She hadn't even packed.

'Mum, I forgot the time. Can you give me a lift to the station? I'll miss the train and Pandora'll kill me if I'm late – failing that she'll probably leave without me and I don't even know where we're going!'

'OK. Hurry up, though. I've got a meeting in college and they're so used to my being late they'll definitely start without me. I've got so much to say to that twit of a Dean that for once I really don't want to miss it.'

Anna James shrugged on an ancient green sweater so

full of holes she sometimes wondered why she bothered putting it on at all for all the warmth it gave her, and started to search for the car keys. She knew that it would take her about the same amount of time to find the keys as it would for Morgan to pack and be ready to leave.

Two minutes later, Morgan was standing by the kitchen door, looking pointedly at the clock. She still had her waist-length red hair held in a knot by a chewed biro, and she hadn't bothered to change out of the dungarees she'd worn to help her mother paint the hall. Anna finally found the car keys under the cat and, shrieking with triumph, rushed out of the door, slamming it behind her before realising that she didn't have the papers she needed for the meeting, and that she'd forgotten her house keys. Morgan laughed as Anna stood by the door looking nonplussed.

'Don't worry, Mum, the Dean would really die of shock if you turned up on time for a meeting. Best not to do that to him when he's so close to retirement. The bathroom window is open, so you'll be able to get back in again.'

Anna sighed. Another afternoon battling with a wobbly stepladder and the dodgy bathroom window was all she needed.

Max, having decided that he'd never find a legal parking space, announced to the doorman at the Savoy that Mr McAllistair wouldn't be needing his car until 4.30, at which point he, Mr McAllistair's driver, would return to collect it. Sam gave Max an amused grin – typical Fyodov behaviour – shook his hand and thanked him for the lift before heading towards a drink and a bath in his suite.

Max leapt into a taxi and told the driver to take him to the Ivy. As the cab headed towards Trafalgar Square, his heart sank. He hated lunching with his father.

Minutes later, he was walking into the restaurant.

'Afternoon, Max,' came the cheery greeting from the coat girl. 'Take your jacket?'

'It's OK – I'll keep it.'

'Your father's at his usual table.'

'Thanks.'

Max headed through the main room of the restaurant towards the corner banquette table that his father always used. As soon as this ordeal was over he could head off to Esher and spend the whole weekend with all those lovely girls – perhaps life wasn't so bad after all. He was smiling by the time he came to kiss his father hello. Andreï grimaced back.

'Max. Nice to see you shaved and put on a tie for me,' he sneered. 'Meet up with Sam all right?'

'Yes, Father. Safely dropped off at the Savoy.'

Andreï's features softened a little. 'How was he? Seem all right? Not too exhausted?'

Max looked up in surprise. For once in his life, Andreï actually sounded concerned about someone else.

'Yeah, I suppose so. Didn't say much, though, just stared at me the whole way to London like I'm some kind of freak or something.'

Andreï snorted. 'No, my beautiful boy. He's just stunned at the likeness between us, that's all. Like it or not, we are very similar. Not every family has a long line of mismatched eyes to distinguish it.'

Max nervously poured a glass of wine from the bottle of Chablis cooling by the table. He got away with this audacity. Andreï had already begun his tirade.

'Projects, Max. Tell me your projects for the summer,' he snapped. 'I imagine you plan to skulk around Europe sponging off my endless generosity, as usual. No chance of you getting a job, I suppose?'

Max sipped at the beautiful Chablis – something to do while Andreï ranted.

'Actually, Father . . .'

'Don't interrupt, boy. No, of course you have no intention of earning a living for yourself. Absurd thought. Do you realise what you cost me every year? Of course not. You lounge about pretending to learn languages you already speak fluently. Chasing women – women with no family, no background, nothing. People like that James girl! I didn't make all this money for you to throw it away on a cheap little tart like her. Things have changed, Max. Gentlemanly pursuits will get you nowhere. And Morgan James is nothing more, probably less than that.'

Max kept his mouth shut and let the ice-cold white wine slip down his throat, cooling the angry words he would never have dared use in defence.

Lunch finished, Andreï left his son on the corner of the street without even a farewell. Max spat on the pavement. As he watched his father head off, he wondered if maybe he should get a job after all. The thought did not inspire him. What was the point of large quantities of inherited wealth if you didn't squander it? He set off to collect his car from the Savoy. House parties were always a perfect antidote to lunch with his father. This one he would think of as a reward.

Pandora Williams lay back on the huge bed and handed her Uncle Rory the joint she'd just lit. Her exceptionally long legs, black hair long enough to sit on, eyelashes that she liked to measure whenever she was feeling down, and the fact that she always wore black from head to toe all made her look like a river of black velvet. Rory looked at her. He hoped she would grow out of that petulant pout one of these days. She was beautiful, but he didn't know anyone else so spoilt, apart, perhaps, from himself.

'Cheer up, lovely, what's getting you down today?' he asked. Pandora shook out her hair and gave him one of her tragic queen looks.

'Darling Rory, I don't know what to do.'

'Let your Uncle Rory help, sweetheart – you know I'm the world's expert on other people's problems. It makes up for being so useless with my own.'

'I'm in a quandary.'

'Which two men is it this time?'

'How do you know my quandary concerns men?'

'Because, my precious, your quandaries always do! Let me guess: some gorgeous delivery boy with those fabulous legs that couriers always have, and a fabulously rich banker, and you can't choose between the two of them? Darling, go for the courier. I know from experience he'll be much less demanding than the banker, and, more importantly, much easier to be rid of when you've had enough!'

Pandora laughed and took back the joint, puffing and stretching at the same time.

'Not quite the two boys I know. They are both going to be at Emily's this weekend and I just can't decide between them.'

'Well, darling, I can't help you until I know what they look like, can I?'

'OK. Boy A is six foot, skinny as anything, with lovely floppy, streaky, blondy-browny hair and little round glasses. He always wears purple velvet trousers and big shirts. He drives a VW Beetle, silver, left-hand drive, and listens to a lot of Van Morrison. He's studying English and drama, is passionate about cricket and he fancies me so rotten he can hardly keep his tongue from hanging out when he sees me.'

'Money?'

'Not to speak of.'

'Parents I care about?'

'No.'

'Yuck – in Putney with his parents.'

'Wants out of life?'

'For Christ's sake, Rory, I haven't even snogged him yet. How the hell should I know what his deepest wishes are? Apart from going out with me, of course!'

'OK. Boy B?'

Pandora sighed and closed her eyes.

'Fabulous, fabulous, fabulous – just the business.' She sat up suddenly. 'But I can tell you now, when I've never got closer than a chaste little hello kiss, that he is the greatest bastard ever born.'

'Fabulous he may be, bastard he may be, but I need to know more than that to be able to help you at all, my little darling.'

'All right.' She shook her hair again purposefully. 'Here goes. He's tall, at least six foot three. White-blond hair slicked back but bits always fall forward. He's seriously clever – you can see from the way he never tries but always knows everything. Wears obvious clothes – falling-apart sweatshirts, ancient jeans, baseball boots. He never goes anywhere without his flying jacket – worth going out with him just for the jacket! Drives a prehistoric Spider which he calls his *danseuse* and loves much more than he'd ever love a girl. Studies French and Russian, lives in London and Paris, paints things, you know, portraits, walls and stuff . . . umm . . . He's just by far and away the most glamorous boy I've ever met.'

'Sounds like there's no contest.'

'Well, there is. Boy A would be so easy to have and get rid of. Boy B would be much too easy to fall in love with, and he's such a bastard . . .'

'Pandora, I despair of you. You are only contemplating Boy A because secretly you are a very nice girl who can't bear to let someone down, and you feel you'd be letting him down by not letting him have his wicked way with you. But you're bound to end up with the bastard Boy B anyway. That's the thing about bastards, they always get the girl.'

Pandora laughed and stubbed out the joint. She jumped up and ran to the wardrobe opposite the bed.

'Can I raid your wardrobe for this house party I'm going to?'

Rory sighed. 'Of course you can, darling. Fat chance I've got of having an occasion to wear anything worth hanging in a cupboard.'

'Why, what's happened to Craig?'

Rory burst into tears.

'It turned out he had a wife and two children in Bermondsey. The children are both under five. I had to send him home to them.' He squared his shoulders and wiped his eyes. 'I may be a slut occasionally, but I will never be labelled a home-breaker!'

'Good for you, darling.' Pandora blew a kiss to her uncle and started helping herself to his collection of clothes.

The doorbell rang and Pandora ran downstairs to answer it. Boy A stood outside with a bunch of wilting sunflowers in his hand.

'Pandora!'

'Nick, you're early. Come upstairs and help me pack and cheer up my uncle – his boyfriend's just dumped him. Don't worry, it wasn't serious, it was just the man who mended the roof for him the other day. He'll be over it by the end of the weekend.'

Pandora turned and ran back up the stairs. Nick followed sheepishly, holding the sunflowers.

'Rory, this is Nick.'

Rory raised his eyebrows questioningly. 'Boy A, I presume?' He held out his hand as if he expected it to be kissed. Embarrassed, Nick nodded, tongue-tied. Rory continued to talk, unfazed by Nick's silence. 'You are sweet, you brought me sunflowers. My favourite. Pandora, go and find a vase.'

Nick thought better of protesting that the flowers were for Pandora, and simply handed them over. Pandora giggled.

'Nick, talk to Rory. Don't worry, he won't bite. I've just got to pack. I'll be back in a minute. And get your own vase, you lazy thing.'

Pandora disappeared, and Nick turned to find Rory looking at him curiously.

'Sit down, Boy A. Aren't you lovely?'

Nick sat nervously on the arm of a nearby chair. Why did this strange man keep calling him Boy A? The only other space in the room was on the bed. Every other surface was covered in a plethora of clothes, shoes, photographs, ornaments and two packets of condoms spilling their contents.

Rory put on his polite, entertaining-people face.

'So you're all off to spend the weekend in Surrey somewhere?'

'Yes, it's a friend's twenty-first.'

'Yuck, you'll have a horrible time getting there. I stopped leaving London by car on a Friday night when it started taking longer to get out of it than before there were motorways.' Rory looked disgusted.

'Take no notice of my horrible uncle,' shouted Pandora from across the landing. 'He's such a townie that if you asked him where Surrey was he wouldn't have a clue.'

'Rubbish, it's next to Richmond – the other side of the world.'

The doorbell rang again.

'Would you be a sweetheart and go and open the door, Nick? I'm sure one of your lot.'

Nick headed down the stairs, relieved to be spared further questioning. When he opened the door, a man in dirty painter's overalls was standing there.

'You tell that man to keep his hands off my brother. He's married to Bianca and doesn't need any extra-terrestrial involvement to distract him.'

Nick looked at the man blankly.

'No good looking at me like that. You're probably one of them too. I'll tell the filthy bugger myself.'

As the man pushed past Nick, Morgan arrived.

'Hi, Nick. Thank God you're here. I've been walking around in circles for hours. I forgot my glasses and had to take my contacts out in the train because they were hurting so much, and I couldn't see a thing. First I bumped into your car, and then I saw your trousers glowing at me like a welcoming beacon. What a relief.'

Nick grinned.

'Welcome to the mad house.'

They headed back up the stairs, bumping into Pandora on the way.

'Come on, you guys. Let's wait for Max downstairs. There's a right rumpus going on in Rory's room.' She laughed and led them back downstairs.

When, finally, Max arrived, swearing at the Friday-afternoon traffic, Rory missed him. All he saw from the first-floor landing was a shock of blond hair and the flying jacket. He watched, amused, as Pandora was firmly seated in Boy A's car while Morgan James and her fantastic Pre-Raphaelite hair was carefully stowed in the passenger seat of the Spider.

Rory went back to his bedroom to call Nina.

'Hello, darling. My boyfriend's being protected. I thought you might like me to do some work.'

'Oh, go away and call me on Monday, Rory. You've missed all sorts of excitements today. Don's coming over next week. Perhaps you'd better get some things together to show him. You know how he likes to fire people who don't appear to be busy enough.'

'Oh, darling, don't worry about me. I've got enough on that old thing to blackmail him for a century. I'm safe. It's you that I'd worry about.'

'Rory, don't be ridiculous. We've only just had a reshuffle. Got to go. Gloria's here. Talk to you later, darling.'

'Wait! What are you doing later?'

'Working, Rory, making up for your lost time.'

'Don't be mean. There must be some moment when I can see you. Or do I have to call your sweet new assistant, that Pandora was so kind to find for you, to make an appointment?'

'Emily has quite enough to do without you wasting her time as well.'

'Why do you have to see Gloria?'

'She's my fashion director, darling. You are simply a paid

gossip. I have to meet with her. Besides, she's shooting in New York this weekend. Remember?'

'If you're not careful, I'll come and camp out on your doorstep until you agree to see me.'

'Why? Where's Pandora?'

'Gone to your assistant's birthday party.'

'Already?'

'Five minutes ago. Hilarious. The man she's after is after Morgan. There'll be fireworks if he doesn't watch it.'

'God, I'd better let Emily go then. Poor thing. At this rate all her guests will arrive before she does.'

'Nina, you are mean.'

'I'd forgotten! Shit. Listen, call me later at home. I need to talk to you about the couture. And Don.'

'Talk to me now!'

'Gloria is sitting patiently in front of me, fuming because I'm making her have dinner with Don tomorrow night. The least I can do is talk to her about her shoot. So no. I won't talk to you now. Call me later.'

Rory put the phone down and sniffed disapprovingly. Gloria indeed. How dull. He began to shuffle through a series of photographs of male models. Ugh, even duller.

Andreï's plane soared over southern England. He would much rather have stayed in London to catch up with Sam, but he knew that Sam would be so exhausted after his trip that he wouldn't be up to much. Besides, Nina would be able to look after him. Andreï had unfinished business in Paris which just wouldn't wait. He closed his eyes, exhausted.

'Are you all right, sir?' Andreï jumped at the pilot's enquiry.

'I'm fine,' he said impatiently.

'Sorry, sir, it's just that you cried out.' The pilot looked nervously at his employer, who had gone a pale shade of green and looked as if he might be sick.

For once Andreï was nonplussed 'Did I? Well, none of your business. How long till we land?'

'Should be there in another half an hour, sir. Le Bourget is alerted and ready for us to land. It's twenty-eight degrees in Paris and . . .'

'Oh, shut up! I couldn't care less about the fucking temperature.'

Andreï sat back in his seat, unsettled, and closed his eyes, only to find that the nightmare face of his dead wife was there, glued inside his eyelids. He grabbed the *Wall Street Journal* that he'd picked up at the airport and tried to concentrate on the news from the other side of the Atlantic. 'You'll not get the better of me you bitch,' he thought.

Almost exactly beneath his father's plane, Max, trying to break Morgan's reserve, was becoming increasingly irritated by her refusal to talk.

'Great weather for a party.' Max kicked himself. Talk about a clichéd way to start a conversation.

'Mmm.'

'Have you been down to Emily's before?'

'No.'

'Good thing I know the way, then.'

'Yes.'

Long pause while Max searched his brain to find something Morgan might be interested in talking about. She just wouldn't communicate. He wasn't to know that she was so frightened of the sheer electricity which pounded out of him that she couldn't think how to speak to him at all.

'Are you going away this summer? On holiday?'

'No. I'm working all summer.'

'Oh. Shame. You could have come out to Paris for a while.'

'Yes, I suppose so.' Morgan closed her eyes and felt the warmth of the evening sun begin to work on her freckles. With any luck he would take the hint and think she was asleep.

'How do you know Emily?' Hmm – another inane question.

'Through Pandora. They were at school together, I think.'

'Right.' Another long pause. Max was getting desperate.

'How do you know Pandora?'

'I don't know – I've known her all my life. My mother knows her Uncle Rory. What is this? Some kind of social categorising?'

'No, no. I'm just curious, that's all.'

'Listen, I'm not one of these mad social London girls who throw themselves at your feet just to become another notch on your bedpost, all right? I don't know why you insisted I came down in your car. We never have anything to do with each other at Bristol, we don't share any friends . . .'

'Except Pandora and Emily.'

'. . . and I really don't see why you have to ask me all these questions.'

'Perhaps I was just trying to be good-mannered. I do apologise if you find my conversation boring. If you're that determined to remain an outsider and nurture your social chips, then I'll leave you alone.'

The rest of the drive to Esher was spent in stony silence, Max and Morgan both staring ahead with identical thin-lipped fury hardening their faces.

Sam groaned as he woke up again. This was totally useless. He'd tried everything to make himself sleep, but nothing short of drugs would knock him out. He called room service for some camomile tea, and decided to unpack and go out to dinner. He wasn't together enough yet to try and see Morgan. He looked so haggard that if he appeared on her doorstep now, she'd probably scream and run away.

He took out the only photograph he had of her. She looked uncomfortable in a party dress, a long shift of dark plum-coloured velvet. Her hair was piled on her head and kept in place with what looked suspiciously like a biro. Same smiled. She had obviously inherited her mother's distaste for dressing up. His stomach turned with nerves as he wondered whether Anna would be interested in seeing him.

After their divorce he had moved to America, and thrown himself into his work as an architect in order to dull the pain of his broken marriage. Anna had made it extremely clear that she would not welcome contact, and so, after twenty years, the only contribution he had made to his daughter's life was enough money to cover school uniforms and books. Anna had refused other financial help.

He jumped as the phone rang.

'Sam McAllistair.'

'Darling, it's Nina, I hope I haven't woken you.'

'Nina Charles, not *the* Nina Charles – how did you know I was here?'

'I happened to have that dreadful old reprobate Andreï Fyodov on the phone this morning and he mentioned that you'd just arrived in town. How long are you here for? What's the trip in aid of? Why haven't you been to see us for 20 years? Will you come and have dinner with me and tell me all about it?'

Sam grinned from ear to ear. Nina Charles, one of the most famous fashion editors in the world, hadn't changed a bit since their Oxford days.

'Of course I'd love to have dinner. I can't even begin to sleep – it's ten a.m. in LA. Where do you eat in London these days?'

'Oh, please, come to my house. I'll whip something up in no time – just give me time to get home and have a bath. Say eight-thirty?'

'Nina, that would be great, I'll see you then.'

Sam had never been so relieved to hear someone's voice. With any luck Nina and Anna would have stayed in touch and Nina might be able to fill him in a little on

Morgan. He hurriedly put on an ancient pair of chinos and a soft denim Ralph Lauren shirt, and decided that he would walk, see if he could remember the way to Chelsea.

Nina couldn't believe her luck. Twenty years after falling in love with Sam McAllistair she was finally going to have him to herself for a whole evening. She silently blessed Andreï for calling her that morning. It was unlike him to be so caring about somebody, but who was she to complain if she got Sam all to herself for a while?

She rushed home in her navy chauffeur-driven Mercedes, and showered as quickly as she could before diving into her closet. It was typical fashion editor stuff: a whole room of clothes, each outfit labelled, and with shoes ranged underneath in rows. Unlike most fashion editors, however, she had kept her favourite clothes from each season and now had a veritable museum of perfectly cared-for *haute luxe* ready-to-wear. From this she chose a pair of écru Saint Laurent pants, lightly belted with an old brown brass-buckled belt, and a pale linen tunic through which you could see her extremely fit body encased in a cream silk Galliano camisole. She slipped pale gold strappy Prada sandals on her feet and ran her hands through her short gold-highlighted hair. She seldom wore make-up, and this evening didn't even look at her bathroom shelf for lipstick, but sprayed herself liberally with Eau de Hadrien, the fresh, lemony scent she always bought from Anick Goutal's little shop in Paris. She ran downstairs, thanking God that she always kept a bottle of Veuve Clicquot in the fridge and that her housekeeper had

had just enough time to nip out and get her the ingredients to make a really good chicken salad.

She put the *St Matthew Passion* into the CD player and set to, chopping salad and frying chicken and pine nuts in lemon juice and olive oil. She wondered if, after all these years, she would feel the same about Sam. Nina had never married, had sacrificed her life to her career. She had never met anyone apart from Sam who had given her the remotest desire to settle down. Of course there had been boyfriends: photographers, editors, publishers. All work-related. These men had always been made absolutely aware that the relationship would eventually go nowhere. Nina had bought herself a beautiful house in the Royal Hospital Road in Chelsea, and until today had been perfectly happy living all by herself in its exquisite rooms. Now, twenty years since she had last seen him, her heart beat unnaturally fast and her hands shook slightly at the thought that Sam McAllistair was actually coming to her house for dinner.

When the doorbell finally rang she carefully flattened her hair, turned down the music and went to open the door.

'Nina, help, I can't bear another Friday night on my own.'

Rory stood on the doorstep, a bottle of Australian Chardonnay in his hand, looking pleadingly at Nina.

Nina didn't know what to do.

'Actually, I've got people coming round, Rory. It's work – advertisers, not your sort. You know I'd love to have supper with you, but tonight I just can't.'

Rory eyed his friend's relaxed attire and wondered who these advertisers were who were to be treated to a virtually naked Nina, Bach and what smelt like the famous Nina Charles chicken salad. This was not the businesslike Nina that Rory knew so well. For business she wore navy Chanel suits and had caterers in to cook.

'Can't I just come in and talk to you while you get ready? We can drink this and then as soon as the first guest arrives I promise I'll leave by the back door. Or I could play *serveuse* if you like? Besides, advertisers love having me around, it makes them feel like they've joined the inner sanctum. They know you don't let me out for just anybody.'

Rory looked hopefully at Nina. Nina didn't know what to do. Please, God, did she have to share Sam with Rory? It would be awful. Rory would talk nineteen to the dozen, and twenty years on, Nina still wouldn't have Sam to herself.

'Please, Nina. I'm sulking because I've had to send my lover back to his wife and kiddies, again. I can't bear it. And you know that everyone else always insists on leaving London at the weekend. There's no one to play with. Imagine, Pandora's *chosen* to go to Esher!'

Nine smiled at Rory. She'd never been able to turn her friend down. Unfortunately she would have to tell him that she'd lied, but Rory would forget. He always forgot almost immediately anything that didn't directly concern himself.

'Come on, then. Come into the kitchen and I'll tell you who's really coming to dinner.'

Rory dived over the threshold with unseemly haste. He'd always believed that possession was nine-tenths of the law, and thought that once inside the house he was unlikely to be thrown out.

'And you can tell me all about Don Elson sliming his way over the Atlantic to see us. And that terrible Gloria. What did you want with her?' Rory hurried into the kitchen and spotted the champagne in the ice bucket. Having hidden his own bottle in his oversized Gucci back-pack, he went for champagne glasses. He poured for them both and perched on the edge of the table, crossing his lilac shantung-clad legs elegantly and flicking nonex-istent dust off his matching *faux* lizard Patrick Cox wannabes. 'Well, first things first. Who is this mysterious guest? I'll forgive you for lying to me only when you tell me.'

Nina wondered if she should tell Rory that Andreï was coming; that would get rid of him pretty sharpish. She decided against the lie. It would be too mean. 'You'll never guess.'

'Why not? Give me a clue.'

'You haven't seen him for twenty years.'

Rory looked up with a start. There weren't many friends they had had in common for that long; certainly only one that immediately sprang to mind.

'Not . . . You must be joking. He hasn't been to London since, well, since the divorce.'

'I know.'

'What's he doing here?'

'Lord knows, but Andreï rang me this morning and

told me he had to be away for the weekend and maybe I wouldn't mind entertaining Sam.'

Rory looked askance at Nina.

'You should know better than to mention Andreï Fyodov's name to me. This once I'll forgive you. But entertain Sam McAllistair! You've been dying to entertain him since the first day you met him! That's why you didn't want me to come in. Well, because you are my best friend in the *world*, I will simply stay for a drink and to find out exactly what he is doing here, and then, like the good little girl I am, I will claim a frightfully important date and leave you to it.'

Nina leaned across the counter and kissed him.

'Thanks, Rory. You are a star. I don't know why, but I'm shaking like a leaf. Is it possible to stay in love with someone you haven't seen for so long?'

'Of course it is. Nuns stay in love with God all their lives, and they don't meet him until they're dead! Don't be a twit, Nina, I'm sure he hasn't changed a bit. And you never know, he might come in here and wonder what he ever saw in Anna. You don't know what's happened to him since, do you? Did he ever remarry, I wonder?'

The doorbell rang.

'We can but ask,' replied Nina as she headed back down the hall, wishing her hands weren't sweating so much, and opened the door.

'Sam . . .' Nina couldn't think of anything else to say. He had aged, but not too much. He was tanned by the California sun, had smiley crow's-feet and the odd worry line, but he stood straight and tall as he'd done at Oxford, and his wiry hair, more pepper and salt than blond now, still made him look as if he'd been dragged through a hedge backwards.

'Nina.' He kissed her, and she felt herself grinning from ear to ear. 'Aren't you going to ask me in?'

'Sorry, come in.' Nina still couldn't think of anything to say and was suddenly grateful for Rory, who she knew would never leave after a quick drink but would stay to chatter for hours like the spoilt child he was.

Rory jumped up as they walked into the kitchen.

'Bitch,' thought Nina. Rory had on his coy, sweet-little-boy look.

'Sam McAllistair, what a fabulously divine thing to happen on this boring old Friday night. Nina, doesn't he look gorgeous? He hasn't changed *du tout*; even the crow's-feet only serve to make him look even crunchier and more delicious. So tell us, Sam, we're dying to know, what brings you back to your native shores after all this time?'

'Hello, Rory. You haven't changed much either.'

Rory preened and batted his eyelashes. 'Sam, really, I look like an old witch, and everything important has dropped so far that my knees are positively crowded with unexpected companions.'

He's ridiculous, thought Nina, and poured Sam a glass of champagne. Then she turned an acid gaze on Rory. 'Rory just dropped in for a quick drink, but you've got a dinner later, haven't you, darling?'

'Oh no, I couldn't leave now. I'm sure the others will understand when I tell them why I had to stand them up.'

Rory smiled his most sugary smile at Nina, who decided that the only solution would be to strangle her old friend immediately and deal with the consequences later.

'Actually, I'm glad you're here,' said Sam. 'You might be able to help me.'

Nina and Rory turned to him curiously and, while Nina doled out plates of chicken salad and re-filled their glasses, Sam explained that he had come to England to try and make amends with Morgan but that he didn't have the first idea how to go about it.

'I don't suppose either of you keep up with Anna, or even know anything about Morgan, do you?'

Rory laughed. 'Keep up with Anna, not that much, but Morgan and Pandora have been friends since they were little girls. Morgan stays with us all the time. She's at Bristol University, but that doesn't stop her swinging into the big smoke occasionally. Pandora looks after her. They've gone off together this weekend, in fact. Some boys took them off earlier to Surrey. Darling, if you want to see Morgan, you just have to hang around my house for long enough and eventually she's bound to turn up!'

Sam looked at Rory in amazement. It couldn't be that easy.

'What's she like?'

'Charming, darling, charming. Could take a little more notice of her appearance. She has the most divine Pre-Raphaelite hair – Lord knows where that came from – which she insists on tying in a knot on the top of her head and keeping in place with a succession of chewed biros. Most unsavoury. Nina is dying to get her hands on her to shoot her for the magazine. Frankly, I think she would be about a photogenic as a boiled egg. Unlike Pandora, she really finds being looked at very uncomfortable.'

Sam had no intention of letting Rory swing the conversation round to the subject of his niece. All he could remember of Pandora was a screaming child with so much black hair you seldom saw her face. He didn't doubt she'd grown up to be just as spoilt as her uncle.

'So Pandora must know Max too, then.'

'Oh no. No one in her life with as good a name as that. My dear, she's becoming so in demand with her modelling that she really doesn't have enough time for men. I might have to speak to her about that. Who's Max?'

'Andreï's son, didn't you know? He's at Bristol with Morgan.'

It had never occurred to Rory that there could be more Fyodov's roaming the world. One was enough, having already ruined his life. 'Ugh, how dreadful, another Andreï to carry on the family tradition of wreaking emotional carnage all over the world. I suppose he's got white-blond hair and different-coloured eyes too, has he?' Rory was scathing.

'Actually he has. He looks just like Andreï used to, hardly any Tatiana in him at all. He collected me from the airport earlier in a battered old Spider which should have been taken off the road long ago.'

Suddenly the penny dropped, and Rory blanched. Max had to be Boy B. There couldn't be that many blond stunners who lived in Paris and studied French and Russian. And the blond boy had been driving a Spider too!

'Are you all right, Rory? You look a bit green all of a sudden.' Nina was genuinely worried. Rory looked as if he might faint.

'Mmm, fine. Look, perhaps I will go to that dinner after all. I really can't let these people down like this. I'm famous enough for my rudeness already; there's no need to make it worse.'

Rory smiled vaguely in the direction of Sam and Nina, grabbed his bag, crashed into the table in his haste, swore loudly and dashed out as quickly as he could.

'What was all that about?'

'God know. Rory hasn't changed, Sam. You still never really know what's going on in that scatty head of his.'

Nina was so relieved that Rory had gone she forgot to worry about the green colour he'd turned at the mention of Max Fyodov.

'So, now Rory's gone, tell me about yourself. What have you been up to for the last twenty years?'

Sam glanced about him. 'Looks like you and I have been about as busy as each other. You never married.' He looked at her bare hands. Her eyes followed his.

'Just because I don't wear a ring doesn't mean that I'm unattached. You're more old-fashioned than I thought you'd be.' She smiled across the table at him, her chicken salad cooling before her, ignored. 'But you're right. I never married. Never found anyone who came up to my extremely exacting standards.'

'I never found anyone either – since Anna, that is.'

'Why not? I would have thought America would be full

of beautiful women dying to look after you and all your money.'

'That's just it. All they wanted was my reputation, my money, the status. None of them ever showed any real interest in me. I'm afraid I've lived a rather monastic life.'

'I would never have thought you'd be able to fight them off.'

'Well you know. The West Coast obviously didn't breed the right sort of woman for me. Maybe I should have stayed in England. I might have stood a better chance of not spending the rest of my life alone.'

'Why did you go to the States anyway?' Nina asked, tentatively.

'Work. I was offered a job helping design a new film studio – it was just the sort of thing I'd always wanted to do. I wasn't really that desperate to finish my PhD. – especially as Anna didn't want me around. It seemed a good way to get out of all that Oxford atmosphere. I thought if I did something totally different and about as far away as I could get, then I could just work myself into the ground and the separation wouldn't hurt as much.' Sam smiled wryly. 'Worked a treat I've been a total workaholic ever since. I'm extremely successful, extremely rich and I live alone.'

'You sound just like me.'

'What was it that all the men you've met lacked?'

'Well,' Nina, said looking at Sam's twinkling eyes, unruly hair, little round glasses, worn shift, 'let's say they just didn't have a certain *je ne sais quoi*.' She hoped she wasn't blushing and scrunched her toes in her sandals to counteract it if she was. She picked at her salad. 'I didn't do much to help the situation by working in fashion. Most of the men are either voyeurs or gay. They're all right – but you wouldn't want to live with any of them. And, like you, a lot of them are after my reputation, or the glamour of it all, or something. They couldn't really care less about me. Besides, normal men seem to find what I do intimidating. They can't compete – I earn more, have a higher profile, you know. It's threatening for men to have to deal with that. I'm surrounded by beautiful, intelligent capable, charming women. A lot of them will never find anyone for the same reasons. We spend our lives being escorted to things by ageing hairdressers. I quite often take Rory. He's a riot.'

'Not an ageing hairdresser.'

'No, but he gets on very well with them.'

'What does Rory do now?'

'He's my style director.'

'Good at it?' Sam smiled.

'Not very, but very good for the magazine. His expense account is so outrageous even I blanch at it. But people like him, he gets out and about for us. I'd rather have him on my side than lose him to the competition. And it means I get exclusivity on Pandora too. She really is beautiful.'

'How've they managed without her mother?'

'Better than you would have expected.'

'Must have been tough on you, though.'

'Luckily I love them enough not to mind. Anyway, they're a good excuse to stop working from time to time.'

Sam laughed. 'Rory really hasn't changed.'

'I know. If only he realised what a caricature of himself

he is, perhaps, he'd calm down a bit.' Nina paused. 'Still, he wouldn't be nearly so endearing if he did, would he?'

'I'm not sure I'd call him endearing.'

'I know.' Nina smiled. 'He never really was your sort, was he?'

"No. Just everybody else's.' Sam sipped appreciatively at his champagne. 'And Morgan?'

'Funnily enough, I've never really met her. Well, not since she was tiny. Pandora always keeps her to herself. But if you want to see her soon, I'm having a party on Tuesday. Pandora could bring her along. What do you think?'

Max was thoroughly enjoying himself. Pandora had spent the whole of dinner sending him kisses down the table and making faces at the boys either side of her. They looked perfectly all right to Max, but she obviously preferred him. Emily had seated him on her right and had gazed adoringly at him all evening, making sure that his glass was full, that he had everything he wanted, that he was the star of the evening, in fact. Now the party was lounging round the pool, luxuriating in the balmy night air.

The only problem was Morgan. It wasn't that she disliked him – she was being perfectly polite – rather it was as if she had a protective shell around her. Max couldn't get through to her at all. He was used to women finding him absolutely irresistible as soon as they'd taken one look at him, let alone been treated to the famous Fyodov charm all the way to Esher. He just couldn't work her out at all. He lay back on the grass and looked around but couldn't see her anywhere. God forbid that some other boy had succeeded where the Fyodov charm had failed!

'Hello, my darling, enjoying yourself?' Pandora flopped on to the grass beside him and shook her hair out, enjoying the fact that two of Emily's other male friends were positively slavering in her direction from the other side of the pool. Max looked at her appraisingly and wondered if he shouldn't just cut his losses and go for this one. She was definitely a stunner, and was equally surely available. Then he remembered Morgan's exquisite profile, the scattering of freckles over her perfect little nose and the pale-pink blush on her alabaster cheeks, and decided that it would be worth waiting for the real prize of the evening. Pandora was too obvious for his taste.

'What's happened to the others?' he asked her.

'There they are, coming through the conservatory doors.'

Max whistled quietly in admiration. She was extraordinary. Morgan had come last through the glass doors and, totally without guile, waited while she got her bearings. She's making the entrance of the century, Max thought, and she doesn't even know it. She had let her hair hang loose, and it shone in a cloud of gold around her head and down her back. She was wearing a white cotton empire-line dress with little capped sleeves. The others were all in richer colours or fabrics, but none looked as beautiful as she did.

Max didn't know about Morgan's problems with her contact lenses and therefore that she really couldn't see a thing in the dark. As she frowned, trying to find Nick, Max went over to her, leaving Pandora fuming by the side of the pool.

'Hello, you look lost all of a sudden.'

She smiled at him and his heart melted.

'I feel so stupid, my contact lenses hurt too much to wear them tonight. I got some grit in my eyes in the train, and I packed in such a hurry that I forgot my glasses.' She smiled at him again, nervously. 'I can't see a thing.'

Suddenly Max was tongue-tied. This was ridiculous; he felt as nervous as an innocent fourteen-year-old with his first crush. 'Would you like a drink?' He couldn't think of anything else to say, and he absolutely had to keep this conversation going.

'Yes please, where are they?'

'I'll lead you. Take my hand.'

Her hand was cool, soft; he never wanted to let it go. They walked slowly across the lawn towards the games room. Max was woken from his reverie by Pandora screaming as Nick threw her into the pool, and the spell was broken.

Emily grabbed Morgan as she ran past, shouting, 'Come on, let's all swim!' She wasn't going to let Morgan steal Max from under her nose, and group hysteria in the pool seemed like the only answer. She and Morgan jumped in together, fully dressed and shouting with laughter.

Max felt left out. He didn't want to play around in a pool with Morgan; he wanted the magical atmosphere of the past five minutes to be returned to him. Disgruntled, he marched into the games room and poured himself a large whisky from the well-stocked bar, determined not to join in with the others.

He was woken some time later by Pandora, who lay

down beside him, a skimpy towel barely covering her. She looked at him from beneath her extraordinary eyelashes. 'What's the matter, Max, don't you want to play with us all?'

As she stretched, Max caught a glimpse of her perfect rounded breasts, which she only covered again once she was sure he had had time to really appreciate them. He laughed. This girl was incorrigible. In spite of himself, he reached out and stroked her hair. It was wet and she had plaited the mass of it loosely down her back. At his touch, he saw the goose pimples come up on the tops of her arms. He let his hand trail loosely over her shoulders, and she shivered. This is too easy, he thought.

Pandora leant back against him and smiled to herself as she felt his erection in the small of her back. She snuggled down and began to enjoy herself, looking up at him and waiting for him to lean down to kiss her. His eyes had a faraway look. She couldn't understand why he wasn't concentrating on her. First of all he insists that she be drive to Esher in Nick's car, and now she was lying in his lap virtually naked he still wasn't concentrating. Pandora let the towel fall open and closed her eyes. She would wait. No man could ignore her beautiful body for that long. Finally Max bent down and kissed her.

He had been looking for Morgan, and had seen her laughing with Nick as she jumped up and down to warm herself up after her swim. She was dressed in a long man's shirt which hid none of the glory of her legs, and her hair was still loose, shining with the water in it. She looked as if the last thing in the world to occupy her mind would be Max Fyodov.

Meanwhile Emily was having a totally miserable time. Her mother had been rude to Max, her father was snoring in front of a video of *100 Great Cricketing Moments*, she could see Max and Pandora snogging in the games room, and she couldn't get Nina's schedule for the Paris collections out of her mind.

She was sitting dangling her feet in the pool, and wondering if she really should go and be nice to everyone, when Nick and Morgan plonked themselves down either side of her and handed her a glass of wine.

'Well, I've seen people look less miserable on their twenty-first birthdays, haven't you, Morgan?' Nick grinned at Emily and put his arm round her shoulder.

Her misery increased. He was only being nice to her because he felt he had to, and the person he was really interested in was snogging Max in the games room. Admittedly, it wasn't surprising that Max had gone for the leggy, raven-haired Pandora instead of the mousy girl-next-door-like Emily, but it didn't make it any easier to bear.

'What's the matter, Em?' Morgan looked really concerned.

'Nothing, but it's never easy to enjoy your own party, is it?'

'I wouldn't know,' laughed Morgan. 'I've never had one!'

'Come on, Em. It's a great party, the people are fab, everyone's getting on really well. Much better than two hundred and fifty of your closest friends dressed like penguins in a steaming tent – I hate those kind of parties.'

'Oh, it isn't just that!'

'What is it?' chorused Morgan and Nick.

Emily sighed. 'It's complicated.'

'At least Pandora's enjoying herself,' commented Nick. 'I would have thought this wouldn't have been nearly glamorous enough for her.'

Morgan laughed. 'I wouldn't call seducing Max slumming it.'

'No, but Esher games rooms aren't her usual hunting ground. I thought she liked to run off with models and hairdressers.'

'No, that's her Uncle Rory who does that.'

'What happened to her mother? I'm surprised she's normal if he's the only influence she's had in her life.'

Morgan and Emily looked at each other and laughed.

'That's just it. She isn't normal. She's about as abnormal as she can be.'

'So take that mournful look off your face, Emily. You can run rings round her, you know you can. After all, you're going to be the one who chooses not to shoot her for your magazine when she's old and grey and has lost all her looks.'

'If I don't get fired for being incompetent first. Nick, stop trying to be sweet. Just because you're in love with her yourself.'

'I'm not.'

'Liar!' Emily punched him playfully and felt much better.

'What did happen to her mother?' Nick was leaning on one elbow, looking longingly in the direction of the games room.

'Died giving birth to her,' answered Emily.

'How awful. Who was her father?'

'Nobody knows. It's a taboo subject.' Morgan lay back and carried on. 'It's odd. She never asks about him herself.'

'Who?' Emily lay back on the grass too and stared at the few stars bright enough to show through the pollution of the English night sky.

'Her father. You'd have thought she'd be curious.'

'What, like you are about yours, you mean?'

'Well, at least I know who mine is, where he lives and stuff,' Morgan responded. 'I just can't remember him. She must walk down the street wondering if every other man she sees is the reason she's alive.'

'Nah – I don't think she thinks about it. Her world consists of herself, Rory and my boss Nina. As long as nothing rocks that little boat, she couldn't care less.'

'Lucky thing.' Morgan sighed. 'I wish I could be so contented with my lot.'

Anna couldn't sleep. She'd put Morgan on the train, rushed home and collected her papers, then cycled to her meeting in college, where she had predictably been late and as usual hadn't said any of the things that she'd wanted to. She'd finally got home at around 8.30, annoyed with the world, and slammed about making herself a cup of soup and some toast.

Not long afterwards she'd gone to bed. She'd fallen asleep easily but had woken suddenly, around midnight, spooked. She was too frightened even to put the light on. The moon shone aggressively through the uncurtained window and all she could do was hide under her sheets and blankets and force herself to breathe normally. She was convinced that if all she thought about was her breathing, then the spooked feeling would finally go away. It was bizarre. She hadn't felt like this since her student days, and then she had always been able to explain it by saying she was nervous of exams or of seminars she had to give. Except that one time. She sat up with a start, feeling sick.

Her hands shaking, she gingerly reached out for the light switch and screamed when something moved at the end of her bed. Thank God, it was only the cat. She took the black ball of fur into her arms and snuggled down again. But Walter didn't begin to purr as he usually did. Instead, he extricated himself from her arms and set off downstairs. She stared at him as he marched out of the door. Even he must be spooked. At last Anna gave into the fact that this panicky feeling was not going to go away, and began to try and work out what it was that was frightening her so much.

As she sat and thought about her work, Morgan, all the little things that might cause a disaster in her life, her mind kept going back to Andreï and Sam, and what had happened while she'd still been a student at Oxford, the city she had loved so much that she had never left it.

She couldn't bear the silence and the thoughts whistling around her head: Miranda dead; Tatiana dead; Rory a nervous wreck; Nina the strong one; Sam in exile; Andreï a murderer; Max, Morgan, Pandora, the children . . . She forced her hand out to the telephone by her bed and rang Rory.

A sleepy voice finally answered her. 'Hello.'

'Rory – I'm sorry to ring so late. It's Anna.'

'Anna, darling, you must be ill to be up so late. Are you all right?'

'I'm fine, sort of. I had a nightmare and Morgan's not here, and I just need to hear someone's voice, that's all.'

'Oh, pickle. You poor thing. Talk to me darling. I'm still very up and feeling a bit spooked myself actually.'

'Liar, you were fast asleep. Do you mind? I'm just all jittery.'

'So, what happened, seen a ghost?'

'Never believed in ghosts,' Anna said shakily into the receiver. 'I just feel as if someone's been walking over my grave with particularly heavy hobnailed boots.'

'Well, something must have brought this on.'

Anna, already comforted, snuggled deeper under her old pink eiderdown. 'Do you ever get that thing when memories just come up behind you and surprise you?'

'Oh, darling. Don't talk to me about memories. I'm surrounded by ghosts that creep up on me all the time. I'm probably fonder of mine than you are, that's all.'

'Sorry, Rory. Of course you are.'

'Darling, Miranda's with me every minute of the day. If you like, I'll send her up to Oxford to keep you company. The only thing is, she hates leaving London even more than I do, and I'm not sure she could handle Oxford at all.'

'I know.'

'Listen, if I were you I'd go downstairs and make yourself some cocoa, talk to that dreadful cat and then call me in the morning. Everything will seem much rosier then. All you have to do is look out of your kitchen window at the dawn on the dog roses in your back garden and everything will fall into place.'

'Rory, you're such a dreamboat. What would I do without you?'

'Find Emily's number and call Morgan there, I expect.'

'Did they all get off all right?'

'Darling, I don't know. The party hadn't even started when I last saw them.'

'I meant in the car to Esher, you twit.'

'Oh, definitely. And your lovely Morgan was being shepherded by a blond bombshell into a Spider. Maybe she's got the boy bug after all.' He didn't tell Anna the boy was probably a Fydov. She'd have gone berserk.

'Rory, you're incorrigible. Of course she hasn't.'

'Well, sleep well, pickle, and call me any time. I'm all shaken up too.'

'Why?'

'Oh, tell you in the morning when I've got less gin in me. Right now I'm not sure you'd believe me.'

'OK. Sleep well.'

'And you.'

'How's Nina, by the way?'

'Fine. I'm still trying to get her to throw out that moth-eaten old leopardskin lounger she's had since we were at Oxford and which she still insists on keeping in her bathroom, but she absolutely won't.'

'Surely there's more to your life than Nina's bathroom?'

'If only you knew, dear, if only you knew.'

Chapter 2

Saturday 15 July

Anna lay in bed, no longer frightened, and watched until the dawn crept over the windowsill. Her final weeks as a student at Oxford seemed so long ago. It had been years since she'd thought back to them. When her marriage to Sam broke up, not long after the birth of their daughter, she had stopped using her married name and had shut the door on the memory of her last few days as a student and her short life as a married woman. Sam had left for America and had never tried to get in touch with Morgan, for which Anna was externally grateful.

In the pale early-morning light, Anna went downstairs to make herself a cup of strong PG Tips with lots of milk and sugar. Walter was asleep on the fridge, as usual, and she decided not to work that day. It was the university holidays after all. She couldn't work all the time.

*

Rory lay in bed, shaking. How he'd managed to get through that conversation with Anna without letting her know that Sam had come back he would never know. He waited impatiently for the hands on the clock to reach 6.30 a.m., when he could call Nina.

'Darling.'

'What on earth are you doing awake at this hour?' Nina sounded astonished.

'Working! What do you think? If Don Elson's gracing us with his presence next week, I'd better have something to give him, don't you think?'

'Rubbish. Work would never keep you awake all night.'

'All right. You win. Anna James, then.'

'What do you mean?'

'She rang me at midnight. Must be a record for her, being awake so late.'

'Don't be bitchy.'

'I wouldn't dream of it. Anyway, guess what?'

'What?'

'I didn't tell her Sam was over. I thought you should have first go.'

'Stop talking about him as if he were a sure thing, Rory.'

'Well, he must be for somebody. I didn't see any rings sullying those lovely manly hands. He must be free, no?'

'Don't be ridiculous. He's just an old friend who's trying to re-establish relations with his daughter. That's all. If we can help we should.'

'You're telling me I should ring Anna back and tell her he's here.'

'No, no. So what did she ring you for?'

'I don't know, she had a nightmare or something. Andreï Fyodov haunting her dreams. I didn't tell her how he was haunting mine too.'

'Why this sudden bout of discretion? Are you ill?'

'Blame my therapist.'

'You haven't got a therapist.'

'What are you then?'

'Your boss! Listen, I really have to go. Some of us have work to do. Why don't you go shopping and call it work? I'll expect a really huge expenses bill on my desk on Monday.'

'Nobody takes what I do seriously. It's not fair.'

'Nobody takes what I do seriously either. I just do it rather better than you.'

'Ouch. Don't you want to know what's bothering me?'

'No, Rory, I don't. Now get up and go shopping. You never know, you might find a story out there somewhere.'

Rory slammed down the phone. Nina could be so useless sometimes.

He stormed downstairs and made coffee so strong he had to throw it away and start again. For an hour he fiddled about in his state-of-the art lime-green and steel kitchen. When everything including the bin liners had been wiped and straightened at least twice, he gave in, made a fresh pot of Colombian-blend Harvey Nichols coffee and rang Nina back.

'We have to talk.'

'Rory, I'm trying to work. Please go shopping. What is this? Boyfriend trouble? I can't help it if your current beau keeps running back to his wife and children. Can't you find yourself a gay boyfriend for once? Someone unattached?'

Furious, Rory leant against the kitchen counter, the phone wedged between his ears and his shoulder, and began to clean his fingernails with a silver toothpick.

'Nina, are you going to talk to me or not?'

'No, Rory, I'm not. I've got to get the September book OK'd before I go to Paris, and so far I've found nothing but typos and bad credits – nothing as interesting as a big mistake. I'm giving a cocktail party for three hundred people on Tuesday, my managing editor does nothing but whinge about the fact that I keep throwing people's boring ideas out and having creative ones of my own, and so far Gloria hasn't come up with one original plan for the couture shoot. I'm *working, darling*.'

'My, we are crosser than I thought we were.' Rory perched on a bar stool and began to sketch on the telephone pad what he imagined Nina's expression would be at that moment. 'Well, I'll just have to wait until we've calmed down a bit and perhaps done a little of the pile of very important magazine editing which we all know you can do brilliantly in your sleep and which really doesn't have to take up your entire Saturday when your best friend's having a nervous breakdown.'

He paused.

'All right, speak to me.' Nina was exasperated.

'I just thought you'd be interested to now that my lovely niece is spending the weekend with a Fyodov, who, if you'd been even vaguely interested yesterday instead of slobbering over a middle-aged man who's already been rejected by one of your best friends, resembles exactly the description of Boy B.'

Nine was lost.

'Who's Boy B?'

'I know I told you all about the boys Pandora was spending the weekend with. Don't pretend I didn't.'

'Rory, I hardly spoke to you yesterday. You didn't even turn up to the meeting I called about November . . . Wait a minute. She what?'

'So, I have your attention at last, have I?' Rory sighed.

'How did she describe this man? How do you know it was him?'

'Blond, studying French and Russian, rich lives in London and Paris? I'd say that fairly well puts the lid on other candidates for the position. If only I'd known there was another Fyodov in the world, I could have protected her from him. I could have stopped her going away from me to that horrible country party with all those ghastly Surrey people.'

'She didn't mention anything about the eyes, though, did she? And don't be such a snob.'

'No, but how many boys are there in the world who study French and Russian and live in Paris and are so attractive that Pandora will let drop another man who's slavering at her feet?'

'She's not like you, darling. May be sometimes she likes a little work to get her man.'

'Oh please, she's exactly like me. She's never been able to resist an easy lay.'

'Do you have to be so explicit?'

'Nina, this is an emergency. Mincing words won't help. We're going to have to tell her.'

'What do you mean, "we"? You mean *I'm* going to have to tell her, because you are too cowardly.'

'No, really. I thought we could tell her together.'

'What, that you do know who her father is after all, and that surprise surprise she's been having a little incestuous love affair with her until now unacknowledged brother.'

'Well, I couldn't have told her about the brother before, could I?'

'Fair enough.'

'Wait a minute. We don't have birth dates, do we? No, of course not. This boy must be younger than Pandora. After all, Andreï was at Oxford when Pandora was conceived. Unless he was impregnating half Paris at the same time as he was sleeping with my twin sister – holiday pastime, so to speak. I wouldn't put it past him.'

'No, darling. Max is the same age as Pandora.'

'Oh, great! And I expect you're his godmother too. No, I don't want to know. More to the point, what are we going to do about it?'

'She's your niece.'

'She's your goddaughter.'

'Thanks. Listen, Rory, I'm sorry all this had to happen now, but I really do have to do some work. We'll talk about it after the party, OK? I must get ready for Don, and Paris, and everything.'

'What if she seduces him?'

'We'll cross that bridge when we come to it. I'll send

her off to Timbuktu for a shoot that lasts a month. Don't worry, we'll think of something.'

'You are taking her to Paris, aren't you?'

'Of course. She's doing half the shows and I've optioned her for my couture shoot.'

'Well, at least that'll keep her out of the monster's way for a little while. You go and work, darling. I'll try and keep calm until you've had a good idea.'

Rory put the phone down, grabbed his fencing foil from the umbrella stand in the hall and launched himself into the garden, his imaginary opponent dying several times before he'd even got down the steps.

'Andreï Fyodov, please.'

'May I ask who's calling?'

'Sam McAllistair.'

'Hold on just a moment, I will find out if he is at home for you.'

Sam sat at the desk in his suite at the Savoy, toying with a biro and battling jet lag with thoughts of his daughter.

'Sam – you arrived all right?'

'Yes, hi. Shame you had to rush off to France. I thought we'd be able to have dinner. You should come over. I saw Nina last night. She's having a party. On second thoughts, don't. Rory's been invited. Understandably he hasn't learnt to let sleeping dogs lie.'

'Well, I couldn't anyway. Business. Max pick you up all right?' asked Andreï, knowing perfectly well that he had.

'Oh yes. Very dangerous car. Why don't you buy him a Land Rover or something more stable?'

'Wouldn't let me. Wilful boy, you know. Totally unlike me, of course.' Andreï laughed hoarsely into the phone. 'Spends his life doing various types of art. Modern. Not very good. And he won't just concentrate on one thing, you know; it's sculpture one minute, photography the next. He seems to be under the impression, mistaken of course, that someone's going to patronise him and make him famous. Useless boy. He'll end up in a bank, I suppose.'

'Good that he has a creative outlet, thought, don't you think?'

'No, not really, not unless he's really gifted, and I've told him a number of times that he's not.'

'Nice to see that you've mellowed in your old age, Andreï.'

'Oh, you know me. Can I help it if I'm a perfectionist?'

"So I'm not going to see you then?'

'Depends. Not in the immediate future. How long are you planning to be in Europe?'

'I've no idea. Things in the States can more or less look after themselves for a while. This is the first holiday I've had for years. I might be here for two months. Depends on Morgan, too.'

'Ah yes, the beautiful daughter. Where did she get that hair?'

'Her mother Anna just keeps hers too short to show its real character.'

'She's just like Anna in a lot of ways, including the little sneer of disapproval of the luxury around her. I never did understand how Anna could disapprove so much of the lifestyle of all her friends and still remain loyal.'

'Perhaps she was in love with me.'

'Yes, perhaps. Very odd woman, Anna. I suppose Morgan will be the same. Have you made contact with the enemy yet?'

'Don't call my daughter the enemy,' Sam snapped.

'I'm not. I was referring to your ex-wife.'

'Well . . . no, I haven't.'

'Slow coach. You've been here for days.'

'A little under twenty-four hours, actually.'

'Yes, well, still slow.'

'Andreï, I have to plan this. I've only arrived. Having dinner with Nina was the first step. She hasn't changed much. Just got even more glamorous.'

'Lovely woman. Charming. Yes, she's the only person I speak to occasionally. Obviously Rory's out of the question, and that charming ex-wife of yours never took to me, I fear.'

'You didn't exactly encourage friendship with her.'

'I was curious to see how far her secret passion for the good life would let her go. I couldn't encourage her; she had to want it in spite of herself.'

'I hope you're not implying you wanted her to lust after you.'

'Would have been interesting, no? We could have compared notes.'

'Careful, Andreï – I'm virtually the only friend you have left. Don't lose me like the others.'

'Oh, don't get all prim on me, Sam. Nothing ever happened. I married Tatiana – remember?'

'OK, OK – all water under the bridge. I know.' Sam

took a deep breath. 'So I'm not going to see you. Don't tell me you have emergency business for two whole months that won't even give you a weekend off.'

'Not exactly. I was just going to suggest that if you have time you might like to come and join me in August for a little rest and relaxation. I have a house in Morocco. Charming place. Perhaps you would like to come there for a whole?'

'Love to. August. How will I find you in the meantime?'

'Call here. Mrs Fischer always knows where I am. She'll put you in touch with me.'

'She's not still around, is she?'

'Alive and well and living at the rue de l'Université Paris septième.'

'I would have thought she'd have popped her clogs years ago.'

'Comes from a very tough strain. They live forever.' Andreï laughed again. 'I doubt if I'll ever be rid of her.'

'I still don't understand why you didn't sack her after that business with Max.'

'Sam – she's a woman. She knows more about bringing up children than I do. He doesn't seem to have suffered any long-term effects from the slightly unorthodox nursing he received after his mother died. besides, she brought me up, and I'm not a total monster, am I?'

'Depends who you're asking,' chuckled Sam.

Rory tried to take Nina's advice. He bought a pale-orange skinny-rib Nicole Farhi top, a bit small for him, but he could always share it with Pandora. He trailed round the DKNY store, couldn't find one thing that didn't have threads hanging from it or badly finished seams, but bought some sunglasses anyway. He looked longingly in at Chanel, but doubted Nina would let that one pass on his expenses slip. He was, after all, going to be in Paris in a week and he should be able to get everything he wanted there. He'd wait until the following weekend, when he would get himself a lime-green cashmere twinset to go with his kitchen. The new Joseph shop didn't have a big enough beige bias-cut satin-backed crêpe Galliano suit. He started making a list of people he had to call for shopping when he got to Paris, and went to have coffee at Nicole's. By the time he got to Boots to stock up on Vaseline and Nurofen he felt almost *soulagé* about Pandora chasing her brother around the Surrey countryside. He jumped in a taxi and headed off to Gucci in Sloane Street. He'd give Nina expense accounts! How dare she patronise him like that?

Pandora triumphantly installed herself in the front seat of the Spider, and waved a regal goodbye to the rest of the party as she and Max roared away from Emily's house and on to the London road. Nick chucked his and Morgan's bags on to the back seat of the Beetle and turned to put his arm round Emily.

'Looks like neither of us is going to get anywhere with our crushes.'

'I never really thought I would.'

'Don't give up hope. They're both so spoilt, the relationship can't possibly last for long – they'll argue all the time. It'll be nonstop fireworks. They're too alike for true love to blossom. There's still a chance for us ordinary mortals.' He kissed the top of her head.

'I can't think why you're so interested in him anyway, Em,' said Morgan. 'You should have heard the way he talked to me in the car on the way down yesterday – first of all it was the Spanish Inquisition on my family background – which, let's face it, is a little *vin ordinaire* for him – and then he started accusing me of being chippy. I'm amazed he even spoke to me after that. In fact, I wish he hadn't.'

'But you are chippy sometimes,' laughed Emily.

'No I'm not. I just have principles which I like to keep, that's all. I don't see why I should become a social butterfly just to make that spoilt little rich boy feel more comfortable with himself.'

'How can you be so horrible about him?' Emily leaned against the porch, a steaming cup of coffee in her hand. 'The poor thing's practically an orphan. His father obviously couldn't care less about him and his mother died when he was tiny.'

'So? My father did a runner when I was six months old and I'm perfectly normal.'

'Yes, but your mother adores you. She didn't have you nursed by strangers and then send you away to school as soon as she could, did she?

'No, but that's no excuse. He's had all the privileges there are and all he's done with them is abuse them. Since when did he ever do anything useful?'

'God, you can be a prude, Morgan.'

'Em, I'm not being a prude. I just think he should give something back, that's all.'

'Yeah, right,' said Nick. 'And what exactly had you in mind on the giving-back front.'

'Oh, I don't know. But I don't think you can excuse people just because one of their parents died when they were tiny and the other didn't love them enough.'

'You let Pandora get away with murder.' Nick laughed.

'Pandora's different. She's funny. And anyway, she's in a worse situation. She's got no parents at all.'

'Emily,' Nick said, 'you and I are so painfully normal compared with all these people, perhaps we should just cash in our chips and get it together ourselves.'

Emily blushed. 'Thanks, Nick, but I've never really thought of myself as a consolation prize.'

New York was boiling, but the Royalton Hotel was kept at a sufficiently frosty temperature for Gloria to wear a spring-weight pale-pink bouclé Chanel suit for her dinner with Don Elson. She curled her long Wolford-clad legs up on to the pale-mauve velvet banquette of the restaurant and curled a coy look at her host, the editorial director of the group of magazines she and Nina worked for, and therefore her ultimate boss.

You would never have guessed from her appearance that she'd had a terrifying day photographing winter coats on girls in ninety per cent humidity and temperatures which threatened to hit the low forties. She'd started at 9 a.m. and by lunchtime had practically managed to drown three girls in their own sweat. She'd also offended Saul

Smytheson, her star photographer, so much that he'd secretly vowed never to work with her again.

She didn't know that, of course, and as Don reached out a podgy, sallow, overmanicured hand and stroked the back of her neck, the gesture predatory rather than sensual, Gloria smiled back at him with all the confidence of the hottest property in world-class fashion styling.

'Hell, girl,' Don began.

'Don?' she simpered.

'So you think you're wasted working for Nina?'

"Well – it's hardly stretching to do the same old things season after season, is it? We both know Nina's a genius, but let's face it – there's room for more than one genius in this market, isn't there?' She made a little moue at the remainder of her curried Thai fish cakes and waved for a waiter to take it away. Gulping at her wine, a not very good Californian Chardonnay, she took a deep breath and began again. 'I heard you weren't too keen on what Knowle's been doing recently.'

'Knowle's a great girl – she just has a few family commitments she has to sort out.'

'You mean she's spending too much time not working on the magazine?' Gloria's voice was horrified.

'Last time she had a baby it cost the magazine three months of her absence. My publications are babies in themselves – they're a full-time job. And now she says she won't come in until the children have left for school, she'll leave the office in time to be home when they get there, and she wants shorter weeks during the school holidays! It's outrageous. Editors-in-chief should move into the office – never leave it. That's a thought. Maybe I should build an apartment for her on the top floor – you know, an enticement for her to be there a bit more.'

'You're so brilliant. I'd love to live at my office. Imagine how much time you'd save travelling.' Gloria put a hand on Don's lemon-yellow cashmere-wrapped chest. 'It must be hard when people let you down like that. I don't know how you deal with the stress and stay sane.'

'Hell, Gloria, I manage.' Don's hand tightened round the back of Gloria's neck. 'Nina's never had a full-time relationship. I like that in an editor. Her total commitment is to me.'

'I wouldn't be so sure.'

'Why? Honey, don't put me off her. I could give her Knowle's job in New York, and then who knows which hot seat could be empty for you in London? It's the obvious next step. Knowle was editor-in-chief in London before I brought her over here.'

'Do you really think Nina'd want to leave London?'

'What is there to keep her there?'

'That terrible Rory, for a start.'

'And?'

'She'd never leave Pandora. She takes her godmotherly duties desperately seriously, you know.'

'That can't really be all. You're holding back on me, Gloria. You know how I hate that. It's disloyal.'

'Well . . .'

'Gloria – tell me or you'll be filing runway slides for the rest of your life.'

'Well – you know about Sam McAllistair, don't you?'

'The architect? What about him?'

'If anyone's the love of Nina's life, then it's him.'

'So? Why should that stop her moving to new York? I'd have thought she'd like to be only a red-eye away from LA.'

'Maybe.'

'What, Gloria? You're not going to go and get all obtuse on me, are you? Look, it's late. You and I both have to work tomorrow. If there's anything else I should know about Sam McAllistair, I suggest you tell me now.'

'Darling – don't get so excited. You didn't think Nina would fall for you, did you? You know she's always refused to mix work and pleasure.'

'Bullshit – the girl's been through every straight photographer in the business.'

'And a few of the bias-cut ones too. But you'd be different. Anyway, as I said, Sam's the great love of her life, and guess what?'

'What?'

'He's just turned up in the UK for the first time in twenty years.'

'So?'

'So he's got over his allergy to England. You don't have to move Nina to the States in a fit of uncharacteristic altruism to let her be near him.'

'Sweetheart, there was nothing altruistic about my plan to move her to the States.'

'Listen, I know it's hardly my place to say anything, but if I were you I'd let things lie a little with Nina. I don't know if she's about to dump a lifetime of crawling to the top of this business, but you should have seen her on the phone to him last night. Her hands were shaking, she blushed beetroot, and then rushed home to play the little housewife and cook for him. I mean, when was the last time she cooked in her own kitchen? And at five minutes' notice? I couldn't bear it if you were let down again, Don. It would be terrible.'

'Bullshit, Gloria. You want Knowle's job and you'll do anything to get it.'

Chapter 3

TUESDAY 18 JULY

ANYONE walking down the Royal Hospital Road the following Tuesday would have been in no doubt that somebody was preparing to give quite a party. Nina Charles was hosting her annual bash, and there were delivery vans queuing right up to the King's Road, where the traffic was accordingly even more held up than usual. Nina always had everything delivered and set up in the morning so that she could get home from work at about noon and dedicate the afternoon to flowers, food and final touches.

The flowers, however, still got delivered in the morning, along with everything else. At 8.30 a.m. the van from Pulbrook and Gould was unloading at the same time as the food was being delivered, the tent low-loader arrived and the wine merchant was trying to get five hundred bottles of Veuve Clicquot into the house. The armloads of July flowers, only English, and largely white, were taken straight to the cool of the cellar, where long tables were ready for the roses, lilies, and whole branches of copper beach to be laid out for Nina's inspection. At the other end of the cellar were bins ready for the ice and the champagne. Nina never served any other drink at her parties. Champagne didn't stain the carpets, and as long as it was good enough quality, the guests could drink as much of it as they liked without suffering from hang-overs. The kitchen had been given over entirely to the caterers, who were preparing trays of the smallest, light-est eats to serve as blotting paper for the champagne. There was a green-and-white-striped awning over the garden in case of rain, but the sides of the tent were never put up. The high garden wall protected the guests from the English weather, and Nina hated the smell of closed marquees.

Leaning back in the cool leather interior of her car on her way home from the office, she forced herself to con-centrate on the conversation she was having with Don Elson, who'd already called her in spite of the fact he hadn't even got in from Heathrow yet. Nina wondered what he was on. Then she remembered.

'Don, welcome to the UK. I'm sorry I'm not in the office. I'm on my way home to make sure my housekeeper isn't arranging flowers fit for a funeral parlour in my absence. You did get the invitation, didn't you?'

'Of course. And don't you worry about me. I've got plenty to keep me occupied till this evening.'

'Really?'

'Absolutely. I hope you've got some lovely girls for me.'

'They're all coming, of course they are. It's everyone's last chance to enjoy themselves before the collections start. Shame you can't stay on for them.'

'Well, you know how it is. I can never bear to be away from the Big Apple for more than a week at a time. It's too good for my ulcer.' He chortled hoarsely, and Nina made a V sign down the phone.

'Don, you're a riot.'

'Where's Rory?'

'Rory?'

'Yes, your style editor. I'd like to see him this afternoon.'

'Shooting.' Nina improvised. 'In the East End somewhere. Tell my assistant when you want to see him and she'll arrange everything.'

'Come on, Nina. Why don't you call him right now and tell him to get his ass over to the office just as soon as he can?'

'Don, he'll be all yours as soon as I can get him.'

'Good. See you later, honey.'

'See you.' Nina hoped Don wouldn't be able to hear the distaste in her voice.

'Oh, Nina.'

'Yes, Don.'

'Where's the September book?'

'With me.'

'Have it sent over, would you?'

'Don, there's too much missing for it to be worth your while.'

'I just had an idea I thought I could go over with your art director.'

'Then I'm sure he'll be glad to print you out as many copies of the book as you like. See you later' She switched Don off. How dare he? Treating her like an assistant. She dialled the number of Rory's house in Oakley Street.

'Precious – Don wants you,' she announced.

'What?' answered Pandora.

'Oh, darling, I'm sorry. I thought I was talking to Rory.'

'Evidently. Who's Don? Would I approve?'

'I doubt it. Where is he?'

'Who, Don or Rory?'

'Stop being pedantic, darling. Rory.'

'I've no idea. I haven't seen him all day.'

'Well, if he does turn up, tell him to get his tight little ass over to the office. His editorial director would love to have a word.'

'That Don.'

'Yes. That Don. Find hi, Pandora, and send him over, would you? I'll see you later at the party.'

'OK.'

'Morgan's still coming, isn't she?'

'Yes, of course she is. Don't worry about a thing . . . Nina?'

'Yes?'

'I've asked a couple of friends as well as Morgan. Do you mind?'

'Of course not, sweetheart. As long as they're presentable.'

'Don't worry. You can hear the comforting rattle of Gucci snaffles at a hundred paces with these two.'

'Not always such a good sign.'

'Ah, but wait till you see the signet rings they have to match. Well, one of them anyway. It's so stunning I'm surprised he can lift his hand off the ground to carry such a heritage.'

'I'll just have to trust your judgement, darling. See you later. And try not to be too late.'

'Promise.'

Nina was putting the first tall vases of white dog roses and copper beach in the drawing room when Rory arrived, breathless, his hair looking as if he'd been dragged through a hedge backwards.

'Nina, I'm having a nervous breakdown.'

'Have you seen Don?'

'No. I put him off. I'm seeing him tomorrow afternoon. Told him a tiny little white lie about having an appointment with the Princess of Wales I just couldn't change.'

'And he believed you?'

'He'll believe anything if you pull rank enough with him. I could hear him tugging his forelock through a haze of Charlie down the phone.'

'How do you do it?'

"It's my accent. It makes him swoon.'

'You're such a snob.'

'Stop it. You're taking my mind off my nervous breakdown.'

'Well, you do look a little the worse for wear. What's the matter darling? Come one, I need a break, tell me all about it while I have my bath.' She turned to her housekeeper. 'Mrs Davies, could you finish up in here? I'm going to have my bath. Oh, and could you ask someone to bring a bottle of champagne up to my room. Two glasses, Mr Williams will be joining me.'

'Certainly, Miss Charles.'

'Come on, Rory, join me in my boudoir.' At least she could get on with getting herself ready while Rory prattled.

Upstairs she ran her bath, pouring in liberal quantities of Eau de Hadrien bath oil. She got out her grey-and-yellow-spotted silk John Galliano pyjamas, which were a few seasons old by now, but which she loved for the fact that they were so comfortable, and that their bias cut showed off her perfect petite figure to its best advantage. She was damned if she was going to wear Chanel like the rest of her contemporaries. She hated looking as if she were going to a business lunch when she was trying to enjoy herself in her own house.

The champagne arrived, and she poured herself and Rory a glass. She was exhausted. At least things were finally coming together. She would bath and change, then rearrange all the placements of the flowers later. Mrs Davies was very good at copying Nina's style, but she always put the arrangements in the wrong place. Nina liked banks of flowers, not one vase every three feet. Otherwise everything was more or less ready. She could relax.

Once she was in the bath, and the pyjamas were hanging off the bathroom cupboard door, their nonexistent creases being gently steamed by the fragrant bath water, Nina called to Rory.

'Come on, sweetie, come and tell Auntie Nina all about it. What on earth can be making you feel so glum on a lovely day like this?'

Rory arranged himself carefully on the rather tatty leopard-print *chaise-lounge* which Nina had had in her sitting room at Oxford and now, in spite of the decorator's pleas to have it re-covered with something more politically correct, was under the window in Nina's bathroom. He picked an imaginary piece of lint off the knee of his navy silk linen mix Dior suit, and sighed. 'Pandora.' His niece's name as pronounced as if it could only herald doom.

'That's helpful. Why the voice of doom? You'll have to be more specific. What's she done?'

'It's not what she's done, it's what she's trying to do. I don't know what to do about it and I'm finding it very hard not to go into a depression over the whole thing.'

'You're still not making sense, sweetheart.'

'I'm going to have to tell her, but I just don't know how. I was so surprised myself – I never knew anything about this other boy, did you?'

Nina sat up in her bath, exasperated.

'Rory, piece of advice – start at the beginning and tell me clearly what the hell's going on. At the moment I couldn't be more lost. What are you talking about?'

'Andreï's son. Pandora's trying to seduce her brother. What on earth can I say to her? She doesn't even know who her father is. How can I dump that one on her and add a little unexpected incest just to spice it up?'

'Oh, God. I knew you should have told her that you knew perfectly well who her father was. I've told you countless times to come clean with her.'

'Thanks, Nina, you're a great help.' Rory was almost in tears.

'Sorry, sweetheart, but it's true. You are just going to have to tell her. There's no other way out of it.'

'But she'll hate me. She'll hate me because I always knew.'

'You say you didn't know about the brother.'

'No, but I could have told her about Andreï. I didn't because I didn't want her growing up knowing that her father was one of the greatest shits that's ever graced this earth. Why should I hang that round her neck?'

'Rory, you and I know what kind of a shit Andreï is. The rest of the world seems to think he's an OK guy. Why don't you let her make her own mind up? You can't spend the rest of your life protecting her from the truth, can you?'

'Well, actually I thought I could.'

'Look, circumstances have proved that you can't. Come on, Rory, you haven't got any choice. She'll handle it. Maybe the real problem is that you can't face raking it all up again. You are finally going to have to act like a grown-up and deal with this one. It's not fair to Pandora if you don't. Don't you see that?'

Rory put his head in his hands and sighed. His champagne sat on the *chaise-longue* beside him, untouched. Nina poured herself another glass.

'Rory? Come on. Make a decision.'

Nina felt terribly sorry for her friend. Apart from the circumstances of Pandora's conception and her mother's death, Pandora and Rory had managed to avoid any real difficulties in their lives. They lived in the house his parents had left them. There was no mortgage, and they were comfortable on the little money they had been left and what Rory made from his job at the magazine. They weren't rich, but their overheads weren't exactly enormous. Whenever things got tight, Rory just abused his expense account a little more than usual. And now that Pandora was modelling for a living, things were a bit easier. She had always had enough admirers to keep her happy. So had Rory. Nothing had ever disturbed their carefully constructed little world. Until now.

Nina, would you tell her?'

Nina looked up in surprise. 'Me? Why?'

'The thing is, if I tell her, I'll get hysterical. I can't possibly give her a fair version of the story. If you tell her then you can be nicer about Andreï than I would be. Maybe he wouldn't come out of it as such an ogre. And you could be calm. I'd freak out. She already thinks there's something seriously heavy going down and keeps asking me if anything's the matter. We, I mean you, have to tell her something soon. I know I can't.' Rory looked hopefully at Nina.

'Rory, I think you've just come up with the most sensible idea you've ever had in your life.'

Rory smiled with relief. 'Will you tell her tonight?'

'No . . . tomorrow. Send her round to have breakfast

with me or something – not too early, about ten-thirty, definitely not before. Tell her I want to talk to her about a shoot. She always comes running when the possibility of her photograph being taken crops up. And if you're in such a foul mood all the time, I should think she'd be grateful for any excuse to get out of the house.'

Nina got out of the bath, wrapped herself in a huge towelling robe, went over to her friend and hugged him.

'It'll be all right, Rory. Your beloved Pandora is stronger than you think. She'll be all right. Don't you worry.'

Rory laughed nervously. 'You're going to kill me, but it's really not Pandora I'm worried about. It's me. I might lose her, Nina. She might want to go and live in Paris.' Rory looked up at Nina, and his eyes were huge with unshed tears.

'I wouldn't worry too much. Do you really think Andreï'll welcome her with open arms?'

'Emily, tell Nina I'll talk to her about the idea for the Morocco story at the party.'

'Emily, tell Nina I can't meet with her on Thursday. It'll have to be Friday afternoon or not at all. And I don't care if she's leaving for Paris on Saturday. This magazine does have a features department, you know.'

'Emily, why hasn't Nina given back the proofs of the Smytheson pictures yet? Honestly, how can I meet deadlines of my editor-in-chiefs delaying things?'

'Emily, tell that woman you work for that I will not do another story with Pandora. She wouldn't let me do what

I wanted and kept having a better idea. I can't be creative with her.'

'Emily, when did Nina reschedule the planning meeting for? I haven't had the memo.'

'Emily, I am managing editor this magazine. Tell Nina to call me about her decision to throw away October and start again. I can't do my job if she carries on like this.'

'HELP!' A smooth American voice interrupted her fumbling attempts to keep control of her boss's life. She stood up.

'Hello. Can I help you? I'm afraid Miss Charles is out.'

'I know. Don't worry about me. I'll just use her office for a while.'

'Um, I'm sure I can find somewhere more suitable for you. I don't think she would care for people using her desk.'

'You're new here, aren't you?'

'Yes.'

'Name?'

'Emily Carlton-Jones.'

'And you've been here, what, three weeks?'

'Yes, well, nearly a month.'

'Well, honey, get to know my voice, and make sure you don't stop me using whatever desk I like. You obviously ain't seen my picture anywhere. Don Elson.' He put his hand heavily on the back of Emily's neck and squeezed. 'Now, I'll have some coffee at Nina's desk.' The diminutive man, hair greased back into a glossy ball of oil, creaking in his brand-new Armani suit, tweaked her cheek before pushing past Emily and into the inner sanctum of her boss's office. Emily nearly burst into tears. She was never going to get this right.

'Hey, girl. Call Gloria for me. Tell me I'm here and ready for her.' He chuckled. 'And if that ageing fag calls in and says he's finished with the Princess, tell him to go jump. I'll see him at the party and tell him where he can put his royalty.'

Emily had no idea who Don was talking about, and didn't dare ask. She called Gloria, who rushed in seconds later all hair wax and vampy Chanel nail polish, still taking on her mobile and kissing Don at the same time.

Pandora's bedroom was a mass of discarded clothes and make-up. Uncaring, Pandora lay on her narrow childish bed and lit a Marlbor Red from the carton on the windowsill. Morgan sat at the end of the bed, legs crossed, face serious, biro keeping her hair away from her face.

'Pandora, you can't seriously want to go out with him.'

'Yes, I can.'

'You know he spent the entire journey down to Emily's trying to find out if I was well bred enough for him to talk to.'

'I expect he was just trying to make conversation.'

'So what do you want with a man who has the social graces of Geghis Khan and who thinks he's so gorgeous everyone should drop at his feet?'

'Did he tell you that?'

'No . . . but you can see it in the way he flicks his hair back – it's all so practised.'

'Well, he's coming to the party tonight.'

'Shit.'

'Don't worry. I won't give him time to come and be horrible to you. I'll drag him off to Nina's bedroom and neither of us will ever be seen again.'

'Why don't you go for Nick? He thinks you're gorgeous, and he's such a sweetheart.'

'I know, sticky sweet. I'd never get him off me. He'd be like chewing gum stuck to the sole of your shoe. He should get it together with Emily. I'd just walk all over him and make him miserable.'

Morgan laughed. 'Maybe.'

'Listen. Max and I are made for each other. We're both spoilt rotten, have no idea how the real world works, think the sun shines out of our respective arses . . . The only difference is that he's clever and I don't have to be.' She tossed her hair back. 'You see, we even throw our hair around in the same way. And the way I do it isn't that calculated so why is it so horrible when he does it?'

'You're honest about it. That's the difference. And I've known you ever since I can remember. I've only just met him and he thinks he has the right to ask me all these questions.'

'Well, don't you worry about him, my darling. I'll take care of him and we'll find you a nice young man at the party tonight.'

'Likely . . . They'll all be gay or chasing the super-models. No one's going to be interested in me. I'll help Emily do the door.'

'I wouldn't. Have you ever seen Emily working? The concentration's frightening. I'll be surprised if she speaks to us. Now.' Pandora stubbed out the cigarette in the unhealthy-looking cheese plant on the windowsill. 'What are we going to wear?'

Pandora made Morgan try on most of her wardrobe before deciding that the only answer was a pillar-box-red mini-dress so short Morgan couldn't bend down without showing her knickers, which unfortunately were black, with BLOOMIES written in large white letters over her behind, and a pair of marvellous stilletos – fake Manolo's; Pandora couldn't wait until she could afford the real thing. Morgan refused and wore the same long white cotton dress that she'd worn to Emily's party, and no knickers – the black ones showed through the thin fabric of her dress. Pandora couldn't understand her at all, but Morgan was insistent that she didn't want to look like a Barbie Doll, and that her own dress was fine. She hated showing off her legs like that, people stared at them all the time. Pandora shrugged, giving up on her hopeless friend. What on earth could be wrong with people looking at your legs all the time?

Pandora herself was in a black Lycra halter-necked top and hot pants which were not long enough to cover the cheeks of her buttocks. She looked ready for anything.

Nina was busy chatting up Saul Smytheson, fashion photographer to the stars, when Morgan and Pandora arrived. They were in the kitchen, using a spare surface to draw flat plans of the pages Saul was due to shoot. Don was standing by the garden doors in the drawing room, holding court. None of the fashion people at the party could afford to ignore him: he held the keys to success for anyone worth their salt or keen enough to lick ass for long enough to get his attention. At this particular second, an up-and-coming photographer was making a rather embarrassing attempt to kiss his hand, while Don had his arm round Tuesday, his current favourite among the supermodels. The crowd hovering round him waiting for a word or a look, made him feel just as important as he knew he was.

He smiled for Gay Smith, the most unpleasant paparazzi photographer in the world, who had elbowed her way to the front of the crowd to photograph him with Tuesday. 'Get out of the way, Gordon,' she hissed at the grovelling photographer, and leaned forward to kiss Don's hand herself.

Gloria was looking very busy on her portable, giving snapped instructions to her assistant, who was still in the office. Don looked at her approvingly. There was a girl who'd not let anything get away if she could avoid it. He thought with pleasure of the night they would spend together later. He knew she was sleeping her way to the top but he didn't care, just so long as she was using her considerable skill to encourage his own lively libido. And the fuchsia Versace dress she was wearing was made up of so many zips he couldn't wait to decide which one he would pull to strip her out of it.

Nina had planned on greeting the girls and introducing Morgan to her father gently, but Saul Smytheson was not a man you could just walk away from. The girls might have been late, but they weren't nearly as late as Nina had presumed they would be, and she wasn't ready for them. Naturally Emily, who'd been posted by the door, didn't miss them, but she didn't dare interrupt Nina when she was talking to Saul. Instead she hissed to Pandora, 'Nina wants to talk to you. She's in the kitchen with Saul.'

'Ugh. Please don't make me work yet. I've just got to get the lie of the land. Who else is here?' Pandora turned the visitors' book round so that she could check the names.

Emily smiled at Morgan. 'Don't worry. Nobody's going to eat you. You look jumpy as a cat.'

'I don't know what I'm doing here. I wish I wasn't so easily persuaded to do things I hate.'

'Think of yourself as moral support for me. It'll make me feel better that there's someone here more nervous than I am.'

'I hope you're being paid overtime for this.'

'Don't be ridiculous. I'm supposed to cry for joy at the opportunity to meet so many fashion groupies.'

Morgan laughed. 'I don't know why you do it.'

"Put it down to a lifelong desire to own a Dior dress. Mind you, since I've started working for Nina, the desire does seem to have waned a bit.'

Pandora shut the visitors' book and turned to look about her.

'Right, Morgan, come on. Let me show you around a bit. We'll go and find Nina later.' She grabbed Morgan by the hand and headed into the throng. 'See you later, Em,' she called over her shoulder.

Pandora and Morgan's entrance caused quite a stir. Most of the room knew who Pandora was, as she had been modelling since she was sixteen, but the beauty at her side was a total unknown. A buzz went around the room. Don didn't miss it. He made a mental note to congratulate Nina on the quality of the models present, and ask her why the hell her magazine wasn't photographing these two together before anyone else got on to them.

Morgan, almost immediately abandoned by Pandora, wandered, feeling lost, into the garden, where she sat looking miserable on an antique teak bench flanked by two huge arrangements of white lilies.

'Boo!'

Emily jumped, and blushed. Max and Nick stood at the door, grinning at her.

'Hey, gorgeous. We're gatecrashing.' Max kissed her on both cheeks and ruffled her hair.

'Don't! You can't gatecrash! Do you realise what kind of party this is?'

'Don't be such a goody two-shoes. Nina probably sent my invitation to the wrong address and it just hasn't reached me yet. Besides, surely she needs some straight men at her party.'

'Max!' Pandora fell on Max's neck and cut him off mid-speech. She dragged him off, leaving Nick and Emily at the door.

'Hi!'

'Hi, Nick.' She smiled at him.

'I'm sorry if we're going to get you into trouble.'

'Don't worry. I've been nearly fired about a thousand times so far this week and it's only Tuesday night. A couple of gatecrashers can't possible make things worse.'

'You take your job too seriously.'

'I know – but', Emily sighed, 'it's what I do. I know it's not going to change the world or anything, but before I started the job I really thought I'd be good at it. So,' she brightened , 'I'd better give it my best shot before I'm proved wrong.'

Nick laughed. 'Good on yer, girl. Come on, I'll help you. What do I have to do?'

'Tuck your shirt in and go and brush your hair for a start.'

'What?'

'No, no. I'm joking. Don't look so horrified. Please.'

By the time Sam found her, Morgan was struggling to keep her eyes open and wondering if she could go home. Emily evidently didn't need any help – she and Nick were having such a good time doing the door that Morgan was loath to disturb them – and, surprise, surprise, Pandora had totally disappeared.

Sam was bored and beginning to wonder whether this daughter would ever turn up. He saw Morgan staring into the distance and did a double-take. This had to be her. Before he could stop himself he was heading towards her.

'Hi.'

Morgan looked up and fell in love. Before her stood the nearest thing she'd ever seen to an ideal man. He was tall and tanned, his blue eyes twinkled mischievously and his wiry hair made him look as if he'd just woken up. He was wearing little round glasses exactly like her own. She knew it must be true love; Pandora always said that when you met the man of your dreams you would know, because you would feel as if you knew him intimately before you'd even exchanged a single word.

'Hi,' she answered. He just stared at her, so Morgan, embarrassed, stood up and held out her hand. 'I'm Morgan James.'

'I know. We've met before. But I don't think you remember me.'

'No, where did we meet?' Morgan was desperately trying to recall when she could have met such a spectacular man without glueing him to her memory. She must have been very young.

'I last saw you when you were two. You were wearing kickers and a red and white dress. Your hair was short. I came to visit you in Oxford.'

'Oh, so you're a friend of my mother's. I'll tell her I saw you. What's your name?'

'Sam McAllistair.'

It was Morgan's turn to blanch. Her father! She sat down hard and stared at him, her mouth open in amazement.

'I'm sorry, I've shocked you. I didn't mean to meet you like this. Nina said she would invite you this evening. I just wanted to see you, see what you looked like, and then go. I was going to ring you at home later. I'm sorry,' he repeated. 'Oh no, don't cry.'

All Pandora's carefully applied mascara was running, and Morgan was wiping her eyes with the hem of her dress.

'I've dreamt of meeting you.' She gulped back her tears. 'All my life. I never even knew what you looked like. We didn't have any photographs of you. I'm . . . I'm surprised, that's all. I'll be all right in a minute.'

'Would you like a drink? I'm sure I can find something stronger than champagne in the kitchen.'

'No, really, I'm fine.' She sniffed loudly, trying to get a grip on herself. 'I thought you never came to England.'

'I don't – didn't, I mean. Somebody sent me a photograph of you and it acted as a sort of catalyst. I couldn't put off meeting you any longer. I waited for your summer holidays to start and came over. In fact, it's quite a relief to have met you now. I would never have got enough courage together to ring you at your mother's. Anna would probably have slammed the phone down on me.'

'Why? I have a right to know you, don't I?'

'Yes, of course you do. But it's been such a long time. Anna and I always had a difficult relationship. I don't know what her reaction would have been to my just calling like that.'

'Why did you never even write to me? You never rang, you never got in touch at all. I thought you'd abandoned me. I thought I'd never meet you.'

'I didn't know how. I'm sorry, that's no excuse. I knew perfectly well where you were all the time, but once you were old enough to call, I didn't know what to say. I thought maybe Anna would have turned you against me.'

'She would never turn anyone against anyone. She's never tried to influence other people. She's just said what she thinks.'

'But she does put her own opinions particularly, finely, don't you think?'

Morgan couldn't help laughing. He was so right.

Suddenly too shy to speak they sat side by side on the bench, staring ahead of them. Morgan didn't even notice Pandora heading towards them, dragging Max by the hand.

'Hi. Trust you to pick the most gorgeous man at the party, Morgan. Look who I found gatecrashing with Nick.'

Pandora plonked herself down between Morgan and her father.

'What are you two looking so glum about? Hello,' she turned to Sam, 'Pandora Williams.' She held out her hand to be shaken and didn't quite know what to do when Sam didn't reply.

'And you are?' She put on her most polite smile and left her hand mid-air.

Sam pulled himself together. They were at a party; of course someone was bound to disturb them sooner or later.

'Sam McAllistair,' he said, forcing himself to smile. 'Hi, Max. How's your car?'

'Fine.' Max looked thoroughly bored.

'Poor darling.' Pandora grabbed Max's hand again. 'He's just been spat at by Rory. I didn't know Rory could be so rude. It was hilarious. Don't worry, darling. I'm sure he's just mistaken you for one of his ex-boyfriends. Or perhaps he thinks you're someone who stole one of his ex-boyfriends. Or perhaps,' Pandora could hardly speak, she was laughing so hard, 'he's playing extremely hard to get.'

Desperate to be on her own, and disappointed in Sam for not getting rid of Pandora and Max immediately, Morgan stood up, surprised to find that her legs were wobbling.

'Excuse me, I need to find a loo.' She walked off as steadily as she could, and didn't see the longing in Max's eyes, or the disappointment in Sam's.

Trying to find a bathroom, she couldn't stop herself starting to cry again. She locked herself into Nina's boudoir, washed her face in icy water and sat, stunned, on the moth-eaten leopard *chaise-longue*.

She didn't know how long she'd been there when there was a gentle knock on the bathroom door.

'Morgan?'

'Yes.'

'It's Nina.'

'Oh, I'm sorry, ' said Morgan, unlocking the door, 'I've been hogging the bathroom. I'll be right in a minute.'

'Oh, don't worry. There are plenty of loos in the house. I shouldn't think anyone's crossing their legs because of you. Are you all right? Sam sent me to check on you. He's worried that you might have freaked out or something.'

'Oh, no. I mean, yes, I am all right. I'm not freaking out. I'm fine. Just a bit surprised, that's all.'

'Don't worry, sweetheart. He's a lovely man. I think he's just as blown away by meeting you as you are by meeting him.'

'Do you know him well?'

'Oh, darling, if only you knew.' Nina laughed the sound tinkling round the room like a shower of diamonds on glass.

*

The last guests finally left at 3 a.m. Nina hurried the staff to finish clearing the drawing room, opened another bottle of champagne and settled down to rake the party over in her mind. She was surprised when Sam walked in, having presumed that he'd left hours before. She wondered if he knew that his daughter was asleep in her bathroom, and ancient quilt keeping away the night chill. He slumped on to the sofa opposite Nina and ran his hands through his hair. Nina passed him her champagne and went to fetch herself another glass. She didn't hear Morgan come downstairs, and when she returned to the drawing room, she found the girl standing by the door, staring at her father, who was fast asleep on the sofa.

Nina took Morgan by the hand and led her to the now empty kitchen. She put milk on to boil and made two mugs of hot chocolate. 'So, how are you feeling?' she asked Morgan, who looked as if she'd been slammed over the head by an old fashioned frying pan. Nina was much too polite to mention this.

Morgan hedged. 'You must be exhausted after having that huge party. Are you sure you don't want me to go?'

'Oh no, darling, please stay. I'm so hyped up I wouldn't sleep anyway. It's a pleasure to have someone to talk to instead of heading off to a lonely bed.'

Morgan was too tired to remember her manners; besides, she was curious.

'You seem to be the only one of this Oxford gang not to have had children or a partner.'

Nina laughed a little harshly. 'I won't die a vestal virgin. Don't worry about me.' She tried to bring the conversation back to Sam. 'What do you think of your father, now that you've had a while to take stock of the situation?'

'I don't know. I mean, I suppose he's an attractive man and all that. But I don't know him, do I? Am I supposed to magic some kind of instant relationship out of the air? I don't know what to think. My mother's going to be furious.' Morgan looked up from her mug of chocolate. 'You must have known them well at Oxford. Did they ever love each other, or was I just a mistake that they married to cover up?'

'Oh, sweetheart. Is that what you've always thought? Of course not. You must never think that. Anna wasn't pregnant when they married. You're young for your year, aren't you?' Morgan nodded. 'There. You see? At the end of Oxford Rory's twin sister was pregnant with Pandora and came back to London to have her. Your parents married that summer. They were doing both Ph.D.s and I think your grandfather gave them enough money to buy the house you lived in then.'

'Still live in,' interrupted Morgan.

'So you? I remember it having very pretty dog roses on the back wall of the garden.'

Morgan smiled. 'Still does.'

'You must have been clever like your parents and jumped a year.'

'Mmm . . . I started school a year early, actually. I don't think it had much to do with my brains. Mum was finishing her Ph.D. and my father had gone by then. I think she wanted me out of the house as much as anything.' Morgan said this without malice.

'And your mother never remarried.'

'No.' Morgan shook her head. 'She's married to her work, I think. It's easy to forget when you're with her that such a gentle person can be so manic about her books. She's a bit schizophrenic like that – either being at home and motherly, or working. There's no grey area between.'

'She was like that when we were at Oxford. I think that's why she made friends with us. We never spent any time on our books. When she was with us she could completely break away from her studies. But I remember, when she was working, woe betide anyone who disturbed her. Even Sam wasn't given that right. She would always go to him when she needed him. He could never just drop in on her.'

'But they loved each other?'

'Oh yes, they certainly did. I never really worked out why they broke up. He rushed off to America at great speed, so none of us saw him again, and your mother kept in touch with us, though we don't often see her. She hates, London, doesn't she? She's still quite close to Rory, calls him occasionally. But not me. We don't really move in the same world. She's so famous for her erudite works I'd hardly dare speak to her if she did contact me.' Nina's laugh was gentler this time.

Sam lay back in the drawing room, listening to the soft voices drifting from the kitchen, his daughter and the woman he knew had always loved him. He closed his eyes and pretended to sleep again. He didn't think it would be fair to go and disturb the quiet conversation. Morgan had had enough to deal with already that night, and so, for that matter, had he.

Chapter 4

WEDNESDAY 19 JULY

MORGAN sat in the train on the way back to Oxford early the next morning and watched the rain lash the windows in much the same way that she felt like lashing a few people herself that day. The man opposite her watched the corners of her mouth turn down to make a little pout. She would have been even more furious if she'd known that anyone thought her adorable at that moment, but luckily her fellow passenger didn't say anything.

Walking in from the bus, she fund Anna in the kitchen, drinking tea and reading the *Daily Mirror*. Walter was on the fridge.

'Hi Mum.' Morgan reached for the rescue remedy on the window sill above the sink and squirted about half the bottle straight into her mouth. She felt sick.

Anna glanced up. 'Listen to this – "Magazine mayhem

looms. Don Elson, editorial director of the biggest magazine group in the world, arrived in the UK yesterday. Rumour is he's here to shake up the sluggish English end of the group." I hope Nina's reading this, or will her hangover be too grim after her party?' She stood and went to kiss her daughter. 'Did you have a lovely time in London? Blimey, you look worn out. Cup of tea?'

'Yes please' replied Morgan. While Anna put the kettle on and got out the cups and the milk Morgan sat at the table looking nervous.

'What's got into you? You look like a naughty schoolchild who's about to be caught out.'

'Mum, make the tea. I need to talk to you.'

'OK, hang on, hang on. Get the sugar out, would you? And some spoons.'

Finally the ritual of making the tea was over and Anna sat down and looked at Morgan.

'Right, what's the matter?'

Morgan, didn't know where to begin.

'What's so dreadful? You're pregnant? You're gay? Come on Morgan, everything's handleable!'

'I met my father last night.'

Anna froze. 'What?'

'Are you all right, Mum?'

'Fuck me, I don't care about me. Are you all right, Morgan?'

'I don't know,' she said, then burst into tears and rushed out of the room.

Anna collapsed at the kitchen table, where she sat pulling distractedly at her naked wedding ring finger and staring into space. The ringing of the telephone interrupted her reverie. Anna heard Morgan answer it upstairs.

'Hello.'

'Hi, Morgan, it's Pandora – how are you?' Pandora was too excited to wait for an answer. 'Guess where I am?'

Morgan sighed. 'No idea.'

'Paris!'

Morgan lay back on her bed and, with minimum encouragement, let Pandora prattle on while she absent-mindedly chewed the biro she'd removed from her hair.

'Who with?'

'You'll never guess.'

'Come on, Pandora, stop teasing, tell me.'

'Max Fyodov! I'm at his father's house. Darling, it's too divine for words. There's no one here except us and a crusty old housekeeper, so I thought I'd ring and get you and Nick over too. Come on a holiday. England's so dull in the summer, all the parties are finished now, and I bet you've never had a proper look at Paris. I've thought it all out. If you and Nick come together in the car, then it'll cost you the petrol and the crossing and you can be here by the day after tomorrow. Go, say yes, please!'

'Don't you want to be alone with lover boy?'

'Well, only some of the time. It would be more fun in between times with you lot too.'

Morgan grinned to herself. Things must be going pretty slowly with Max if Pandora wanted friends there for diversion.

'I'll think about it. Give me a number where I can tell you. I'll have to check with Mum. I'm supposed to be working, remember?' Morgan didn't mention her father.

'Oh, please, don't bring that work thing up with me. These are your student days, remember; you're supposed to be irresponsible and carefree. After all, you're going to have to work for the rest of your life afterwards. Have fun while you can. Listen, I'm going to ring Nick. Call me back before the end of the day. Promise?'

Morgan grinned in spite of herself.

'Promise.'

When Nick rang half an hour later, Morgan agreed to meet him at Paddington station the following day at noon. They would catch a mid-afternoon shuttle to France and be in Paris for dinner.

'Emily, it's Nina. How're you feeling this morning?'

'Fine. Nina?'

'Yes?'

'I didn't get a chance to tell you last night, but I thought you should know that Don Elson spent some of yesterday afternoon in the office. He was only using the phone. I tried to stop him but he wouldn't let me.'

'He what?'

'He used the phone in your office.'

'How long for?'

'An hour or so.'

'Who was with him?'

'Gloria, most of the time. And a few other people. But mainly Gloria.'

'He told me he wanted to spend the afternoon in the art department . . . Oh well, it's not your fault. Listen, sweetheart, clear my desk, would you? Put everything in the locked filing cabinet behind you. I know there's a spare drawer. Just leave the photographs and so on. Make a big space in the middle and if he's there this morning tell him I had you clear it for him. I'm not coming in.'

'OK. Should I tell him where you are?'

'Meeting at my house. He can call me here on the office phone if he wants me. If not, I'll meet him at lunch. Any messages?'

'About a thousand from yesterday afternoon. Do you want me to give them to you over the phone?'

'No, send me my mail file with the car, will you? And tear up the message about the Smytheson pictures. They were so awful I threw them away. Apparently he and Gloria had a screaming match in the middle of Columbus Circle and it kind of shows in the photos. She'll have to reshoot after the couture, when he's calmed down. If Gordon Whitacker calls, make an appointment for me to see his book after the couture. And confirm Smytheson for the couture shoot. Tell him he can bring his boyfriend, but not his ex as well.'

'Gay rang again.'

'I bet she did. What did you tell her?'

'That you were in retreat before Paris, concentrating your mind. It's odd, she seemed to understand.'

'You'll learn, Emily, that there are some very strange people in this business. You never know what to expect next.'

'Yes, well . . . I'll send the car over with the faxes and your mail file at twelve-thirty, then, as you asked.'

'Right, and Emily . . .'

'Yes, Nina?'

'Try not to call me over lunch.'

Nina dialled Rory's number.

'Rory, sweetheart, it's Nina. Send me Pandora and I'll deal with her now if you like. And if I were you, I'd get into the office and lick a bit of ass. Don didn't look that thrilled with you last night, and I know you didn't speak to him. I'm meeting him at the Croucho Club at one, so you've got a while to smarm up to him.' Nina watched the Alka Seltzer fizz in the glass of Evian she'd poured. She had a teeny hangover to deal with before she met Don for lunch. Redoxen fizzed in another glass beside her. 'I've even had Emily clear my office for your meeting. You can sit in my chair and make him feel small if you like.'

Rory wailed on the end of the phone. 'I can't. She's gone.'

'Why? Who's gone where?'

'Pandora, upped and left. She's left a note saying she's gone on holiday for a while, not to worry and that she'll ring when she gets there.'

'Isn't that a good thing? Where's she gone?'

'I don't know – except, of course you can imagine who might have dragged her off to some awful den of iniquity.' Rory had on his most dramatic voice.

'Rory, don't be ridiculous – and turn the Mahler off. I won't help you with that music making everything worse. She's probably gone off with one of her girlfriends. Why would she go away with Max when she's only just met him? I'm sure it's all perfectly innocent. Besides, the couture starts on Saturday. She'd never miss that, and she's confirmed for Versace, so just calm down.'

Rory continued to howl and Nina gave up, put the phone down, gulped down the Alka Seltzer and the vitamin C, and headed out of the house. Oakley Street being only round the corner, she had decided that Rory would be easier to deal with face to face than over the phone. She looked at her watch. As long as she was back in time to change for lunch with Don she would be fine. She hurried down the road, eager to sort out the day's Rory and Pandora problems as quickly as possible.

Letting herself into the Oakley Street house with the key she'd had since the days when she lived there during Pandora's mother's pregnancy, she headed into the immaculate shining green and steel kitchen where she knew Rory would be bent over the counter by the telephone, doodling frantically on one of his pads. She found him in tears, three-quarters of the way through a pile of lilac silk handkerchiefs. He was still holding the telephone receiver to his ear as if it were about to impart some fascinating piece of information, and Mahler continued to blare out from the CD player in the drawing room. She opened the window, turned the music off, fetched herself a glass of Perrier from the fridge and perched, bird-like, on the other end of the kitchen counter.

'Right, where's the note?' she said as she leaned over and put the phone down. 'Piece of advice, Rory, if she's going to ring, it's a good idea to make sure the phone isn't off the hook.'

Rory passed her a postcard of Michelangelo's *Pietà*, and she read: *Darling, off for a teeny break. Back soon. Will call when get there. Bisous, P.* She wondered if the postcard wasn't a clue that Pandora had gone to Rome. But somehow she doubted that her goddaughter had any idea where this particular sculpture lived.

'When do you think she went?'

'I don't know. I don't think she even came back last night. Of course, I can't be sure, because I'm so upset by all this Fyodov boyfriend thing that I took a little tiny dose of sleeping pills. The only clue I've got is that her room looks the same as it did last night before she went out, clothes all over the place, you know. There's no space where anyone could have slept at all.'

'All right, let's be sensible about this. How close do you think they've got?'

"How close?' screeched Rory. 'You think she's going to tell me the specifics? Oh no, all I've had is her waltzing around the house clutching a cushion, pretending to dance with him, and lots of clandestine phone calls in her bedroom. She never makes clandestine phone calls. She thinks her life's much too interesting to keep it to herself. We are totally open with each other about everything.'

'Oh, don't be so prissy, Rory. You've been hiding something from her too. Maybe she's been talking about that.' Nina tried to prevent herself from looking at her watch, and failed. Time was passing, she couldn't be late. 'Listen, she's said she'll ring. You know she will. Apart from anything else, she's never been able to prevent herself crowing to you about her conquests. She's bound to call.' Nina stood. 'I've got to go. You may not be interested in talking to Don, but unfortunately I haven't got any choice. If she rings me, I'll let you know, but I'm sure she'll be in touch. We'll see her in Paris in time for the couture shows, I promise. She'll be fine.'

Nina hurried out of the house. If Pandora was with Max, then she could be at Andreï's London apartment, or his Paris house. She thought the Paris house much more likely. Pandora wouldn't want to leave the comfort of her own home just to go elsewhere in London. Nina would give her time to get to Paris and ring her there later in the afternoon.

But first she really had to pay a little attention to her job. Putting Pandora and Rory out of her mind, she changed quickly into fashion editor mode – navy Chanel suit with classic white trimming, dark glasses firmly on her nose, mobile phone clutched in her hand, and large chauffeur-driven Mercedes – and set off for lunch with Don. At least the panic about Pandora had solved one problem: she hadn't had time to feel nervous about this lunch.

'Don.'

'Darling.'

'Precious. How's the hotel?'

'Ugh. Claridge's. You know. It's full of royalty who get in the way all the time.'

'You must hate it. Why not try another hotel? Blakes is fabulous now they've finished the works on it.'

'Old habits die hard, Nina.' Don blew his nose a little too gently into a monogrammed handkerchief.

'I know. Enjoy the party?'

'Fabulous. Who's the new girl with the hair?'

"You must mean Morgan. She's a friend of Pandora's.'

'I hope you're shooting her.'

'Bluestocking, not interested. She'd fight the camera. It'd be a waste of time.'

'Pity. Can't she be tempted?'

'I doubt it. Her mother's a world-famous feminist. She's been brought up to think that fashion magazines are morally wrong.'

'Too bad. Can you imagine her in pictures? Virtually naked, on horseback.'

'Mmm . . . a little pornographic for my taste.'

'You think so?'

Nina smiled with her teeth.

they ordered a lunch neither would eat. Nina drank Evian and Don vodka. Nina's phone rang.

'Yes?'

'Nina, Saul wants to know where you are. He's furious about something. What shall I tell him?'

'I told you not to call unless it was important, Emily.'

'He's on his way here. He's going to sit here until I tell him.'

'Well, just don't. Is that all?'

'Yes.'

Nina put the phone down beside her plate. She looked back at Don, her *foie de volaille* salad sitting untouched before her. 'So, Don, what's this trip about?'

'Changes, Nina, changes. We need to up-shift some of your people, and frankly, I think we could down-shift a few others.'

'Who exactly are you keen on shifting, and in which direction would you like them to be shifted?'

'Come on, Nina. Don't get antsy. It's difficult to be clear about things when you're in the middle of them. That's why I'm here: I have a better overview of the magazines, and it's easier for me to see the weaknesses.'

'And where precisely do you see the weak points in my team?'

'Rory?'

'Not Rory. I know you don't mean that. Where?'

'Art department.'

'Mmm . . .'

'I've a features editor I'd like to try out with you before I bring him back to the States.'

'Oh, great. You want to try someone on me and then take them back. Meanwhile I lose a great features editor. Thanks.'

'Nina, Nina. This is how the system works. You know that perfectly well.'

'OK. Who else? Gloria? Me? Would you like me to down-shift out of your life?'

'Nina, you're taking this the wrong way. Of course you position's safe. How could we do it without you? No, no. And Gloria's fine where she is. Rory . . . Well, if you insist, he can stay – in spite of his expense account, which is costing the company about the same as everyone else's salaries put together.'

'You must agree he's vital. We couldn't possibly let him go to the other side. His relationships are too valuable to lose. He can get through doors even you might find slammed in your face.'

'I'm not sure anyone's ever slammed a door on me. As far as I can see, he never does anything except send thousand-dollar bouquets to ageing socialites who have him to lunch.'

'Don, you don't see him on a day-to-day basis. I couldn't possibly work without him. He has a clearer perspective than anyone on how the industry works, because he always knows the whole story. He has to do his lunches to get the background. Anyway, you know he's the most brilliant sittings editor there is, when he has to be.'

'When he's forced, you mean?'

'No, I mean I have a brilliant sittings editor in Gloria, so I use Rory elsewhere.'

'Humph.'

Nina's phone rang again. She picked it up and turned it off. She really was going to have to talk to Emily. This was just not good enough.

By that evening Rory still hadn't met up with Don. He was pacing the little-used drawing room in Oakley Street like a sentry mounting guard over the fireplace. He thwacked the air occasionally with his fencing foil, ready to use it should a Fyodov burst into the room, an idea he was easily drunk enough to accept as possible. He wore a heavy purple velvet dressing gown, bald in patches but the only thing in the house that he found near enough in colour to royal mourning. He held a large gin, from which he took gulps each time he turned to retrace his steps. He was smoking. He'd found a carton of Marlboro Reds in Pandora's room and had fallen on them in relief. You couldn't be really stressed without a constant stream of cigarettes. Naturally, he hadn't thought to make sure the phone was on the hook. It buzzed, ignored, on the kitchen counter, the noise drowned by the Mahler which boomed once more throughout the house.

Don had to hammer on the front door with all his considerable strength before Rory finally heard him. He opened the front door, fencing foil in one hand, gin in the other, and with tears pouring unheeded down his face.

'Oh,' said Rory. 'It's you.'

'I would have thought I'd get a warmer welcome than that from one of my favourite employees.' Don opened his arms wide and went to hug Rory, who stepped backwards, grimacing, just in time, so that Don nearly ended up with his nose embedded in the doormat.

'Come in. I hate drinking alone.'

'It's never stopped you before,' snapped Gloria, who leaned sulkily against the door jamb.

'Don't be bitchy, Gloria. Rory, darling, I thought we could go out. I haven't really partied yet and I've been here thirty-six hours.'

'Don't you ever tire?'

'Never. Well, if you don't want to go out, we could always play here. Can I use your bathroom?' Don patted his breast pocket and winked. 'You want some?'

'I've given up.'

'Honey, that's not your style. You were always the first to enjoy a little Charlie.'

'I saw the effect it was having on Saul's boyfriend and decided to stop. You know he has to hold his nose when he's drinking anything hot, to stop the insides falling out?'

'You're exaggerating.'

'No. But help yourself to the bathroom anyway. I haven't taken away the mirrored surfaces yet.'

'Great.'

Don grabbed Gloria's hand and bounded past Rory and down the hall. Rory sighed and headed back into the drawing room. When Don and Gloria returned from the bathroom, he was standing in an unfriendly position by the fire, still holding his fencing foil.

'So, Rory, what makes me such an ogre you have to avoid me all the time?' Don was lounging on the sofa, fondling Gloria's legs as a crocodile might those of a victim. He smiled at Rory, his eyes glittering with cocaine and dislike.

'Work, sweetheart. You know what a workaholic I am. I can't just drop everything like everyone else can' – I hear Rory shot Gloria a look of pure venom – 'when important people make surprise visits.'

'And what is it you're working so hard on now?'

'Darling, the couture. Haven't you heard my fabulous idea?'

'No, of course not. You know Nina likes to keep her beloved magazine entirely to herself until it's hit the news stands.'

'In that case perhaps I'd better not tell you.'

'Go on. Force yourself.'

'Well, put it this way, four of the greatest designers alive today have been working with me on a very special project to celebrate this season's couture.'

'Which is?'

'Just a few pieces, you understand. But some of the boys and I got together right at the beginning of their work, and I've been following the pieces with them since conception, you know, photographs, sketches, inspiration and so on. And then finally we'll shoot the finished project with Saul and the most magnificent girls in the business.'

'Bullshit,' Gloria spat.

'It's true.'

'Why don't I know about it?'

'Because I didn't want your sticky little fingers pinching the ideas and gluing your own name all over them.'

'But I should know about this. I'm doing the shoot.'

'Darling, just because you're a stylist doesn't mean that I have to tell you everything Nina and I are working on. Besides, from what I hear, you and Sauly had a teeny little contretemps in the old US of A and he might refuse to shoot the couture if you're the sittings editor.'

'I think you should you know Gloria's a talented girl. Her input could be very valuable on this.'

'Her input is given its exact value by Nina on a day-to-day basis. I cannot dictate to my editor-in-chief what she does and doesn't divulge to her junior staff.' Rory's voice was icy. He'd had enough of these people. 'And now, if you'll excuse me, I have a heavy week ahead of me. Gloria obviously feels she has time to go out raving, but I'm afraid I'm past all that, and I need my beauty sleep before the couture starts.'

'Where's Pandora?' Gloria's voice was sugar-sweet.

Rory blinked back new tears. 'Paris . . . for fittings. Why?'

'Just wondered. She might have liked to come out with us. She's more our generation, isn't she, Don?'

'Hmm. Lovely legs too.' Don made his way to the door, Gloria trailing behind. 'See you, Rory, I hope you'll learn to be a bit more helpful to Gloria in the future. You might have to.'

Rory slammed the door behind them and leaned back on it. How on earth did such a horrid little man get to be so powerful? And what was he doing sniffing cocaine with Gloria? He marched down to the kitchen, poured more gin, frowned at the telephone receiver, which sat on the kitchen counter, ignored it and took his glass to bed.

Nina was feeling relieved. She'd found a message from Pandora on her machine when she returned from lunch.

'Nina, hello, darling. I'm in Paris with Max. Can you tell Rory? I think he's left the phone off the hook – it's constantly engaged. Shouldn't be here for too long. Max says we can't stay after his father gets back, and apparently that's in a couple of days. Anyway, I need to talk to you about him. He's very strange. He must like me, obviously, but I have to behave like a complete harlot to get him even remotely interested in sex. We still haven't done it. Do you think he's gay?' The message ended, but another one came immediately afterwards: 'Can't you leave more space for messages on your machine? Anyway, I'm going to keep trying, with the sex, not Rory. He'll run out of excuses sooner or later, he must, surely. Tell Rory I've got loads of fittings and am being terribly cultural and going to all the museums in my spare time or something. Lots of love.'

The girl has no shame, thought Nina as she sank into a long, hot bath, exhausted after a conversation with Don which had left her feeling as if she'd been involved in a gun fight, the results of which still hadn't been decided. She groaned as she remembered the five hours she'd had to sit there and be nice to that man. And that silly girl Emily had interrupted her train of thought by ringing her four times to ask questions which a three-year-old who'd never seen a couture suit, let alone knew the name of one designer, should have been able to answer in her sleep.

Nina let the scent of Eau de Hadrien float over her and tried to put all thoughts of Pandora and of Don Elson out of her mind. The July haute couture collections would start to be shown in Paris in a few days' time, and Nina always enjoyed the trip. These were the least hysterical of the collections; fewer people came, everybody was in a good mood because of the summer weather and she could relax knowing that other people would have to shoot the stuff and she could make up her mind about it later, once she returned to the UK. Pandora would still be in Paris. Perhaps that would be the perfect time to tell her about Max. Nina nearly laughed: she could kill several birds with one stone, and introduce her to Andreï, too. It wasn't really funny, but the situation was a little ridiculous, surely?

Getting out of the bath she wrapped herself in a huge towelling dressing gown and dialled Rory's number. Getting an engaged tone, she decided, rightly, that the phone must still be off the hook, and thought she'd go round there the following morning. After she'd had time to talk to Pandora, perhaps. Switching on the answering machine and putting in her ear plugs, she let her bathrobe drop to the floor and crawled into bed. Her last thoughts were not of the magazine, or of Pandora, but of Sam, wondering where he was and how she could help in the next step of his getting to know his daughter.

Sam was in Oxford, sitting in Morgan's place at the kitchen table in Anna's little workman's cottage, warily keeping an eye on the cat, who'd declared war when Sam had arrived by sinking his teeth into Sam's calf. Sitting across from him, Anna saw no reason to bury the hatchet. Even if he was Morgan's father, he was still the arrogant, self-opinionated twit she remembered. He hadn't changed at all. She wouldn't put it past him to have had a hairdresser arrange his hair in that delicious crunch, messy look, and his tan, it was so obvious! The thing she hated most about her relationship with Sam was her disappointment with it. She was disappointed in herself for having been misled for long enough to marry and have a child by this man, this fool, this ordinary person.

Sam felt like a child who had been invited to impress the diners at a grown-up dinner party and then hadn't known how to do it and ended up crying. Anna's cool intelligence and quiet self-sufficiency still made him feel inadequate.

They'd got over the introductory pleasantries and had run out of things to say. There was a long silence before Sam finally spoke.

'What's Morgan like?'

Anna thought for a moment.

'Well, she's not like either of us. She won't be an academic and I don't think she's ambitious for a career, or she certainly hasn't talked to me about anything if she has plans to specialise. She's perfectly clever, though.'

'What else?'

'Well, you're seen her, so you know she's beautiful. She doesn't like that. She doesn't like being so tall. In fact, she doesn't like anything about herself that makes her stand out. That's why she goes to such lengths to ignore her appearance. She also seems to have got in with a rather fast crowd at university. You know, too much money and not enough sense, that sort of thing.'

Anna rose to make more tea.

'Haven't you got anything stronger?' Sam pleaded. 'I used up all my courage coming here and I could really do with something to keep me going.'

Anna reached for the whisky bottle and a couple of tumblers. She didn't offer Sam ice, which after all his years in the States he longed for. He didn't ask for it.

'Did you know you were going to see her at the party?'

'Yes, but I was going to have a look and leave. But when I saw her I couldn't just walk off.'

'You were going to have a look and leave?' Anna was

stunned. 'What an extraordinary thing to do. What were you going to do next?'

'Well, then I was going to ring here and come and visit.'

'Oh, and when she said, 'I saw you at a party the other day', what were you going to say to that?'

'Same signed. 'OK, Anna, it was a stupid idea. But it's easy for you, you know her. I had a daughter I'd hardly ever met and who didn't even know what I looked like. I thought if I rang here you'd probably slam the phone down on me. I didn't know what to do. Nina told me she would be at the party. I thought it would be a start. Then if I lost my nerve and went back to the States without doing anything about it, at least I'd have seen her in the flesh. Don't look at me like that. I had to start somewhere, agree at least on that point.'

'But she was so upset about it when she got home that she stormed off upstairs in tears and we never talked about it,' Anna retorted. 'Now she's gone to France to escape both of us and – most unlike her – isn't dealing with the problem at all. Why on earth didn't you contact us before? You've had twenty years to get in touch!'

'Anna, you didn't exactly encourage contact after we split. I didn't want to make the atmosphere around my baby daughter an aggressive one. She needed peace and quiet and love, not you and I shouting at each other.'

'You sound so American New Man!'

And so the conversation went on. The level of the whisky bottle dropped lower and lower, and suddenly Anna realised it was getting light outside. For some reason she was embarrassed, and this made her furious. She slammed the tea cups and the whisky glasses into the sink and started to wash up with a vengeance. She hardly mumbled goodbye as Sam stood up to leave. Frustrated, he kicked the garden gate closed and set off frowning, his shoulders hunched around his ears against the early-morning chill.

Chapter 5

THURSDAY 20 JULY

'HELLO, Mrs Fischer, it's Nina Charles. I'm sorry to call so early, but I was wondering if Pandora Williams was staying here?'

'She is,' came the guttural reply.

Charming as ever, thought Nina. 'Would it be possible to speak to her?' Nina was on her best telephonic behaviour with the formidable Fyodov housekeeper.

'Hold on.' The disapproval in Mrs Fischer's voice deepened. 'I do not know if she is yet awake.'

Nina settled down for a long wait. She knew how big Andreï's Paris house was and that Mrs Fischer neither ran nor shouted, and therefore she had to be patient while Mrs Fischer shuffled off to fetch Pandora. She turned up the radio and listened to news of the latest cabinet reshuffle. She and John Major seemed to always do it at the same time. After her boxing-match lunch with Don the day before, the office was as rife with rumours and counter-rumours as bulletins from the *Today* programme.

Pandora, breathless, interrupted her thoughts.

'Nina, darling, how are you?'

'I'm fine, sweetheart. More to the point, how are you?'

'Oh, darling, I'm having a marvellous time. The house is to-die beautiful and Paris is too heavenly for words. I'm gong to have to live here. Perhaps I'll get myself a Paris agent and forget London.'

'Darling, you can't, you only scraped your GCSE French. You've always said you hated languages.'

Pandora sighed. 'Don't pour cold water on my little plan, Nina. Anyway, who needs languages in fashion? Everybody just speaks the language of the most famous person, and when that's me, they'll speak English, won't they? Now listen.'

Nina settled herself deeper into her armchair and reached for the cup of Darjeeling tea Mrs Davies had brought her.

'I'm listening.'

'What do I do about Max? I wish I could talk about it with Rory, but for some reason just the mention of the name Max makes Rory go quite green, and he clams up entirely. I can't see why. He's perfectly harmless. At least, in spite of all my encouragement he hasn't managed to harm me at all yet.'

Nina wondered whether now would be a good time to tell Pandora that the man she was chasing was her brother. She decided against it. Max must be pretty steely to have lasted this long. Nina had witnessed Pandora's seduction of men ever since, at the age of three, she had won over Don Elson by lolling about on his lap and pointing out with a charming pout that she had the longest eyelashes that any Pears Soap baby had ever had.

'What does he do exactly when he turns you down?'

'Well, the first time we snogged was at Emily's party. Remember when we went to Surrey for her twenty-first? That was easy. I just lay down and let my towel slip a little and Bob was your uncle, so to speak.'

Or Max your brother, thought Nina. 'And then what happened?'

"Well, it was a very sort of parenty weekend. You know, all the boys slept in this sort of playroom they had in the garden, and the girls in the house. There wasn't much opportunity for real hanky-panky – too many people around, you know what I mean, and I've never been that much of an exhibitionist.'

'Pandora, you sound so like Rory!'

'Do I?'

'So carry on with the story.' Nina poured herself a second cup of tea from the Georgian silver tea service on the tray in front of her. Pandora's voice continued from the other side of the channel.

'Well, the next time was your party. I didn't see him in between. It was only a couple of days, and I thought that absence might make the heart grow fonder. Besides, he had about four thousand clubs to go to with Nick and I wouldn't dream of disturbing the boys when they're doing that mad rushing about from one warehouse to another, comparing DJ's like Rory does vintage couture.'

'Yes, go on.'

'So, nothing happened then because there was all that carry-on with Morgan and her father. Isn't he gorgeous?'

'Stick to the point, Pandora, we'll talk about Sam McAllistair later.'

'All right, all right, keep your pants on. Anyway, nothing happened then, and later, at the end of the evening, Max said he had to go because he wanted to catch the Shuttle early so that he wouldn't have too much traffic getting back to Paris, and I said, Paris! and he said, yes, Paris, and I said, can I come too, and he gave me that divine drop-dead grin he has and said, of course you can, come on, let's go, so we did. I had to buy underwear and jeans and everything when we got here cos I didn't bring anything, not even my purse. That's almost the best bit. He's so rich he's paying for everything and not evening mentioning the fact that one of these days perhaps I ought to pay him back some of it.'

'So how long have you been in Paris and failed in your seduction?'

'Oh, don't say that,' Pandora wailed. 'I haven't failed yet. We've only been here one full night – the first one we were driving and he might have crashed. Last night was so romantic. Oh, Nina, you'd have died! He took me to a tiny little restaurant in Montmartre where there's a courtyard with vines growing up the walls. It's not in the touristy bit, it's behind somewhere. I'd never be able to find it again. And we had scrummy food. It was lovely. He said, shall I order for you? in this delicious, masterful way, and I said yes, and he ordered things that I'd never have chosen because the only thing I understood on the menu was steak frites, and we had this lovely long dinner followed by three cognacs. Oh, Nina, it was heaven. And then we walked home, all the way to the seventh arrondissement. Paris by night . . .I didn't even notice that it was five a.m. when we got back. Oh, by the way, Mrs Fischer, who you spoke to, she's this hideous sort of housekeeper creature who Max says brought him up. Can you imagine how horrible? Anyway, she was at the door looking thunderous as we came into the courtyard, and Max was suddenly like a little boy again. Mrs Fischer didn't even say anything. He just ran in and up to his room, which for some reason is next to hers. He was like a puppy with his tail between his legs. It was pathetic. I swept past her as grandly as I could and went to sleep alone in my cold little bed the other end of the house from Max.'

'Pandora, piece of advice, Mrs Fischer's probably listening to every word, so do be careful what you say about her. I've known her for years, and she can be a toughie.'

From her vantage point rearranging already perfectly arranged flowers halfway up the stairs, Mrs Fischer saw Pandora redden and wondered what Nina had said to her. Pandora was an impertinent little cow, with her long black hair and lethal eyelashes, and her designs on the young master. Really, she didn't even have a title!

'Pandora, are you still there?'

'Sorry, yes, I'm just checking around, if you see what I mean?'

'Don't worry, sweetheart, she'll be fine. Just be careful

of her, that's all. At the end of the day she's only a housekeeper, and really, what can a housekeeper do?'

This sounds like a French farce, thought Pandora, as she dropped Mrs Fischer from her thoughts and returned to more important matters.

'So, what do I do?'

'Maybe Mrs Fischer locks him in after lights out?'

'Pandora laughed, 'I wouldn't put it past–' She stopped herself. 'Well, it's not impossible, is it?'

'So you're stuck. How far has it gone?'

Pandora sounded crestfallen. 'Well, in fact, we've only snogged the once, at Emily's party. It's ridiculous, we have a fantastic time, and we keep doing all these lovely romantic things, but . . . well . . . I just don't understand it. I mean, let's face it, Nina, I don't normally have to chase men, do I? Do you think he's gay?'

'Darling, how should I know? I hardly know the boy. I couldn't say. Does he remind you of Rory at all?' Nina knew perfectly well Max wasn't gay. After all her years in the fashion industry, she was pretty discerning. She knew, from a previous holiday, that Max had proved himself undoubtedly heterosexual. But she wasn't about to broadcast the fact to Pandora.

'No. He can't be gay,'

'How do you know?'

'I've seen his bathroom.'

'Nothing in it?'

'And it's not that clean.'

'Fair enough then. He's not gay. So what do you think is the problem?'

'Oh, Nina, I'm going to have to admit it.'

'What?'

'I think he fancies someone else.'

Nina smiled. This was a first for Pandora: a man she found attractive not responding.

'You can't be serious. You're always so confident that all men fancy you.'

'Well, I've got a horrible feeling this one's different. But I can't be too cross about it, can I? I've never been turned down before, and I'm really more embarrassed than anything else.'

'Why?'

'Well, since I always presume that no one can possibly resist my delightful charms, I never play silly games or anything. There's no need. So I'm in this rather sticky position of having made it perfectly clear where I stand, and now that it looks as if he couldn't care less, I'm stuck here in Paris with him, and the others are on their way here and they think we're together.' Pandora's voice became more conspiratorial. She whispered, 'Nina, it's my image I'm really worried about – what can I do about that? There are too many witnesses here.'

Nina couldn't reply for the tears of laughter pouring down her cheeks. Only Pandora could suffer her first major love-life let-down and worry more about her image than the fact that the man she hankered after didn't hanker back. Nevertheless, she pulled herself together.

'Listen, my darling goddaughter, I'm sure you'll get over it, and if it's Morgan and Nick we're talking about, then I'm sure they'll be loyal enough to you not to plaster posters all over the place when they get back advertising your failure with the famous Max Fyodov. Perhaps he just doesn't like dark-haired women?' Nina stroked her golden cap of hair reflectively.

'You might be right. He never stops drooling over Morgan, and she's got red hair. Can you imagine? I thought people with red hair smelt and had bad tempers.'

'Does Morgan smell?'

'No.'

'Does she have a bad temper?'

'Well . . . I've never seen her in one.'

Nina couldn't carry on being mean. 'Perhaps she's not a natural; try having a bath with her and see!'

It was Pandora's turn to laugh. She had visions of herself taking sly looks at Morgan's pubes and Morgan getting the wrong idea. Morgan would probably run a mile!

'I've got to go, sweetheart. Some of us have to work for a living. Keep in touch, though, please, Pandora. You know you can always leave messages here or at the office.'

Putting the phone down, Pandora remembered what Nina had said about Mrs Fischer and looked about her quickly. She thought she saw a shadow move halfway up the stairs, but told herself not to be so stupid. She ran back to her own room, where she found Max ensconced on her bed, legs crossed, reading a battered old copy of *Asterix and Cleopatra* in French.

He looked up as Pandora walked in, and she couldn't help her heart turning over just a little at the way his hair had fallen forward over his white-blond eyebrows. His eyes, one green, one brown, shone even when there was no light reaching them from the window behind him. To distract herself Pandora struck a pose in the doorway and said:

'Don't you find me just irresistible in the morning?'

He grinned sheepishly. 'Actually, that's what I've come to talk to you about.' He put down book and shook his head. 'Pandora, you've got to help me. I don't know what to do.'

Doing her best early-morning Marlene Dietrich impression, Pandora slunk over to the bed and lay down, letting her hair fall to the floor. Looking up from under her eyelashes she realised that she could have been doing a Maori war dance for all Max cared, and sat up straight. He was staring at the tiny Russian icon hung above the bed-head. Perhaps he's praying, Pandora thought. This was obviously serious.

She absent-mindedly began to plait her hair, leaning back against the Napoleonic bedstead that filled most of her room. She sighed. Should she play friendly confidante? If she did, and Max declared undying love for her, then she'd be caught out – no one wanted to declare undying love to Auntie Pandy! Surely they needed Randy Pandy for that? Oh well, it didn't seem to matter, he wasn't looking at her anyway.

I've got to being somewhere, she thought, and said gently, 'What is it, Max? What's the matter?'

Carefully, she stretched her legs into his line of vision, in case he needed to collapse on to them during his declarations. He did no such thing. He put his head in his hands and stayed silent. Pandora was becoming increasingly exasperated. First of all this divine creature ignored her advances. Then he marched into her bedroom first thing in the morning, a heinous crime for anyone else, though she would forgive him just this once. Finally, the ultimate transgression, instead of spilling the beans *mucho fasto* as he really should, he was just using up levée time.

Eventually he looked up at her, and Pandora was shocked by the passion burning out of those gorgeous different-coloured eyes.

'I'm in love. It's awful. I don't know what to do.'

Well, that's a start, thought Pandora. All she needed now was the name of the object of his passion. She smiled encouragingly.

'Pandora, you must help me. The thing is, I've never been in this situation before and I don't know what to do. I mean, I've never . . .' He looked up at her and grinned. 'This is an awful thing to say and you're definitely the only person I can say it to; anyone else would kill me for my arrogance. You know what it's like to always be the most attractive person in the room, don't you?'

Pandora nodded; of course she did.

'So what do you do when someone doesn't find you attractive?'

'Who's not finding you attractive?' she replied, astonished.

'Can't you guess?' He sounded wretched.

Now she was in a real pickle. She couldn't very well name herself could she? She leant forward and ran her hand through the white-blond silk of his hair.

'Are you sure she doesn't fancy you?'

His face was pure misery as he looked at her.

'Positive. She hardly seems to acknowledge me . . . Come on, Pandora, you're one of her best friends. Hasn't she talked to you about the situation?'

Pandora was torn between being offended that the love object was definitely not herself and curiosity as to who exactly it was. Not liking to admit that she didn't know whether he was talking about Emily or Morgan, she hedged.

'No, she hasn't said anything.'

'Pandora, I have to say you're being about as helpful as Mrs Fischer would be.'

'Well, the thing is, I don't know what you do in a situation where someone doesn't fancy you back. It's never happened to me either.'

'Bullshit!'

Pandora was dressed and ready to go. Nick and Morgan wouldn't arrive till the evening and she knew Emily would be too rushed off her feet, getting ready to come to Paris, to gossip on the phone. She had to think of something to do to keep Max and herself busy for the afternoon. She wound her hair round like Morgan did and gazed at herself reflectively in the mirror. She did look quite like Audrey Hepburn. Fittings. That was what would keep them both busy. She reached for her battered black calfskin phone book and flipped through until she found the number of the Chanel studio. She might as well start at the top.

Some hours later Max was bored rigid and Pandora was getting her pound of flesh. He should never have admitted to her that he fancied someone else. She stood with her arms stretched out while a slip of white chiffon someone had ambitiously described as a dress was pinned to her body. Jurgen and Jurgen, the hairdresser's most junior assistants, were doing the Audrey Hepburn thing to her hair, while Gavin Cheveux, their boss, watched, his eyes narrowed in thought.

'Darling, could we put in skunk stripes for the show?' he pleaded. 'Audrey looked fabulous with them.'

'You dare. I'll never get the colour back.'

'But sweetheart, all the other girls colour their hair. They don't mind.'

'None of them have hair that's as naturally beautiful as mine.'

'Maxy, you're an expert. Don't you think a few fabulous fanfares of blondeur would do the trick?'

'I wouldn't' have a clue.'

'Please, Maxy. Help us persuade her.'

Max turned and stared out of the window at the shimmering July heat reflecting off the Paris rooftops. 'Sorry, mat. No one's ever persuaded Pandora to do anything she didn't want to.'

'Ough, Pandora, precious, what's up with Mr Sulky?'

'He's in love.'

'No. Who with? I thought Max Fyodov was unavailable to anybody.'

'Not so.'

'Who is it?'

'Well,' Pandora began.

Max whipped round. 'Shut up, Pandora. How long are we going to be here?'

"Ooh, we are cross. Max, you shouldn't invite people to stay if you can't be bothered to entertain them.'

'I'm not entertaining you. This ageing queen in a white coat and a pincushion is.' He marched over to the door. 'I'm going. You don't need me for this. I'll see you at home later.'

'Max . . .'

'What?'

'Sorry to be quite such a bore, but I haven't got any money. I can't get home.'

Max threw a five hundred franc note down on the table by the door.

'That should do you. Unless you smoke it first.' He slammed out.

'My, he's really unhappy. Perhaps he's struggling with his sexuality,' muttered the hairdresser hopefully. Jurgen and Jurgen giggled at each other. Imagine, Max Fyodov available!

'I wouldn't bet on it.' Pandora, suddenly bored, dropped her arms and sighed.

'Oh, darling, don't do that! Quick, back to where you were, just for a tick. Jurgen, a Polaroid. Quickly, quickly, our lovely little Pandy's tired, aren't you, darling?'

Pandora posed for the Polaroid before dropping her arms again. 'I'm parched. Isn't there anything to drink here?'

'Champagne, champagne. Champagne for the lovely Pandora. Nothing like it to take the edge off the heat of a July afternoon.'

'I don't know. Air-conditioning might help. How is it that most of the great fashion houses in France have no air-conditioning, lifts to the studios that you virtually have to crank up yourself and people who work so slowly I have to stand with my arms in the air arguing hairstyles for hours at a time?'

'Darling, sit down. You're obviously very tired.'

Pandora collapsed on to a tiny gilt chair with a pink velvet seat. She suddenly felt bad. 'I'm sorry. I'm just having a girlie moment.' She smiled gloriously at the people around her: the designer, the man who'd made the dress, the *premier main* from the atelier who'd beaded the hem with thousands of tiny pears, Gavin and the two Jurgens. She knew that she was being unfair, that these people had been working their socks off for her dress for months and that they were all exhausted and longing for the show to be over. 'Come on.' She jumped up and kissed the designer. 'One glass of champagne and I'll stand with my arms over my head for the rest of my life if I have to.'

The Jurgens clapped their hands, 'Oh, she's too precious!' and the whole rigmarole started again, this time with a grass-green paper taffeta pant suit which reflected emerald sparks into Pandora's eyes.

Nina and Rory sat in the armchairs at the far end of Nina's huge office. Emily sat disconsolately just outside it. It was 7.30 at night. She was desperate to go home, but the list of things that needed doing before they left for Paris was about five pages long, and she (a) wanted to get some of it done before she left and (b) didn't dare ask Nina if she could go for fear of getting her head bitten off for the thousandth time that day. She sighed and picked up the phone to call Paris. At least the fashion houses seemed to be finishing their days later and later too, so she knew that she could still get through to people. She dialled Dior, the telephone receiver jammed between her ear and her shoulder, while writing in huge letters at the end of her list, 'Pick up dry-cleaning or you'll have nothing to wear in Paris!' She just hoped she'd have time to do that on Friday. Otherwise she'd have to swan around the Crillon in jeans and a T-shirt. She could hear the low voices of Rory and Nina in the background. At least she wasn't the only person working late.

'Right, we're agreed,' Rory was saying. 'We'll go with the Dior, the Givenchy, the Chanel, the Versace and the Saint Laurent. Oh yes, the Lacroix too.'

'We should do some Ungaro, really, for the advertisers.'

'Nina, we have never – nor do we intend to start now – sold advertising on the back of editorial.'

'I know, but you know what the publisher's like. He'll have our guts for garters if we don't.'

'Look, Nina. He's already made me promise to go to all those parties, and I'm having lunch with about fifty of these people. Do we have to photograph their clothes as well? It'll compromise the story.'

'We could always do two couture pieces.'

'No we can't. One couture story's enough. Don't confuse the reader. Besides, September's all bound up and ready to go except for these pages. You can't put in more.'

Nina sighed and relaxed in her hair.

'I know, I know. OK, we stick with the story as agreed.'

'Shooting?'

'We'll see. I'm sure Gloria knows what she wants to do, and depending on the collections, I'm quite happy to go along with that. She's never let me down yet.'

'What do you mean, "we'll see"? Honey, you have to know what you're going to do before we get there. Everyone and everywhere will be booked otherwise. We can't fuck around on this. You know how little time we have. I'm not going to have my life ruined because you don't make your mind up till the last minute. Some of us have other things to do apart from photographing couture at your convenience, you know! Besides, if Gloria's so brilliant, why isn't she here now, reassuring us?'

'She has a dinner. She told me about it. Calm down, Rory. What are you so antsy about? If you've got such a busy life just leave the couture to me and Gloria. I don't care. Besides, you've done your bit. It really is up to Gloria now.'

'Oh, I see. The famous stylist with the jumped-up title's getting all the credit, is she? You know she turned up and Charlied around in my bathroom the other night, lovely Don Elson in tow.'

'Yes, Rory. You did tell me.'

'So. You still trust her?'

'She's my fashion director. I have no reason not to trust her. And if she feels she needs to spend time with that slimeball, then that's entirely her affair. I'm not about to distrust her.'

'Well you should. What happens if she lets you down?'

'She won't.'

*

At about eight o'clock that evening, Nick and Morgan arrived at the Fyodov house. They'd had a typical sort of journey down: queues for the train, shock at the exchange rate with the English pound, too many motorway snacks, and then an hour and a half lost in central Paris trying to follow Pandora's completely inaccurate instructions.

'You go to St Germain and head south,' she'd said in her usual throwaway manner. They had done just that, and kept finding themselves snarled up in the one-way system round the Tour Montparnasse. By this time everything was closed so they couldn't buy a map. Finally Morgan had insisted Nick park illegally outside the Church of St Germain des Près while she attempted in very dodgy schoolgirl French to ask directions from a waiter at the café opposite. Luckily the waiter spoke some English, and eventually she discovered that Pandora should have said north instead of south, and that for the past hour and a half they had been only about half a mile from the house.

'You go down ze rue Bonaparte zat way and you take ze firrrst turrn on ze left,' the waiter told her. 'You follow ze rrroad till after ze next fire and zere you find ze 'ouse. She is just near Mr Lagerfeld, on ze left.' Morgan thanked him profusely and jumped back into the car.

'That way,' she cried, pointing back towards the river. About five minutes later they were parked next to Max's Spider in the courtyard of a large seventeenth-century house in the rue de l'Université, a forbidding Germanic woman looking down disapprovingly at them from the top of a flight of steps.

'I thought bay trees were supposed to keep the devil out of a house,' whispered Morgan to Nick, when she saw the woman who introduced herself gutterally as Mrs Fischer. Nick stopped himself from laughing and marched, square-shouldered and determined, towards her intimidating bulk. He introduced himself and Morgan and asked if Pandora and Max were there.

Mrs Fischer, who gave no sign of inviting the two friends into the house, addressed them in her thick German accent, unsoftened by a lifetime of Paris. 'They went out. They didn't say when they would return. They told me you were expected. However, I must warn you that I did not prepare dinner for you. Young Master Max left no instructions and I have enough to do preparing for the return of Mr Fyodov. You will have to eat out and I will give you a key so that you can let yourselves in after your dinner. I always retire by twenty-one-thirty hours.' She held a key at arm's-length for Nick and shut the door in their faces. They watched through the glass doors as she disappeared down a long hall.

'Well,' said Morgan, turning to Nick. 'What do we do now?'

'What the fuck does Max think he's doing, inviting us down and then not being here?' Nick was all manly outrage. He was furious with Max for putting them in this embarrassing position. Ever practical, though, he decided they go and eat, as Mrs Fischer had suggested, and shout at Pandora and Max later. Apart from anything else, he was starving. He led the way out of the courtyard and turned right. He had no idea where he was going but hoped that sooner or later they would find a cheap restaurant. At least they could leave the car safely in the courtyard.

They headed back towards St Germain and eventually came across an old-fashioned little bistro, the Petit Saint Benoit, which served slapdash French country food. Apart from the fact that Nick ordered liver when he thought he was ordering veal, and that andouillette turned out to be white blood sausage which Morgan really couldn't eat, they felt much better as they finished their meal with hot tarte tatin with crème fraiche and tiny cups of steaming espresso.

By the time they got back to the house in the rue de ;'Université, Pandora and Max had returned, and the four friends settled down to catch up on what they'd been up to for the last couple of days. They were all in a good mood, partly brought on by wine and the excitement of being away.

Morgan lay back on the huge white linen sofa in the drawing room and thanked God she'd left Anna and Sam behind to deal with later. Max couldn't stop himself from watching her. Her hair had come out of its knot and fell in a shimmering stream over the arm of the sofa. He wanted to bury himself in it. Pandora caught Max staring longingly at Morgan. Why should he be so relentlessly intent on her when he had Pandora to distract him? Perhaps the thing was to feign total indifference, as Morgan did. Though Morgan really was indifferent, and incapable of feigning anything. Nick lay back, looking at the exquisite baroque ceiling and wondering if he would ever earn enough money to be able to afford something like this. He decided he didn't care. All he really wanted was Pandora.

Chapter 6

FRIDAY 21 JULY

NINA looked around the table in the conference room. This was her team, waiting expectantly for her to start the last meeting they would have before most of them set off for Paris the following morning. They were there to put the final touches to their plans and to the stories that they would write if the news they'd gathered in advance of the shows proved true. If the designers had done a mass turnaround behind their backs, then the stories would have to be changed. Usually, however, the shoots could be set up in advance, the photographers, studios, outside locations and most of the models booked ahead of the shows. They were only waiting for Gloria. Nina's lips were set in a thin line. She didn't like waiting for anyone.

Emily knocked nervously and entered the room. She was exhausted. She hadn't got home until 10.30 the previous evening, and still hadn't picked up her dry-cleaning. The last thing she needed was to be disturbed by her boss every three seconds.

Nina sounded charming. 'Darling, do you think you could nip down to Gloria's office and find out whether she's going to be joining us? I don't think any of us want to wait all day.' She smiled to show she wasn't cross with Emily, and turned back to her agenda. With her face set in deep lines of concentration, she carried on writing. Sam's name down the margin.

Two minutes later Emily was back.

'Gloria's just called from her mobile. She says she'll be here in two minutes. She had a meeting.'

Nina fumed. Gloria wouldn't get away with this. There'd been too many clandestine meetings for Nina's liking lately. There would be some explanations or Gloria would be in serious trouble.

Gloria had been Nina's first assistant, and thanks to hard work, she had an encyclopaedic knowledge of fashion and an eye that even Nina had to admit made her one of the best sittings editors around. She had become indispensable to both Nina, who had rewarded her with a position as her fashion director, and also to the magazine. She did four out of every five fashion sittings, coming up with an endless stream of ideas and fantastic cover shots. The Paris couture collections would be shot exclusively under her eagle eye. Still, Nina didn't like her being late. She tapped her Chanel ballet-slippered foot against the leg of her chair and pursed her lips. Rory looked up from the other end of the table and sent her an 'I told you so' smile. Nina wanted to slap his Penhaligon-hair-oiled head, and refrained from the impulse by writing Sam's name another fifty times in the small space left at the end of her agenda.

When Gloria finally bounded into the room, waving files and portable phone with dangerous energy, Nina knew that something was definitely up. Either Gloria was off to another magazine or she was planning a takeover on Nina's turf. Nina had never seen her right-hand woman so excited. The couture was fun, but it was unlikely to break any fashion barriers that season. What was Gloria on? Nina smiled silkily down the table.

'Lovely to see you at last, Gloria. Do you want to call your assistant quickly and tell her you'll be lunching with me? Emily,' Nina looked up as Emily came through the door again, 'set my office up for lunch – two people – and call out for pizza, would you?' As Emily bowed out, Nina smiled down the table at a furious Gloria. Gloria, a diet fanatic, knew she would not get away from lunch with Nina in this kind of mood without a whole pizza inside her. She sighed and loosened the skirt of her sharp Prada suit in readiness.

That same morning the object of Max's passion was tucking into a steaming bowl of coffee and a pain au chocolat in his Paris kitchen. There had been no sign of Mrs Fischer when everyone had come downstairs. Someone had made a pot of coffee, which sat grumbling on the pre-war stove, and a huge plate of breakfast delicacies was waiting on the table, so Morgan had decided she should just help herself.

Max and Pandora were evidently disporting themselves upstairs in a manner which didn't invite interruption, and Nick had disappeared, claiming he couldn't possibly start the day without a newspaper. Morgan gazed out of the window at the small formal garden, in the centre of which stood an exquisite eighteenth-century fountain depicting a small girl pouring water into a basin from a jug on her shoulder. It was almost the kitchest thing Morgan had ever seen, but in the special clear, pale light peculiar to Paris and the dappled shadows from the limes around her, the girl looked divine.

Suddenly Nick slammed back into the room slapping a copy of the *Times* on to the table.

'Fifteen bloody francs for this. Can you imagine it? It's daylight robbery. If it weren't for the cricket I wouldn't have bothered. And they didn't even have a copy of the *Sun*.' He sat down and hid behind the sports pages, occasionally snorting with continued fury.

Morgan laughed out loud. 'Honestly, surely you could live without the sport for a few days, couldn't you? Imagine if I had to run out and buy papers for the fashion pages or something all the time – I'd be permanently broke.'

'Watch it, Morgan, Pandora does!' Nick caught sight of the coffee pot and the croissants and immediately forgot all about the paper. He poured, grabbed a croissant and dunked it in his bowl. 'So what are we going to do while we're here?' he said, his mouth full.

Morgan shrugged, 'It looks as if true love is going to take up most of Pandora and Max's time, so I think we can probably entertain ourselves. What do you think of going to Versailles?'

'Mmm . . . not bad, a bit grand for me. Can we go to Giverny too? We can balance the two and then won't go back with too drastic an idea of the French.'

Morgan smiled, noncommital, and picked up the discarded half of Nick's newspaper. And so, once again, she missed Max's look of longing as he walked through the door, hand in hand with Pandora. Nick didn't, and wondered how Max could get away with constantly panting after Morgan like a labrador after its master. Pandora never seemed to bat an eyelid.

'Good morning, children.' Morgan glanced up to see Max silhouetted in the sunlight pouring through the south-east-facing windows. He looked like a Greek god. He was wearing soft old jeans, belted with battered black leather, and nothing else, and was staring at Morgan as if she was the only thing in the room. She found herself blushing and kicked herself under the table. Don't be ridiculous, Morgan. Not only is this man going out with one of your best friends but you have nothing in common with him. She went back to studying the newspaper and waited for the red flush she could feel clashing so attractively with her hair to calm down.

Max helped himself to coffee and leaned against the scrubbed oak dresser which took up the whole of one of the kitchen walls.

'So, what do you guys want to do now you're here?'

'Well, Morgan wants to go to Versailles and I want to go to Giverny.'

'Oh, please! You're all such tourists,' exclaimed Pandora. 'Doesn't anyone want to go shopping?'

'No, shopaholic – we don't. Is that all you want to do?' Max playfully pulled the black satin ribbon loosely holding Pandora's hair back. 'Don't you have enough trinkets already?'

Pandora grabbed her hair ribbon back out of his hands, laughing.

'Of course I want to go shopping. Unlike you lot I've done enough touristing in Paris to last a lifetime. Nina always used to bring me here when I was little. Now I just want to lunch at the Floré and shop. Does no one want to come with me?' Pandora looked questioningly round her group of friends finishing off the coffee and croissants. 'Well,' she stamped her foot in mock irritation, 'I think you're all philistines. I'll just have to go alone. That is,' she smiled winningly at Max, 'so long as my beloved will lend me enough money to get me through the day. Did I tell you the story of my flight from England without even a five-pound note to sort me out in emergencies?' And Pandora flounced out of the room in mock annoyance.

The others agreed that they would go to Versailles that day and Giverny the next, and having seen Pandora off with five thousand francs in her pocket with which to amuse herself. Max tucked Morgan into the front seat of the Spider and Nick squeezed himself into the back. Max tried not to look too excited. He'd even had the foresight to warn Morgan that Versailles could turn into a dust bowl in the summer so she might prefer to wear her glasses rather than her contact lenses, and she'd smiled like an angel and thanked him. As usual, she was unaware of Max's discomfort.

Without the others, Pandora thoroughly enjoyed herself. She'd done all the fittings she needed to do the day before, and now she wandered around the little streets full of tiny shops behind St Germain. She bought herself a selection of vastly expensive goodies. The best part, she thought later, as she settled down to lunch at the Café Floré, was that all the shops gave you very thick card bags with rope handles, even if you'd only bought a couple of drawer handles, you felt as if you'd spent a fortune, and when the waiters at the Floré caught sight of the absolute – the Prada bag – you were treated as if you had a similar fortune to spend on them.

She settled back on the banquette, glad that Max's jeans fitted her to perfection and that he had such a large collection of pristine white T-shirts. Shame she hadn't been able to whip his flying jacket for the day, but *tant pis*, at least she'd got rid of him. She felt as Parisienne as an English girl could: understand elegance, little details giving away the fact that she just couldn't help being glamorous even though she'd never thought about it in her life . . . much. She smiled lovingly at the flat snakeskin Prada sandals that had been her real extravagance of the morning – after all, there was a limited amount of time that she could force herself to march about in her party shoes. She ordered a kir and scrambled eggs on toast for her lunch and opened her newspaper. She'd bought the *International Herald Tribune*, as she didn't want people to be able to tell what nationality she was, and she settled down behind it to watch the people around her.

She was deep in an inspection of Lauren Bacall, who was sitting with a group of what looked like grey-haired intellectuals, when she was interrupted.

'Excuse me. Do you mind?'

Pandora looked up to find the man of her dreams gesturing at the empty seat next to her. The voice was unplaceable, international, not even half one accent and half another. Pandora had never heard anything so sexy. Covering her eyes with the famous eyelashes, she took in the details of a tall, distinguished-looking man, blond like Max, and with a scar slashed across his face, unbalancing his looks just enough to make them perfect.

She smiled her most devastating smile. 'Of course. Please.' She even pretended to move up a little.

'I do apologise for disturbing you.' His eyes had a mischievous glint in them.

'Not at all. I was getting thoroughly bored with the paper.' Her lunch arrived and she put the paper away and tucked in, buttering the thick slices of toasted pain de mie that had come with the scrambled eggs, and smiling at the man next to her winningly. She prayed that he wouldn't stop talking. He was heaven.

'May I ask what you are doing in Paris?'

Oh God, thought Pandora, thank goodness I'm not with Max. I would never have come across this man if I'd gone off with that youth. She tried to look cool.

'I'm staying with some friends. Just a trip to go shopping and so on, you know.' She waved at her expensive shopping bags dismissively. 'And then there are the shows. They start tomorrow.'

'So you're not a tourist?' His eyes were boring into her. She hoped she wasn't going to blush.

'Oh no. No, I know Paris quite well actually.' She simpered. 'My godmother always used to bring me here when I was little. Frankly, if I saw another group of Manets or even the Rodin museum once more I think I'd die.' She gave a little tinkling laugh. She hoped she wasn't going over the top, but this man looked as if he was about to offer to show her around, and the last thing she wanted from him was a tour of the Musée d'Orsay!

'Good, so you spend your time familiarising yourself with the real Paris, the living city?'

'Yes, I suppose so.' In front of her the scrambled eggs began to coagulate; the toast, which had looked so delicious, got colder and more leathery by the minute. Pandora gulped at her wine and stared, spellbound, at her neighbour. The man looked directly back at her. She held his gaze, even though she knew she was blushing.

'This café is hot, don't you think? My house is just round the corner. May I invite you to lunch?' Without speaking, Pandora simply stood, waited for him to pay for her virtually untouched eggs and followed him down the street back towards the river. He took her elbow and carried her shopping. She would have been in seventh heaven if the divine snakeskin sandals hadn't been rubbing uncomfortably against her little toes, making walking in an elegant fashion almost impossible.

The shock came when he turned into the courtyard of

Max's house. Of course – this man was Max's father! Pandora hugged the knowledge that, having been jilted by the son, she'd get her own back by seducing the father, and tried to keep a straight face as Mrs Fischer opened the door for them, bowing as she did so.

'We'll have lunch in the small drawing room, Mrs Fischer. I think smoked salmon and the Montrachet. Bring two bottles and then leave us.'

He led Pandora to a wing of the house which she had not yet discovered and into a little room furnished with exquisite Louis XVI chairs and tables, the walls hung with pale gold and green silk. He pulled out a chair for her and waited for her to sit down, then sat on the other side of the table. Neither of them spoke. Minutes later Mrs Fischer carried in a large tray holding a plate of slices of brown bread and smoked salmon, two glasses and two bottles of white wine submerged in buckets of ice.

'Thank you, Mrs Fischer. I am not to be disturbed.'

The housekeeper threw a foul look at Pandora and left. Pandora sat quite still and waited patiently for the man to make the first move. He sat and watched her from the other side of the table. Neither of them had spoken to each other since they had left the Floré. There was no need. For the first time in her life Pandora was speechless.

Eventually, after what seemed like an hour, the man spoke.

'I think it better if we don't know each other's names,' was all he said.

'OK.' she answered and tried to swallow. Her mouth

was unaccountably dry. She wanted to stand and walk round the table to him. Max's jeans were rubbing the insides of her thighs. He'll take them off, she thought, and smiled at him. He would reach forward and pull her towards him. She would stand between his knees and he would snake his arms around her back and slowly stroke her buttocks through the jeans. She forced herself to wait. Bloody hell, he was passing her the salmon!

'Thank you,' she said, and piled her plate with thin slices of bread and fish.

Andreï was equally confused. He'd been under the impression when he'd asked this girl home with him that she was one of the high-class call girls who usually touted for business in all the grander cafés in Paris. But she couldn't be. She'd be halfway through her act if that was the case. He looked across the table. This girl was tucking into the smoked salmon! He didn't want salmon now; it was for afterwards, and for him, not her. She would be long gone by then. Now she should be getting on with the job in hand.

He studied her more closely. She was very young to be successful enough to have spent money on Prada sandals. Her hair was extraordinary. Somehow she reminded him of his mother, the slant of her eyes, the way her hair grew straight back from a pronounced widow's peak off a high forehead, eyes so dark they were almost black. Perhaps she was new to the Café Floré scene. He could tell her about it, fuck her later. He opened one of the bottles of Montrachet, expertly drawing the cork so that it hardly made a sound and pouring the pale golden liquid into fine long-stemmed glasses. He passed her one of them. He watched with pleasure as she sipped the wine, her natural grace giving even such a mundane movement a beauty that he thoroughly enjoyed. He still hadn't said anything. But the silence now was so all-encompassing that neither of them could break it. He didn't seem to mind it. And why should she ruin the atmosphere of gilded calm which held them? The hustle and bustle of Paris, only yards outside the window, was a lifetime away. She smiled at him. He smiled back. The silence held.

'So, you've been coming to Paris for many years?' At last his voice broke the mood.

'Yes, my godmother comes often and she used to bring me. This time I'm visiting friends. They are terrible tourists and have rushed off in this heat to Versailles or somewhere. I couldn't bear the idea of the people they would have to queue with, so I begged a day off to shop. I love it here.'

'It is one of the most beautiful areas of Paris. One of the oldest. All the little streets have been here since long before the Revolution.' He said the word Revolution with some disgust.

Pandora was almost swooning, his voice was so gorgeous. 'Really.' Ugh, she hated people who said that; it made them sound like a secretary in a Philadelphia cheese advert.

'Do you know the rest of France at all?'

'No . . .' She was stuck. 'No.'

His different-coloured eyes flashed and he fingered his scar meditatively. She wondered where he'd got it.

'You should take the time to explore the other parts of France. They can be much more beautiful than Paris.' He paused. 'So, you are new to the girls at the Floré, are you?'

'I'm sorry? Which girls?'

'You are working?' It was a statement, not a question. 'All this conversation is really irrelevant. You must be new or you wouldn't be wasting so much time.'

'New to what?'

'Please, let us stop playing games. Stand up and come here.' She came round the table obediently and stood before him. He got up and circled her.

'You are lucky it is I who have collected you today. You could behaving a horrible time elsewhere. Where are you working from?' Pandora was completely lost. 'No matter. You don't have to tell me if you are embarrassed. You are right. You should always go with the man, then your own place need not embarrass you if it is a little,' he searched for the right word, 'ordinary for your guests.' He picked up her ponytail and untied the ribbon that held back her hair. 'Mmm, if you take my advice you will always wear your hair back like you did today. It is so extraordinary when you let it down. Really, there are things you could do with your hair that could make you a specialist. Much more lucrative. Did you think of that?'

Pandora barely took in what he was saying; she was only aware of his hand running through her hair, weighing it like gold. She was disappointed when he dropped the mass, and she automatically went to tie it back again. He held the ribbon away from her and looked her up and down.

'You could wear clothes which are a little more obvious, to. After all, if you are new to the game you might not have too many regular clients. Dressing as you do is really for the hardened professionals. If it weren't for my experience in such matters, you would never have attracted me. I am always drawn to things about which I am slightly unsure. Yes, I think to make a real success you should show your legs a little more, nothing overtly *putain*, but you could wear a short skirt instead of jeans.' Andreï had a sudden urge to take this innocent young tart shopping, to fit her out like he had Max when he went away to boarding school. 'Take your clothes off.' Andreï sat down again, crossing his legs and putting the ends of his fingers together thoughtfully.

Pandora didn't dare disobey. She took another gulp of her wine, and her jeans and T-shirt dropped to the floor, leaving only the Calvin Klein underwear. Andreï whistled. She was a pearl, her skin such a beautiful colour it looked as if it could only be man-made, and all framed by that stunning hair.

'Yes, you will make a lot of money.'

Pandora gave in. She didn't care if she looked stupid, she had to know what on earth he was talking about. 'A lot of money at what?'

'Why, modelling, of course. This is what you do is it not?'

How was Pandora to know that Andreï was using a polite term for whoring? She smiled and sat down, sipping at her wine. She had no intention of dressing again. She just longed for him to make the first move towards her. He walked behind her chair and lifted her hair again, letting it fall slowly before beginning to run his fingers over her shoulders. Pandora shivered in anticipation.

Mrs Fischer chose that moment to walk into the room. Pandora blushed.

'Get out! I told you, no disturbances.'

'Sir, I am aware that you wished only to be disturbed in an emergency. But your driver called. Armand is on his way to Fontainebleau. I thought you should know.'

'I said get out. And don't disturb us again.'

Andreï turned to Pandora, his expression hard and his eyes suddenly mean. Pandora was almost frightened of him.

'You should dress,' he said, looking at his watch. 'I'm afraid this has taken rather longer than I intended. I have business to attend to. But I wish you great luck in your career. Learn the right moves and you might get somewhere.' And to Pandora's amazement he laid a bundle of five-hundred-franc notes on the table in front of her and politely turned his back while she dressed. She stuffed the money in her jeans pocket and tied back her hair. She was thoroughly confused.

Andreï took Pandora's arm and led her to the front door, then kissing her lightly on the lips, he turned back into the house. Pandora waited for a longing look from him, but only the cute-looking driver of a huge black Mercedes parked in the courtyard threw her an appreciative grin. Pandora shook herself. Back to the matter in hand. He hadn't even suggested that they meet again. Perhaps she should sit and wait for him at the Café Floré until he turned up. She wondered where he really lived. Obviously not in the house while Max was there, or she'd have seen him before, wouldn't she? She marched back to the Floré and ordered coffee. When it arrived, she sipped at the thick foaming espresso and began to think.

Emily was trudging through the afternoon's tasks. Now she had two lists, one for work and one for herself. Her own list read:

Dry-cleaning
Ring Mum and tell her you're going tomorrow
Pack
Go to Boots
Cancel cleaner
Pick up shoes from menders
Order taxi for the morning

The work list was about fifty times longer and never seemed to decrease in length. Every time she managed to get something done, Nina gave her another five things to tackle. She was beginning to think she needed an assistant herself. She sighed, exhausted, lit a Silk Cut, opened a can of Diet Coke, wiped the sweat from her brow and picked up the phone again. Her personal list would just have to wait.

'Hello, this is Nina Charles' assistant in London. Could I have the press office please?'

'*Comment?*'

'*Parlez-vous anglais?*'

'*Non. Vous voulez qui?*'

'Um.' She thought hard and finally stammered, '*Le bureau de presse, s'il vous plaît.*'

'*Ne quittez pas.*'

Emily breathed a sigh of relief. She was halfway there.

'*Allo.*'

'*Oui. Bonjour. Ici le bureau de Nina Charles à Londres. Parlez-vous anglais?*'

'Yes. A leetle.'

'Thank goodness for that. I'd reached the end of my French.'

'What is it?' The voice was not friendly.

'I was just checking that Miss Charles' invitation will be sent to the Crillon.'

'Yes. It will be. We know ziss. I really don't 'ave time to go over ziss any more.'

'Yes. I understand. Just one more thing.'

'What is it?'

'Could you give me her seat number please? I need it for her schedule.'

'Oh, please. I am 'ardly going to give 'er a standing ticket. She 'as a front-row seat. Ziss *rédactrice en chef* get front row. Why you insist to waste my time like ziss? I already 'ad your Paris office on ze line four tines for ziss. For ze last time you can tell Nina Charles she 'as a very good seat. It is 1A4. She is in ze middle of ze end section, far away from ze Americans. I put zat pop star she like near 'er, behind.'

'Thank you. And could you tell me Rory Williams' seat number too?'

'E tell me 'e don't want a seat, zat 'e will be backstage ssroughout. I send 'is pass already to 'is 'otel. Tell 'im not to be late, please. Last time 'e put ze 'ole backstage organisation off track.'

'I will. Thank you so much for your help. Um . . . there was one more thing I wanted to check.'

'Yes? I really 'ave to go.'

'Yes. I understand. But has Pandora Williams been for her fitting?'

'Yes, she come yesterday. Very bad mood and brought Max Fyodov wizz 'er. 'E was in a bad mood too. I 'ope ssings improve before ze show, ozzerwize zere will be problems.'

'Thank you so much.' Emily put the phone down and ticked off on her list the third of the houses she had to call. At least Pandora was still in Paris. That should calm Nina down a little. She squared her shoulders and prepared to make the next call.

Pandora spent the rest of the afternoon mulling over coffee at the Floré and smoking half a pack of Marlboros. It wasn't something she would normally do – she dreaded ending up with stained teeth like Rory's – but this was an emergency! The problem was that Andreï had just left her, let her leave without a backwards glance. Somehow she had to make sure that she saw him again, and she couldn't presume that by turning up at the Floré on a sufficient number of consecutive days she would. Eventually, despondent, she headed back to the house in the rue de l'Université. She'd come up only with a series of useless answers to her problem and was becoming more and more convinced that she'd never see her dreamy man again. As she turned into the courtyard, she stopped short. The huge black Merc was still sitting there accusingly.

Distracted by the cute driver leaning on the bonnet smoking a cigarette, she forgot that Andreï didn't know that she was staying at the house and flounced past the car, making sure her hair was swinging about to its full advantage. She threw the driver a dazzling smile, and he grinned back and slowly ground out the stub of the cigarette on the cobbles. Pandora ran up the steps to the front door, torn between the desire to chat up the driver and the need to know whether Andreï was in the house.

The door swung open before she had time to reach for the handle.

'Get in,' hissed Mrs Fischer. 'Go straight upstairs. He will be gone soon. He does not need to know you are here.'

The housekeeper glared at Pandora with such authority that Pandora meekly obeyed and ran upstairs, but not to her room. She hung around on the landing, admiring a large painting of a woman seemingly being raped by a swan – something she frankly found perverted – and listening hard to what was going on downstairs. A door slammed, and she heard footsteps hurrying down the hall. Then the front door opened and Andreï's voice rang out.

'See to it, Mrs Fischer. I will be at Fontainebleau until further notice. I expect all deliveries to be sent straight to me. You will not forget to call my driver.'

Pandora tried to hear Mrs Fischer's reply but could

have sworn that she didn't say a word. The door closed and Pandora ran to the window to watch the car ease through the high arch framing the heavy doors which closed the courtyard off from the rest of the world.

Pandora sat down heavily on the window seat. Damn – how far away was Fontainebleau? No point in hanging around in the Floré now, was there? The only way she would get any further with Max's father would be to get information out of Max himself. So, all she needed was for Max to return from his culture-vulture session with Morgan and Nick. Unless . . . She jumped up and ran downstairs to the telephone.

'Mrs Fischer, Mrs Fischer.'

'What is it, Miss Williams?'

'Sorry, what's the international code for London again?'

'Nineteen forty-four, and you leave out the zero.' Mrs Fischer turned on her heel and disappeared towards the kitchen, disapproval written all over her back.

'Right.' Pandora dialled her home number. No answer. Odd. She tried the office.

'Yes?'

'Rory!'

'Precious! Where are you?'

'Paris, you dimwit. Remember, the collections start tomorrow.'

'Oh Yes. And are your dresses too divine for words?'

'I can't tell you. The Lacroix is arguably the most beautiful thing I've ever seen.'

'And you've been a good girl and done nothing but go to fittings?'

'Not at all. I've met a man.'

'Who? Would I approve?'

'Well, Max was such a little boy.'

'Never my type. I knew you wouldn't like him for long. Have you moved to the Crillon yet?'

'No, I'm still here, at the rue de l'Université house. Very convenient for a lot of things.'

'Like what?'

'Falling in love at the Floré. You know Max, don't you?'

'Never me the boy.'

'Rubbish. He was at the party.'

'I just had a look at him, precious. I wouldn't want to contaminate myself by getting any closer.'

'Why, what's wrong with him?'

'His father. You haven't met Andreï, have you?'

'Why, what's wrong with him?'

'He's a murdering swine, and you keep well away from him. He's evil and a bastard and disgusting and wrong and horrid and amoral and . . .' Rory ran out of words.

'My, whatever did he do to you to deserve such vitriol?'

'You're too young to know.'

'Tell me, Rory. You know I'm not squeamish.'

Suddenly Rory's voice changed. 'Watch it, Pandora. Don't get involved in things to big for you. Andreï Fyodov is about as unpleasant a character as it's possible to find, and I'm telling you to keep away from him.'

'Telling me!'

'Yes. And if you disobey me, I'll never forgive you.'

'Rory, have you gone out of your mind?'

'No, Pandora. I've never been so sane in my life.'

'You have no idea what effect you ordering me around like this has on me.'

'Quite frankly, my dear. I couldn't give a flying fuck. Leave him alone. In fact, if you've any brain at all you'll move into your room at the Crillon this afternoon and save yourself a lot of trouble.'

'I won't.'

'You should. I can't force you. But make sure you're there by the time Nina and I arrive tomorrow.'

'Yes, Uncle Rory.'

'I mean it.'

'I know you do.' Pandora stared at the receiver. Rory had definitely gone mad. How dare he order her around? 'Just one question, Rory.'

'What? I'm busy. I'll talk to you tomorrow.'

'Where's Fontainebleau?'

'Three-quarters of an hour from Paris. François the First's hunting lodge. The model for Versailles. Nice place. Big château. Fab shops. Now, darling, *get away from the Fyodovs and move into the Crillon*.'

"Bye, Rory.'

Pandora jumped when she heard a car enter the courtyard. She had been fast asleep, stretched out on a landing window seat, and she had lost all idea of time. She didn't even know where she was. It took her a couple of moments to realise that Paris was still Paris and that the car below was Max's Spider, and that he was laughing with Morgan! I'll give her something to laugh about, the witch! she thought as she ran downstairs, thunder taking the place of sleep in her eyes. She looked at her watch – it was almost 8.30! How dare they leave her alone for so long? She'd forgotten that she'd insisted that everyone go off without her, and her fury transformed her face into the usual spoilt pout. Max looked up at her as she burst through the doors, and made the mistake of giving her a thumbs-up sign behind Morgan's back. Right, thought Pandora, you're all for it! She forced herself to smile and opened her arms wide in welcome.

'You look like the mistress of the house, Pandora,' said Morgan as she unfolded her long legs out of the car. Pandora couldn't help noticing that they looked slightly burnt.

'Darling, I hope you didn't spend all day in the sun with your delicate skin. You know you can do lifelong damage to it in one afternoon.'

'Never mind about my skin, Pandora, we had a lovely day. What did you get up to?'

'Oh, nothing much. You know, shopping, lunch . . . Do you like my sandals?' She waved one of her elegant little feet. Morgan laughed; Pandora was incorrigible.

The two girls ran upstairs, and Pandora sat on the ottoman in the bathroom while Morgan rinsed her feet with the shower attachment.

'So, darling, how was your day with lover boy?' Pandora's voice was acid.

'Who's lover boy?'

'Max, of course.'

'Rubbish.' Morgan blushed.

'Please,' said Pandora. 'You two are all over each other

and both of you refuse to see it. Oh, don't blush, Morgan, it clashes with your hair.'

'Don't be such a bitch, Pandora.'

'You don't believe me, do you? You'd better go and have a sneak about his room, then, hadn't you? It's a studio.'

'Really?'

'You think he takes happy snaps with that camera of his! Oohlala, I've never seen so many things made totally unrecognisable by a Fyodov Fuji mix. And he paints.' Pandora said with some disgust.

'How do you know all this?' Morgan laughed.

'Because I'm a nosy old cow, that's how. I've been sneaking around looking in places where I haven't been invited.' Morgan looked shocked. 'Well, how else am I supposed to find out what's really going on in the world? Nobody ever spells things out, do they?' Morgan laughed again. 'So go look in his studio. and you'll believe he's in love with you, I promise. Now, don't you want to know about my day?' Pandora asked, raising one of her eyebrows quizzically.

'All right, what did you get up to?'

'Well, apart from the investment in these divine sandals, which would have been quite enough for most girls to be getting on with, I had an adventure with a man.'

'No, who?'

'Well, began Pandora, 'I was just sitting minding my own business in the Floré, staring at Lauren Bacall and wondering if it really could be her, when this gorgeous man came and sat next to me.'

'Yes . . .'

'Imagine, tall, blond, grey linen suit, oh, divine. And,' she sat up to make sure Morgan was paying attention, 'he had a scar slashed across his cheek. It was so perfect I had to check it wasn't make-up.'

'A scar?'

'Yes, a scar. I didn't ask him where he got it; we never had time,' Pandora said mysteriously.

'So what happened?'

'Well, I was eating an innocuous little lunch and he asked me to come to his house with him!'

'What was his name?'

'We didn't swap names. It wasn't like that.'

Morgan couldn't help herself. 'You tart!' she exploded.

'No, I didn't sleep with him either. We just talked. We had smoked salmon and this lovely white wine that I can't remember the name of.'

'What did you talk about?'

'Well, this is the odd part. He kept asking about how I made my living and how I was doing. I think he knew I was modelling, but I'm not sure what kind of modelling he was talking about. I mean, he made me undress so he could check me over. I thought we were going to make mad passionate love on the carpet, but then he had to go. It was so frustrating, I can't tell you.'

'You are a tart!' repeated Morgan.

'No, I'm not.' Pandora was all innocence. 'Nothing happened.'

'But you took all y our clothes off in front of this strange man. You didn't even know his name!' Morgan was genuinely shocked.

'Will you see him again?'

Pandora sighed. 'Lord knows,' she said. 'I mean, I can't very well spend the rest of my life sitting at the Floré waiting for him to turn up, can I?'

'No.' Morgan laughed. 'You are impossible, Pandora. You don't even know who this man is. He could try and white-slave you to Latin America.'

'Oh, don't be so dramatic, Morgan, people don't get white-slaved any more. They're just abused on their home ground.' Pandora tossed her hair and changed the subject. 'So, what are we going to wear tonight? I've done enough seducing for today, but you are in an ideal position to look your best and pull your man.'

The chauffeur eased the huge black Mercedes through the gates of Andreï's country house, a seventeenth-century manor, and drew up before the imposing scrubbed oak doors which swung open on silent hinges. He hurried to open the car door. He wasn't fast enough. Andreï brushed past him and marched into the house, heading straight for his private study. He slammed the door behind him and locked it.

He turned on the CD, and the notes of the Mozart clarinet quintet floated out over the beautiful garden, rolling away from the french windows. He poured himself a straight vodka and settled down into the Boule chair which his dead wife had brought with her as part of her dowry. In spite of all this, Andreï did not look like a relaxed man, a man whose problems were under control. On the contrary, his face was creased into a series of worry lines and he kept running his hands distractedly through his hair. A businesslike expression of tired concentration settled on to Andreï's face like an old enemy come home to roost.

Andreï was a gambler, playing for stakes higher than most people could begin to imagine. Having inherited virtually nothing from his parents, he had gone to work in Paris for one of the American brokerage houses. Over the next few years he gained as much experience he could about the world's financial markets and the ways in which they were run. At first he had simply traded a little on his own account. He had found that he was good at it. He accrued a large enough sum to repair the house in the rue de l'Université, send Max to the best English schools, and, finally, live the kind of luxury which he had always known was his destiny. Working for other people had not lasted long. Andreï had soon branched out on his own, and thanks to carefully nurtured contacts and a certain amount of discreet insider dealing he soon found himself a very rich man.

Now, for the first time in his gambling career, he had a problem. He sipped at his vodka. Andreï did not lose money, ever. His frustration was mounting; he wasn't used to wasting time or money, especially on a deal about which he'd had doubts from the beginning. He slammed down the glass. Only the fact that he'd been marginally overstretched before the deal was proposed to him and persuaded him to take it. Andreï didn't like it when his funds looked low and, of late, his gambling hadn't been as successful as usual. He'd lent money for a quick return. He didn't need a useless associate to renege on his word, not now. Briefly he allowed his mind to drift over his memory of the call girl's perfect body. His mood snapped back to fury as the internal phone rang. The butler announced that his business associate had arrived. Should he tell him that the master was not at home?

'Of course not, you imbecile!' Andreï hissed into the phone before slamming it down and heading to the drawing room.

He strode down the hall, imposing in his finely cut pale-grey linen Savile Row suit, the steel caps on the heels of his custom-made Italian shoes clipping the flagstones of the ancient floor, sharp as gunshot. By the time he opened the drawing room he was masked with the famous, if steely, Fyodov charm. He went forward, hand held out in welcome.

'*Armand, comment vas-tu?*' He kissed his visitor on both cheeks and gestured to a narrow, rather uncomfortable Second Empire sofa. Without waiting for an answer, he walked over to the drinks table, where he began to fill a glass with ice cubes.

'Your usual I suppose?' His eyebrows raised in a question mark, he reached for the bottle of Scotch which Armand preferred. Armand sat up and accepted the drink, looking relieved. Perhaps this interview wasn't going to be so terrible after all.

Andreï sat in an armchair across the room from Armand. The late-evening light shining through the windows behind him left Andreï's face in darkness. The room was heavy with the residual heat of the afternoon and the nervous energy which emanated from Armand's hunched shoulders and sweating fact. Andreï sipped his vodka, the ice clinking against the crystal glass the only sound in the stillness of the room.

'So.' Andreï's voice was icy. 'What's the story?' He sat back in his chair, crossed his legs and waited.

'there's been a hitch . . .'

Nina let the answering machine reply to the ringing phone and settled into her bath. It had been a long day: the staff reshuffle was going to cause a lot of upset, she'd got nothing out of Gloria at lunch, and she didn't feel like talking. From her bathtub, she heard Pandora's voice. She reached for the portable on the *chaise-longue*.

'Hello, darling, hold on . . .' She paused while the tape switched itself off. 'Now where are you, sweetheart?'

'Still in France.'

'How's it going with the wayward Max?'

'Oh, him. Nina, I've decided he's really not my type.'

'So is Nick going to finally get a look-in?'

'Nick?'

'You remember, you told Rory you couldn't decide between the two of them.'

'Oh . . . yes.' Pandora paused. 'Actually I've decided to take a break from boys altogether.'

'How very unlike you. What on earth can have taken your attention away from them?'

'Well, you know. After a while the whole thing begins to pale, don't you think?'

'Very philosophical of you, Pandora. What brought this on?'

'Oh, you know . . . Nina?'

'Yes, darling?'

'What's *putain*?'

'A *putain* is a prostitute.'

'Really! And Nina . . .'

'Yes, darling?'

'What's Rory got against Max?'

'That's why you've dropped him? Good girl, listening to your elders and betters for once in your life.'

'But what did he ever do to him?'

'Long story. One day when you're about seventy-five years old and I'm in my dotage and Rory's dead and gone I'll tell you.'

'I just spoke to Rory, Nina. He told me I should leave this house before I'm contaminated and then he ordered me to the Crillon.'

'Well . . . Look, Pandora, I will tell you the story, but it's really too complicated to do over the phone. Wait till I'm in Paris. I really would rather tell you then.'

'What's that matter? What's so awful? I've been working as a model for ages. What's left that can shock me? I'm my uncle's niece, after all. I've hardly been overprotected all my life.'

'Pandora, drop it, ' Nina said firmly. 'I'll tell you in Paris, OK?'

'Fine, treat me like a five-year-old. I couldn't care less.' Pandora slammed the phone down.

Nina decided to finish her bath and then call Pandora back. She was due to leave for Paris the next morning. Better idea. She would ring as soon as she'd booked into the Crillon and tell her face to face. Now it was too late to do anything constructive, and Nina was totally shattered.

Late that evening Andreï had disposed of Armand. The man was still alive but would never again do business in the world that he was used to. A few well-chosen telephone calls had seen to that. Andreï had made sure that Armand would spend the next few years in jail for fraud and tax evasion. His fury at allowing himself to be dragged into a deal which had proven not only unprofitable but finally a loss-maker was taken out on his arrangements for Armand's financial demise. He made one final call. The relatively comfortable open prison where Armand should have served his time was suddenly full. The man would spend his sentence in a much less salubrious place, and there the physical punishment for having crossed Andreï Fyodov would be of a more violent sort.

Andreï was still shaking with anger when he poured himself one more vodka. He wanted that girl back. He would take her away. He would take her to his retreat in Morocco. There he could leave the worry of his business behind for a while. He would play with her instead, and this time she would not get away with sitting pretty. She would have to sing for her supper, like all good whores did.

Chapter 7

SATURDAY 22 JULY

NINA groaned as her alarm and the phone rang in quick succession. Why couldn't people call at a civilised hour? This was hardly what she needed when she was supposed to be making herself beautiful for her trip to Paris. She groaned again: a whole week of having to look glamorous morning, noon and night, just to be a spectator. She could hear Emily talking to the answering machine downstairs and reached to pick up the phone.

'It's OK, Emily, I'm here. What on earth's dramatic enough to call me at home at this hour of the morning?'

'Sorry, Nina. I just thought you should know Knowle McLulack's resigned. I just saw it on the news. I thought I should tell you before the press start badgering you for your opinion.'

'Which station?'

'CNN.'

Nina grabbed the remote control from beside her bed and flipped on the television. Her American opposite number's over-made-up face stared back at her. Bloody hell, Nina really didn't need this today. Paris would be rife with gossip. The most important glossy editor-in-chief didn't go without a bang. And no thanks to Don Elson for warning anyone, either. Didn't they realise that when people were fired like this in the middle of the night the least they could do was to warn the other editors. Thank God Emily had cable TV and was an early riser! Nina collapsed back into bed. She couldn't even call New York to find out what was going on until later that afternoon. She would have to arrive in Paris without knowing a thing until she was given some answers from the top. She swore to herself and turned back to the telephone.

'Emily, what time are you picking me up?'

'Ten-thirty.'

'You'd better get me hair and make-up now, then. I don't want to be faced by a barrage of cameras looking like the Medusa I resemble at the moment. Oh, and has Gloria left yet for Paris?'

'Yesterday evening. She said she had some important dinner she didn't want to miss.'

'Of course, I'd forgotten. Great, so she'll be none the wiser either.' Gloria had better be none the wiser. Nina needed Gloria. Only she could make the shoots work, leaving advertisers, designers and models happy with the result.

'I'll call Tim right away,' said Emily. 'See you at ten-thirty.'

Nina forced herself out of bed. It was 6.30. Nobody should have to get up at this hour, and especially not to news like that. She showered quickly, roughly towelling her hair, but leaving it wet enough for her hairdresser to turn it into the cap of gold for which she was famous, and which certainly didn't come without a little effort. By 7 a.m. she was in the kitchen, making herself a citron pressé and searching in her Filofax for the number of Gloria's hotel. For the moment she'd forgotten all about Pandora's phone call of the evening before. Her goddaughter's well-being would just have to wait until she knew more about what was going on at work.

Nina couldn't get through to Gloria and was frowning with concern when the doorbell rang. She looked at her watch. That was quick; Tim had a long way to get to her from Peckham. She ran to the door to find both Tim and Rory standing on the doorstep, Rory eyeing up the young man appreciatively and smoothing down his already perfectly greased-back black hair.

Nina kissed Tim hello and stood by to let him pass.

'I'll set up in your boudoir, darling,' he called as he bounded up the stairs.

Nina put her hands on her hips and turned to Rory, who was not being welcomed into the house. Dressed in pale pink linen, he mirrored Nina's stance and pouted back at her.

'Hello, darling. I won't say I told you so. I'd better come in and make you some real coffee. I promise not to chat up your hairdresser, but obviously you have a crisis on your hands.'

Nina reluctantly led the way back into the house.

'Just because Knowle's gone, doesn't mean I have a crisis.'

'No, not in the slightest. You just haven't got a clue who's replaced her. At least you hope you haven't. Where's Gloria?'

'Paris.'

'And? You've spoken to her of course.'

'Don't be pedantic, Rory. It's eight in the morning over there. She's just not answering her phone yet.'

'Like fuck she's not answering her phone. Where's Don?'

'The States. He left yesterday.'

'And you saw him on to a Kennedy-bound plane yourself, did you?'

'No. But Emily confirmed it, ordered the car, made sure he got there in time.'

'And Emily checked he arrived, did she?'

'Darling, I've no idea. She might conceivably have had other things to worry about last night. The Couture for instance?'

'Well. Let's make the coffee and just talk about the awful possibility that Gloria Wharton's been promoted over your head, behind your back, and that you're going to have to deal with total ignorance of the situation with the press camped outside your room in Paris until Don the Godfather deigns to discuss it with you.' Rory waved Nina upstairs to her bedroom and headed, sniffing with disapproval into the kitchen where he would make Turkish coffee for the three of them. Nina headed back upstairs. She prayed Rory was wrong.

A few hours later Nina sat back in the relative comfort of the first-class carriage of the Eurostar which was chugging through the Kent countryside at a reassuringly English pace. She hadn't been able to speak to Gloria and wasn't much the wiser as to what was going on as far as her American equal was concerned. Nina just hoped that Knowle hadn't had the misfortune to hit Paris before the announcement was made. If she had, the whole fashion world would be there to witness her demise and Paris was not a comfortable place to end a successful career as a magazine editor. For that was what had surely happened. Nobody ever resigned from the top of the magazine's slippery ladder; either they were promoted to even higher places or they were fired, fast and usually ignominiously.

Rory sat opposite Nina, looking holier than thou in ecru linen; the pink was a little precious for a train journey. He was going through their preparation for the couture and was racking his brain for ideas for a shoot. He was convinced Gloria had deserted a potentially sinking ship and he knew that the onus would probably fall on him to be the stylist on the shoot, unless Nina decided to do it herself, which was unlikely but possible.

Saturday morning in Paris dawned with Pandora running round the house in the rue de l'Université looking very businesslike. Her small amount of luggage was piled by the front door, and she quickly said goodbye to Morgan and Nick, who were still half asleep, before turning, glowing with happiness, to Max.

"Bye, darling. I've got to go. You do understand. The couture starts tonight. My first show's Versace at six-thirty and I've got hair and make-up at three. I should really go and ensconce myself at the Crillon in case of emergencys and to get in the right mind-set for the shows. I'm going to be so exhausted by the end of them.'

'How many are you doing?'

'Six! Can you imagine, in as many days. I'll need a fortnight in a health spa to get over them.'

'I'll see you tonight then.'

'Will you? Where?'

'You won't miss the Versace party, will you?'

'Not in a million years.' Pandora kissed Max lightly on both cheeks and skipped down the steps of the house. It was 9 a.m. She had loads of time.

Knowing that the others would be preoccupied with breakfast and deciding what disgusting touristy activity they would indulge in that day, Pandora headed for the Floré. She wouldn't be disturbed there. No one except Max could afford it. She ordered coffee and peeled a hard-boiled egg from the basket the waiter put on her table. It was still warm and was delicious dipped in a little salt and freshly ground pepper. Absent-mindedly she plaited her hair and tied it with her little black satin ribbon. She had four thousand francs. She would take a taxi.

She finished her egg, slurped down her coffee, left much too much money on the table, headed to the taxi rank on the other side of the Boulevard Saint Germain and leapt with relief into the air-conditioned car which was waiting there. Even at that hour of the day the July heat was oppressive. Pandora smiled to herself. She would arrive as cool as a cucumber. It wasn't even as if she had much luggage to complicate the situation; only her Prada bag with her party clothes in it and a spare T-shirt that she'd stolen from Max. The cab driver looked at her with delight when she announced where she wanted to go. This was the ride of the week.

As they pulled out into the thick, aggressive Paris traffic Pandora should really have turned back and looked at the Floré. She would have saved herself a fair amount of cash. Andreï's chauffeur was pulling up in the huge Mercedes. He had strict instructions to keep his eyes open, for Andreï had been convinced that the girl would be there again.

After a long wait and a drive home tinged with trepidation at returning empty-handed, the chauffeur drew up in front of the Fontainebleau house to find a quantity of luggage piled on the steps. Inside, an impatient Andreï was pacing the drawing room while the gorgeous girl he had been instructed to find sipped delicately at a glass of straight vodka on ice and looked for all the world as if she'd been there all her life. How the hell had she got there?'

In fact it hadn't been too difficult. The taxi driver had dropped her at the centre of Fontainebleau, and Pandora had marched about until she'd found the street with the most expensive shops in it and installed herself in a café there. She'd flirted outrageously with the waiter who served her, who had quickly divulged that there was a man with an unmistakable scar who lived in Fontainebleau. Nobody knew much about him except that his wealth meant he ordered dinner from the best restaurant in town on his cook's night off and they delivered to his door. The house was a little way outside Fontainebleau, on the way to Milly le Forêt, only ten minutes' drive or so. The waiter lived that way and his shift would finish in half an hour. If Pandora waited for him, he would give her a lift on his bike.

Pandora sat back and grinned to herself. Good thing the waiter was taken in by the batting eyelashes; she was down to her last three and a half thousand francs and didn't want to waste more on a taxi ride to Milly le Forêt only to find herself stranded with the wrong scarred man! True to his word, half an hour later the waiter came back for her, changed out of his uniform of black waistcoat and long white apron and into a Grateful Dead T-shirt and tight black jeans. He'd added an earring to finish the effect of rather drippy biker, and showed Pandora to an ancient Vespa. She perched gingerly on the back and they set off at a very gentle pace out of town.

Nearly half an hour later Pandora was dropped at the gates of Andreï's country house. The waiter waved as he trundled off, looking back to see if he could catch a last glance of the English stunner and narrowly missing a large oak which stood at a bend in the road. Pandora laughed as she watched him wobble round the corner, before turning back to the house and wondering how she should approach the situation. Now that she was here she'd slightly lost her nerve. She squared her shoulders and set off over what seemed like a mile and a half of perfectly raked gravel towards an imposing and very shut front door. The heat weighed heavy and she could feel beads of sweat threatening to appear on her top lip. She rang a huge old bell which pealed somewhere in the far distance, and stood, waiting in the glaring sun for something to happen.

Finally, apparently independently of human force, the door opened on silent hinges. A butler peered out.

'*Mademoiselle?*'

'Er . . .' Pandora stumbled around in her brain trying to find sufficient French to explain why she was there. 'Um . . . *Monsieur Fyodov, c'est maison Fyodov?*'

'*Oui, mademoiselle.*' The butler made no move to ask her in.

'*Um . . . Monsieur Fyodov, il là?*' Pandora waved her hands in the air helplessly, hoping that the butler might make himself a little more amenable and not leave her in this searing heat for the rest of the day.

'*Oui, mademoiselle.*'

Pandora gave up, drew herself up to her full height and put on her best Chelsea accent. 'Then would you be so kind as to tell him that I am here to see him?' Leaving her Prada bag on the doorstep she marched past the butler and into the house. There she found Andreï heading towards her from the other end of a long hall, fortunately with a wide smile on his face.

"How did you find me?'

'I happened to be passing and thought this looked like a house worth visiting. I had no idea you lived here.'

'Oh, please, explain. You know I sent my driver back to try and find you. I wanted to invite you here, but since I didn't know where to look for you I just asked him to wait at the Floré until you should come there.'

Pandora was stuck. She didn't want to admit that not only was she a friend of Max's but she'd been staying in his house for several days and had got out here on Fyodov money with a little daring thrown in.

'No, really. I cam out to Fontainebleau to visit the chapel at the château.' Pandora prayed that there was a chapel at the chateau worth coming back for. 'I come every time I am in Paris. It's one of my favourite places in the world. Then I took a walk. I found your house by chance, really.'

Andreï smiled and took Pandora's elbow. He led her into the drawing room and offered her a seat, then rang for tea.

'So, now you are here, what are your plans?'

'I don't know. The couture collections start this evening and I'm working. After that, nothing. I'm free for the summer.'

Pandora poured the tea into the bone-china cups which the butler had laid on a side table next to her. She passed Andreï a cup and a plate of patisseries. He took the cup and waved the cakes away. Pandora looked at them longingly, but she never ate sweet things – well, nearly never, and certainly not between meals.

Conversation ran out. Pandora sipped her tea, trying to

look demure. She was nervous. Andreï seemed totally at ease, lounging in his armchair, back to the light as usual.

Pandora looked about her. Above the fireplace was a large painting of what looked like a market somewhere in north Africa. There were men in long hooded dresses, donkeys loaded with panniers of kindling, a woman cooking over a pot in a corner. The colours were beautiful, the whole scene lit with a strong sunlight which reflected off all the surfaces. Having totally ignored an expensive education, she had no idea that this was a respected Delacroix, but being naturally curious she wondered where the place was. She got up and went to have a closer look. Andreï followed her.

'It's beautiful, isn't it? It's a painting of one of the old souks in Fez.' Andreï looked at Pandora; she evidently didn't have a clue where that was. 'Morocco,' he added.

'I've never been there.'

'It's a beautiful place. I have a house there, in the mountains behind Fez. It's cooler up there. I usually go in the summer.'

'Do you go alone?' Pandora knew perfectly well that Andreï wasn't married, but she had to check that she hadn't been misinformed. He might have an acknowledged mistress, or, God forbid, a boyfriend.

'Usually. Sometimes I have a friend to stay. It's my retreat from the world. I go there to think.'

Taking a deep breath, Pandora turned, held out her hand and said, 'Then let me introduce myself, Jane Smith, a bored model from London. Won't you take me to your Moroccan retreat?'

Andreï laughed, the unfamiliar sound crackling in his throat. She was extraordinary, this girl. Jane Smith indeed. If that were her real name then he was John Jones – but if that was the game she wanted to play then he was perfectly happy to go along with it. And of course he would take her with him. That was what he'd intended to do all along.

He stopped himself laughing. She was looking offended.

'I do want to go. I shouldn't presume, though. I don't even know who you are.' Pandora was suddenly embarrassed and made as if to go and pick up her back. Andreï grabbed her arm.

'Don't go. I'm sorry.' He held out his hand. 'Andreï Fyodov. I am delighted to make your acquaintance. Let's leave this evening?'

It was Pandora's turn to laugh. 'Whoopee!' she cried, and did a little dance around the room. 'You know I came out here to find you. I've never been to the château. I have no idea if there's a chapel there.'

Andreï sat in his usual armchair and watched the extraordinary girl stretch luxuriously. She was throwing herself on his mercy. He could rape her, steal her, keep her prisoner. Evidently nobody knew where she was.

'There is a chapel. But I'm not sure it's one you'd rush to see time and again.' Andreï headed to the door. 'Will you excuse me? I must go and arrange the packing. I presume you would like to have your luggage collected from Paris?'

'Oh no. I've brought all my paraphernalia with me. I'll just wait like a good little girl until you're ready.' Pandora jumped up. 'Do you mind if I look round the house?' Andreï bowed his acquiescence and left the room.

When Nina arrived in Paris, she found the usual state of panic at the start of the collections, exacerbated by the untimely end of Knowle McLulack's career. She, Rory and Emily, in that order, made the required entry to the Crillon. They were followed by five trolleys of luggage, mostly Rory's. Nina and Rory smiled with their teeth at the press gathered in the foyer of the great old hotel and didn't comment on any of the questions thrown at them. They just marched, their smiles a tiny bit forced, towards the lift. The concierge showed them personally to their rooms. Emily was stunned by the whole charade.

Nina locked herself into her suite and told Emily to hold all calls while she tried to find out what was going on. Rory had to go straight to Versace and then would have to spend the rest of the time until after the show backstage. Nina had to make do without him. She called Gloria. Still no answer. She called the Paris office. They were in a terrible state. Half of the people there worked for the American magazine, and not only did they not know who had replaced their boss, but their own jobs were on the line until the new editor-in-chief was confirmed. At least everyone Paris-based knew that the magazines couldn't do without the Paris offices – a vast percentage of the editorial content of glossy fashion magazines came straight from them.

The clock crawled towards the 3 p.m. mark, when Nina could call New York. This, after all, was the world of magazines, not famous for early risers. Eventually she reached Don Elson's office. Naturally he was out. He would, of course, call her as soon as he could. Nina was becoming increasingly uneasy. The wall blocking her from information was proving thicker than it should have. She'd worked out by now what must have happened, but she needed New York confirmation fast. Her first show, the first time she would have to appear and answer questions on the situation, was three hours away. She sighed. There was little she could do. She wanted the truth from the horse's, or rather, Don's mouth, and until she spoke to Don, she would just have to wait.

She decided to find out which room Pandora was in. She may as well try and speak to her at least. But before she could pick up and dial, Emily ran into the room, a strange, desperate look on her face. In a loud stage whisper she proclaimed, 'It's Don.'

'Well, put him through then,' Nina snapped closing the door and waiting for her bedroom phone to ring.

'Don,' she began.

'Nina, I'm sorry I wasn't here to take your call earlier.' Liar, she thought – after all his years in the business he still couldn't resist power games, and one of them was making people wait. 'I've had meetings – you couldn't imagine.'

'Don, I can well imagine. What's going on?'

'Well, we've been making a few changes. As you know, the business side of the magazine has recently been brought up to date a little , and now we feel we need to do the same on the editorial side, that's all.'

'So who's the replacement?'

'I'm sure you'll be thrilled for her . . .'

'Yes?' Nina could hardly keep the anticipation out of her voice.

'I'm afraid it makes things a little difficult for you, though.'

'Who is it, Don?' Nina asked sharply.

'Haven't you spoken to her yet today? I thought you always had early-morning telephone meetings. That's why I didn't call you last night. I thought she'd like to tell you herself.' It was confirmed – Gloria. The bitch, thought Nina, she jumps to the best glossy-magazine job in the world and I'm not even consulted. With an effort, Nina put on her most sugary voice for the man she loathed most in the world.

'Naturally I would have spoken to her this morning – but you know, getting to Paris, and late meetings . . .' she lied. All she wanted to do now was get off the phone so she could find Gloria and give her a piece of her mind. Of course she'd congratulate her, too, but how dare her old friend leave her in the lurch like this? Don was prattling on and eventually said that his busy schedule was going to prevent him from talking much longer. 'Much though I enjoy it, I really do,' he said sweetly.

Fuck you, thought Nina, and sent a sugary goodbye down the phone. Right, she thought, Gloria. The phone rang again.

'It's Rory.'

'OK. Put him on.' Nina waited while Emily fumbled with the phones.

'Come on, Emily. You've just done this two minutes ago.'

'I know. Sorry.' Emily felt sick with nerves. Nina was so tense, Rory was so tense. Emily was convinced she was just going to get everything wrong and therefore make things worse. Finally she managed to put Rory through.

'Rory, you were right. It's Gloria.'

'Great. Just what we need.'

'We'll manage. If you see her congratulate her. Our party line is going to be "Fabulous, we couldn't be more pleased, and no, we haven't chosen a replacement but have lots of ideas." We'll talk about that later. Don was disgusting.'

'I bet he was. Nina, we've got another small problem to sort out. Pandora's not here. Get Emily to find her, would you?'

'What do you mean? Have you tried her room?'

'She hasn't checked in. That's the problem. Maybe she's still at Max's.'

'Emily, call Mr Fyodov's house and get Pandora for me,' Nina yelled through her bedroom door to Emily's makeshift office in the sitting room of the suite.

'The London house?'

'What would Pandora be doing there when she's been in Paris for days? Come on, Emily. Try and concentrate.'

'Sorry. Yes. Right away.' Emily started riffling through her handbag to find her work address book. She just prayed she hadn't left it behind in the rush.

'Rory? Give me the backstage number. I'll get Em to call you back.'

'I'll murder her.'

'Emily?'

"Pandora. How dare she be late?'

'Darling, let's not bother with that now. She'll be there in a minute. Calm the hair and make-up people and tell them to get on with someone else first.'

'Nina, you don't understand. The hair takes three hours to set or it won't work.'

'Well, they'll just have to do her hair as soon as she arrives.'

'She'd better get here fast or I'll wring her scrawny little neck.'

'Rory, calm down. She'll be there. What's your number now?'

After a couple of misdials, Emily finally got through to the Fyodov house in the rue de l'Université.

'Hello, this is Emily Carlton-Jones. May I speaking to Pandora Williams, please?'

'Hold the line.'

'Em?'

'Max!'

'Hi, sweetheart. You're looking for Pandora?'

'Yup. She's supposed to be in hair and make-up at Versace but she hasn't turned up.'

'What?'

'I know. Trust Pandora to make everybody late. Rory'll kill her.'

'He won't be the only one. Versace will never use her again.'

'So can I speak to her?'

'Em, she's gone. She left first thing this morning for the Crillon. Where are you?'

'At the Crillon. She hasn't booked in.'

'Oh, shit.'

Nina, having overheard half this conversation, grabbed the telephone from Emily.

'Hello, Max, it's Nina. How are you?'

'Fine, fine.'

'What's going on? Where's Pandora?'

Max sighed. 'I don't know. She went to book into the Crillon earlier on this morning. If she's not there, I don't know where she is.'

Nina's voice was icy calm. 'Then I suggest you put your mind to thinking about where she might be. I have enough to worry about without having to traipse around Paris finding missing models.'

'Don't worry, Nina. She'll turn up. She's like a bad penny. She always does.'

'Oh, you make me feel so much better, Max.'

Later, Max and Nina left together for the Versace show. They decided to present a united front. On the way, Nina quizzed Max further.

'You're sure she didn't say anything to you?'

'Not a word. She was all business this morning. I know she didn't intend to miss the shows. I had to go to all those terrible fittings with her.'

Nina couldn't help smiling. 'Yes, I heard you didn't enjoy them all that much.'

'Yes, well. Not really my thing, is it?'

'And nobody else said anything?'

'No. I mean, I don't know if she said anything to Nick and Morgan.'

'And where are they now?'

'They've gone.'

'Where?'

'Home.'

'Why? That must have been the shortest trip to Paris in the history of university holidays.'

'Morgan and I had . . . we had a fight and she made Nick take her home.'

'Darling, don't look so coy. I couldn't care less if you're fighting with Morgan. She is, however, one of Pandora's best friends. You'd better ring her as soon as we get to the show.'

'No point. They only left an hour ago. Nick's not quite up to a car phone yet.'

'All right. As soon as they get home them. You'd better talk to both of them.'

'Can't you ring her?'

'Oh, grow up, Max. I'm editor-in-chief of a magazine that's just lost its fashion director during one of the busiest and most high-profile weeks of the fashion year. I'm really not going to faff around getting hold of your girlfriend just because you had a little tiff.'

'Emily could ring her.'

'No, Max. You ring her. You've got nothing else to do. Emily and I have. Oh, and one more thing . . .'

'What?'

'Try and be your most charming with Rory. You've never met him before, but he's liable to fly off the handle when he sees I've brought you along.'

'I have met him. He spat at me at your party the other

day. Literally. I had to go and wash my face afterwards. It was disgusting. What's his problem?'

'It's a long story. Just watch him. He'll be all right, and remember, it's not you he's angry with.'

'Fine. I'll just ring Morgan for you and be hated by the people you work with.'

'Sometimes you sound so childish.'

'Thanks for the support.'

'You're welcome.'

The car drew up outside the Ritz Hotel. The driver opened the door.

'Come on then. Let's h it the fray.' Max helped Nina from the car, and they put on their smiles for the bank of photographers who greeted them.

'Gloria, darling. Congratulations.'

Oh, John. You are kind. I'm thrilled, as you can imagine. What a challenge.'

'What does Nina think?'

'Darling, I haven't even had a chance to speak to her. I'm sure she'll be just as thrilled as I am. We can be trans-Atlantic comrades.'

'But darling, your magazines are competition for each other.'

'No reason for anyone to get nasty, is it? I mean, I'm not sure there's any real competition, is there? I think the Americans have already won, don't you?'

Nina sat ramrod straight on her chipped little red velvet and gilt chair, listening to this exchange. Her face gave nothing away. She was even ignoring the pop star behind her. Max sat beside her. He'd been given a seat in the VIP section but Nina had had it changed. She needed support and insisted he help in giving it. Across the catwalk, Jurgen and Jurgen steamed in identical black Lycra and hoped their matching peroxide hairdos weren't crinkling in the heat. They leaned against a pillar, sweating profusely but thankful they'd got in at all. They couldn't resist a bit of bitchery.

'Nina Charles looks like she's about to kill someone,' said one.

'And eat them. She's got a face on her like a cat's bottom. And her back's so straight it looks as if she's got a broom handle right up her arse. Look at the way she's got Max Fyodov by the hand. Poor child. He'll never get away from her. I never knew she was into cradle-snatching.'

'Oh, very peculiar tastes. Well-known fact. Never stays in a relationship for more than about a week at a time. Boyo there's going to have a terrible time. She'll kill him, chew him up and spit him out before the couture's over. Doesn't matter, though, he's got that thinking-model look. He's probably so dumb he won't even notice.'

'Give her something to do, though. Nobody's talking to her.'

'Gloria looks fabulous.'

'Doesn't she? How does she get away with suits like that? She must be boiling.'

'Not her, always an ice maiden, even in this heat.'

'And the hat! It's extraordinary.'

'Philip Treacy.'

'It would be with that feather. Oops! Nearly poked an eye out there.'

Gloria was posing, a huge smile stretched across her face, while the fashion world came to pay homage. Nina thought she'd never seen so much air-kissing in her life. She herself was in a little Galliano slip dress, cool in the July heat. She had intended to wear Versace, but it was just too hot.

Nina leaned towards Max. 'We're being talked about.'

'Are we?' He kissed her on the nose. 'That'll put the cat amongst the pigeons.'

'You can be very sweet sometimes.' Nina smiled at Max and kissed him back, full on the mouth. There was an audible intake of breath around them. They couldn't help laughing.

'What did you fight with Morgan about?' she asked, whispering in his ear.

'Oh, God. She got all uppity, and it was her own fault for being nosy. I got so angry. How dare she?'

'Darling, a little clarity would help.'

'OK. She went sneaking around in my studio.'

'And?'

'She found a portrait I was painting of her.'

'And?'

'She found it offensive.'

'Why?'

'It's a nude.'

'Well done, Max, well done.'

'What do you mean? If she hadn't gone poking around where she wasn't wanted, she would never have seen it and everything would have been fine.'

'OK. Let's not talk about it. People will think we're having a row already.'

'Yeah, right. And here come some lovely plastic dresses for you to get all hyped up about. I wonder which of his boyfriends did the music this time.'

'Don't be bitchy.'

'Come one, Nina, don't tell me you'd pay thousands of pounds for half a yard of PVC? Surely you can get that at your local bondage store in Soho?'

'It wouldn't be nearly so well cut.'

'Don't make me laugh.'

The show over, Nina had gone backstage to make her duty call of congratulations. Everyone knew Pandora was her protégée. With her arrival, the temperature dropped to a grim chill. Mr Versace had given Nina a rather steely smile and she'd returned it. She had no excuse for Pandora and wasn't about to start making things up. Rory stood hopelessly behind her, his once immaculate orange shantung suit rumpled and a little damp round the armpits, his hair flopping out of control over his very shinny face. Not a successful moment for Nina's team. Max, however, was swarmed over. Everybody, girls and boys alike, thought him the most divine creature on earth.

It wasn't over yet. They had to make an appearance at the post-show party, air-kiss a few more colleagues. Nina told everyone that she thought it was wonderful that Gloria was being given a new opportunity and wasn't it clever of her to have kept it all so secret for so long? She repressed a longing to shout and finally collapsed into her car, still holding Max's hand. Rory followed, hair smooth once again, but churning internally.

Emily hurried after them. If her mother could see the kind of party her beloved daughter had just been to, she'd be shocked to the core, and for that reason if for no other, Emily was determined to see this fashion thing through. With or without a Dior dress, she would make it past the air-kissing parasites and climb right to the top of the whole glittering heap.

Back at the Crillon, Max sat nervously on the fake Louis XVI chair in Nina's sitting room. There was an untouched chef's salad before him, but his glass of white wine was empty. Nina was glaring at him from across the table. Pandora was definitely lost. The cosy atmosphere of the show had evaporated. Rory had spat at Max's feet before storming off to his room, and now Max was being verbally whipped by Nina. He didn't know what to say. Pandora had chosen to go, she'd said she was going to book into her hotel. What more could he have done about the situation?

'You let her away with saying she'd find a taxi! I thought you knew her better than that.'

'Nina, I know she usually likes to be driven about, but I had other people staying too. I couldn't just desert them.'

'It would have taken you a maximum of twenty minutes to get her here. Don't try that one on me.'

'Nina, honestly, if never occurred to me that she was going anywhere else. She never stopped talking about the couture, the collections, her work. I really didn't see anything odd in her going off this morning.'

'Did she ask you if you would see her later? Did she ask you for taxi money?'

'She said she'd see me at the Versace party and she didn't ask for money. She's not a child, Nina.'

'Fat lot you know about that. You two are the most overprotected people I know. It'll be a miracle if either of you ever stops being a child. Did she say anything to Mrs Fischer?'

'Nobody ever says anything to Mrs Fischer unless they absolutely have to.'

'Point. Right. Well, we have to assume she met somebody else that she'd rather be with. Did she say anything to you? What did you do with her, where would she have met people?'

'I don't know, Nina. We were together most of the time, apart from the day she went shopping and the rest of us left Paris for the day.'

Nina pounced on this idea. 'So where did she go? Come on, Max. I need some answers. It's only a matter of time before Rory really loses it. Let's try and solve this before he does.'

'I don't know,' Max repeated. He wished he didn't sound so much like a scratched record. He thought back. 'OK – I think she bought some sandals and some doorknobs, and a wrap thing for the beach. Apart from that she really didn't say anything.' He looked up. 'Apart from having lunch at the Floré, that is. But you hardly chat up people at the Floré, do you?'

'Shows how well you don't know Pandora,' said Nina, her lips thin with fury. 'Go home, Max, and think about it.

My first show is at eleven-thirty tomorrow. Call me before then. I don't want to have to hound you to find out more. Let's try and clear this up quickly.'

Nina couldn't help sounding brusque, but really she'd had enough. She was bushed. Not only had Pandora disappeared and Gloria defected to the American market, but she had nobody to do her couture shoot for her. She could leave it to her ordinary fashion editor but wasn't convinced the girl was up to it – she was OK for sportswear, but these couture clothes always needed a special touch to make them come alive. Usually she could ask Rory to do it, but if Pandora didn't turn up he'd have collapsed by the end of the week. She had a horrible feeling in the pit of her stomach that she was going to have to do the job herself.

Morgan and Anna sat at their accustomed places at the kitchen table, Anna with her back to the sink and Morgan with her back to the dresser, big mugs of tea in their hands. The Brandenburg Concertos played softly on the record player in the sitting room. Anna had told Morgan of her conversation with Sam. He was staying at the Randolph and would like to see his daughter whenever she was ready. They'd left the back door open and could hear the soft summer rain gently washing over the house. At last they got round to talking about Morgan's holiday.

'Where did you stay?' asked Anna.

Morgan brightened. 'Mum, it was great. Central Paris. I went to Versailles, to the Musée d'Orsay, all over the place. We even had dinner up the Eiffel Tower. Max said it was terribly touristy but the view was fantastic. Max has lived there all his life so he knew where to take us. Shame he's such a wan–' She stopped herself.

'Who's Max?' Anna asked.

'A friend from Bristol. Not my type – you know, too much money for his own good and spoilt rotten. I didn't like him much before and I still don't. I only went because Pandora was there, and you know Nick – he's a sweetheart.'

Anna felt the teapot and realised it was cold. She got up to make more tea and to rummage around in the food cupboard for another packet of chocolate Hob Nobs. They'd finished off what had been in the biscuit tin.

'I hate to say it, but it sounds as though you've rather fallen for this Max person. He must be rich if he lives in Paris and goes to University in England and takes you to places like the Jules Verne for dinner. I presume he paid.'

Morgan laughed. 'Of course he did. He's so rich he gave Pandora five thousand francs in cash so that she could go shopping while we went to Versailles for the day. Oh Mum, remind me to ring White's tomorrow. I absolutely have to work now till the end of the summer. I'm totally broke and only serious waitressing will keep the wolf from the door next term.'

'I saw the restaurant manager in the street yesterday. She was asking when you were due back. Apparently they're short-handed. Now, this mystery man. What is it you dislike so much about him?'

Morgan blushed. 'You know, he's just spoilt. I've never liked people like that much.'

'You like Pandora enough.'

'But Pandora's hilarious. This guy isn't funny at all.'

'He can't be that awful if you all rushed off to Paris to stay with him. Or were you just using his house as a hotel?'

'It wasn't that calculating. I mean, he's not that dreadful and Pandora was sort of going out with him. Anyway, I've never been to Paris. I wanted to see what all the fuss was about.'

'And did you like it?'

'Oh, Mum, it was beautiful. I could live there.' Morgan paused, slowly winding her hair around a biro. 'Anyway,' she tossed her head back and her carefully arranged chignon fell out, the biro clattering to the floor, 'that's all beside the point. Max Fyodov is a bastard and Paris is a pipe dream. Besides, he could do with a little playing-hard-to-get in his life. I doubt he's ever had any. I think he assumes that after the row we had I'm going to run back to him and ask his forgiveness.' She smiled. 'Imagine me running to that spoilt brat's house and asking to be taken back into the royal favour! Humph, likely possibility, I don't think.'

Fyodov!' Anna's voice was icy. Her face had gone quite white, apart from two little red spots of astonishment in her cheeks.

'Yes, Fyodov – what's so terrible about that?'

Pandora and Andreï left that night for Tangiers and then Fez. Did Pandora think to call Rory? No, of course not. For a second she thought she might ring Nina and tell her where she was going, but then decided that this would only complicate things. Was she responsible enough to inform the poor overworked organisers of the fashion shows in which she was supposed to feature that she wouldn't be there? Not in a million years. Pandora was in love and everything else faded to insignificance beside the fact that Andreï Fyodov, the father of the man who'd rejected her advances, thought her worthy of whisking off to his Moroccan hideaway.

Chapter 8

Sunday 23 July

Pandora stretched and warily opened her eyes. She and Andreï had arrived at his fortress house in the mountains above Fez late the night before. There had awaited them a feast of goat's cheese, unleavened bread and a thin red wine. There was a dull ache at the back of her head, and her mouth was dry. She'd forgotten to clean her teeth before she'd gone to sleep. She winced as she focused on the fierce Moroccan sun pouring through the slats in the shutters high in the turret roof above her head. She turned over, away from the light, and jumped when she saw the shock of blond hair beside her. She sat up too quickly, and groaned as the effects of the wine hit her from behind. She hadn't slept with him, had she?'

Her sudden movement disturbed him. He turned over, opened his eyes and reached out to trace her profile with one long, manicured finger, smiling good morning. They were lying on a bed made of piles of large cushions, covered with linen throws, and with huge bolsters for pillows. They were all much too white for Pandora's thudding head. The room was octagonal, large, and there were other arrangements of cushions, smaller than the one they had slept on. The carpet-covered floor was punctuated with low tables made of intricately carved brass trays. There was no ceiling, and the eight walls of the room soared unbroken into the high roof, where narrow, loosely shuttered windows filtered light into the room. On a little table by the bed were the remains of their midnight snack, and beside the table sat a huge pot-bellied hookah. She grimaced; the evening was coming back to her now. She knew from painful past experience that mixing hashish with alcohol was never a good idea.

Andreï stood up. Pandora saw with relief that not only was she still dressed, but so was he. It wasn't that she didn't want to sleep with him – she just wanted to remember it if she did. He smiled at her and tugged at a bell pull next to the fireplace.

'Saida will look after you, show you to your quarters and get your bath. If you want anything, just ring for whatever it is. I'm afraid I must take care of some business this morning. Please, amuse yourself. We will meet for lunch later.' He turned and left the room, leaving Pandora nervously sitting on the edge of the bed and wondering what she'd got herself into.

A few minutes later a small wizened maid came to show Pandora to her rooms. As Saida began to run a bath scented with musky oils, Pandora opened french doors in her adjoining bedroom and looked out. Below her was a huge courtyard, in the centre of which was a long wooden table shaded by potted palms at which Andreï was tinkering with a portable computer. It all looked like something out of a Mafia movie, equipped with everything from a battery of telephones to two heavies in suits standing at a respectful distance. Pandora wanted to shout down and ask what the bad guys were for, but thought better of it. A bath was more important.

Clean and relaxed after soaking in oils, she wrapped herself in a huge soft bath towel and meandered back into the sitting room, where she found breakfast laid out for her – slices of fresh fruit, more unleavened bread, freshly churned creamy unsalted butter and a pot of steaming mint tea. Saida poured and then left Pandora to lean back and luxuriate in the embrace of the huge sofa. She sipped at her tea. This is the life, she thought. She didn't need anything more to amuse her, at least not for today.

Nina woke that morning, warm and comfortable in her huge Crillon bed. She had a few seconds' peace before remembering where she as and what was going on. A knock on her bedroom door announced that Emily was already there and probably hard at work counting Nina's invitations for the day for the hundredth time. Nina sat up, squinting at the bright sun which splashed through the windows, making everything in the room look slightly overexposed.

'Morning, Emily,' she croaked, leaning over to her bedside table and fumbling for the glass of water she knew must be there somewhere. Blinded by the light, she not only took a while to find the water but when she looked up she thought she must be imagining things. The light wasn't that bright; it couldn't transform Emily into Don, could it? He stood there laughing, in his hands a tray of breakfast, which he carefully placed on the end of the bed.

'Morning, madame,' he said, marching to the windows, pulling the half-open curtains wide and throwing open the windows. 'It's a beautiful day. I trust madame slept well.'

Nina, now completely blinded, was trying to flatten her hair, which stuck up all over her head in a decidedly un-chic manner. What the hell was Don doing in her bedroom? Magazines were supposed to take over the lives of the people who worked for them, but surely not to the extent where people had the right to march into one's bedroom at that time in the morning?'

'Don,' she managed to scrape out, 'what on earth are you doing here?'

'Come to check on all my staff, darling. The only time I can guarantee getting everyone together in one town. I thought I'd give a little dinner tonight. You'll be there, won't you?'

"Of course.' Nina sighed and made a mental note to cancel the dinner with Christian Lacroix that she had had Emily arrange. Perhaps he wouldn't be too put out by her asking if he wouldn't mind just meeting for a drink instead.

'I'm supposed to be dining with Christian Lacroix, but if you'd rather, I'll cancel it.'

'No, no, don't worry. I'll have notes on the dinner sent to you afterwards. You mustn't let your pet designers down.'

Pet designers indeed! Nina wondered if this man would ever understand that they owed their jobs to the fact that the designers existed, not the other way round.

Don sat down at the end of her bed. He looked horribly as if he was about to settle in for a little chat. Nina wanted to call Max and ask if he had found out any more about where Pandora might have gone. She couldn't do that with Don there. Don didn't expect you to have a private life if you worked for him.

'Any ideas about what you'll be doing for your couture shoot? Sorry I took Gloria away from you. I hope that doesn't mean you'll have to shot the collections yourself.'

'Actually, I'm quite glad of the opportunity. It's years since I've done a sitting myself.'

'And what exactly do you plan to do to outshine your contemporaries?'

'I thought I might shot– No, let me surprise you, Don.'

'Well, as long as you don't lose sales.'

Nina put on her most sugary employee voice. 'Don, really. When have I ever let you down?'

Max sat at the kitchen table of the house in the rue de l'Université, racking his brains to find Pandora's possible playground. He finished his coffee and gave in to the inevitable. He was going to have to ring Morgan. He ran upstairs to find the notebook that served as his address book. Back at the kitchen table, he riffled through until he came to a scrawled number. Morgan's handwriting really was appalling.

He fetched the portable and lit a red Marlboro, knowing how much the cigarette smoke would irritate Mrs Fischer, before dialling the number.

'Hi, I'm ringing for Morgan James. It's Max Fyodov here,' he began when he got through. To his astonishment, the woman at the other end swore and slammed the phone down. He wondered if he'd got the wrong number and tried again. This time she snatched the phone when it had hardly begun to ring.

'Listen, Fyodov, she spat, 'we don't want anything to do with you. Keep away from my daughter, all right? There's nothing between you and Morgan; she has a boyfriend already. Take a hint and keep out of her life.' The line went dead again.

Not being someone who could be shaken off lightly, Max persevered and tried again.

'Didn't you understand what I said?' cried the voice before he'd had a chance to say anything.

Max decided to try the very polite approach. Before she had time to slam the phone down on him again, he drew breath and spoke as quickly as possible.

'I'm sorry to bother you again, and if you insist I'll try not to have anything to do with Morgan, but a friend has disappeared and I need Morgan's help to find her. Would you mind telling her that Pandora's gone missing?' Finally he seemed to have got through. The line stayed open.

'Where?' the voice asked.

'Here in Paris. I wanted to ask Morgan if Pandora said

anything about where she was going. I was under the impression that, she was going to her hotel to get ready for the couture shows, but evidently not. Max decided that he'd captured this mad woman's attention sufficiently to try and actually speak to Morgan. 'Is Morgan there? Any information she has might help.'

'No, she's gone to work. Some of us have to, you know,' Anna added gratuitously.

'Would you ask her to call me then, or can I ring her at work?'

'No, you can't. Ring her here after five this afternoon; her shift should have finished by then. I'll tell her to expect your call.' She didn't try and hide the contempt in her voice.

'Thank you for your help.' Max put the phone down, puzzled. What on earth had he done to offend this woman so much?

Nina escaped as quickly as she could from the Lacroix show, hardly showing her face backstage before rushing outside to find her car and get back to the Crillon. She wanted to talk to Max and see if he'd got any further.

'Nina, I could hardly get through at all.'

'What do you mean?'

'Whatever did I do to Morgan's mother?'

'Why? What did she say?'

'She only slammed the phone down on me about five times. Anyway, Morgan's working. I can't speak to her till five this afternoon.'

'So you'll try again.'

'Yes, Mummy.'

'Don't call me Mummy.'

'All right. How's the nightmare going?'

'It was better when I had you on my arm actually, people were more worried about you than they were about whether I was likely to still have a job this time next week.'

'I can always come and help.'

'Don't bother. Find Pandora, darling . . . Unless, if you're hungry I'm lunching with Gianfranco at the Ritz. You could always drop by.'

'Deal.'

'As long as you promise to blank Gloria if you see her. She's always fancied you.'

'No problem. See you later.'

Nina climbed into yet another new outfit, this time Dior and jumped back into her car. She gave Emily strict instructions to call her on her portable if there was any news about Pandora.

While the car sat stuck in a traffic jam on the way to the Ritz Bar where she was to have her lunch she tried Sam at the Savoy. Mr McAllistair was staying at the Randolph Hotel in Oxford; would Miss Charles like the telephone number of this establishment? She took it in case. No, they didn't know when he would be back, he'd left his suite. Fuck, she thought. She didn't know how Sam could help with the Pandora situation, she just thought he might be able to calm her down a little. The car stopped outside the Ritz as she was dialling. Nina put the phone away.

Grimacing at the photographers, who had found out

that Gloria was lunching at the same place, Nina slipped past them and ran headlong into Don who was evidently waiting for Gloria too. She forced herself to skid to a halt and smile sweetly at her boss.

'Darling, I was looking for you. Who are all these people? I've never seen half of them before. Can you type me a list of all the important people in Paris with a little description by their names? Then I won't feel so lost.'

'Don, do you have a secretary?' Nina's tone was icy.

'Nina, little Nina, don't get all prickly. I see your lunch date is here. You mustn't keep him waiting, and mine!' Gloria had arrived and Nina wrinkled her nose with distaste as Don kissed her a little too close to her mouth on both cheeks and posed for a photographer just behind them. She stormed off, getting tangled in a rogue handbag strap hanging off the back of a chair on the way. By the time she'd reached her table she wished she'd stuck to her Galliano slip dress. The restaurant was steaming, and she hoped that Gianfranco wouldn't notice the gleam of sweat on her upper lip.

She'd hardly had time to kiss her lunch date hello before her telephone rang. Excusing herself, she answered, hoping it was news.

'Nina, it's Emily. Sorry to disturb you.'

'Yes. Did Max ring?'

'Max?'

'Yes, Max. Remember I told you on no account to disturb me except to tell me if he had rung.'

'Oh, yes. Well, in that case this can wait.'

'Emily – what is it?'

"Well I just wanted to tell you that Don was looking for you and I found out that he was lunching at the Ritz too, so you can see him there.'

'Thank you, Emily, but I've already seen him.'

'Oh.'

'Was that all?' Nina hoped that Emily could hear all the exasperation in her voice. Really, this girl was impossible.

'Yes, yes, it was.'

'Well, now you can leave me to lunch in peace, and only call if Max has any news.'

'Sorry.'

'And stop apologising!' Nina tried to slam the phone down but couldn't because it was a portable. Instead she threw it into her ancient Hermès Kelly bag with unnecessary force. 'I am sorry,' she apologised to her guest. 'Paris is just one thing after another. You can't get anything done because everyone spends the whole week rushing round making sure that they know what everybody else is up to.'

'Nina, my dear, you look exhausted.'

Nina relaxed and tried to enjoy her lunch. She'd known Gianfranco for years. He took her mind off things for a couple of hours. Better still, Rory turned up too and, being an old friend of Gianfranco's, they gossiped away like a pair of magpies and left her to relax a little. Then Max arrived, blanked Gloria and Don at their corner table and was made much of by Nina's party. Rory controlled himself and managed to be civil, just.

By the time Nina left the restaurant she was in a much better mood. She loved the way Rory made so much noise that everyone presumed that her table must be the most happening one. Even Don looked a little put out . Nina noticed that he and Gloria were left completely alone. Ha ha, she thought. Maybe Gloria's rise to fame wasn't going to be paved with so many air kisses after all. Rory, glorious in French blue linen piped with crushed raspberry velvet, and – Nina couldn't help laughing – patent leather shoes and spats, shone like the only star in the firmament and made the whole restaurant revolve around the people he was with. Nina relaxed and even drank a glass of wine, something she never usually did when she was working.

As she left, Max on her arm, there was a spring in her step, and she didn't notice Rory and Gianfranco exchanging knowing smiles.

'Man trouble,' announced Rory. 'She looks awful! Max is a little younger than her. She must be exhausted. You know he's a pervert, don't you? He must be, his father being the biggest bastard on earth.'

'My dear. How vitriolic you sound!'

'I'll tell you about it one day, but not in the Ritz bar. I'll cry in front of everyone, and it never does to cry about one's own tragedies in public.'

First day at work over, Morgan found the phone ringing as she arrived home. She could hear it clearly through the back door, which stood wide open. She threw her bag down by the kitchen table and shouted:

'Hi, I', home.' Silence. She shrugged and picked up the receiver. 'Hello.'

'It's Max Fyodov again. I'm sorry to disturb you, but I wonder if Morgan is home?'

'Max, it's me!'

'Thank God for that.'

'When did you ring before?'

'Your mother slammed the phone down on me about five times this morning. She told me to get out of your life and stay there. What did I ever do to her? She spoke as if I had a contract out on your life or something.'

'Strange to say, but she seems to have some pathological hatred of you, and I still haven't got to the bottom of the story.'

'Are you all right? You sound exhausted.'

'No, I'm fine. Really. Just a bit shattered by my first day back at work, I suppose. I'm waitressing,' she added by way of explanation. There was a pause. 'Anyway, I would have thought I was the last person you wanted to speak to. What do you want?'

'Do you know where Pandora is?'

'No, modelling at some show, isn't she?'

'Well, here's the thing. She's not. I mean, she's supposed to be. But she seems to have gone off somewhere.'

'Well, I can't help. As far as I knew she had some fashion modelling to do in Paris. That's where she told me she was going when she said goodbye anyway.'

'That's what I thought too. But she never turned up yesterday at Versace, and she still hasn't shown. She's been gone for twenty-four hours. Her uncle's going berserk and Nina's not much happier. Are you sure she didn't say anything to you?'

'No – I mean, I'm sure she didn't. She was all excited about the shows and those horrible dresses she was going to wear and everything.' Morgan tried to be helpful. 'I'll ring Nick if you like and see if he knows anything. Call me back later. I can't call you – Mum'll go berserk about the phone bill.'

'What if your mother answers?'

'Oh, grow up – she's only another human being. Just tell her it's about Pandora – she can't stop you looking for someone, can she?'

'No, no, I suppose not, Morgan . . .'

'Yes?'

'Nothing. I'll call you later.'

Morgan ran upstairs to find her phone book and call Nick.

No answer.

Mrs Fischer had a short conversation with her conscience. If she told the young master that his father had been canoodling with the girl with the disgusting eyelashes in the morning room it would be disloyal to Mr Fyodov. But if she didn't., it would be disloyal to Max. She would do anything to preserve her position. She thrived on her loathing of it. Mrs Fischer thought that Pandora deserved to be lost. However, she wasn't. The butler at Fontainebleau had told Mrs Fischer where Pandora had gone. The housekeeper decided to keep her mouth shut. The little slut was probably getting what she deserved. She saw no reason to try and save her.

Morgan jumped guiltily when Anna got home. For some reason her mother was in a foul mood. Morgan put the kettle on and took Anna a cup of tea. She found her mother sitting at her desk crowded with papers , with her head in her hands.

'Here, Mum, tea.' Morgan put the cup down and went to leave the room.

'Wait, Morgan. That Fyodov boy rang this morning.'

'I know. I've spoken to him.'

'Pandora seems to have gone missing.'

'Yes, well, you probably couldn't care less, seeing that you seem to loathe all my friends.'

'Morgan, I do care. She's the daughter of a friend of mine.'

'Well, stop being so cross all the time. I'm going to call Nick. I need to try and find her.' Morgan slammed out of the room.

Back in the kitchen she sat on the edge of the dresser and tried Nick's number gain.

'Hello, Nick?'

'Morgan, how are you?'

'Fine. Thanks for driving yesterday.'

'Piece of cake. What's up?'

'Pandora's disappeared off the face of the earth.

'What?'

'Yup. You know she said she was going off to do all her fashion shows? Well, she didn't.'

'How do you know?'

'Max ran. She's just disappeared.'

'Didn't she say anything to her uncle?'

'Nope.'

'Where's she gone?'

'I don't know. That's why I'm calling you. I thought you might have some ideas.'

God. She could be anywhere. Knowing her, she's rushed off with some man she's picked up somewhere just to get back at Max for not falling in love with her.'

'Oh my god. You're right. She met someone that day we left her to her own devices. She met him at the Floré and then went and had lunch with him at his house. All we know about him is that he has a scar.'

'Well, that's going to get you a long way. Where's the scar. Somewhere the rest of the world could see it, or somewhere that only Pandora would know?'

'On his face, slashed across his cheek, she said. But that's not going to get us very far. Millions of people have scars, and Pandora's so addicted to exaggeration I expect he'd just nicked himself shaving.'

'Yeah. Must be a red herring. I'll have to think about it. I mean, she was too busy slavering over Max to speak to me.' Nick paused. 'And you. You must be speaking to Max now?'

'Only as far as I can help find Pandora. The bastard. I'm still shocked.'

'I think you're being too hard on him. You know he's been keen on you for months.'

'So? That's hardly my problem, is it? And it's hardly a reason to paint pornographic pictures of me in his bedroom.'

'It's not his bedroom.'

'It is. He sleeps there.'

'Yes, but it's not his bedroom. Have a little charity, Morgan.'

'Oh, go jump, Nick. I'll be nice to Max the day you finally manage to tell Emily how you feel about her.'

'Pandora, you mean.'

'No, Nick. I mean Emily. Put that in your pipe and smoke it.'

'Well, that's going to get us a long way.'

'Sounds like we're both going to die innocent.'

'All right, all right. I'll let you know if I hear anything from Randy Pandy, though why she'd ever get in touch with me, I have no idea.'

'Only a week ago you were slavering over her as if she were the last woman in the world. She may well call you and demand that you service her.'

'Morgan!'

'Don't sound so prudish. It's just the kind of thing Pandora would do.'

'Nina? Hi, it's Max.'

'Hello, darling. Any news?'

'No, nothing concrete. Don't you think we should tell the police?'

Nina sighed. She supposed they would have to. She hedged.

'What did Mrs Fischer say?'

'Odd, actually. She looked dead shifty when I asked her. I mean, more shifty than she usually does, if that's possible. But she said that Pandora had given her no indication of her intentions. You can imagine her expression. She looked as if I'd asked her to defecate in public.'

'Still insisting on pretending to be the least curious person in the world, then?'

'Yup.'

'Where's your father?'

'I don't know, haven't heard from him for ages. I thought he was coming back here, but not a word.'

'Hm – does he still have that lovely house in Morocco?'

'Yes, though I haven't been there since I was about twelve.'

'Have you got any photographs of it?'

'I don't know, I'll have a look for some. Why?'

'I thought I'd do something a little different for the couture. Can I come round later? Maybe I'll have made some kind of decision about Pandora by then, and perhaps Mrs Fischer will be a bit more forthcoming with me.'

'I wish you luck. What time?'

'About eleven. I've got a dinner, but it shouldn't go on for too long.'

'Deal. I'll see you then. If I'm out, it won't be for long. I'll tell Mrs Fischer you're coming.'

'See you later.' Nina dumped the phone on the bed and changed again, into a pale-lilac silk taffeta evening dress trimmed with black lace. It was a dream; luckily Mr Lacroix made clothes that she loved wearing when she had to see him. He was always a good excuse to go shopping on expenses. She touched up her make-up and hurried out, passing Emily in the sitting room miserably counting invitations.

'Haven't you got a date tonight, darling?' Nina was suddenly feeling charitable.

Emily sighed. 'I thought Jerry Cawlfield's assistant was going to call, but he hasn't.'

'Don't worry sweetheart, he's gay anyway.'

Emily looked more miserable. 'This industry's impossible; there are no straight men to play with.'

'Well, at least the gay ones are almost guaranteed to be more fun.'

'But who do you sleep with?'

'In this day and age you avoid sleeping with anyone. It's much too dangerous.' Nina smiled at her assistant. 'Don't worry, some day your prince will come. In the mean time you've got my portable number should Pandora or Max call me. Otherwise, no repeat of your lunchtime performance.'

Emily smiled nervously. 'Don't worry, I think I've learnt my lesson. If you don't want to hear from anyone, you *really* don't want to hear from them.'

'Precisely. Listen, call room service and get them to send up something really delicious, and a video. That should cheer you up.'

'Thanks, Nina.' Emily was relieved. She'd really thought she'd lost her job earlier in the day. 'Your car's waiting for you. I told him you'd need him throughout dinner and then he could probably go home.'

'Actually, I'm going round to Max's house afterwards. Why don't you go and have supper with him and I'll bring you back?'

'Oh, I don't know . . .'

'Come on, ring him. He's not doing anything. All right?'

'All right.'

Much later Emily lay back on the huge white sofa in the red lacquer drawing room in Max's house, a large cognac in her hand.

'Have you heard anything from Morgan?'

'No, not a squeak. I tried to ring her earlier but there was no answer. Maybe I should call her now.'

'I wouldn't. It's eleven-thirty at night. If you've already offended Anna, there's no need to make sure it gets worse. They all go to bed at about nine o'clock in that house.'

'I'll ring tomorrow morning then. How's work going? You look a little worn at the edges, I have to say.'

Emily was drunk enough not to care what she looked like.

'It's a nightmare, Max. Nobody ever speaks less than three languages at once and I'm supposed to be a clairvoyant and know what they all want in advance. I suddenly find myself in charge of things which I thought were other people's responsibility, and Nina shouts at me morning, noon and night, and about really stupid things, like her tights being the wrong thickness or something. I don't know how long I'm going to be able to put up with it.'

'Why do you do it, then?'

'I love the clothes. Stupid reason to stick a job, but there you are. I'll do anything just to be able to see the seaming on a Givenchy party dress.'

'Don't worry, Em. You'll get used to it. Just thank your lucky stars it's the couture and not the ready-to-wear? That'll really sort you out. This is a piece of cake in comparison.'

'It's all right for you. You're everybody's blue-eyed boy and can't put a foot wrong. You're a VIP, for God's sake. I'm killing myself and I haven't even been to one show yet.'

'Are you going to any?'

Emily, shook her head.

'I'll take you to one if you like. They always let in the people I go with.'

'But Nina's monopolising you.'

'I'll make her give me a day off.'

At that moment the phone rang on the Boule desk in front of one of the windows, and Max stood to answer it.

'Hello.'

'Bastard!' said the person at the other end of the phone.

'What?'

'Listen, while you're swanning round Paris pretending to be in an episode of *Absolutely Fabulous*, the fact that you're a bastard doesn't escape the world. You should hear the things they are saying about you. We know you're perverted. We know you stink. We know you are nothing but an evil little worm sent into the world to kill and maim. Go back to Russia where you belong. I hope you freeze to death.' The line went dead.

'Well, said Rory on the other side of town, reaching for his gin and filling the Jurgens' glasses from the bottle by his side. 'That should shut him up. Arrogant little shit. I should scar his face too and then there'd be no mistaking him for Andreï Fyodov's son.'

'Wouldn't know.' The Jurgens were getting thoroughly bored. They wished Rory would let them get what they'd come for.

Rory reached up and stroked one face. 'Are my little boys getting a teeny bit pouty because Rory's not concentrating? I know, you didn't come all the way here to talk about Pandora, did you, darlings?'

'We haven't got all night.'

'Ooh, love, another appointment, have we? You should be careful, boys. You might catch something.'

'Oh, a girl knows how to look after herself.'

'Does she now? Shall we prove it, then?'

Nina arrived exhausted at Max's house. She took the file of photographs he'd got out for her and hurried Emily to the car. There was no way she was up to discussing Pandora's possible whereabouts or the potential locations for her couture shoot at this time of night.

Tomorrow was Monday. She had to shoot by the end of the following weekend to get her couture pages into the September issue. It wouldn't be easy. She slipped down in her Crillon bath and sipped at a glass of Sancerre. At least Lacroix and Dior were on for it; now she just had to get a little Saint Laurent, some Chanel, a touch of Givenchy and she supposed she should get Versace too, just to keep the ad agency happy, and then she could start working on logistics. Oh yes, and she was going to have to declare

Pandora a missing person. There was nothing else she could do.

Pandora was teaching herself how to deal with older men, or so she thought. She'd spent most of the day asleep in her luxurious quarters, missing lunch entirely. She'd curled up in her comfortable robe and upon awakening had found Saida laying out the clothes she'd brought with her, now washed and immaculately pressed. This is the life, she thought, as she changed into Max's jeans and his crisp white T-shirt. Then she headed off to try and find her way to the courtyard where she'd seen Andreï earlier in the day.

Andreï was on the phone as Pandora came through the vast carved wooden doors and posed at the end of the courtyard. He waved her towards a chair and turned to finish his conversation. Pandora, a little put out that he hadn't dropped everything to come and pay her attention, perched, pouting, on the arm of a chair and waited impatiently for him to finish. He murmured instructions into a phone and eventually, at least three minutes later, he came and kissed her on both cheeks. They were in a part of the courtyard which she hadn't been able to see from her rooms. It was laid out like an English drawing room; there was even a grand piano in a corner. Andreï went over to the drinks tray.

'What would you like? vodka again?'

Pandora smiled in acquiesence and dived for a bowl of cashew nuts on another table. She hadn't eaten anything since breakfast and was starving. Andreï passed her straight Absolut on ice, and she perched on the arm of a sofa. 'How was your day, dear?' she asked.

'Ugh – let's not talk business, it makes me so bored.' Andreï sat back in an armchair and admired his companion. She was beautiful, especially when that spoilt little pout settled on her face, as it had at that moment.

'I'm not a child, you know. I'd like to know what you do. Tell me.

'Darling, it's hardly polite to talk business while we eat, is it? But,' he paused and looked at her, eyes narrowing, 'we can play a game if you like.'

'What sort of game?'

'Come and eat first. You must be hungry.' Andreï stood and took Pandora's elbow, guiding her to a table laid for dinner with a gleaming white double damask cloth and a blinding array of glass and silver. He pulled out her chair and waited for her to sit down before taking his own seat. Silent men in long white djellabas tied round the waist with red sashes served a crunchy french bean salad topped with slices of foie gras. Pandora licked her lips and reached for a piece of hot toast, balanced as much foie gras as she could on it and put it in her mouth all in one go. Andreï smiled as he watched her. He still couldn't get over how delicious this girl was, especially when she ate. She enjoyed it so much it was a pleasure to watch. Absent-mindedly he spread a piece of toast with a little foie gras and popped a bean in his mouth.

The salad was followed by a delicious lamb stew filled with Moroccan spices and served with sweet couscous. Andreï watched Pandora wolf it down. Finally, lemon soufflé finished, he ushered her back indoors for coffee and liqueurs. She accepted a cognac.

'Now, Jane.' Pandora winced. 'First of all, I think you'd better tell me your real name. Every time I call you Jane you jump a mile in the air.' Andreï was laughing. 'No, wait. Let's start the game. The game is to guess what we really are. Let's face it, your name is hardly going to be Jane Smith, is it?'

'No. All right then. You'll never guess.'

'If you were more European I would give you a Russian name. Perhaps you are. Perhaps this English thing is a cover-up. After all, my son's French-Russian and he sounds English.'

'That's only because you sent him to Eton.'

'How do you know?'

'Obvious. You wouldn't send him anywhere else, would you?' Pandora kicked herself for gaffe.

'What else can you guess about me?' Andreï lay back in his chair and waited.

'Wait a minute. You're supposed to be guessing my name.'

'Pandora.'

'How did you know?'

'Never mind.'

'You've been snooping through my things.' She was outraged.

'And what does that matter? You shouldn't leave things lying around. I was checking you were not intent on spying on me.' He laughed. 'Pandora's a good name for you – you are, after all, a box of surprises, aren't you?'

Pandora preened and tossed her hair. 'Yes, but most of the surprises are supposed to be bad ones. It's only when you reach the bottom of the box and find the hope sitting there and I become really useful.'

'You've done your homework.'

'Being stuck with a name like this, it's good to have an explanation. My uncle called me Pandora because my mother died and I was all the hope he had left in the world.'

'Your mother died. You have a father somewhere?'

'No. He's the great mystery in my life.'

'You just have an uncle?'

'Yes, and a godmother who loves me.'

'And does your uncle not worry about you being so far away?'

'Frankly, after the way he spoke to me last time I rang him, I couldn't care less.'

'Good. I'd hate it if you suddenly wanted to leave because of guilt or family responsibilities. Now,' continued Andreï, 'what can you tell about me?'

'She leaned back in her chair and sipped at her cognac. She looked at Andreï. The expression on his face had changed. It had become hard, aggressive, competitive.

'Would you think I was the kind of man who could kill his wife?'

'No. You don't have a wife.'

'I did have one. She died. My son was very young . . .' He seemed lost in the golden depths of his drink.

'What did she die of?' Pandora had wanted to know this ever since she'd met Max.

'A drug overdose. She was a heroin addict. She killed

herself, or I killed her, what difference is there? She died. She never knew her son.'

'Was he born a drug addict too?'

'No. I took him away from her at once. She never nursed him. She never fed him. She never knew him.'

'Who did look after him then? I bet you didn't.'

'My housekeeper.'

'And who accuses you of killing her?'

'No one.'

'So why did you ask the question?'

Andreï looked up from his cognac and caught her staring. His face hardened to a blank sheet of iron. Pandora suddenly understood how vulnerable she was. He didn't know she was a friend of Max's. She was to all intents and purposes his prisoner here; he could do anything he wanted with her.

'How did you get your scar?' The tension in the atmosphere changed as she reached out and traced its length until she reached his lips. He kissed her fingertips gently and took her hand, kissing her palm softly.

'I got it in a duel.'

Pandora sat up, interested. He pulled her down beside him on the sofa.

'How did you get in a duel? It's such a beautiful scar, it looks as if you had it put there by a plastic surgeon.'

'No, please. At the time it was very painful.'

'Who were you duelling with? Was it over a woman?'

'Yes, I suppose it was.' Andreï looked away into the distance and remembered the sweet faces of Rory and his twin Miranda, both so eager to please him. 'She was a lovely girl. I knew her when I was studying. The duel was with her brother.'

'Her brother! He can't have been vying for her attentions, was he?'

'I think he was a little bit jealous. Perhaps their relationship was incestuous. They were extraordinarily close. You know, families are strange things. I've never had one so I have never understood why people get so upset and protective about them.'

'What happened?'

'Well, it wasn't exactly pistols at dawn; we were using fencing foils. Do you know anything about fencing?'

'No, but my uncle is very good. He says it is such an elegant sport it should be called dancing.'

'He's quite right. It is elegant.'

'But duelling's illegal.'

'So?'

'Did you win?'

'Oh yes. He came off much worse than I. He was a little, how shall I say it, fey. Is that the word? Yes. And I was stronger and fitter than he. So I won.'

'What kind of scars did he come out with?'

'I think they were emotional rather than physical. I don't ever leave my opponents with simple injuries. Andreï stood and walked towards the grand piano in the corner. He began to play a Chopin nocturne. 'No, one should always leave one's opponents with something to think about. Broken bones are easily mended. Still, I threw him out of a window and he broke some ribs along with his heart, the fool.'

Pandora was impressed. The power this man was exuding was almost intoxicating. He looked up at her and she was mesmerised by the different-coloured eyes flashing in the shadow. She went over and leant on the piano.

'You play beautifully.'

'Thank you. I learnt when I was a little boy. I learnt to fence then, too. The fencing is more useful, but the piano is good for relaxation. When I'm frustrated I turn to my piano.'

'Not to fencing opponents, then.'

He smiled at her. 'Not any more. No, these days I have less messy ways of dealing with people who annoy me.'

'Do you always "deal" with people? Do you not just leave them to get on with their own thing?'

'You will learn that a little revenge is a useful thing. I doubt anyone has ever crossed you, yet.'

'No, they haven't, except my uncle, who won't tell me what it is that's bothering him. He keeps ordering me around and being mean to me.'

Andreï stood and took Pandora's hand.

'You poor thing. I will make you feel better about your uncle. Come with me, I want to show you something.'

Pandora luxuriated in the warmth of the hand that guided her out of the room and up a narrow, winding staircase to the roof of the house. Andreï led her to a parapet and let her look. She gasped, not from breathlessness but from the view. The house was high on a mountain. In the far distance she could see the lights of a village, but all around the house was total darkness. Only the glitter from a multitude of stars silhouetted the hills around them.

'This is what is important. This is fantastic. Man can never conquer the earth. Remember that. We are just little bugs rattling around on the surface of it. It doesn't matter what we do. We are irrelevant. Sometimes I try to make my son understand this, but he thinks the people around him are too important. He will learn.'

Pandora changed the subject. 'It is fantastic.' She leant on the parapet and let the soft night breeze stroke her hair. She turned and looked at Andreï.

'You are so little,' he said, stroking her cheek with a gentleness that surprised him.

'I'm not. I'm nearly six foot tall.' Pandora was indignant.

'No, so innocent, so childlike. You remind me of the girl I duelled over. She was like you, daring on the outside, but inside she was so frightened of the big wide world. Are you frightened inside too, Pandora?'

'Not now. Not here.'

Andreï bent down and kissed her forehead. She breathed in the scent of the skin of his neck. His lips a wandered over her face, exploring it, and she stood still, content to feel his breath on her cheek, his hot, dry lips heading inevitably for hers. He let his hand creep round to the back of her neck and pulled at the ribbon tying her hair so that it fell in a shimmering stream over her shoulders. He buried his face in it, searching for her neck through the sweet-smelling weight of it, beginning to get to know her, his own black swan.

Chapter 9

MONDAY 24 JULY

'DARLING.'

'Darling? What are you darlinging me for? It's seven-thirty in the morning!' Rory's disgruntled voice did nothing to boost Nina's confidence.

'I know it's early but I just wanted to check in.' Nina was secretly praying that Pandora would have turned up in the night. 'Everything OK?'

'Fine. Apart from the fact that there's still no sign of Pandora. Can we talk later? It's the middle of the night.'

'No, I've got to work. Remember I'm doing these collections without my fashion director. Things are a little hectic.

'I know. I'm here with you, remember? Or are you too involved with that ghastly little Barbie Boy Fyodov to notice that I'm trying to help too? I'm beginning to think the rumours around town are true.'

'Which rumours?'

'That you are practising paedophilia with a known devil worshipper.'

'Well, in that case it wouldn't matter about his age, would it? Rory, bury it. Max can't help who his father is. All things considered, I think he's remarkably well adjusted.'

'Ugh. You are falling for him.'

'No, I'm not. Anyway, he's deeply in love with Morgan James.'

'Oh great. Anna'll be thrilled.'

'Be honest, Rory, do you really think he'll get anywhere with Morgan?'

'Fair point. OK, what are you ringing me about at this unearthly hour?'

'I think we should inform the police.'

Rory began to howl.

When Nina had put down the phone, she went to fetch Max. She needed him to come with her to the Préfecture Police. Rory had refused point blank to accompany her. He said that if they reported Pandora missing it was tantamount to burying her alive. Nina slammed out of the hotel, furious with Rory. She and Max didn't have much time; she had a show at ten-thirty and hadn't yet OK'd the faxes which had come through overnight. She hurried to her car and had the driver speed her to the rue de l'Université, where Max was up and eating breakfast, yesterday's *Sunday Times* spread before him on the drawing room.

'Come on enough dreaming about with the papers, we've got to declare Pandora missing.'

'Not before you've had a cup of coffee. Look, Mrs Fischer even laid a place for you.' Max giggled. 'I think she thinks you stayed the night!'

'Just like old times, eh?' Nina's voice was grim. 'OK pass me the Style section. Let's see what the *Sunday Times* has to say about the demise of Knowle's career and the bright beginning of Gloria's.' She opened the paper. 'Oh, great, just what I need. "Glorious Gloria Beats Nobody Nina to Top Job".'

Rory opened the door to a pair of policemen who'd come to take a statement. He was already dressed in morning, a black armband round the sleeve of his moss-green velvet jacket.

'Oh, darling Nina, I really don't need a strippagram to cheer me up. I would have thought you had better taste.' Rory turned to the policemen. 'Thank you for coming. My boss sometimes doesn't get the right end of the stick. I don't think a pair of Chippendale *manqués* are really going to help right now.'

The policemen drew themselves up to their combined height of about fourteen feet.

'I'm sorry, sir, if we give ze wrong impression, but we are real *agents de police*.'

'You can't be, you're much too good-looking.' Rory looked the two of them up and down. 'And much too young.'

The produced badges, and Rory blushed.

'Good Lord, how embarrassing. I really thought you were, well, working boys!'

'We 'ave come to take ze statement about your missing niece, Miss Williams.'

Rory, suddenly the gracious host, asked them to sit, and called room service for coffee.

Anna jumped as the phone rang. She was having a determined clear-up, and was in the middle of the sitting room surrounded by bags of various sorts of rubbish. She struggled over the mess to the hall and into the kitchen to answer it.

'Anna, it's Rory.' He was in tears.

'Hello, pickle, how are you? I heard about Pandora. I am sorry.'

'Anna, it's a total disaster. Apart from anything else, she's more or less ruined her career by not being here. None of us have any idea where she is. I just had to make a statement to the police.

'You poor thing. Did they think they'd find her?'

'Well, we haven't got much to go on. She just walked out of Max Fyodov's house and was never seen again.'

'Oh, that little toad. He's been ringing Morgan to see if she's any the wiser. Of course she's not.'

'Well, at least you agree with me on the toad front. Nina's going full tilt towards marrying the boy. I keep reminding her she's old enough to be his grandmother, but she just tells me to shut up and mind my own business, and that he's well adjusted.'

'I shouldn't think that's possible, bearing in mind the

kind of upbringing he's probably had. So what are you going to do?'

'Well, I'm just praying Pandora's only doing this because she's annoyed with me. The only possible clue I can think of is that she rang before and started asking me about Fontainebleau. You don't know why, do you?'

'No idea. There must be more than that for you to go on, surely?'

'I know. I know. Now, is Morgan there? I want to pick her brains.'

'No, she's working. She's doing the lunchtime shift so she should be back in a minute. She's probably just grabbing something to eat herself . . . Wait, here she is. Hold on.'

'Hi, Rory. I'm sorry about Pandora. I'm sure she'll turn up. I mean – she's more capable of looking after herself than we all give her credit for, I think.'

'Thank you, Morgan.' Rory sniffed away his tears and put on his best schoolmarm voice. 'Now, tell me exactly what happened before she disappeared.'

'Well, there isn't much to tell, really. All Nick and I could come up with was that maybe she'd gone off with this man with a scarred face. She met him at the Floré.'

'What?' said Anna and Rory in unison from either side of the Channel.

'But we decided it wouldn't be Max's father. Too obvious. Anyway, he wasn't in Paris when we were.'

'Wouldn't put it past him to try and seduce her, though. He'd love to steal his son's girlfriend.'

'Oh, she wasn't going out with Max, he wasn't interested.' Morgan blushed.

'I see,' continued Rory. 'And who on earth could be more interesting than Pandora?'

'Well, I didn't mean that Pandora isn't attractive, it's just that . . .'

Anna grabbed the phone. 'I would have thought you'd be thrilled he wasn't going out with Pandora. That would really have put the cat among the pigeons.'

'What do you mean?' asked Morgan.

'Never mind,' said Anna, at the same time as Rory said, '*Pas devant les enfants.*'

'Oh well,' said Morgan, offended. 'If you guys are going to talk about things I'm too immature to deal with, then I'll just leave you to it.' She took the handset back from Anna. 'Rory, that's all she said, really. I can't imagine it would have been Max's father or we would have heard about it, surely? Why doesn't someone just get Interpol on to the situation?'

'We have informed the police.' Rory was trying hard to keep control. He'd done well so far, but for Pandora to rush off with Andreï . . . 'Did this man have different-coloured eyes?'

'She didn't say. She would have, wouldn't she? I mean, it's the kind of thing you notice.'

Max thought he'd worked out where Pandora was. He'd finally spoken to a reluctant Morgan, who'd mentioned the man with the scar. He wouldn't' have thought any more of it if Mrs Fischer hadn't reacted so strangely. The day before, she'd said she knew nothing about Pandora's whereabouts. Today he'd asked her if she knew where his father was.

'No.'

'What? You always know where he is.'

'Well, this time I don't. You have all his telephone numbers. You could always call yourself and ask the servants. They will surely know if he is at one of the houses.'

'Mrs Fischer, you do realise this is making me suspicious.'

'You can be anything you like, Max Fyodov. I do not know where he is.'

'You know that my friend with the long black hair has gone missing.'

'And what has that to do with the price of eggs? I do not listen to other people's conversations. You should know that.' Mrs Fischer was looking deeply offended. She drew herself up to her full five foot two inches. 'And I will thank you to stop looking at me accusingly like that. I cannot be expected to keep track of your father or of your friends.' She sniffed disapprovingly. 'I am, after all, only a housekeeper, not a detective.' She marched out of the drawing room, fury written all over her ramrod-straight back.

She must be with Andreï. The only question was, which house had he taken her to? London? Unlikely, not at the end of July. Fontainebleau? Possible, but dull for long periods of time. Morocco? Obviously. Max went to call Nina.

Nina was exhausted. She hated not feeling in control of her life. Lying in her bath, she began to dictate to Emily, who sat on the loo seat taking notes.

'OK, here goes: Confirm the outfits by fax with Givenchy, Dior, Lacroix, Chanel, Versace and Saint Laurent. You'd better get on to Manolo and see what kind of shoes he can lend us. Get them to fax us a list. And tell him I don't want anything complicated. If he gives me horrible things I'll photograph the girls in bare feet. But I can't possibly use the Chanel shoes, they are always so dreadful, and none of the others are much better. I wish the designers would draw the line before they hit the feet. They should concentrate on clothes and let Manolo and Christian Louboutin and Filippa Scott and people worry about the leg ends. Tell Manolo that if the worst comes to the worst we can have them picked up from London. Tell him thirty-nines or bigger will be OK. Those girls' feet are enormous.' She looked reflectively at one of her own perfectly pedicured, dark-red-nailed size three and a half feet. 'You can choose which ones we'll take when the list comes. You can manage that, can't you?'

Emily blushed with pleasure. Nina continued, ignoring the fact that she'd just given her assistant her first tiny little break.

'Tell everyone the carnet will have to leave Friday afternoon and that the clothes will be back in Paris Monday morning, by lunch. And get the Paris office to get on to their temporary export people. You'll have to get the carnet list to them by eight a.m. Thursday so they can deal with the paperwork. I'm afraid you are going to be exhausted, Emily, but never mind. It'll be worth it.

'Get someone at the Paris office to tell you where you

go for twenty pairs of Wolfords, ten nue, sheer and ten black, sheer. And you'd better get some nue strings for the girls, they never remember to bring their own. Get five, M and S have perfectly good ones. Go to the avenue Haussman. Get the Paris office to give you a seven-thousand-franc float. I've signed the chit for you, it's on the desk in my sitting room. And don't forget to keep all your receipts.

'Quickly fax Saul's assistant in NYC and confirm him. Tell her I'll take the boyfriend but nobody else, but you'd better just check if he has any new foibles. Knowing him, he has. Tell Gay I want all her backstage pictures here to look at this afternoon by four. Fax the managing editor's office in London and tell them everything's under control. Then check Rory to make sure he hasn't died of shock after giving his statement to the police. No, don't worry, I'll do that. All right? Are you clear on everything?'

'Yes,' Emily lied. Did nobody ever say please and thank you in this business?

'Oh, and one last thing, you'd better get the credits for everything we're taking with us in advance; it'll make the last-minute stuff a lot easier. After all, we go to press next Wednesday.' Nina laughed.

Emily nearly cried. 'Yes. But who are we going to shoot on, Nina? Shouldn't I confirm the model agencies?'

'That, my darling, is my little secret. If I tell you, then someone might start bleeding the information out of you, and I think that would be disastrous for everyone.'

'And where? Hadn't I better confirm the location people?'

'No, darling that is the other secret. I don't want anyone knowing anything about this. Am I clear?'

'Yes, Nina.'

'OK. Put on your list that I have to deal with the insurance. It's going to be astronomical, but never mind. And I need a light table and a loop sent over from the office. OK? Oh, one last thing, we'll need five cars Friday morning at nine a.m. One of them should be an Espace with all the seats except one taken out. You can sit there and guard the luggage. Clear?'

'Fine, Nina. I'd better go and get on.'

'Yes, darling, I think you better had. What time's Chanel?'

'In an hour.'

'Right. I'd better get dressed. Off you go.'

At 6.30 that evening the phone rang in Nina's suite. Deep in thought about pink satin evening dresses, Nina picked it up, and swore as someone knocked at the door at the same time. How was she supposed to work like this? She'd had to let Emily go and have a break. The poor girl had that white look about the eyes that assistants got when they were about to burst into tears on you. Nina would much rather Emily went and had a huge gin and tonic and then carried on. A little Dutch courage made all the difference at this stage. After all, she could hardly offer the girl tranquillisers, could she? Still, she had to have dinner with Karl and she wasn't dressed and she couldn't do fifty things at once. At least he would feed her magnificently, and his house was so beautiful it was a joy to go there.

Telling the person on the other end of the phone to hold on, she opened the door to find don standing there.

'Hi, hang on a minute, would you? I'm just on the phone.' She hurried back across the room.

'Hello?'

'Nina, it's Max. I think I've worked out where Pandora is.'

'Wow – how did you do that?'

'Well–'

Nina cut him off. 'Listen, darling, are you at home? Can I call you back in a second. Someone's just arrived.'

Max was disappointed. 'OK.'

'Better, I'll come round, I'm having dinner with Karl. Can I drop by for a drink beforehand, in about half an hour?'

'OK.'

'Don't sound so piqued, sweetheart. I'm working I won't be long.'

She put the phone down and kissed Don hello. He smelt of alcohol.

'You'll have to talk to me while I change, I'm afraid. I'm due at Karl's in an hour and a half and I've got about five thousand things to do before I leave.'

Don followed her into her bedroom, wondering if this might not be the come-on he'd always rather hoped for from Nina. 'What are you wearing?'

'Chanel. I wish it wasn't so bitty, though I hate all those buttons.'

'Don't wear anything for a while, then.' Don put his hands on Nina's waist and kissed the back of her neck.

She whipped round. 'Darling. I never thought you cared. I thought you were sleeping with Gloria.'

'No rule against a little infidelity, is there?'

Nina tried not to slap him, and only just succeeded. Wanker! 'Sweetheart, I couldn't do that. Gloria's one of my oldest friends. It would be too disloyal.'

'You're not seriously rebuffing me?'

'Fraid so. Come one, Don, don't look so furious. Take it as a compliment,' she hedged,' or as me playing hard to get?'

Nina struggled out of the wide-bottomed navy Chanel pants and skinny Chanel T-shirt with a camellia at the neck that she'd worn for the show, threw on a slip of a silk dressing gown and went to the wardrobe to find the black mousseline Chanel cocktail dress that she'd brought with her, pretty except for the gold buttons with the crossed Cs which went down the back making it extremely uncomfortable to sit down in. She slipped it over her head, and put a little scent behind her ears and on to one finger. Then she turned to Don, who'd followed her across the room, and dabbed the end of his nose. She laughed coquettishly, wishing he'd just bugger off. 'Now Gloria'll think you've been unfaithful even though you haven't. Won't that do? She always did love a bit of competition.'

'No, that won't do, you little bitch. You think you're better than the rest of them, don't you? You think you're clever, you think that what you do is important.' He shoved her slightly; she stepped backwards to find her balance and hit the wardrobe door.

'What's gong on, Don? We've worked together for

years. Why suddenly this? Our relationship's always been so professional!'

He leaned in close to her face; she could smell the whisky on his breath and see the coke glitter in his eyes. Maybe if she thumped him he wouldn't remember.

'You, Nina Charles, are nothing but a jumped-up little tart. I know all about your affairs, I know all about the men you've seduced and used on your way to the top. Well, now you've got as far as me. Come on, Nina, you'll enjoy yourself I'm sure I can do a better job than Max Fyodov.'

He lunged at her and she heard the dress rip as she dragged herself away. He fell to the floor but was up in a second. She couldn't get past him; he stood between her and the door, breathing heavily, sweaty jowls shivering in anticipation. There was nothing for it. She brought her knee up and heard him groan as he slumped to the floor. She ran to the bathroom and was sick. Then, shaking, she rang the concierge.

'Could you send a doctor quickly? There's someone in my room. He's not well.'

He was trying to stand up. Before he had a chance to come to properly, she whacked him over the nose with her Prada bag. He was out like a light. Still shaking, she went to change. She still had to see Max and then dine with Karl. She would think about resigning, or suing, later, when she was alone. Hoping her ordeal didn't show too obviously on her face, and that Don wouldn't remember much in the morning, she watched as he was lifted on to a stretcher and carried to the hotel infirmary. Then, in her trusty Galliano, she left the hotel and jumped into her car. She hoped Max had a glass of whisky ready for her. She needed it.

'Andreï! Hi, how are you, *where* are you? This number is bizarre – where am I calling?'

'Sam, what a pleasure to hear from you. How is your daughter?'

'Coming round. She's not concentrating on me much. She's been staying in your house in Paris.'

'Has she now? Mrs Fischer said Max had had guests. Shame I missed her. Is she as charming as you hoped she'd be?'

'She's very like her mother.'

'How unfortunate.'

'You forget, I loved her mother once.'

'And as far as I can see still do. Still, doesn't mean I have to adore her too, you know. Loyalty doesn't have to go that far, does it?'

'No, Andreï. Anna doesn't think much of you either. She freaked when she discovered that Max and Morgan seem nearly to have got it together. Luckily they had a big bust-up and I don't think it'll go any further, but Anna was surprisingly shaken about it.'

'Telling you what she feels, then, is she? Perhaps she's still in love with you too?'

'No chance. You know she always loved her books more than me.'

'No, she loved you. She just didn't love me and couldn't see why you had to have anything to do with me.

Remember when you came to stay in Paris and she had a nervous breakdown about how I was choosing to bring up my son? What a mess she made of things then.'

'You were drugging him to shut him up, Andreï!'

'I was doing no such thing. I sacked the nurse immediately when that was discovered.'

'You did wait until Anna discovered it for you.'

'No lectures, please. Max has grown up without any major scars from the experience. I just wish he took after me a little more.'

'How could he when you were never there for him to copy?'

'Why is it you are the only person I will let get away with this kind of comment?'

'I'm your good conscience, Andreï. Someone's got to be.'

'And a lot of good it has done you, my friend. So, are you coming to visit? I'm in Morocco. I'm having a lovely time, too much business to attend to but a charming girl to keep me company. Come and share her with me.'

Sam laughed. 'You're incorrigible. Perhaps she doesn't want to be shared.'

'She might not have any choice.' Andreï wasn't joking.

'Well, I thought I might come next weekend. England is cold and miserable, and I think Morgan's more or less had enough of me. Would that be OK?'

'Marvellous. I'll send the plane for you. Let Mrs Fischer know when you want to come and I'll have her arrange everything.'

'Don't send a plane. I'll just fly to . . . Where are you?'

'Not far from Fez. You fly to Fez and then I'll helicopter you up here.'

'Andreï, I'm perfectly capable of getting there myself.'

'Don't be foolish. Why turn down a little luxury? It didn't work last time, did it?'

'No.' Sam laughed. 'OK, I'll let Mrs Fischer know. The end of the week, then.'

'Yes. Look forward to it.'

Sam chuckled to himself and let himself out of his room, heading downstairs and down St Giles towards Anna's house, buying iced champagne on the way from the off licence.

The scene he found at Anna's house was not one he was expecting. Anna and Morgan were standing either side of the kitchen table, arguing.

'You call,' Morgan snapped.

'No, you do it,' said Anna. 'Anyway, we've all agreed that's not who she's with. It would be too much of a coincidence.'

'So let's confirm it and we can strike him off our list of suspects.'

'Such a long list! It'll leave us with nothing.'

'You're not suggesting we don't call just because then we won't have any other leads?'

They turned round and saw Sam, and carried on in unison.

'You can ring!'

'Ring where?'

'Andreï, direct, no need to go via Paris or Max.'

'He's in Morocco.'

'Why?'

'On holiday. He's got a house there. I'm going at the end of the week. What do you want to talk to him about?'

'Pandora!'

'Why?'

Pandora lay in the quiet of the dark room and tried to get her bearings. Gingerly she felt the bruises on her legs and arms. She knew nothing was broken, she could move it all, but she knew also that the damage must be serious. Why else would it hurt so much? She carefully moved her legs and found that they were all right. The blood ran cold in her veins. He had told her he would be back for more. She had no idea of what time of the day or night it was. Her eyes searched the darkness for some pinprick of light, anything to give her her bearings. Nothing, the room was pitch black. Slowly turning so that she could get on to her hands and knees, she decided that she was just going to have to explore by feel Gingerly she began to move about, and as she did so she realised that she was in a large room. There were rugs on the floor, but otherwise it was unfurnished. The strangest part was that however many times she went round the edge of the room, she could not find a door. Eventually she sat back and leant against the wall. She was stuck, a prisoner. She contemplated screaming for help but decided that would only bring more trouble. She knew she had to save her strength for the next time he came to visit her.

'Good evening, Mrs Fischer. Max is expecting me.' Nina swept past the old housekeeper, who made a face at her back, and marched into the drawing room, where she found Max poring over a map laid on the floor. He hardly looked up as she came in.

'Hi – I know where she is.'

'Where?'

'With my father.'

'Don't be ridiculous. He doesn't even know her.'

'Yes, he does. He picked her up at the Floré.'

'But why would he take her anywhere?'

'Because she's a pretty girl and he likes pretty girls.'

'So where is she? Paris? London?'

'Oh no, nothing so simple. He's taken her to Morocco.'

'Great. And how can you be so sure? Have you rung and asked him?'

'Oh, yes. That's really going to go down a bundle. He thinks he's on holiday with a little tart he's picked up off the street, and when he finds out she's a friend of mine and I'd really rather he didn't abuse her, he's going to apologise and send her back on the next plane.' His voice was filled with caustic sarcasm. 'I don't think.'

'I don't see why he shouldn't. He doesn't even have to send her back. She must be more or less safe there, surely? Except . . .'

'Precisely.'

'Precisely what?'

'You know how violent he gets.'

'With girls?'

'Don't you?'

'Max, what are you talking about?'

'What are *you* talking about?'

'Nothing. What do you mean, violent?'

Max sat back on his heels and stared at Nina. How much would he have to tell her to make sure that Nina left this situation well alone? If she rushed in demanding Pandora's return, Max knew his friend stood little chance of returning unharmed, emotionally or physically. He had witnessed his father's anger taken out on women before.

Nina walked over to the drinks tray, laid out between the tall french windows which led into the garden. The cool evening breeze played with the white lawn curtains. Nina, oblivious to the beauty of the room, poured herself a large vodka, straight, on the rocks. She didn't pour a drink for Max. She went back to the centre of the room and looked down at the map.

'Have you got a cigarette?'

He jumped up and fetched his Marlboros from the mantelpiece. He offered her one, then leant forward to light it for her. His manners were impeccable, like his father's had been at Oxford.

Nina had precisely twenty-five minutes before she was supposed to arrive at Karl's, a house where one was never late. She wondered if at some point she would come to the end of her tether and freak out; Pandora was gone, to the arms of a monster it seemed, Don had tried to rape her, and she was going to have to spend the evening being charming in order to endure her continued place among the high and mighty of the fashion fat cats. She drew heavily on the cigarette and let the nicotine rush over her.

Nina leaned on the end of the mantelpiece and flicked her cigarette ash into the fireplace. On any other occasion she would be enjoying this: an illicit cigarette, straight vodka, a beautiful, exquisitely proportioned eighteenth-century room where the soft breeze of a Paris evening was lifting the weight of the day's heat, and the best-looking young man in the world. She sighed. She supposed she wasn't going to have a nervous breakdown. She was just going to get on with the matters in hand, even if there were ten of them, each more important than the last. Max lit a cigarette himself and perched on the arm of the sofa.

'You don't know about Dad, do you?'

'Get on with it, Max. What is it that's making Pandora so unsafe with him?'

'He beats women up. I think it's something to do with the fact that my mother died. He thinks she deserted him and he's not sure if he was the one who killed her, or whether she would have died anyway. So he takes his fury out on other women, she being unable to answer the question, so to speak. He's a mess.' Max blushed. He hated talking about sex with someone old enough to be his mother. 'He has this routine. First he charms them, then he quizzes them about what sort of man they think he is, and then he beats them up to show them how stupid they were to trust him in the first place. Usually the girls are paid and usually they get away. I suppose he thinks Pandora's a professional.'

'What?'

'Sordid, isn't it? But I expect you knew he could be violent. You were at Oxford with him, after all. But the point is, we have to work out how to spirit Pandora out of there.

We can't just ring him up and tell him to lay off her. He's too volatile.'

'But what if he's already beaten her, done things?' Nina was frantic.

'I've already decided. I think the only thing is for me to go there. I can get there without him knowing I'm coming.'

'I'll come with you.'

'Don't be ridiculous. You still have several days' couture to go, and then you've got to shoot it.'

'Yes, but what if I shot it in Morocco? I could kill several birds with one stone.' Nina looked at her watch. 'Listen, darling, I've got to go, Karl hates it if people are late. I won't stay long, and I'll come straight back here afterwards. We'll decide what to do then.' Nina picked up the four-metre-long piece of black mousseline which served as her shawl and threw it round her shoulders. She kissed Max. 'In the meantime, don't do anything silly.'

'Andreï? It's me, Sam, again.' Sam stood at the phone in Anna's kitchen, Morgan and Anna's expectant faces staring at him.

'Great. Coming earlier, are you? Had enough playing happy families for the moment?'

'No, not at all. I've just got rather an odd question for you.'

'Yes.'

'The girl with you, is she, um . . .' Sam searched for an appropriate world, 'a professional?'

'Oh definitely. I'm training her, so to speak. She's a gifted little thing. Why?'

'Just curious. Pretty girl, is she?'

'One of the best. Legs to die for, such long eyelashes I think she must have a secret stock of falsies to put on, I can't tell you how pale her skin is.' Andreï laughed. 'Beautiful, you'll love her. But you might not be able to meet her after all. I think she'll be gone by the weekend. She seems to have other plans. If you like, I'll arrange some local girls for us.'

'It's OK. I think I can live without.'

'Ah, a stronger man than I. Why do you want to know all this?'

'See you next weekend, Andreï.' Sam put the phone down. 'Well, it's not her.'

'How do you know?'

'The girl's a prostitute. And who would describe Pandora without mentioning her hair?'

Anna was unconvinced. 'What else did he say?'

'Listen, it's not her, all right? I mean, can you think of anything more ridiculous than her being picked up and rushed off to Morocco by her own father?'

'Her, father!' Morgan was stunned.

Chapter 10

TUESDAY 15 JULY

MAX left the house without a backward glance, a small holdall slung over his shoulder. Mrs Fischer was out doing the week's shopping. She wouldn't miss him until that evening. He'd left a note saying she could get him at the London flat. He jumped into the Spider without opening the door and drove it round the corner, where he parked it in an underground car park. He stopped at a hole in the wall and took out ten thousand francs on his gold card. Finally he hailed a taxi and directed it to the Crillon, where he planned to say a quick farewell to Nina and make sure that she had everything clear in her head for their plan.

Paris shimmered under a haze of heat and pollution, but Max ignored the weather and headed into the cool hall of the great old hotel where Nina was staying. He saw her cross the lobby towards him, her hair reflecting glints from the chandeliers far above her. She was stunning, her understated cream linen suit only serving to underline her natural beauty. She kissed him.

'Good luck. I'll see you on Friday.'

'Thanks, Nina. If anything happens I'll call you. But as of the day after tomorrow there might not be any phones. Anyway, we'll be fine. She'll be fine. We'll get her out of this.'

'Why are you doing this, Max? What makes you care so much about Pandora?'

'She's a nice girl.' His voice hardened. 'And I wouldn't want anybody to be stuck with my father a million miles from anywhere and entirely at his mercy.' Suddenly he laughed. 'Don't worry. I'm not in love with her. I seem to be *persona non grata* with parents at the moment. I'm going to remain young, free and single just to save potential girlfriends from their parents' wrath.'

'Was Anna that bad?' Nina took his arm and headed for the bar. She had time for coffee. 'What time's your flight?'

'Two hours.'

'Then what?'

'Spend the night in Tangiers and then the train to Fez. I'll be in Tounetz by tomorrow evening, and I'll head for the hills as soon as I can arrange it. Probably Thursday morning, unless I can persuade them to get me up there during tomorrow night.'

'I won't ask who 'them' are. Are you sure you'll be safe?'

'I've known these people all my life. I'm certainly safer with them than I am with my father.'

'If you say so. I hope so. I'm fond of you too, not only Pandora.'

'Thanks. That's reassuring.'

'Well, I try to help where I can. What did Anna say to you?'

"Told me to keep out of Morgan's life, and that they had had enough of the Fyodovs to last a lifetime. What on earth did my father ever do to make her hate me so much?'

'I'll tell you about Anna and all of us one day. Someone should. After this weekend.'

'What do you mean?'

'You said your flight was in a couple of hours? Not long enough, I'm afraid.'

'Come on, Nina, you can give me the bare bones, surely?'

'Nina stared at the ceiling for inspiration and found herself looking into Rory's face. He looked thunderous. She breathed a sigh of relief.

'Hello, darling,' she said, leaping up and kissing him before he could spit at Max.

'Precious.' He kissed her hand and threw a look of pure venom at Max. 'Glad to see you're entertaining your toy boy.'

Max grinned, grabbed his holdall and kissed Nina goodbye. 'Sorry to have ruined your day Rory. You'll be pleased to hear I've got to leave town for a while. You'll be able to breathe again. And it'll mean you can stop setting your alarm for the middle of the night to wake you up to make those charming phone calls.' Rory blushed. 'See you

Friday, Nina.' Max headed out of the lobby, turning heads as he went.

'Rory, you haven't been making nasty phone calls to Max?'

'Me? Never.' The blush slowly abated, and he sat down next to Nina on the little two-seater sofa. She sat up straight and reached for her coffee. 'Anyway, my nightly activities seem to be nothing to yours. You, my precious little friend, are cradle-snatching, and it's not good for your health. You should watch out. What do you think Andreï will do when he finds out? He'll have your guts for garters, that's what.'

'No, he won't. Why, he invited me to relieve Max of his virginity at one stage. I made a valiant attempt but unfortunately was already too late.'

'Oh, you are disgusting. Besides, Andreï's more unpredictable than that. He might get jealous.'

'Rory, keep your voice down. This is a public place.'

'So what are you doing hobnobbing with him here?'

'It is precisely because I have strictly nothing to hide that I met him here.'

'Pull the other one, it's got bells on it.' Rory waved a beringed finger at a waiter and asked for fresh orange juice. 'You're planning something with him though, aren't you? I can see it in your guiltily hunched shoulders.'

'I am not planning anything.'

'Yes, you are. Where are you shooting, Nina?'

'Spying for Don, are you? Or for Gloria?' She tapped the side of her nose. 'Wait and see, nosy parker.'

'Nina!' Nina looked up to see Don bearing down on

her, his nose bandaged and a huge black eye making his usually oily face a little more interesting.

'Good Lord. Whatever happened to him?' whispered Rory.

'I'll tell you later.' Nina stood and smiled with her teeth. 'Hello, Don.' Did he remember the previous evening? She looked at him and could see no further than his good eye. His expression wasn't giving anything away.

'Can I join you for breakfast?'

'Oh, Don, I'm sorry, I can't. We have a show in three-quarters of an hour, remember? And I've got proofs to OK and pictures to bin and an assistant to wipe up off the floor before I even think about what to wear.' She headed off toward the lifts.

Rory watched this little scene with amusement.

'Odd things going on with that one, Don,' he said. 'I think she's having an affair with the Fyodov boy. That's why she hasn't been seen around that much. Where's she shooting the couture?'

'No idea. Bitch won't tell me.'

'Darling, no need to be so vitriolic.'

'If only you knew.' Don sat down, holding his head, and shouted for coffee.

'Whatever happened to your head dear?'

Without waiting for his coffee, Don turned on his heel and headed out towards his car. He couldn't bear to tell Rory that he didn't have the slightest idea where his black eye had come from.

*

Max had half an hour to spare at the airport. He wanted to call Morgan but squashed the impulse, sat down at the dirty little bar in the departure lounge, ordered an espresso and lit a cigarette. The bustle of the airport went ignored by him. He avoided thinking about what his father's reaction would be when he turned up out of the blue. It wouldn't be pretty. Andreï didn't appreciate being interrupted by uninvited guests, and Max, if anything, was even less welcome.

Orly Airport smelt of the people who inhabited it at that moment – a strangely attractive sweet-smelling mixture of spices, rotting fruit and unwashed humanity. Max knocked back his shot of caffeine, ground his cigarette out on the floor and allowed himself to be carried along by the throng towards the Air France flight to Tangiers. His mind drifted in other directions: Morgan – stupid girl. She wasn't so perfect herself, was she? What was it that she'd particularly hated about his pictures of her? It wasn't the fact that she was naked, of that he was sure. She'd said something about the look on her face. Her face was beautiful. He'd caught her thoughtful expression, her air of slight detachment perfectly. That was all. Why take such umbrage? He shrugged, ignoring the safety instructions being given by a sweating air stewardess, and stared, unseeing, at the shimmering tarmac below. Well, he would see if she could keep up her anger, as long as Nina's plan worked.

Max had imagined that Morgan would be working. In fact she was taking a long way round to the restaurant. She had half an hour to spare and in order to appease her mother, who had begged her to make an effort with her father, was walking along the Cherwell with Sam. Bored, Morgan sat down under a willow tree and took the biro out of her hair, letting it fall shining in the light of the late afternoon sun.

'Tell me about the Fyodovs. Why does Anna hate them so much? What did they do to her? And why do you still see them if they're so dreadful?'

'They're not that bad. I only met Max once or twice. Seems all right to me, considering he's had a pretty uncared-for childhood. Nice guy. You know he paints?'

'Don't remind me. He painted me, naked.'

'Was the picture good?'

'That's hardly the point, is it? How dare he? He's never seen me naked. You should ask permission before you do things like that.'

'That's not why you don't like him. There must be more to it than that.'

Morgan sighed. 'He just makes me feel uncomfortable that's all. He stares at me all the time – he looks right through me and his eyes are so ale you can't see what he's thinking. And because they're different colours you can't quite decide if one of them's looking at you and the other's busy doing something else. He's the kind of person who always makes sure the light's behind him so you can't see the expression on his face.'

'You don't think he does that so he can see you in your best light?'

'Why should he?'

'Well, if he wanted to paint you and was too shy to ask you to sit for him, he'd have to do his studies of you in other ways, wouldn't he?'

'He should have bloody asked, instead of slyly sizing me up without my knowing it.'

Sam laughed. 'Are you always this cross with people?'

'Only when they take advantage of me. I don't like not knowing where I stand.'

'You can't always know where you stand. Life would be dull if you did.'

'Yes, but you'd be prepared for things. I don't like surprises.'

'Like your mother.'

'What did Andreï Fyodov do to her, then? You're avoiding the subject.'

'No, I'm not. It's just that I'm not sure. I mean, she didn't think much of him after he had an affair with Pandora's mother and Rory at the same time.'

'Wait a minute. I'm still not clear about this. Andreï Fyodov had an affair with Rory *and* Miranda Williams at the same time, knowing they were twins and presuming they wouldn't mind. Miranda got pregnant, didn't tell him about the baby, had Pandora and died haemorrhaging in the delivery room. Of course Anna didn't think much of him! And he's never even acknowledged Pandora. That's an outrageous thing to do. I'm surprised anybody speaks to him after that.'

'Hang on. He still doesn't know about Pandora,' Sam explained. 'Rory and Miranda decided they didn't want anything to do with him. So when Miranda died Rory carried out her wishes and didn't tell him about Pandora.'

'And none of you ever thought to tell him either?'

'You can't go against other people's wishes. Especially at such an awful time. Besides, Rory always said that when Pandora was old enough he would tell her about her father. You can't judge people just on their actions, Morgan. You have to put things into context. It's probably better that Pandora didn't know who he was until now. Andreï's not that terrible. And as for Anna – I think she was frightened of how attractive she found him. She didn't think she should for all the same reasons you think you should disapprove of Max. You shouldn't, you know. It's not fair on either of you. Andreï was very like Max, not just in appearances. When he was young he had the same energy bursting out of him. It's a shame he never let himself use it constructively. He never dared.' Sam looked wistfully at the water drifting past them. 'Now he's bored.'

'But if Andreï had an affair with Rory, he must be gay, then? Or Bisexual?'

San paused. 'Neither, I think. At that stage we would all do virtually anything to get a kick. We were middle-class people caught up in the sexual revolution. All of a sudden, anything went.'

'He wasn't middle-class. He's a White Russian prince or something, isn't he?'

'That's one of the problems. He's not nearly as grand as he tries to make out.'

'Why do you still see him, then?'

'Perhaps because I'm his only friend and I don't want to let him down.'

Morgan raised her eyebrows at Sam. How could he accuse her of being holier than thou? He sounded like a particularly charitable missionary.

'Is he really Pandora's father? I mean, Rory's sister could have been sleeping with all sorts of people.'

'She wasn't. Pandora is Andreï's daughter, without a shadow of a doubt.'

'So she's Max's sister.'

'Yup.'

'Good thing nothing ever happened between them, then.'

'No thanks to her trying, from what I hear.'

'Well, she wasn't to know. Since you grown-ups have this ridiculous thing about not telling her about her true parentage, Max is still fair game for her, isn't he?' Morgan thought for a minute. 'You know, I bet she's run off to get back at Max.' She looked at her watch and jumped up. 'Shit, I've go to go. I'm late for work.' Shyly she turned to her father. 'Come and eat there tonight if you like. I'll make sure you sit in my bit, and then you can see what I do in my free time.'

Sam grinned at her. 'Love to.'

Emily sat exhausted before the telephone in Nina's sitting room. Nina had rushed off to another show and Emily's list of tasks just wouldn't get any shorter. She prayed for the end of the week and stared out of the window, giving herself a minute's rest. The main problem was that Emily spoke perfect English and passable French, but this fashion business seemed to have a language of its own. She couldn't understand what anyone was talking about, whatever language they were speaking. She was relieved to finally get Rory on the phone. At last, someone she knew, even if he was going to talk about his missing niece.

'Don't I know that lost little voice?'

'Yes, Rory, it's me.'

'How's it going? Nina behaving like a slave-driver?'

'A bit.' Emily wounded tearful.

'Totally lost, are you? Haven't got a clue what anyone's talking about?'

'Absolutely. What is this language that fashion people speak? I've never heard anything like it. And all they do is call you darling and expect you to know in advance why they're ringing and to have the answer to all their questions at your fingertips. I think they need clairvoyants doing this job, not normal people.'

'You're' absolutely right. And don't believe anyone who calls you darling. The more endearments they use, the more likely they are to stab you in the back at the first opportunity.'

'Thanks for the confidence boost, Rory.'

'Well, I like to help where I can. Nina at a show, is she?'

'I think so. She said she'd be back at about eight, and then she was going to spend the evening going through September's book.'

'So I can get her later?'

'Yes. Shall I give her a message?'

'No. No, it's all right. Wait a minute. Tell her I spoke to Morgan and Anna. They weren't much help. All right, darling?'

'Rory, wait, one more thing.'

'Yes?'

'What's a loop?'

'A what?'

'Nina asked me to send over to the Paris office for a loop and a light table. What does she mean? I don't know whether to get a removal van or whether this is lingo for things that'll fit on a bike.'

'Poor baby. Call the Paris office and they'll sort it out. You'll find out what they are when they get to the hotel, won't you?'

'And Rory, what's a carnet?'

'Oh, darling, if you don't know that yet, you're in real trouble. have you not shot abroad before?'

'I've never had anything to do with any shoots. Till now Gloria's assistant always did all this stuff. I haven't got a clue what Nina's on about half the time. Before Gloria went I just planned lunches and fashion shows and hair appointments and shunted articles and artwork around London following Nina wherever she went and got shouted at by all the magazine staff. I wish Nina would find another fashion director. I can't do everything. I'm, going to have to ask for an assistant for myself soon. I've only been here a month and I'm so exhausted I'm ready to retire. So, what is a carnet?'

'It's the suitcase of clothes you're taking with you to shoot with, and all the temporary export papers to go with them. Are you doing it?'

'No, just the list, and then the Paris office are doing the rest.'

'Then you'll be all right. Give them the list and they'll do everything else, that's what they're there for.'

'Thanks, Rory. You're a great help.'

'Do my best. Talk to you later.'

'Hello?'

'Anna?'

'Yes, who is this?' Anna looked at the clock beside her bed. It was almost midnight. She'd been asleep for hours. She turned on her bedside light and Walter, deep in his own dreams at the end of the bed, yowled in protest and buried himself under the eiderdown.

'I'm sorry to ring so late. I tried earlier and there was no answer. It's Nina.'

'Nina Charles. My God, the past is catching up with me. Sam's ensconced in the Randolph, and I keep getting that horrid little Fyodov boy on the phone. Are you about to turn up with Andreï and Rory to complete the reunion?'

Nina laughed. 'Not today. How is Sam?'

'Fine. Circling Morgan like a wolf with his prey, which I don't like very much, but I suppose she's old enough to make her own decisions, and I suppose they should get to know each other before she decides anything. He's got a lot older, hasn't he?'

'You mean wiser.'

'Well . . .'

'Come on, Anna, gone is the spoilt little boy who always thought he was going to get his own way, and in his place is a fine example of what all of us could possible want in a man.'

'If we want a man at all!'

"Well, I do. Don't you?'

'It's been a long time, Nina. I've managed well without one for all these years. Why rock the boat now?'

'Because it might make you happy?'

'But I am happy.'

'Lucky you.' Nina stopped.

Anna broke the embarrassed silence. 'It's good to talk to you, Nina. It's a shame that it takes a crisis like this to get us all together. When are you back?'

'Next week. I'm shooting at the weekend. I've got another friend of Morgan's working for me – Emily. Do you know her?'

'Yes, Morgan brought her down here with Pandora one weekend earlier this year.'

'Well, I'm teaching her how to become married to her work. She's a good pupil. Hasn't been out once this week, apart from to see Max, that is.'

'Are you married to your work? Is that how you never came to get hitched?'

'No, I never married because I was always in love with your ex-husband and you frightened him off to the States.'

'Oh, Nina. Not still.'

'Let's not talk about it.'

'No. Let's not.' Anna was relieved to change the subject. 'So where do you think Pandora is, then?'

'Aha, therein lies the rub. We think she's with Andreï.'

'That crossed our minds too, but we dismissed it. It's too far-fetched. We decided the scarred man was a red herring. There must be hundreds of them around Paris. Besides, didn't Sam tell you? He rang Andreï and asked him. Andreï has got a girl with him, but she's a prostitute.'

'No. He may think she's a prostitute, but it's Pandora. The poor little thing's so naïve she probably thought she was playing a hilarious game. And now she's got herself into something she'll never be able to manage. I know you've been talking to Rory. If he calls you, please don't tell him where we think she is. We need to make sure she's safe before he goes thundering off with his fencing foils to balance the scar he's already inflicted. And Anna, there's another thing you could help me with.'

'What?'

'Well, as usual I'm trying to kill about fifteen birds with one stone. I'm going to get Pandora at the end of the week. All being well, Max should already be there keeping an eye on her. And I'm going to shoot the couture for my next issue there.'

'Where?'

'Andreï's house in Morocco.'

'You're not going to rescue her straight away? You should get Interpol on to it. God knows what they could be getting up to!'

'I don't think twenty-four hours will make much difference. They've had since Saturday to get up to whatever they like. So Max has gone on ahead, he should get there late tomorrow night if all goes well and then I'm going too. I think it's time somebody told them they are father and daughter, don't you?'

'Well, yes. But what if she's . . .'

'I'm praying that she won't be. Anyway, I wondered if Morgan could come to.'

'Whatever for?'

'Then Pandora will have her two best friends there to support her. And Morgan's just met her own father. She might be able to help.'

'But we can't afford it.'

'I'll pay. She can come as a model. I want to shoot her, Anna.'

'She'd hate that.'

'Tell her my job's on the line and I'll be eternally grateful. See what kind of a response that gets.'

'Listen, Nina, I'll try. But she's been through a pretty tough time herself lately. I can't force her to do anything she doesn't want to.'

'Of course not. Just ask her. For Pandora's sake.'

'I'll ask. I can't promise anything. Morgan may be fond of Pandora, but at the moment she's trying to earn enough money to get her through next term. She'll probably say Pandora got herself into this situation and it's up to her to get herself out. Sam said he was going to see Andreï at the end of the week. Won't he do?'

'He's not Pandora's best friend, is he? I'm glad he'll be there, though. He's the only person who was every any good with Andreï. So,' Nina's voice was suddenly brisk, 'she can come with him then. Thanks, Anna. I knew I could rely on you.'

Anna put the phone down exhausted. This was all too far-fetched to be possible. She lay back and stroked Walter absent-mindedly. How on earth was she going to persuade

Morgan to model for a fashion magazine? Modelling, they both knew in their heart of hearts, was morally wrong.

Max spent the night in an ageing hotel whose days of grandeur had gone with the twenties. Deep in the heart of the Tangiers Medina, facing the sweep of the Mediterranean, it smelt of wood smoke and hashish. He left his passport with the old man at the hall desk. The lounge was a relic of a bygone age, decorated with English hunting prints, a mouldy grand piano and three ancient leather-covered armchairs. Lugging his holdall up to a tiny room, he asked for coffee, which duly arrived, sweet and milky. He poured in a generous slug from the whisky bottle he'd bought in the duty-free shop at Orly and lay back on his bed. The train to Fez left at six the next morning, before the heat, and would arrive at the antique town in the middle of it. He needed to sleep.

Pandora, shivering with fear, sat pushing her back into the wall as if at any moment it might give and let her out of her prison. Andreï sat opposite her, dressed in only jodhpurs and riding boots. A riding crop lay across his knees. He sipped at a glass of vodka.

'You see, Pandora, I did kill my wife. I murdered her as surely as I'm going to murder you.' Pandora tried to hold back her fear, but a sob escaped her. 'Shut up while I speak.' The riding crop whipped across her knuckles, drawing a fine line of blood. 'She had my child and then I killed her. You see, she'd served her purpose, hadn't she? So I injected her with the shot that killed her. It was a horrible death. It took days. She suffered more than I've ever seen anyone suffer before or since. And believe me,' he smiled at his whimpering prisoner, 'I've seen enough suffering to last ten lifetimes.'

Pandora shivered.

Chapter 11

WEDNESDAY 26 JULY

PANDORA sat huddled in the darkness, half wishing that Andreï would come to her just so that she could get some idea of what time of the day or night it was. She was ready to do anything for him so that she could have a bath. She stank. Her hair was rank. Her mind focused on soap.

Still, she knew they would be looking for her by now. Nina would have reached Paris and found her missing and put Interpol on to it straight away, surely. So much for being white-slaved to Latin America! She'd willingly allowed herself to be abducted to the nether reaches of Morocco. Fool! It still never occurred to her that she really might not get out of this alive, or sane. Proof that she didn't give Andreï enough credit for his cruelty. He had hardly started.

*

Emily thought she was finally making progress. There seemed to be a pinprick of light at the end of the tunnel of work she'd been stuck in for weeks. At this rate she might even find time to ring Morgan and have a gossip!

She'd called the offices of all the people she'd faxed the previous evening to make sure they'd received the messages and were clear on what they had to do. Right. That was Gloria's shoot ruined.

As far as Nina's shoot was concerned, she almost had the itinerary of the trip finished. Well, there was the huge gap of where the shoot would take place and who would be there. But what could she do if Nina refused to tell her anything? The hair and make-up were confirmed. The photographer was ready. For an astronomical fee Saul Smytheson and his boyfriend were coming. These two reprobates were everything that was horrible about the fashion industry, but Nina had explained to her that this was a make-or-break shoot, and although she was taking a risk using unknowns for the models, she couldn't afford to take any chances with the photographer. Emily thought she could do just as well as Saul with her fully automatic Nikon, but didn't really think it her place to say anything.

Now she started making a list of things she thought they would need: tape measure, double-sided Sellotape, pins, a rolamatic to get bits of lint off the clothes, reams of extra tissue paper for packing on the way back, tights, skin-coloured underwear. She would have to pack the carnet for the return trip, and she wasn't taking any chances. She was so deep in her lists that she didn't notice the door open and Don sneak up behind her.

'Boo!'

Emily screamed.

'Hey, lovely. Don't jump, it does nothing for your blood pressure.'

Emily stood up nervously. 'Yes, sorry . . . I mean . . . I'm sorry I didn't see you come in.'

'Don't look so frightened, you poor little thing. First time at the couture, isn't it?' Don arranged himself on the sofa, a little small for him to pose on but it would do. He looked warily at the fire irons.

'Yes. I'll get used to it.'

'Not quite the same as the London fashion day-and-a-half, is it?'

'London fashion week, you mean?'

'Hardly a week. Not enough houses to make it worthwhile, all those horrible dresses on fat models flaunting themselves around the dinosaurs at the Natural History Museum. Total waste of time.'

'Well . . .' Emily didn't dare protest her theories on how British fashion led world trends and how with a little governmental and industrial support . . . If she'd learnt one thing this week in Paris it was that nobody could care less about her opinion and certainly didn't want to hear it. 'Paris isn't that different.' What did Don want? Nina hadn't told her she was expecting anybody, and Emily didn't think she'd be back before lunch. She had meetings and then lunch with Gloria in her suite. What should she do with him?

'Getting ready for the big shoot, are you?'

'Yes, I am.'

'Where's Nina taking you all off to this time?' Don feigned indifference, paring the exquisitely manicured nails on his podgy hands with the sharp edge of the huge gold pendant that had been lying ready to be packed on the sofa.

'I don't know. She hasn't said anything to me.' Emily's chin jerked up, defying him to get secret information out of her.

'Abroad, though. You're not shooting in Paris?'

'I don't think so. I really don't know.' Emily was determined not to let Nina down. Careful not to let Don see what she was doing, she glanced at her desk to see if there was anything particularly giveaway about it. Nothing. She should be in the clear.

'And Saul's shooting it for you?'

'Yes.' This Emily knew wasn't a secret.

'And which girls are you taking with you?'

'I don't know.'

Get real. You mean she hasn't booked anyone yet? Really, she's stupider than I thought.' Don made a mental note to get Gloria to option all the girls, do a dinner party scene if she had to. That way Nina couldn't have them. 'Carnet ready?'

'Should be.'

'Hmm – well.' He stood up and kissed her hand. 'It's been delightful. I'm sure I'll see you again before you go. Oh,' he turned as if he'd just remembered something, but it was too calculated, and Emily wasn't stupid, 'do you have the number of the Fyodov boy? I've got a project I want to talk to him about.'

'I think he's away,' said Emily charmingly. 'But this is the number. Mrs Fischer, his housekeeper, will tell you where you can reach him, I expect.'

Max shrugged his holdall on to his shoulder and got off the train at Fez, looking about him to get his bearings. The sun was high in the July sky, turning the town around the railway station into an oven of breezeblocks, the trees lining the streets wilting under the weight of the midday heat.

Max's plan was to walk to the medina and go and see the great uncle of the woman who'd looked after him at his father's Morocco house. He needed to get warning to the villages in the mountains through which he would be passing that he was coming and that they should let him pass. He needed to get to his father's house in one piece, and the hash fields which surrounded the place for miles and miles were well guarded. He was wearing scuffed old gym shoes, ancient jeans, and a long-sleeved T-shirt. A grey baseball cap covered his shock of hair, and his odd eyes were pale in the unforgiving light of the Fez afternoon sun. He started to walk, ignoring the offers from the guides who followed him from the station. Ten minutes later he realised that there was still someone following him. He turned and smiled in recognition.

'Akim!' He held out his hand and found himself being taken in a bear hug in return. 'Good to see you.' He spoke in French; his Arabic was not up to much. 'How did you find me?'

'No work. I was hanging around the station to see if anyone needed a guide. I saw you get off the train and followed. I wondered how long it was going to be before you noticed me. I even thought you might not recognise me. It's been too many years.' The two young men walked slowly along the orange-tree-lined roads heading towards the medina where Akim lived with his family.

'I know. I should come more often. But holidays with my father . . .'

'You could come on your own. We would always welcome you. My father often speaks of you.'

'I know, I know, but now I am at university. I have to work hard,' Max lied.

'What brings you here then? You should come when it's cooler. And your father is here now. You know you will have to see him. And he has not changed either.'

'I know. But don't send word I'm on my way.' Max's face was set hard. 'It's a long story. Is your father at home? I need your help and his.'

'Sure – no problem. Why don't you want to tell your father you're here? If he's beating you you don't have to come here now you're a man. You don't have to listen to him.'

'It's not me. He's got a girl with him.'

'Oh, yes, I heard.' There was no need for Akim to say more. His aunt had cleared up the mess Andreï left of his women for years. 'Well, a lot of the family are at your father's house, as he's here. But you'll be welcome here. My father will help you. He's an old man now, but he'll do what he can.'

'All I need is safe passage up there.'

'I'll come with you.' Akim grinned. 'Good to get out of

the city while it's so hot. And there's nothing else to do.'

'Come on, then. Let's go.'

They entered the ancient city under a gate plastered with an intricate pattern of faded azure and gold tiles and headed swiftly through the winding streets where the buildings almost met above their heads. At a corner where a small girl was twisting silk on to a spool from a skein she'd hung fifty yards away, they turned into a darker series of alleys. Even after all his years of visiting Fez, Max knew he would never be able to find his way around his own. He was relieved that Akim had found him. Without protection here a blond man, evidently well off despite his grimy old clothes, was likely to be taken off by somebody – especially deep in the old city, with its hidden dead ends and dark corners. Akim ducked under a low doorway and Max followed into the dank lower courtyard of the ancient house. He followed his old friend up a winding stone staircase, hugging the wall in order not to slip down into the hollow below.

'Watch out, there's a new hole on the landing.'

Max edged round, following the dark shadow before him. Finally they came out into a light room at the top of the house, a huge unglazed window giving on to the roof outside, where another city lives, a city of washing lines and aerials and in the evening groups of people enjoying the dying sun. Akim's room was spare: a bed, walls lined with narrow mattresses on which to sit or sleep, a low table in the centre.

'Sit here. Smoke if you like. The pipe is by the bed. I will go and tell my mother you are here.' Akim headed out.

Max and Akim had grown up together, summer playmates throughout their childhoods. Max noticed that Akim was now more formal with him. In spite of their life-long relationship, Max was now a member of the employer class. He sat back in the two-foot-thick window recess wondering if this change in relationship would prevent Akim's mother from coming to welcome him. If Farah did not come now, he would probably never see her again. Her place was with the women, not with strange men, whether she'd known them since their birth or not. He lit a cigarette and pulled thoughtfully on it, staring over the rooftops to where he could see the purple bruise of the mountains against the horizon.

'Maximilien!' Max jumped up as a stooped old man bent to enter the room, arms wide in welcome. 'So, you are chasing your father's woman!'

'Sort of.' Max smiled at the man, whose sun-lined face and white hair added at least another twenty years to his real age. Akim's father lowered himself heavily on to the window sill. Max sat on the floor and watched as Akim, who'd followed his father in with a tray of sticky sweets and a pot of mint tea, poured for the three of them. Farah was obviously not coming.

'And you think I'm going to help you get up there?'

"Akim said he'd come with me.'

'Stealing women off your father is not something you should do.'

'She's not just a woman. She's a friend of mine and she doesn't deserve what I think she's probably getting.'

'Oh, your father, he is old-fashioned with women.'

'With respect, he is cruel. This girl wouldn't be able to handle it. She is no professional.'

'So you will sneak up on him like a thief and try and slip this girl away.'

'No, I have another way of getting her out. I just need to see how the land lies first. I might not need to take such drastic measures.'

'And what is this girl to you that you would deprive your father of her?'

'Just a friend.'

'I see.' The old man smiled at Max. 'Just a friend for whom you would sneak through those dangerous mountains, taking my son into danger with you. I hope I have friends like this is ever I need them.'

'Gloria!'

'Darling – will you ever forgive me for not letting on?'

The two editors-in-chief kissed each other – well, kissed the air about three inches away from each other's ears. Nina led the way to the table she'd had set up in the sitting room of her Crillon suite. A discreet waiter poured champagne, removed the covers from the lunch of moules marinière followed by steak tartare – both dishes Nina knew Gloria hated – and withdrew.

'Of course not. But we'll be working together until one or other of us gets put out to grass. Let's get on with it until then.'

'Nina, I never thought you'd take it so hard.'

'I'm not used to my friends letting me down.'

'Well, you must admit this wasn't an opportunity I could pass by.'

'Oh yes, it's an opportunity all right. I just thought we were close enough for you to trust me with the news.' Nina smiled across the table. 'I was wrong.'

'I'm not being that nasty. I came to you to have lunch, didn't I?'

'Respect for your elders. Maybe I managed to teach you one thing in all the years you worked for me. Also, you need me more than I need you. And you know I hate showing off at the Ritz. I might not have come.' One of Nina's eyebrows rose a fraction of an inch. Perhaps she was going to enjoy this after all.

'Come on, Nina. Let's drop it. You're right – we still work for the same guys. there's no point in bitching at each other for ever.'

'No.' Nina took a long swig of her champagne, looked at her moules with distaste and lit a Silk Cut.

'Darling – smoking!'

'Darling, yes. So . . . you're sleeping with Don.'

'I might be.'

'Oh, please, you two are like two sides of a clam shell, with all that gooey stuff visible in between.'

'Nina, that's disgusting.'

'So's sleeping with a man twenty years your senior and half your height. I'll save the lecture about his drinking and drugs habits for another time.'

'What do you know? It's none of your business anyway.'

'Listen, you ambitious little bitch – I'm warning you. I wouldn't get too involved with him. I may be furious with you for taking Knowle's job without talking to me about it first. I may be stinking mad about the fact that you have decided that sleeping your way to the top is the only way to do it. But I don't hate you enough not to warn you about him. He's a slimy little number, and if you can't see that, then you're not as clever as I thought.' Nina slammed down her glass. 'You're intelligent and able. What was it that had such a dramatic effect on your self-confidence that you stopped believing in yourself and decided to rely on your body instead?'

'Nina, stop it. I cam here to make up.'

'Bullshit. You came here to talk about your shoot. You're not sure about it and you wanted to clear your ideas with me, make sure I didn't pooh-pooh them. Listen, honey. don't you trust your bedmate for that kind of advice? After all, he's the guy who has the right to bin all of our work.'

Nina stood and threw the end of her cigarette into the fireplace. 'OK – tell me about the shoot and I'll tell you what I think. But I have no intention of giving anything away about mine. Not after you sent Don here to spy for you. Come on, honey, take the innocent look off your face. I didn't think you'd sink so low.' Nina sat in Don's place on the sofa, suddenly soft in her favourite Galliano pyjamas. 'OK, fire away. Tell me your idea and I'll tell you if it sucks or not.'

'I'm afraid you're going to say it's been done before.'

'Darling, haven't you learnt that there's nothing either of us has ever thought of that hasn't been done before?'

'Well, that might be true. But we do try and do it differently, don't we?'

'No. Well, you might. I just try and do something so beautiful that it doesn't matter if someone had the original idea a thousand years ago. We just do endless cover versions – and do our best to stop them being boring.'

'What made you so cynical all of a sudden?'

'You?'

'OK, OK. Well, my boring old idea that I expect millions of people have done before is this. I thought I'd do an end-of-the-war thing. You know, a girl getting out of her uniform and into a ball dress.'

'Yes, and where are you planning to do this, the boiler room of HMS *Belfast*?'

'I was, actually.' Gloria looked so put out, Nina couldn't help laughing. 'Is it that obvious?'

'No, sweetheart. I think it's a fine idea. I'm surprised you got permission.' She thought for a moment. 'Of course. Your father's a rear-admiral, how could I have forgotten? When do you shoot?'

'Tomorrow. All the clothes have to be back in Paris by midday on Friday – for you, I expect.'

'I expect so.'

'So – do you like the idea?'

'Yes. Who are your girls?'

'Tuesday.'

'Fat.'

'Beautiful.'

'You'll have to pour her into the dresses. Photographer?'

'Gay.'

'That's challenge. She doesn't do set-up shoots.'

'She does now. I want it to look like her paparazzi stuff. I'll set up the lighting and so on. I just want her to get Tuesday getting ready, like she usually does. She's done it before, and she does it well. I thought it would make a change – stop the couture looking so formal. And she and Tuesday have such chemistry between them.'

'They're sleeping together, that's why. You'll have your work cut out to stop the pictures being pornographic.' Gloria looked crestfallen. 'OK, OK. It'll work. Just don't let Gay get too big for her boots. You know what a nightmare she can be.'

'I know. Actually, I need a favour. Can I borrow Rory for the day? I need him just for twenty-four hours to shut Gay up when she gets too stroppy and to stop me being too modern about the clothes. After all, they're so beautiful they should be photographed in their entirety – you know I have a bad habit of changing things around and throwing in a pair of jeans or something to take away from the formality. And he's brilliant. I'll give him – you, your magazine, anyone – credit. But I do need him.'

'Aren't you afraid he'll make your shoot horrible just to get his own back? He's pretty upset with you too, you know.'

'He won't. He's incapable of doing anything hideous, however hard he tries. Please, Nina. Just for the day. I know you'll be totally organised, you always are. And I need him. What do you say?'

'So you won't be so far removed from your predecessor after all, will you?'

'Stop it, Nina – I've got to try.'

'I'm sure you'll do a very good job, my dear.'

'So can I have Rory?'

'I suppose so. You'll have to ask him yourself, though. I can't tell him what to do. And you'll be billed for it.'

'I don't care. Don's given me *carte blanche* for my budget.'

'Good girl. You really have got him by the short and curlies, haven't you?'

'Nina! Stop it.'

'OK, OK.'

Gloria settled into a tiny imitation Louis XVI chair across from Nina.

I'm sorry about Pandora. Is there any news?'

'No, there isn't.'

'Do the police have any idea where she is?'

'No.'

'Poor girl. And she'll never be used again by any of the big houses – they won't trust her to turn up. All those dresses made especially for her, thousands of hours of work . . .'

'I know, Gloria. You don't have to rub it in.'

'You and Rory seem remarkably together, though.'

'We haven't got much choice, have we? Not with you running off to the other side and Don breathing down our necks waiting for us to make the slightest false move. Who's he got waiting in the wings to jump into my shoes? Or doesn't he quite tell you that much?' Gloria blushed. 'Don't worry, you don't have to tell me. I don't want to know.'

'I don't know, Nina, I really don't. Can't you tell me anything about your shoot?'

'Nope.'

'Don says you won't tell him either.'

'It's not in my contract that I have to discuss my ideas with him in advance. I'll show him the photos afterwards, and if he doesn't like them then he can bin both me and them.'

'You wouldn't resign?'

'Sure would. You can tell Don to put that in his pipe and smoke it. Make a change from the cocaine.' Gloria looked uncomfortable. 'Gloria, for your own sake, try and keep out of all that. It doesn't do anyone any good in the long run. You and I have both lost enough friends to drugs. I may be mighty pissed off with you at the moment, but I wouldn't want to lose you too.'

'You sound like an agony aunt.'

'Thanks.'

'I don't need lectures, Nina.'

'And I don't need spies. No – you're old enough to make your own mistakes.' Nina stood up, ready to dismiss her erstwhile friend. Neither of them had touched their food. The phone rang.

'Nina, it's Max.'

'Hello, darling. Where are you?'

'Well on my way. I'm off up the mountains first thing in the morning. I'll see you Friday night, yes?'

'Yup – no change in the plan.' Nina paused, desperate to talk but prevented by the presence of her unwelcome colleague. 'Have you had any direct news?'

‘She’s there. I don’t know how she is. I’ve met up with an old friend, who’s taking me up there. How are you doing the last leg?’ Nina looked across at Gloria arranging a huge swathe of lime-green velvet around her shoulders over a lime-green version of a Versace dress Nina could have sworn she’d seen the Princess of Wales wearing. The dress didn’t look any better on Gloria, and it was still a bad length. Nina stopped bitching in her head and made herself reply.

‘It’s a surprise. Use your loaf and you’ll work it out. There aren’t that many options.’

Max chuckled. ‘I can imagine. See you Friday then.’

‘Lots of love, and take care of yourself, Max. I don’t want to get there and find both of you in a mess.’

‘You won’t.’

‘’Bye.’

Nina turned to find Gloria staring at her.

‘So you are cradle-snatching. Don said you’d been seen smooching around with Max Fyodov. Where is he?’

‘Never you mind.’

The air-kissing of half an hour previously was repeated, and Gloria headed for the door.

‘You be careful too, Nina. You may joke about leaving – but Don doesn’t.’

‘Thanks for the warning.’

‘Nick?’

‘Max! Hey, where are you? How’s it going? Is there any news?’

‘Not really. We’ve got a hunch, and I’m on my way to investigate it. Can you help?’

'Sure. How?'

'Can you get back to Paris?'

'Too broke, Max. Sorry. No way I can wing it unless I rob a bank or something.'

'Listen, take my credit card number and use that to reserve your ticket. Go on the Eurostar. Nina'll put you up when you get there.'

'Nina?'

'Yeah, you know, Emily's boss. The woman whose party we crashed.'

'Why should she look after me?'

'Because she's desperate and will welcome with open arms any help she can get.'

'Right. Now do I find her?'

'Go to the Hotel Crillon on the Place de la Concorde and ask for her suite. Piece of cake. You'll probably find Emily there. Poor girl, Nina hasn't let her out of that room for more than five minutes since they got there.'

'She'll live.'

'Yeah, but you know Emily. She's so oversensitive about things, and she tries so hard. She's exhausted, poor thing. She'd really appreciate your being there.'

'Really?'

'Don't be such a fool, Nick. You must know how she feels about you.'

'No. I always thought it was you she lusted after.'

'Not really. She'd rather have you. You're safer.'

'Thanks. I always thought I exuded a dangerous magnetic charm . . . not. So. What's the story with Pandora?'

'I think she's with my dad here in Morocco.'

'No – Morgan and Anna thought she might be there but we decided it was a red herring.'

'I can't decide whether I hope it was or not. If she's there, at least we've found her, but the state she'll be in might make me wish she was still lost.'

'Your dad's not that bad.'

'You don't know him.'

'He was always perfectly nice to me. I mean, a bit scary, but not dangerous.'

'Yeah, well. We'll see.'

'Why haven't you just rung him up and asked him whether he's got her?'

'Because he's liable to deny her existence and have her murdered and thrown down a gully.'

'don't be ridiculous.'

'I'm not.'

'Listen, Max, I'm sure you're exaggerating. Nobody behaves like that. Not in real life, anyway.'

'Precisely. My dear papa has spent his life believing that he is an all-powerful invincible creature and that therefore he can do what he likes with the women he picks up in passing. Nobody ever got him for what he did to my mother.'

'You have no proof about that, do you?'

'No. But I have no mother either.'

'Doesn't mean he killed her, Max. That's ridiculous. Anyway, if he's so dangerous, why don't you just send in the police?'

'Because the police can't get to my father's house. It's

beyond the point where they're prepared to go – high in the Rif mountains, among the hash fields, hours away from anywhere. Nobody gets up there unless they are taken by locals, and even then they have to be pretty careful.'

'So how are you going?'

'I've found some friends here in Fez. They're taking me up there.'

'And then what? You drag her out of there?'

'No. I neutralise the situation – just to sound like a bad film – and then you guys arrive.'

'But you just said we couldn't get there without invitations from the locals.'

'You can if you arrive in helicopters and you're expected. Which you will be, once I get there.'

'Right. Sounds dead complicated to me.'

'Maybe. But will you go to Paris and look after Nina and Emily for me?'

'Sure. London's boring as hell. Everyone's gone on holiday or got a job. I'll jump on a train just as soon as I can.'

'Right. See you Friday, then.'

'Yeah – take care, Max.'

Pandora lay in the dark, counting her bruises and longing for respite. How long would it be before she went mad? Would he kill her first? The comfort of the thought caressed her. Death . . . oblivion . . . She knew he came to her through a doorway high in the wall, down a step ladder. But thoughts of escape were too slippery to catch. Oblivion would be easier, a warm, comfortable darkness never ripped with searing light or pain, or him, or it, or . . . She lost consciousness once more.

She was jolted back to reality by the pain of a blow to the head, at the same time as a shaft of light pierced the midnight of her prison. He stood above her.

Pandora stood up shakily.

'What do you want me to do?'

'How dare you question me?'

The slap came from nowhere and Pandora heard the thud of her own head hitting the floor. She forced herself to stay calm and waited for more. She could see his excitement through the riding breeches he still wore. He strode forward and lifted her, holding her against the wall, preparing to strike again. She could taste the blood in her mouth. She stared terrified at her attacker, and he slapped her twice more, cracking her neck from side to side.

'It's not really painful, is it? No. You see, you know nothing about pain. I'll describe it, shall I? It's all in the mind, my little Pandora. Real pain gets to your mind.' He yanked her hair so hard she heard her neck crack back. 'As I explained to you the other evening, it is always more interesting to leave emotional scars. That's where my strength lies. Nobody ever managed to get into my mind. So nobody ever hurt me. But you, little girl, I think it's time to get inside your head, isn't it?'

As Andreï's words slowly sunk in, something new occurred to Pandora. With sudden clarity his Achilles' heel came into focus. She reached out to the idea and grabbed it, holding on hard.

'What makes you think you're so invincible, so brilliant? You aren't interested in the psychology of pain. I can see through you. You're just a man who's trying to play a role and you can't do it. You don't have the imagination to be a really bad guy.' She didn't know where the words were coming from, but she prayed for time. The longer she had, the more likely it was that this would work. 'Nobody hurt you? That's because they never worked out where your real weakness lay. But I know. Max is your weakness, Andreï isn't he?' Taking advantage of the shock which was slowly registering on his face, she shoved him back. He lost his balance, falling awkwardly and crying out in pain, and she stood over him, pressing home her advantage. 'Well, you'll have to kill me now or I'll tell Max. I know him, you see. He's my other lover,' she lied. 'I just wanted to know what it was like to have the father and the son. Now I'll tell him.'

And before Andreï had time to grab her, she was off to the opening in the side of the room. The ladder was gone but she was tall, she thought she could reach it. Hanging from the door sill, she kicked out wildly when she felt his hands on her ankles. She may have been almost as tall as Andreï, but he was much stronger. She didn't stand a chance.

Chapter 12

THURSDAY 27 JULY

PALE aqua edged the pre-dawn sky as Max and Akim set off for the bus station *en route* to the mountains. Fez was already busy, waking up early to profit from the cool hours before the medina boiled over once more. Max had left the holdall with his friend's family and had borrowed an old brown djellaba which he wore over his jeans and T-shirt. His money and passport were tied around his waist in a money belt; the whisky was buried deep in a pocket of his djellaba. The two men could have been brothers had it not been for the white hands of the one contrasting with the calloused brown of the other. They walked in silence towards the bus station, deep in their own thoughts, passing scenes which had changed little since Delacroix had painted them one hundred and fifty years before. If their luck held out they would reach the fortified house in the hills late that night.

They piled on to a bus headed for Tounetz, the last town before the hash fields began. Max squeezed himself in beside a huge Berber woman, her face tattooed in a fine pattern of small brown dots, her luggage bags of floor, sugar, things she had exchanged for the animals she had brought down with her to sell in the market. Surprised that he already didn't mind the smell, Max remembered that he hadn't had a bath for forty-eight hours. Slowly the bus creaked out of the town and headed across the flat plain, the Rif mountains rearing purple ahead of them. The sun began to beat relentlessly down on the harsh landscape, broken by tiny dry river beds and an occasional boy herding goats.

Back in London, Rory was sitting on a coil of steel rope on the deck of HMS *Belfast*, arms folded, a stern expression on his face. He looked again at his watch.

'If she doesn't arrive soon, you'll have to cancel. What can have happened to her?' He crossed his navy-sailor-trousered legs and unfolded his Gaultier-inspired Breton navy and cream long-sleeved T-shirted arms, and smiled sweetly at Gloria.

'Don't be ridiculous. It's only six-thirty. The call was for six. She's barely half an hour late.'

'Should have booked Pandora, shouldn't you?' Rory said, flippantly.

'Pandora's lost. I can't have her. I don't want her. And Tuesday's perfect for this shoot.'

'As you like, darling. But I thought you wanted me here for my valuable opinions. That's my opinion. And where's Gay?'

'Getting atmosphere downstairs.'

'Oh. I wondered for a moment if she might've been doing an alternative shoot in her girlfriend's bedroom and we were never going to see either of them again.' His eyebrows shot up. 'I hope she's not going to start thinking of herself as an artist after this.'

'Rory, if you're going to be bitchy all day, maybe it would be better if you weren't here.'

'All right, sweetie. I'll just nip back to Blakes for a little snooze and work out my invoice for you. Oh, sweetheart. Don't look so furious. Are you still steaming because I wouldn't stay in my own house for this shoot? Darling, you know I couldn't have done that. It would have been much too friendly and cut the costs of this little débâcle. So Blakes was essential. You do understand, don't you?'

'Oh!' Gloria stamped her foot.

'All right, I'll stay. Pass me the phone. I want to call Emily.'

But Tuesday arrived before he had time to dial the number.

'Oh look!' cried Rory, leaping to his feet to kiss her. 'It's the queen of the elephants.'

'Shut up, Rory, or I'll crown you.' Gloria turned to Tuesday. 'Darling, where've you been? We were about to send out a search party for you.'

'It wasn't my fault I'm late,' wailed Tuesday. 'The stupid driver wouldn't come up to my room to get me because his car was parked on a double yellow line, and I can't walk through hotels without protection. I'd get molested by all those terrible people in the lobby. You should have got me bodyguards.' She slumped heavily against a nearby gun turret. 'Where's Gay?'

Pandora opened her eyes warily. The room was light. There were shutters high in the roof that had been opened. Andreï sat across from her in a folding director's chair, a glass of clear liquid in his hand. She was starving, and her mouth was so dry she didn't know if she'd be able to open it. She didn't move, but stared at Andreï's hooded eyes, waiting for him to speak.

'So – I find that my son has sent a spy to check on me. Does he know where you are?'

'Of course he does,' Pandora's hoarse voice lied. 'He told me I had a week and then he'd come and get me. He'll be here any day now.' She hoped her voice sounded more convinced than she felt. Nobody knew where she was. She lay on the floor, waves of hunger breaking over her. She would have done anything for the glass of liquid in Andreï's hand. She rolled over to sit up, and felt her hip bones crunch sharp against the floor. She crawled to a sitting position and leant against the wall.

'You'd like some of this, wouldn't you?' Andreï held out the glass. She leant forward, greed lighting her eyes. The vodka crashed against her face, stinging. The glass shattered against the wall beside her, splinters catching her face and arms. He stood to leave.

'How dare you? How dare you come here, you conniving little bitch? You and that son of mine . . . I should have let him die when I murdered his mother. He'll never get here, however hard he tries. He'll die in the attempt. And you – I'll just let you starve to death.' He started up the step ladder.

'Wait!' He turned and looked back at her, his face an iron mask. 'Talk to me, Andreï – please. Please stay. I can't bear to be left alone again. Either kill me or talk to me. Just don't leave me. It's OK, I'm used to weirdos. You should meet my uncle – you can't get weirder.' She knew she sounded gauche, but she didn't have time to think of anything more sophisticated to say.

He leant against the wall and looked back at her, suddenly tired.

'How do you know Max?'

'Through a friend.'

'Who?'

'Morgan James.'

'Indeed?'

'Shaking, Pandora tied back her hair. The blood on her arm was drying into scabs. She examined her scratches.

'And how do you know Morgan James?'

'You're worse than Max. He always wants to know how people are related, how they met.' Their conversation was beginning to sound like cocktail party chatter.

'An inherited trait, perhaps. Answer the question.'

'Well, Morgan's mother was at university with my mother and my uncle, who were twins, and also with my godmother. So I've known Morgan for years.'

'Really.' He paused, staring at her through narrowed eyes. 'And Max?'

'Oh no. I only met Max when I went down to spend a

weekend at Bristol with Morgan and I saw him at a party. We've been inseparable ever since.'

'Your mother and your uncle were at which university?'

'Oxford.'

'Of course they were. What are their names? I knew Morgan's mother. Perhaps I knew yours.'

'Miranda and Rory Williams. Miranda died having me, and Rory brought me up.' Pandora looked up from the scratches on her arms. Andreï's face was impenetrable.

'How old are you?'

'Twenty-one – nearly, in October.' She met Andreï's impenetrable stare. 'Why?'

'

Tuesday, supermodel and superbrat, was struggling without any help into a pale-duck-egg-blue Dior party dress. Rory held his breath and listened for the sound of ripping satin. Tuesday'd been to one or two cocktail parties too many during the couture week. Gay Smith, an assistant and a lighting assistant stood over Tuesday. Gay was breathing heavily down her neck, snapping at a rate of about thirty-six shots a second.

'Gloria, forgive me for having yet another strange idea, but shouldn't Gay be trying to get a picture of Tuesday and the dress, not just Tuesday's cleavage surrounded by pale-blue satin?'

'We need all angles, Rory.'

'Indeed? Your American readership isn't exactly famous for its predilection for pornography thinly disguised as fashion photography, is it? Or are you taking pictures for *Playboy* too?'

'Shut up, Rory.'

'All right, Gloria. Look,' he giggled, 'fingers on lips! Wait – there's someone missing. Where's Don? I would have thought he wouldn't be able to keep himself away.'

'New York. I'm not the only thing on his agenda, you know.'

'Ooh, darling – you shouldn't put yourself down.'

'Oh, shut up.'

'Easy, tiger. No need to get so hot and bothered. He likes Emily, though. Did he tell you? Yes.' Rory thoughtfully buffed his fingernails. 'He told me he thought she was going to go far. And with Don behind her, how can she fail?' He stood up and went over to Tuesday, looking at her thoughtfully. 'Now, what can we do to rescue this terrible shoot? It is terrible, isn't it, Gloria? And you can't afford to fail, can you? No. Not in your first issue.' Slowly he circled Tuesday. The rest of the people on the shoot held their breath. The famous Rory Williams was about to pronounce Even Gay shut up for a moment. He shook his head.

'No. I think there's nothing we can do short of recasting and getting new clothes. And what on earth made you choose these accessories? They have the charm of the contents of a cut-price Aladdin's cave. Take them off.'

Reluctantly Tuesday removed the huge purple plastic earrings she was wearing and handed them to a panting assistant.

'Right. We're stuck with the dress. It doesn't fit. Tuesday, bend over as if you're doing up those terrible shoes, and pretend you haven't had time to do the dress up yet. Let's have a little carefully arranged disarray around here!'

'Saul, darling, so glad you could make it. Sit down, please. And you brought Bobby, oh, I am glad, he's always full of ideas, aren't you, sweetheart?' Nina kissed Saul Smytheson and his boyfriend and showed them into her Crillon sitting room.

'Emily, call for ice tea, would you? Unless you'd rather something else, boys?'

'Bourbon,' answered Saul.

'Bourbon then.' Nina sat on the sofa and curled her legs under herself.

'Nina, I gotta tell ya – this whole thing's makin' me noivus.' Saul had a pure Brooklyn accent.

'Why, Saul? It couldn't be clearer.'

'But who are the girls? I don't shoot just any girls.'

'Saul, your fee for this weekend will earn you more than most people on this magazine get in a lifetime. Surely it doesn't matter who the girls are?'

'It matters,' said Saul, as if he were explaining to a fashion student the basics of how to cut on the bias, 'because my material changes depending on the girl, that's why.'

'So bring it all.'

'Oh, yeah. And all the film in the world too? Great, that'll leave tons of room for the clothes. Or do you want to take a plane just for me, Nina? That would be fine.'

'Well, who would you shoot on if you could shoot on anyone?'

'Pandora and that girl who came to your house in

London the other day. That's who. And I'm not just saying that to be difficult.'

'Of course not, precious. You never do anything just to be difficult. Well, I'll have to see what I can do.'

'Oh, right, magic Pandora out of the secret lair she's disappeared to and magic her phone book to get the address of the girl she brought with her. Dead feasible, I don't think.'

Nina didn't blink. 'Saul, come on. Be reasonable. You've seen the Polaroids of the clothes; it's pictures of the clothes I want, not the girls. And remember, the set's divine, and you've done most of the work already with your follow-through of the dresses through the whole design process. You can't let me down now.'

'Reasonable! Your budget won't even let me take my own cook! How do I know I'm not going to be poisoned?'

'Saul, listen. We are going to one of the most exclusive private houses in the western hemisphere. Even Don's never been there. I promise you'll eat like a king. It just has to be a secret until the pictures are complete. You do understand that, don't you?'

"No. No, I don't. In fact, that was my next problem. Honey, I can't go nowhere unless New York can get me any time of the day or night. You have to fax all the information to my office before I go. So tell me now. Come on, Nina, you know I won't come otherwise, and you won't get your pictures and your career's up the spout – if it isn't already.'

'Lovely way you have of putting things, Saul.'

'Thanks. Where's the bourbon? All this talk's giving

me quite a thirst.' He laughed uproariously, and Bobby fell about in hysterics too. Nina couldn't quite see the joke but forced a smile. This meeting could be going better.

'Saul, would it help if I said that this had something to do with Andreï Fyodov?'

Saul and Bobby's laughter stopped in mid-cackle.

'Who?'

'Andreï Fyodov.'

'What has he to do with it?'

'Darling, there's no need to look so stunned. He's invited us, that's all.'

'Where?'

'I'm not telling you, but it's one of his houses.'

'Does he know I'm coming?'

'He knows I'm bringing a photographer but, you know, he hasn't exactly much to do with the fashion world. It hasn't even occurred to him to ask who.'

'Is Max going to be there?'

'Oh, definitely.'

'Can I shoot him?'

'If you like. I thought we could put him in with the girls.'

'Deal. Definitely. No problem. We'll be there.' Saul looked at his boyfriend. 'That's if you still want to come.'

'Stay behind while you seduce that blond bombshell! Not in a million. Honey, I'll handcuff myself to you to make sure you don't get too close to that boy.'

'No need to wash our dirty linen in public.'

'Well, don't threaten to leave me. I'll be there. Maybe we could toss for him?'

Saul and Bobby began to laugh again. Nina sighed and poured herself a glass of bourbon. In his excitement her photographer had forgotten his thirst.

'Emily?'

'Hi, Rory. How's it going?'

'Oh, I'm having a lovely time pretending to be helpful. I'm afraid I'm taking your name in vain, telling Gloria how much Don likes you.'

'But he doesn't. I wouldn't let him spy on Nina through me.'

'You loyal little thing. That's just it – loyalty's his favourite thing and you have tons of it.'

'I wish I were a little better at my job, that's all.'

'Don't worry, pickle. Last time Nina took a new assistant to the couture, the poor girl collapsed halfway through and had to be air-lifted to the Chelsea and Westminster on Nina's employer's insurance. Her parents sued the magazine for emotional abuse. You're doing fine.'

'But am I ever going to be able to do anything?'

'You *are* doing things. Who chose the shoes?'

'I did, but only because Nina didn't have time.'

'And don't you think she could have asked me if she hadn't trusted your judgement?'

'Well . . .'

'And has she changed your choices?'

'No . . . but . . .'

Rory interrupted her. 'Well, there you are then – today the shoes, tomorrow Chanel. Your time will come.'

'Thanks – if it wasn't for you I would probably have had to be air-lifted out too.'

'Nonsense. You're tougher than you like to make out. Is Nina there?'

'She's got Saul and Bobby with her.'

'Ugh. I bet Saul's wearing that horrible ten-gallon hat which clashes so badly with his accent.'

Emily laughed. 'Too right – and frightening new Stars and Stripes cowboy boots covered in rhinestones.'

'Wait – I'm just going to be sick.'

Emily laughed again. 'Do you want to speak to her? I'm so tired I don't care if she minds being interrupted. If she fires me I'll just go home to my mother and go to sleep for a month or two.'

'No – just tell her Gloria's panicking, Gay's giving in to all her natural tendencies in the name of art and Tuesday's got so fat we keep having to Sellotape the dresses together and she screams blue murder when we take them off. If this shoot ever hits the news-stands I'll eat three or four of Saul's hats. It's marvellous. She'll have to reshoot in New York and so she won't be publishing her couture until about next January. Nina has them all by the short and curlies.'

'Great.'

'You were fab too.'

'You mean the accessories scam worked?'

'Absolutely – not one dress has the accessories it should, thanks to your neatly timed little faxes to the fashion houses. Got to go, darling. I made them order lunch from Caviar Kaspia. I can't let them go so far over budget without eating some of it myself.'

White's was busy with lunching tourists and Morgan, beetling about taking orders, didn't notice her mother enter the restaurant and sit down in her area. It wasn't until she saw there was a newcomer and headed towards her with a menu that she realised Anna wasn't going to let this Morocco business lie. Morgan had had her usual problem with her contact lenses and once more had forgotten her glasses. Waitressing in this state was difficult. The last person she needed around was her mother.

'Mum, what are you doing here? I've told you already, I'm not going.'

'I totally understand you don't want to. And I know you will fee you're letting the people at White's down. But for me, please, do it.'

'I don't understand; one minute you don't want anything to do with all these people, and the next Sam's ensconced at the Randolph ready to take me on a private plane to Morocco and you're willingly sending me to a Fyodov hideout. All this for Pandora? You never even liked her.'

'I'm going to say something you must never repeat to any of my students.'

'What?'

'It's a woman's prerogative to change her mind.'

'Oh, get serious. You don't change your mind. You've never changed your mind about anything in your life.

You're the only person I've ever met who has always, categorically and logically, been right. You don't change your mind. You work out the right answer in the first place. Come on, Mum, none of this makes sense.'

'Well, maybe I did make a few mistakes . . .'

'And now I have to sort them out for you? Why don't you go and rescue Pandora yourself?'

'Because Nina doesn't want to take photographs of me.'

'That too. You're sending me off to a Fyodov house to pose for a magazine which perpetuates everything you hate about this patriarchal society. Mum, you've totally lost your marbles.'

'Morgan – table four is ready!' another waitress hissed at her as she passed.

'Mum, I can't talk about this now. Can't it wait till I'm home? I'm not supposed to ring you when you're working, so you should leave me alone when I am.'

'I'm not going to give up. Why don't you get me some lunch and I'll wait till you're finished?'

'I'm not going to give up. Why don't you get me some lunch and I'll wait till you're finished?'

'I'm doing the late shift, as well you know. You'll have a long wait.'

'I'm sure they'll understand if you want an hour off in the middle. You have to eat at some point, don't you? Get me a backed potato with that lovely sour cream and chives and bacon stuff they do here, and I'll read till you're free.' Anna got her *Guardian* out of her bag, smiled at her daughter and settled into her chair. 'I told you, Morgan, I'm not going to give up.'

Morgan jumped as a hand landed on her shoulder.

'Hello, my favourite girls!' Sam sat down opposite Anna.

'Oh, great – so you planned this, did you? The allied forces besieging the poor innocent little daughter who's just trying to get on with her life.'

'Total coincidence!' Sam's eyes were wide with innocence.

'Yeah – like fuck!' Morgan stormed away. 'Claire,' she called to another waitress, 'would you mind looking after my bizarre parents for me? I haven't got time for them at the moment.'

Rip! A forty-five-thousand-pound Lacroix dress split down the side seam, a seam which had been hand-rolled and embroidered with a mixture of crystal and semi-precious stones. At last Gloria gave in and began to cry as the thousands of beads rolled off into the dark corners of the HMS *Belfast* boiler room. Tears were pouring down Rory's cheeks too – he couldn't help it, it was too funny for words. Tuesday stood half-naked and helpless in the middle of the room.

'It wasn't my fault. The dress wasn't too small. It was just fitted wrong. You should have had a new one made for me!'

Max followed Akim to a small breezeblock-built house at the side of Tounetz marketplace. They were nearly there. This, hopefully, was the house which would provide them with the car for the last leg of their journey. Akim knocked, and a slim woman opened the door, a small boy hanging on to her legs and giggling. She smiled at Akim and, without speaking, opened the door wider and showed them into a small room, the walls lined with mattress-covered chests, ideal for sitting or sleeping. Max sat down and waited. The woman spoke briefly to Akim in Arabic and then disappeared. The child stayed, staring wordlessly at the blond stranger. He'd never seen a Caucasian before. He thought perhaps the man was a ghost. He looked normal, but he spoke a funny language, and his eyes were different colours. The little boy was transfixed by the eyes.

Akim grinned and swept the boy into his arms.

'This is Marouan. He is the first-born of our driver, the man who taught me French. He's a fine boy, don't you think?'

'Fine.' Max smiled at the child, who buried his head, suddenly shy, in Akim's shoulder, and when his mother returned to the room wriggled to be put down. The woman brought them bowls of thick soup and a loaf of freshly made bread. Eyes lowered, she left them as soon as the tray of food was put on the central table.

'It's odd being old enough to be ignored by the women.' Max picked up one of the bowls of soup and began to drink. 'The last time I was here I was still allowed into the kitchens.'

'You are a man now.'

'It's sad. I realised last night that I'll probably never see your mother again.'

'And you wouldn't see this woman if it weren't for the fact that the house is too small to avoid it. She says her husband should be on his way back from school now. He will eat with us and then we will go. As long as the car is working. She said they haven't used it for a while. It might need a little warming up first.'

'We'll be able to get up there tonight, though, won't we?'

'I hope so.' Akim looked at Max. 'It's more dangerous, though, travelling in the dark.'

'I know, but you're with us, and this man, the driver, he's known too, isn't he?'

'Yes, but the darkness gives cover to mistakes. We would be safer if we stayed the night here and left at dawn tomorrow.'

'No. We have to leave tonight. Even if it means walking.'

'We can't walk! It's a two-hour drive and then an hour's walk.'

'No wonder my father likes to use a helicopter. Akim, we have to go tonight. If we stay any longer then someone will get there before us and tell my father we're coming. I have to get into the house without his knowledge. I have to find Pandora before he finds me.'

Akim leant back and lit a carefully rolled cigarette. He looked at Max.

'You have a strange expression, my friend. You look as if you are out to prove something. What is it? Saving a girl from your father is not something you have to do. You could leave her there.'

'I have to save her. I have to prove that I'm not totally useless.'

'So that this girl will love you?'

'No, for somebody else.' Max grimaced. 'The ridiculous thing is that she too will think I'm doing this for Pandora. Unfortunately the girl I'm interested in doesn't need saving at the moment. She's far too well organised for that. She doesn't need anything.'

"So why are you interested in her? If she doesn't need you, then there is no relationship. You must need each other for something. Is this girl not interested in your wealth?'

'No. She hates my wealth.'

'Strange girl.'

'No, just independent. She's determined not to need anyone. Besides,' he added, 'my father is my responsibility. I should be there when they come for him.' He gave a wry grin. 'I never thought I'd have to look after him. He's spent all his life making sure that I will never be able to do anything for him. Now it looks as though he won't have any choice.' He got the whisky out of his deep djellaba pocket. 'Do you mind?'

Akin shook his head. 'Go ahead.'

Emily sighed as someone knocked at the door. She was tired and confused, and Rory had only perked her up for about half an hour before she began to panic again. She couldn't persuade Nina that she didn't know what she was doing and that therefore it really was in Nina's interests to look over the arrangements. As a result, she kept on checking and rechecking, desperate to spot the things she'd forgotten and increasingly unlikely to do so. She opened the door, a waif with huge black rings under her eyes, trying to stop her hands from shaking and giving away how close to the end of her tether she felt.

'Hi, fatso!'

'Nick!' She looked over his shoulder. 'Nina!'

'Hello,' Nina put out her hand to Nick. 'I'm Nina Charles. And you are?'

Nick grinned shyly but remembered his manners and shook Nina's hand. 'Nick Fremantle. How do you do? We met at your party; well, not exactly met. I gatecrashed it and helped Emily on the door.'

Sweet, thought Nina. He's so English. 'I remember. And what brings you to Paris, me or Emily?'

'Um, both, actually.'

'Well, then. As at last I am free for an hour or so and Emily has done the organisational job of the century and we are all ready for tomorrow, why not dump your bag over there? We can go to the Café Marly and have tea.' She looked at Nick, at his honest, earnest face and horrible flowery shirt – just the kind of man she needed to be seen with in the street! Perhaps it would put paid to the rumours about her and Max. Emily looked a bit odd, was she hot or blushing? Nina threw down the rough copy of the September edition, a huge empty space in the middle waiting for the photographs she hoped to be able to take that weekend, and grabbed Nick and Emily. 'Come on, what are we waiting for? Let's go and play.'

Her car whizzed them down the Faubourg St Honoré to the Louvre and left them at the archway that led to the café in the recently restored Richelieu Wing. Nina was greeted by an effusive maître d' who knew exactly who she was, and they were installed inside, the terrace being too much like a furnace that afternoon. They relaxed into comfortable armchairs, enjoying the soft air-conditioned breeze that came from the fan above the open door.

'So, Emily, your boyfriend has come out for a night of romance before we go, then?'

'I . . .' Emily stuttered, 'I . . .' She blushed. 'He's not my boyfriend.'

'We're just good friends. I'm the man who saves her from a fate worse than death whenever she works too hard. Aren't I? I'm what's known as a useful bod to have around in a crisis.'

'Really? And what crisis have you come to save Emily from this time? Am I that terrible a boss?'

'No, not you. I mean . . . I'm sure you're great to work for. No, actually, I had Max on the phone last night.'

'Oh, you're a friend of Max's too.'

'Yes. I'm at Bristol with him. He rang and told me what's happening.'

'So, you're coming with us tomorrow?'

'If I can.'

'Of course. The more the merrier. Andreï can hardly kill us all, can he?' Nina was not quite joking. She waved at a waiter. 'Now, what shall we have? Is the sun over the yard arm yet?' She looked at her watch 'Five-forty-five. It'll take them a few minutes to get the drinks – come on, shall we have some champagne?'

Nick and Emily both nodded silently. If this glamorous fashion editor wanted to buy them champagne in the rarefied atmosphere of a neo-Napoleonic air-conditioned restaurant, who were they to refuse?

A deferential waiter opened the champagne, and Nina lit a Silk Cut. She would worry about her smoking when the weekend was over. Now the smoke curling from the illicit cigarette gave her such pleasure that she almost wished she were alone. But curiosity got the better of her.

'So, you spoke to Max. Did he tell you much? He rang me and I couldn't talk to him for long. I had a visitor.'

'He just said he was on his way with some old friend he'd met up with. He told me about your end of the operation and asked me to help. I think he wants some support himself for when we all get there. Is he really as frightened as he sounds of his father?'

Nina nodded. 'Yes, and with reason.' Emily looked even more nervous. 'But you needn't worry about that. There will be a lot of us, you know. Morgan and Sam, Max and this friend of his, me and Emily – and all the crew and Saul and everyone. We're all there as back-up. And Rory, of course, though I doubt he'll be much help.'

'What time do we leave?'

"Two p.m. tomorrow. We fly straight to Fez, and helicopter to the house. We should be there by early evening.'

'Does Andreï know we're coming?'

'No. Well, he knows Sam's coming. That's how we got the helicopter. It's marvellous – it's cut my budget by about half. Apart from Saul's fee, of course.'

'Who's Saul?' asked Nick.

'The photographer. The most expensive photographer

in the world and his even more costly boyfriend are my insurance policy. I'm praying that they'll do the stuff they are paid such vast quantities of money to do, and everything else will fall into line with them.'

'But,' Nick was confused, 'do they know that we're not expected?'

'Of course not.'

'How do you know there's enough room for all of us? How do you know the house will be suitable?'

'Andreï Fyodov is a luxury addict. I helped him find some of the things to decorate this particular house with years ago. It is *easily* big enough for all of us. The helicopter pad is on one of the roofs – you get my drift? We will all be comfortable, whatever it is we want.'

'Sounds amazing.'

'Make the most of it. Until Max inherits I doubt any of us will be invited there again.'

'Max said he knows his father has a girl with him, but how can we be sure it's Pandora?'

Emily snuggled deep into the corner of the sofa and let Nick ask the questions. She just hoped she wouldn't fall asleep while they talked.

'What is this, Nick? Twenty questions?'

'Sorry, I didn't mean to be aggressive. I just want to know what's going on.'

'Fair enough. Well, we won't be sure it's Pandora until we're all there. I can't decide whether I hope it is or not. If it is, at least we'll have found her, in whatever state he's left her. If it isn't, then she won't have gone through the Andreï Fyodov treatment, but she'll still be lost. It's a chance we have to take. Either way it's the best place in the world to take photographs.'

'You can't take any photographs without Pandora, can you?'

'Morgan's coming. I could always do her alone.' Nina hoped she sounded more sure than she felt. Morgan hadn't guaranteed anything yet. Oh, Anna, please don't let me down, she begged silently.

'She'd never do it. It's against her religion, politics, everything she's ever stood for. That's why Max has never got anywhere with her. She's too prudish for your glamorous world. I can't believe you've got her to come at all.'

'I know. I'm amazing.' Nina laughed as if she hadn't a care in the world. 'Just watch me. My powers of persuasion can be pretty impressive when I turn them on.'

'What makes you all so sure Pandora's there?'

'A mixture of things. Largely Mrs Fischer.'

'Yuck – that old cow.'

'Yes, that old cow. She thinks she's being discreet, but Max knows her too well to let any little lie pass him by. We've no proof, we may be wrong. But I have a gut feeling she's there. It would be so like Pandora to go off with the father of the man who wouldn't have her, just to teach Max a lesson. Unfortunately she'll be learning a few lessons herself at the same time.'

Nina stopped suddenly. She should tell Pandora about her father before she started telling the rest of the world. She refilled their glasses and nibbled on a crisp – crisps and cigarettes! Next thing she'd be going to McDonald's!

*

Morgan knew she looked like a spoilt little girl having a sulk, but she didn't care. She did not want to go and be photographed by some stupid magazine, or save Pandora from her fate. Typical, she thought, I have two cross words with Max and all he can do is rush off and save the girl who turned him down first. So much for any budding relationship I might have imagined. Morgan stuck her hands deep in her white apron pockets, put her feet up on a nearby chair and stared out of the window, barely listening to Sam, who was waffling on about parenthood again.

'Morgan, are you listening?'

'Sort of.' She took a sulky slurp at her Diet Coke.

'You've got to go. Pandora needs you.'

'No, she doesn't, she's got her loving brother to look after her.'

'She needs you because she doesn't know he's her loving brother, and neither does he.'

'He's going to get a shock then, isn't he?

'Morgan, you're behaving like a three-year-old.' Anna was shocked.

'I'm behaving like a three year old? How dare you two accuse me of being childish? You haven't spoken to each other since before I can remember, and now you're all chummy again, you expect me to just deal with it and help you save a couple of spoilt brats from each other.'

'How can you be so hard?'

'Easy, just don't get involved. I never asked to. You're the people putting the pressure on.'

'Is it the photographs that are really bothering you?'

'Mum, you're asking me to do a shoot for something you've railed against all your life! How can you be so . . . so . . .' Morgan was lost for words.

'Sometimes you have to be charitable first and worry about the consequences afterwards.'

'There's charity and then there's featuring on news-stands all over the world. I'd rather go and work for free as a social worker for the rest of my life.'

'That is virtually working for free, isn't it?'

'Don't split hairs, Da–' the word stuck in Morgan's throat, 'Sam,' she finished lamely. She sighed; they weren't going to give up, were they? She stared out of the rain-streaked window, imagining Morocco, then turned back to her parents.

'OK. Since I'm such an expert, I'll go and play amateur psychologist to Pandora when she's introduced to her long-lost family.' She got up and started furiously clearing the table. 'Just don't ask me to be any good at it, that's all.' She headed off towards the kitchen, shouting over her shoulder, 'Or any good at being photographed either!'

'Em, stop it. There's nothing more you can do. If you've forgotten anything we can sort it out in the morning. You've got to get some sleep. I've never seen anyone look so tired.'

'Thanks for the compliment. I can't go to bed yet. I've just got to go over this one more time. If I forget anything I'll get fired.'

'Are you sure that wouldn't be a good thing? Wouldn't you rather have an ordinary job where you worked from nine to five and didn't have to have a nervous breakdown about skirt lengths four times a year?'

'You are good to know the collections are four times a year.'

Nick started to sing the jaws music and snaked across the room, his hands sticking up above his head like a shark's fin. 'Der dum, der dum, der der der der der der der der. Watch it Emily, they're going to get you.'

She began to laugh, the sort of laughter that was so near tears it was almost impossible to tell the difference. She threw herself down on her bed. Nick landed on her and started snapping his teeth inches from her nose.

'You'll die murdered by bitchy fashion editors and hairdressers. Imagine the headline: "Innocent girl from Surrey washed up on the pavement outside Harvey Nichols. From the state of her hair and make up it was evident she'd been mauled by fashion people!"'

Emily wiped her eyes on the hem of her nightie. 'I'm so glad you came. I really need you to put all this stuff into perspective for me. I can't do it on my own.' Suddenly she sat up. 'You know what really scares me?'

'What?'

'I'm never going to meet a straight man in my whole life. I'm going to end up like Nina, all hairdressered up and alone.'

'She's not that alone. I bet she's had thousands of boyfriends.'

'I know, but she never found anyone to live with forever did she?'

'Maybe she's just fussy.'

'I'm not that fussy . . .' Emily looked down at herself. She could see nothing even vaguely attractive. 'Nick, am I hideous?' She sniffed and blew her nose. 'I mean, when I'm not blubbing my eyes out in hotel rooms.'

'Of course not!'

'What's the matter with me then?'

'Nothing. What's this all about, Emily?' He sat up and hugged his knees to his chest.

'I can understand that Max would go for Pandora – everybody does. But, why's he after Morgan now? Nobody ever fancies me.'

'Yes they do.'

'No, they don't. I just long for people from afar. I never get anywhere with anyone. And I do know some straight men – well, you and Max, for a start.'

'Em, you're being too hard on yourself. I think you're lovely.'

'Yes, but you're no good, you're my best friend.'

'I suppose you're right. Friends is good.' He wished that other parts of his anatomy would agree with his brain. What was he supposed to do? She was sitting at the end of the bed in a totally see-through white cotton nightie. He could see the outline of her nipples in the lamplight, and he wanted to groan.

'Nick, will you stay here with me?'

He gulped. 'Of course.'

'I'm lonely and I can't bear to think of everyone else getting all the attention. I just want someone to hug, that's all.'

'Fine. Come on, then. I'm not staying up all night

while you check more lists. Turn the light out.' She did and Nick moved over to make room for her and wondered how on earth he was going to hide his excitement. There weren't even any blankets to crunch up in a convenient arrangement. It was much too hot.

Emily crawled back into bed and kissed his cheek. 'You're such a mate, Nick,' she said, before turning over to lie with her back to him.

Nick reached out and stroked her hair. 'You're' lovely, Emily. Don't worry, your knight in shining armour is bound to come along one of these days.' And I'll kill him when he does, thought Nick, and stopped stroking her hair. It wasn't helping.

'Don't stop, that was nice.' Emily snuggled back into him.

'Oh God, Emily, don't do that.'

'Why not?'

'Because I've got an erection the size of anything you'd find at Cape Canaveral, and it's embarrassing.'

'You have? Because of me?'

'I keep telling you you're lovely, and you were sitting there all see-through in your nightie. What do you expect?'

He grabbed her round the waist and pulled her gently towards him. 'Unless you protest, I'm going to have to forget all this just-good-friends business and get on with it.'

'Get on with what?' Emily turned to him.

'This.' His mouth closed on hers and he held her so tightly she could hardly breathe. 'Will I do in place of Max Fyodov?'

Emily came up for air and kissed him lightly on the nose. 'Carry on and I'll think about it.'

Needing no further encouragement, Nick dived in, nuzzling at her soft, sweet-smelling neck and wondering how he could ever really have lusted after Pandora. Emily was so clean, so gorgeous and . . . he moved down to her small round breasts.

Darkness fell late in Morocco in July, but by the time Max, Akim and Hassan, the old French teacher, left it had been dark for some hours and the moon was up. Hassan had come back from school with the local policeman, the mayor and two other teachers, all of whom had wanted to see how the young Fyodov had grown up. They oohed and ahed over his resemblance to his father, told him, roaring with laughter, that all he had to do was go and get himself a scar, and then smoked the local black hashish until Max wondered if anyone was going to be able to see their way up the mountains in the dark, let alone get him to where he wanted to go.

The ancient Mercedes wheezed its way along the winding roads. Once past the last post, the place where most people stopped and beyond which the police and the army held no sway, Max sensed the nerves of the people in the car heighten. Even if they were locals, even if most of Akim's family did live at the Fyodov house, if they were mistaken for other people then their lives would be in danger. The car drove slowly now for ease of identification, not because it couldn't go any faster. Hassan didn't want anyone taking potshots at them from the side of the road. He didn't want Max's pale face to draw any attention either, so Max sat slumped in the back seat, the hood of his djellaba pulled low over his forehead. They hardly needed headlamps; the silhouettes of the mountains reared around them, menacing in the light of the ice-white moon.

Two hours later the car stopped at the side of the road. Max could see no sign to indicate that they were there. He didn't even recognise the road. Hassan motioned for the boys to get out. He gave Akim a note for a cousin of his who was working the fields around the Fyodov house, in case they were stopped, and Akim began to lead the way down what was hardly a path, certainly not a road. Max stumbled, trying to keep up. He wished he were fitter, and that his shoes had thicker soles. Akim strode ahead, sure of his direction. It was all Max could do to keep him in sight. Now he blessed the moon. Without it they would certainly be lost.

Chapter 13

FRIDAY 28 JULY

MAX woke to the sound of threshing in the barn behind him. He sat up. It was early and the air in the mountains was still cool. He shivered. Akim sat across the room from him, drinking mint tea and eating bread with freshly churned unsalted butter. Max wondered if Pandora were getting the same treatment. He doubted it.

He and Akim had finally arrived at the farm at about two a.m. they'd bumped into Akim's uncle, who'd bundled them out of sight before they were caught by anyone who might raise an alarm. Max had laughed as all the men on the property materialised as if from nowhere. They squatted silently, smoking, around the walls of the room while Max asked questions. Yes, there was a girl with Andreï, yes, she did have long black hair a pronounced widow's peak, alabaster skin . . . He was tempted to ask if she was wearing Prada sandals but decided not to be facetious. No, no one had seen her for a few days. They thought they'd heard him call her Pandora. Eventually Max had slept, images of Pandora and his father circling his dreams, ominous, repetitive.

Rubbing his eyes, he reached for a glass of the steaming tea. Akim grinned at him.

'Good news, my friend.'

'What?'

'She's alive.'

'Well, that's a start. What about injuries?'

'Don't know. But he's been with her all yesterday and all night. There was no noise this time.'

'Is he still with her?'

'Apparently.'

'Where is she?'

'The tower room.'

'My father's bedroom?'

'No. The other one.'

'Right.' Max pushed his hair out of his eyes and went outside to pee against the wall. Back in the shed where he and Akim had slept he squatted down and tore into a piece of bread.

'I'd better go for it then,' he said, his mouth full.

'Do you want me to go with you?'

'Yeah, you can be the emergency back-up.' Max laughed and stood up. 'You can just stand behind me to catch the bits of Pandora as I throw them up to you, OK? Come on – let's go in through the kitchen. He's not likely to be sitting in there breakfasting with the staff, is he?'

The house sat the other side of the barn, a tower at each end giving some kind of balance to the ramshackle old fort. Max looked up at the first tower. He couldn't decide if the shutters were closed or not. He hoped they were at least halfway open. It would help if he had some light to help him. Well, if they were in there, he might as well go and find them. No point in putting it off any longer;

The kitchen door was open, chickens scratching around it looking for scraps. From inside came the voices of the house staff breakfasting together. The voices stopped short when the two boys cut off the light from the doorway. Max nodded a greeting to the staff around the table. Akim followed him through to the other side of the house. Neither of them spoke.

The upstairs landing was silent. Max leant against the door and listened. Nothing. How should he do this? Slam the door open and jump down the ladder? What if Andreï had a gun with him? Unlikely. Still . . . He stared for a long time at the ceiling. Well – he wouldn't know until he tried, would he? He took a deep breath and grasped the door handle, ready to throw himself into the room. He thought there was only about a six-foot drop.

At that moment he heard the whimper from inside, and before he had a chance to reconsider, he threw wide the door and jumped in, hoping he was clear of the ladder. He landed cat-like on all fours in the middle of the room and threw himself towards the sound of crying. To his astonishment he landed on his father, a crumpled heap on the floor. It was Andreï who was crying. Pandora, huddled beside the ladder, looked dirty, tired, drawn. She hardly seemed to notice Max's arrival. Ignoring Andreï, Max pulled her to her feet and helped her up the ladder, Akim hauling her up the last few steps. Then he turned to Andreï who hadn't moved.

'Hello, Father.'

Andreï didn't answer.

'Father?'

Slowly Andreï turned over and sat up against the wall. His face was streaked with tears. His scar was livid against the porcelain of his face. Very slowly, and concentrating as if his life depended on it, Andreï was sick, the vomit pouring over his crumpled shirt into a puddle in his lap. Max just watched, mesmerised by this muddled version of a man he'd never before seen out of control.

Andreï looked up at Max and spread his hands in despair. Max went and knelt before him.

'What's going on?'

Andreï shook his head.

'Father, please. What is it?'

'She's my daughter.'

'What? Who is?'

'That girl. The one who came here to get her own back at you for not falling for her. Revenge runs in the family.' Andreï laughed, hoarse, choking. 'Seems I killed her mother too.'

'Don't be ridiculous, Father. Come on, let's go. We'll talk later. Pandora will be all right now. Come on, let's get you out of here.'

Very gently Max pulled his father up. Andreï was the taller man, but now he was bent, older, worn out. Max led him to the step ladder. At the top of the stairs Akim waited. Pandora had gone, sent off to the caring hands of Saida. Between them the two young men led Andreï to his quarters. Max ran a bath and helped his father undress. Andreï let himself be put in the bath, washed, dried and dressed again. Eventually, sitting on the side of his bed in the room where Pandora had woken on her first day, he began to cry again.

Max rang for a tray of food. He knew that Pandora would be taken care of. His priority was the welfare of his father. He offered Andreï the soup that had been sent up. Andreï brushed it away and lay back on his pillows, his eyes closed.

'Get me a drink.'

Max rubbed his eyes – how long had he been asleep? He forced himself back to reality. Andreï was still lying on the bed.

'No.'

'Get me a drink, boy. Now.'

'Father, please, talk to me first. Tell me what all this is about. I'll get you a drink later. Tell me now, while you're sober.'

Andreï opened his eyes and stared at the ceiling. He shook his head.

'I can't.' He looked up at his son. 'Go away, Max. Leave me alone. I don't want you now.'

Max had never disobeyed his father in his life, and he wasn't about to start now. He left the room and crouched down in the gloom of the passage beside Akim, who had been waiting there. He accepted the offer of a cigarette.

He drew on the rough local tobacco and stared ahead at his father's door. A servant arrived with an ice-cold bottle of Absolut and a glass on a tray. Max took it from him, saying that he would give the drink to Andreï himself. Instead he stayed where he had stationed himself, guarding his father's door, staring blindly at the sweating bottle and the puddle of condensation forming around its base.

'Ready, Morgan?'

'Ready. Let's go.'

Morgan turned to kiss her mother. She still looked sulky, but she was going. She didn't have to shout for joy about it, did she? She slid into the back seat of the car beside her father and didn't look back as they pulled out into the narrow lane behind her house. They were taking the taxi all the way to the airport. She couldn't believe the extravagance of it.

The shows were over. Nothing had surprised Nina much: Dior came and went, exquisite white organdy blouses with huge dramatic cuffs, ideal for January; Chanel, jokes in amongst the Coco-inspired suits; Valentino, classic, dull, finished, commercial; Saint Laurent, colour-me-beautiful in featherlight fabrics; Galliano's glorious collection for Givenchy; Lacroix, luscious as usual; and all of this with an average price tag of over ten grand.

Nina had had enough and was thrilled to get out of Paris.

'Good thing the plane's big enough for all of us,' she said brightly as she led the small army of people who were going to Morocco for her make or break shoot. Dressed in a cream linen shirt and black capri pants, black patent-leather Gucci flip-flops on her feet and the trusty old Kelly bag on her wrist, she knew that at least she looked like a fashion editor, even if she felt as if she were lost and had been mistakenly left in charge of a band of unruly school-children.

Emily and Nick led the cavalcade, followed by Saul Smytheson, his boyfriend and three assistants laden with luggage. After them came Gavin Cheveux, Jurgen and Jurgen, make-up artists with two more assistants and then the porters with the carnet – four huge suitcases filled with valuable clothes. Le Bourget airport had never seen anything so glamorous. Right at the end, straggling a little, were Sam and Morgan. Morgan had had an attack of nerves. She'd never flown before and the journey so far had been bumpy enough to put her off for life. Morocco was a lot further than London to Paris. Sam half pulled, half carried her along towards the steaming tarmac where Andreï's jet waited to carry them on the second leg of their journey. There was no sign of Rory.

They were all buckled in for take-off when they heard the screaming from the tarmac below.

'Listen, you stupid little halfwit. I am supposed to be on that plane and it cannot leave without me.'

Nina looked out of the window. She would never have mistaken that voice anywhere. She jumped up and ran down the gangway.

'Rory! Where on earth have you been?'

'Darling, this man wasn't going to allow me to go with you, and you know you can't do the shoot without me.'

'Of course I can't. Darling, the fight Saul and lover boy are having about Max Fyodov is enough in itself to make your presence essential. Somehow you're going to have to calm them down. And Morgan looks about as photogenic as a boiled egg; I hope I haven't made a mistake there. Oh, Rory, I've never been so pleased to see anyone in my whole life.' She took his arm. 'And frankly, darling, we are going to need everyone we can get to diffuse the tension when we arrive.' She looked about her as they stepped into the plane. 'Everybody, you all know Rory Williams. Luckily for us, he's coming too.'

Rory waved at the assembled company, regal and gleaming in scarlet Versace, then settled himself beside Nina.

'What's going to be so tense?' he asked in a stage whisper.

'Oh, darling you're going to love it, it's going to be like the end of a really good trashy novel, only you won't have had to read the whole thing to get there.' She still hadn't told him they were going to collect Pandora and saw no reason to warn him that they were heading for Andreï's house. He might demand that the plane detour to London so he could collect his fencing foils.

Rory was completely lost. 'But I still don't understand. Where are the girls.? You're not going to rely on Morgan, surely? The girl's never stood the glam side of a Pentax in her life.'

'You'll see, sweetheart, you'll see.'

Rory lay back in his seat and began to tell Nina about Gloria's shoot in London.

'Oh, darling, I screamed. Do admit – Gloria and Gay together are already a comedy due worthy of Friday night on Channel Four. Add Tuesday as their special guest star and it becomes priceless.'

'Did you take any nice pictures?'

'Very dull. Nothing that hasn't been done a thousand times before. And Gloria so stressed, and Gay so demanding. Don had already gone back to New York, totally exhausted. I think his roving eye's moved on from Gloria. She was dead touchy about it. And Gloria's going to the States today to start her job and the poor love hasn't even had time to pack her house up. She's taken her assistant, by the way. None of the others have gone with her, though. You're lucky. You could have found yourself with a staffless magazine. It seems you're more popular than Don gave you credit for. Do a good shoot and he'll start wondering why he didn't send for you for the American magazine.'

'I wouldn't sleep with him. I'll never get the American magazine now. Not that I ever really wanted it.'

'What? You mean he's tried it on?'

'I still haven't decided whether to sue for attempted rape.'

'That's where the black eye came from!'

'Mmm. I'm stronger than I thought.'

'He won't talk about it. I don't think he can remember how he got it.'

'I'm not surprised, he was so coked up it's a miracle he had any nose left for me to whack.'

'Darling! Such violence! Now then, I still don't know where we're going.'

"Oh, Rory – let it all be a surprise. You're going to love it.' She patted his manicured hand. 'I hope.'

Paris dropped away beneath them. Morgan felt her stomach stay behind and reached for a sick bag. She couldn't even bring herself to talk to Nick and Emily, who were sitting behind her. Sam looked grim. Nina was at the other end of the plane with Rory. The gold cap of her hair bobbed up and down as she talked to him. Sam took Morgan's hand and held it, and she didn't pull away.

The airstrip at Fez was so tiny, Morgan wondered how the plane was going to avoid crashing into the city. She gripped the arms of her seat and closed her eyes. She must be clinically insane to be there at all. Somehow they landed, and there in front of her were two helicopters. They couldn't seriously expect her to get into one of those, could they? Yes, they could. Sam led her by the hand and put her into a seat. Only Sam, Morgan and the luggage were going in the first machine. The others would come in the second. The helicopter couldn't possibly have taken everyone. The pilot looked around.

'Room for one more,' he called down to Nina, who jumped on herself.

'Rory, make sure everyone gets on the other helicopter. I really don't want to lose anyone at this stage. Saul, come back. there isn't time for shopping trips in the medina. You'll have to come here another time. We have to go now.' She turned to Morgan and Sam. 'Hi, you guys. Nearly there then.'

Morgan had gone pale green. 'Couldn't I come with the next lot, with Emily?'

'No, darling, I think you'd better stay with us. Off we go them.'

Nina's face had lost its jolly look. Her eyes were grim. She had no idea what was waiting for them. She was taking the personal and professional risks of a lifetime. Sam saw her bleak face and took her hand as well as Morgan's.

An hour later they were high in mountains, the two helicopters bobbing over the rough scree, keeping close to the ground. It would be easy to miss the fort.

'There it is,' cried the pilot, pointing to the collection of miniature buildings nestling in a distant fold in the hills. The helicopter pad glared like a white tattoo on the roof of the biggest building.

Max heard the whirr of the first helicopter. He was still sitting outside his father's room, the vodka now warm, the puddle of condensation at its base almost evaporated after the afternoon's heat. Akim had slipped off. Max was alone. He didn't move. There had been no sign of Pandora, but he didn't care. Nina could look after her. He stood and looked through the window of the passage at the huge courtyard below, imagining the shoot that would take place there the next day, and then at the sky, the helicopters, growing dots on the horizon.

The door behind him opened. Andreï stood there, tall and starched, the man Max had always known.

'Come here, Max.' Max hesitated. '*Now!*' He jumped, swallowed back the nausea that the sight of his father inspired and followed Andreï into his room. Andreï had taken the vodka bottle. Max found him calling to the kitchens for a cold version, and this time for two glasses.

'That's Sam arriving.' Andreï had heard the helicopter too. Max wondered whether now would be a good time to announce that it wasn't just Sam, everyone else too. He decided against it.

'We will not see him yet. The servants will look after him until dinner. I want to talk to you first.'

'Yes, Father.'

Andreï installed himself in an armchair, his back against the light so that Max couldn't really see his face. Max perched on the end of the bed and waited. The vodka arrived and Andreï poured, slamming back the first shot and pouring again before Max had even tasted his.

'You have a sister.'

'That's ridiculous.'

'Yes you do. That girl upstairs, that girl I brought here with me, is your sister.'

Andreï knocked back another shot. He was calm but pale. A slight drip of vodka sat on his chin – the only sign that this fastidious man was shaken to his core. Max focused on this and forced himself to concentrate.

'How can she be my sister?'

'I knew her mother at Oxford.'

'Oh, right, so some woman you fucked while you were fucking *my* mother is therefore the mother of your daughter. It's not possible, Father, she's the same age as me!'

'Oh, it's possible all right.'

'Father, you're not making sense. Pandora cannot be my sister. You have one child. Me. You've been a pretty useless father with me, what makes you want more children now? What makes you think you'll do a better job with her than you did with me?'

Andreï, exhausted, forced the tired words out.

'I was having an affair with Miranda Williams during the spring term before our finals. I was also sleeping with your mother. Your mother told me she was pregnant. I married her. Miranda did not. I didn't . . . I didn't even think about it. She left Oxford without saying goodbye. Her brother attacked me,' Andreï fingered his scar, 'but I thought it was for other reasons. I never saw them again. I never knew she had a child. She's *my* child, Max. Miranda was many things, but I know she was faithful to me for the time we were together.'

'More than you were.'

'I never pretended to be a paragon of virtue.'

'No, it never even occurred to you to try.'

'Be careful, Max. I'm telling you this because you can choose whether you want this sister. I cannot deny her her birthright. I will acknowledge her.'

'Father, we are not in the sixteenth century. She might not want you.'

'Of course she does. Every man wants a daughter.' He stopped and corrected himself. 'I mean, every girl wants a father.'

'Am I so much of a disappointment to you? Is a son not what you want now?' Max was trying hard not to cry. He was being disowned, he knew it. Andreï had just picked some random girl to adopt. Max was being let go, fired, the useless child. 'You could have killed her. You would never have known.'

'Max, listen to me. You have a sister. That's all I'm saying. I'm as surprised as you are.'

'No. You listen to me. I may not have been the son you wanted. I know you hate my painting and sculpture. I know you think I'm a waste of space. I know you think I'm just a flake who's bent on spending all your money. I know you want me to grow up grand and Russian and be everything that you've never quite managed to be, everything my murdered mother was. But if you've decided that I'm just not good enough for you at all, then that's fine. I resign. I'm no longer a Fyodov, Father. I'm no longer your son.' Max stood and went to the door. Before he left the room he turned. 'You probably think I cam here to save Pandora from you. I didn't. I came here to save you from yourself. But if you don't want me, then I'll just leave you to it. Here, have the warm vodka too.' The bottle smashed at Andreï's feet.

Max slammed the door behind him and headed for the fields outside the house. He needed to think. In the distance he could hear the commotion of the first helicopter landing. He hurried. He had to escape them. The last person he wanted to see right now as Morgan James, with her holier-than-thou look and superior toss of her head. She could go and look after his 'sister'. He headed down to the pool at the bottom of the fields.

*

Nina jumped down from the helicopter, ignoring the helping hands offered by the servants waiting to welcome them.

'Where is she?' she asked of no one in particular. The servants and Sam began to retrieve the huge quantity of luggage from the back of the machine. Morgan stood dazed, staring at the magnificent view. In the distance she saw a small figure picking its way down a rocky ravine towards a pool she could see glinting in the distance. She turned back to the scene on the roof.

'Yes, where's Pandora?'

Saida appeared at the top of the staircase which led to the roof.

'*Madame, s'il vous plaît, suivez-moi.*' Nina took Morgan's hand, and leaving Sam to fend for himself, the two women followed Saida down to Pandora's rooms, where they found her sitting in bed, a huge tray of food in front of her. She was eyeing the food suspiciously.

'It might have been poisoned, you see. He might still be trying to get rid of me. All the servants are in his power. Don't believe anything you see. Appearances are dead deceptive round here.' She didn't seem to recognise them.

'Pandora.' Nina rushed over to the bed and took the tray away so that she could sit down. 'It's all right now. We're here. You'll be fine. Are you all right? Did he hurt you?'

'Hurt me?' Suddenly Pandora seemed to come to, her eyes focused on Nina and Morgan, hovering over her with such concern. 'Nina. How did you find me?'

'A little light investigation work by Max, actually.' Nina

looked her goddaughter over and decided she could be worse. Nothing seemed to be broken. Apart from the scratches on her arms there didn't seem to be any bad bruising. Her face was unmarked.

'Pandora, what's been going on? Are you all right?' Morgan was shocked at Pandora's gaunt pallor.

'Oh, fine, fit as a fiddle, as you can see.' She jiggled her legs up and down and waved her arms about. 'Look, nothing broken.'

Morgan sat down on the end of the bed. 'How did you get here? How did you meet him?'

'He picked me up at the Floré. The day you guys went off on your school trip to Versailles. I told you about him.'

'You didn't mention the eyes. If you had, we might have worked out where you were sooner. And then what?'

'I found him at Fontainebleau and persuaded him to bring me here.'

'And now you're' – Morgan searched for a suitable word – 'Lovers?'

'No. I don't know why. Good thing in the end. You know he claims to be my father!'

Nina and Morgan blanched in unison.

'How do you know?'

'He suddenly announced it last night. Apparently he was screwing my mother and Rory at the same time as the wife he claims he killed. That's where the scar came from. Rory attacked him with a fencing foil before Andreï threw him out of a first-floor window on to a bed of wallflowers which broke his fall. It's a miracle he's alive really.' Pandora's face hardened. 'It all makes painful sense, doesn't it? What I don't understand, though, is how you, Nina, who must have known all about it, chose not to tell either of us, leaving us to pick each other up in a Paris bar. He could have killed me and it would have been your fault. And you, you saintly little marvel,' she said to Morgan, 'you knew too and didn't tell me either. That's why they brought you. You witch! Was this specially organised, Nina? A let's-get-the-girls-to-meet-their-fathers summer? I wouldn't put it past you.' She got out of bed and opened the door. 'Go away. Go away both of you. I need to think. And I don't need you two little know-it-alls to help me. Go on, get the fuck out of here before I'm not the only one with bruises to nurse.

Nina and Morgan left the room, stunned. Saida was waiting for them and led them to a series of rooms next to Pandora's. Morgan plonked herself down on a sofa.

'Blimey!' She let her hair out of the clutches of its biro and shook it out.

'I've never seen her so angry.' Nina leant against the mantelpiece and lit a cigarette.

'I've never seen her angry at all.' Morgan shook her head and went to look out of the window at the courtyard below. The photographic equipment was being piled under the mezzanine, at the other end of the courtyard from the drawing room. 'Is that where you're going to do your famous shoot?'

Nina followed Morgan's eyes. 'Yes. Seems I took a good risk about the location. It's perfect. I'll use the roof too.'

'And did you see the path going down to the pool below?'

'I think we'll have to be careful about shooting outside the house. We can't have the magazine associated with drugs, can we?'

'Is that what all this stuff growing round here is?'

'Yup. This, Morgan, is a hash farm.'

'A hash farm!'

'The ground's too rocky for any other kind of cash crop. That's why we flew in. We'd never have got up here in a car.'

'Wow.' Morgan was suitably impressed.

Sam, abandoned, decided to go for a walk. He found Max, head between his hands, sitting on a large rock overlooking one of the most beautiful little waterfalls that Sam had ever seen.

'Hi.' He sat down next to Max. 'You don't look so good.'

'Thanks for the understatement.'

'Pleasure. Anything you want to talk about?'

'Not really.'

'OK.' Sam looked about him. The dying afternoon sun was warming the terraces, bathing them in a soft glow. The pool lay beneath him, a natural swimming bath so clear he could see the pebbles gleaming far below.

'Mind if I swim?'

'Go ahead.'

'Join me?'

'No thanks.'

Sam stripped and dived in, his lean, fit body slicing open the water in a neat curve. Thirty feet further on he came to the surface, spluttering.

'You could have warned me it would be so cold.'

'Mountain spring water. You didn't think it would be warm, did you?'

Sam started ploughing through the water to warm up.

'Where's the rest of the circus, then?' Max asked.

'Coming now. There wasn't room for everyone. We took two helicopters.'

'How many people?'

'A lot more than I expected. I hope Andreï won't mind. He's really going to have a full house.'

'He'll probably bill Nina for it.'

'I shouldn't think she'll mind. The magazine'll pay.' Sam started back to the far end of the pool.

'Is Rory coming?'

'Yes.'

'Great. More abuse from him. I hope he doesn't go mad.' Max was silent for a while, then he said hopefully, 'She's not really my sister, is she?'

Sam turned and swam back, hauling himself out and shaking the water from his hair like a dog. He roughly dried himself on his shirt and put his jeans back on, letting his back dry in the sum.

'Fraid so.'

'You knew it. Everybody knew it.'

'Yes.'

'And I nearly slept with her!'

'But you didn't, did you?'

'It was close. If I hadn't been so obsessed with Morgan, I probably would have done.' Max stared ahead at the evening sky, streaked with red, as angry as he was.

'And now he doesn't want me any more. Now I've got no one.'

'What do you mean, he doesn't want you?'

'Pandora is the ideal child for him. She won't use her brain, in spite of the fact that she has a perfectly good one. She looks the part, she'll be perfect on his arm at official functions. And she'll never embarrass him by having strange longings to do something as useless as art!' Max spat out the last word. 'Or by hanging around with badly bred people like your daughter.'

'What?'

'Yes. I'm supposed to avoid Morgan because her mother's a title-free feminist. He can't think much of you either, if he wants me to avoid her.'

'Come on, Max. He's not serious about any of this.'

'What happened, Sam? You all got together when Pandora and I were born and decided that since he had me there was no need to tell him about his daughter? It can't have been much more complicated than that. Probably a good thing. He might have kidnapped Pandora and done away with her mother as well, except she died anyway, didn't she? He probably arranged that too, knowing him.'

'Max, you're not making sense.'

'Aren't I? You know perfectly well that my father administered the fatal shot of heroin that killed my mother. If I know that, then you must.'

'Max. I was there.'

'Oh, great. You helped, I suppose. And now thanks to you lot, I don't have anybody.'

'Max, I know you're in shock, but if you seriously think

you don't have anybody, who do you imagine we're all here?'

'I had to ask Nick to come myself.'

'I'm not talking about Nick. I'm talking about me and Nina and Morgan.'

'Yeah, she's really come for me. You're all here to save Pandora from the clutches of her wicked family. Hey, her father's a murderer and her brother's a mad artist who has no idea there's a world outside the privileged one he grew up in.'

'You're being childish. Your father did *not* kill your mother, you do have a perfectly good idea of how the real world works and I think we're here to bury the past and save all three of you from each other.'

'Well, I wish you luck. With my father in the mood he's in, I'll be surprised if he's still around by morning, when on his behalf I'll throw you all out and Nina will have to do her precious shoot somewhere else.'

The other helicopter landed in the space left by the first one leaving. Rory and Saul directed the shoot preparations from the courtyard. The assistants organised everyone, and only the servants actually picked anything up. Rory, Saul and Gavin Cheveux were running around the courtyard screaming with delight at the setting. Emily was hanging all the clothes in a spare sitting room on huge racks that had miraculously appeared out of the luggage. Rory kept rushing in and hovering menacingly with a portable steamer.

'Emily, where's Nina?'

'I don't know, Rory. Careful!' Rory leapt out of the way as Emily, who was arranging the train of a red satin dress, tried to find a way to keep it off the floor.

'Don't you careful me, young Emily! And the only way to keep that dress clean is to put the train on a separate hanger.'

'Sorry. I'm just so sure something's going to go wrong and it'll be all my fault. Are you pleased with the location?'

'Darling, it's too fabulous for words. We can have the servants in their lovely white nighties standing behind Morgan with trays of things for the pictures. I wonder whether they'll sign personality release forms? You don't think they'll mind being photographed, do you?'

'I haven't got a clue. Where can I lay the jewellery out?'

'On that table. Wrap everything up again once you've checked it. We don't want things doing disappearing acts during the night, do we, darling?'

'I thought I might sleep here and guard everything.'

'All on your own?'

'She won't be on her own. I'll help. Can't I?' Nick stood in the doorway. 'As usual I feel like a spare part. I've come all the way here to answer Max's call and I can't even find him. I might as well make myself useful here.'

'Wait a minute. What's Max got to do with this place? You are talking about that Fyodov boy, aren't you?'

'Yes. It's his house. Didn't you know? We're her to save Pandora as well.'

"What?' Rory collapsed on to a nearby chair. Emily

began some frantic fanning with a jewel-encrusted Valentino clutch bag.

'Oh, shit. Didn't he know?' Nick was shocked.

'Of course not,' Emily wailed. 'Oh no, not now, Rory. Nick, can you go and get some water or something? And have someone go and find Nina.'

'Deal.' Nick headed towards the door.

Rory hauled himself to his feet. 'No need. I will find that scheming woman myself.' Green and sweating, he marched into the centre of the courtyard and began to shout. 'Nina!'

Nina stuck her head out of her sitting room window.

'Yes, darling?'

'Are we in a Fyodov safe house?'

'Yes, darling. And before you go berserk, I think you should know that Pandora is safe in her room eating a delicate little tray of goodies, and there is hardly a scratch on her.'

Rory grabbed a light stand and waved it threateningly.

'Where is he? Where is he? I'll kill him.'

'No you won't. He's hiding, darling. I haven't seen him myself yet.'

'And where's that worm of a son of his?'

'I've no idea. But before you start abusing him, I think you should know that it was Max who risked life and limb to get here before we did and make sure she was all right. I'm afraid you're going to have to bury that hatchet, sweetheart.'

'So where's Andreï, then?'

'I told you, I've no idea.'

'I'll kill him.'

'No you won't. Now stop going round in circles and Saul get the set finished. You know he can't do it without you. Can you, Saul?' Nina called to the perfectly competent photographer, who needed no help with anything and who was lounging in the drawing room, his feet on a side table, helping himself from the drinks tray. 'Saul, I can tell you who your girls are now, if you're interested.'

'Too late to change anything anyway. Tell me, then.'

'Pandora, and the gorgeous girl who came to my party.' Saul's face lit up. 'Glad someone's pleased with something. Rory, put that light stand down, you'll do someone an injury.'

'Then I suggest you keep out of the way, or I might inadvertently take a swing at you!'

Dinner was an inevitably tense affair. Pandora ate in her room. Morgan, Emily and Nick sat at one end of the table, Sam, Nina and Rory at the other, the rest of the team between them. Hardly anyone spoke. There was no sign of either of their hosts. Sam made a valiant attempt to keep the atmosphere light.

'So, everybody ready for tomorrow?'

'As long as Bobby gets out of his mood so we can all work. Honey, we can't wait until you feel less premenstrual. We only have the weekend to shoot in.' Saul's tone was icy.

'I don't see why I shouldn't be in a bad mood. We got dragged out here on false pretences. I thought this was where Max Fyodov lived. No sign of him yet, is there?

And they don't have the right kind of mineral water for me.'

'Ooh, look at her. She'll collapse for the wrong type of materials. Get a life for yourself, Bobby. Not all of us are going to spend the whole of our own lives running round you as if you were a bitch on heat.' Rory stabbed a piece of chicken with extra venom and then dropped it.

'You leave my boyfriend out of this. I won't have Bobby abused in public.' Saul was furious.

'No, darling, you like to keep that little hobby private, don't you?'

'Just because he turned you down . . .'

'He turned me on, actually. And not too long ago. London is quite a place for misbehaving, isn't it, Nina?'

'I have no idea what you're talking about, and I'm certainly not interested.' Nina stood. 'Please everyone, I hope you'll excuse me, I'm exhausted. I'll see you all tomorrow. The six a.m. call still stands.' She smiled around the table. 'Good night.'

'Wait.' Sam stood. 'Feel like a walk?'

'OK.'

Sam took her arm and led her out of the solid oak doors and down the path through the terraces to the pool, where the stars reflected a million diamonds on to the surface of the water. Sam sat on the large flat stone he'd found Max brooding on earlier. Nina stood and stared, mesmerised, at the jewelled velvet of the night sky. The air was warm, but she shivered and pulled the pale-pink Chanel cashmere closer around her shoulders.

'You OK?' asked Sam.

She smiled ruefully. 'Not really.'

Sam stood and put an arm round her. 'You must be exhausted.'

'Relieved, actually. I'm so glad she was here, that we took the right risk, that she's OK. I'm worried too, though. Rory's going to go berserk when Andreï finally surfaces. With any luck he won't till we've all gone, and then you can deal with him next week.'

'Someone should look after Max a bit too. He's feeling rejected. He thinks he's a failure.'

'Poor boy. It's not his fault . . .'

'No. Nina . . .'

'Yes?'

Her face was inches from his. He gently pushed back her fringe and kissed her forehead.

'You need looking after as well, don't you?'

Her eyes were suddenly bright with tears. 'Sometimes.'

Sam kissed her cheeks, one at a time. 'Like now?' His arms went round her, encircling her tiny body with too much ease. 'You're so delicate, like a bird.'

She laughed through the tears. 'And you're more poetic than I ever gave you credit for.'

'Nina, I'm . . .'

She put a finger to her lips. 'Shh . . . later.' And she reached up to kiss him back.

After dinner, Pandora sat in her sitting room with Morgan. Emily had wanted to come too but was too frightened to leave her precious charges hanging on the racks on their own. Nick was keeping her company.

'Morgan, this is absurd. Why did nobody ring up and warn me? I mean, Max must have worked out where I was days ago. You could have prevented all this happening.'

'Max wouldn't let us call. He said it was too dangerous.'

Pandora wished Morgan wouldn't look so earnest. It make her look like a frog, and she didn't want to be photographed with a frog; it would never make the front cover.

'How ridiculous. I can look after myself.'

'Evidently not,' replied Morgan.

'What do you mean? When Max arrived I was quite safe.'

'Only because you and Andreï had managed to work out your relationship on your own. How did you do it?'

'I told you already. I told him about my mother dying, and about how she and Rory were twins and were at Oxford, and suddenly he went all white, threw up and announced that I was his daughter. Can you imagine? Shocked! Neither of us spoke for about an hour and a half. Him because he's so thrilled to be related to me and me because I discover that after twenty-one years of happy innocence I find I was fathered by a pervert! If he thinks I'm going to be all chummy and daughtery with him, he's got another think coming.'

'Is he really that disgusting?'

'Morgan, I can't even begin to describe it. Even if he weren't my father – a fact I'm beginning to doubt the more I think how foul he is compared to my general perfection – I'd be in emotional turmoil. He practically raped me for days and days, and the worst part is that he never quite did – I just lay there in the dark dreading it and wondering when he would come back and hit me. I presume you're here to help me with the emotional turmoil of finding a father, but what about the rape part? You're no expert in that, and Nina's next to useless. I'm serious when I say I'm fucking furious with you both.'

'I didn't know until just a few days ago. Be furious with Nina by all means, but I haven't been hiding secrets from you.'

'No. You wouldn't hide anything, would you?'

'I'm not that perfect.'

'I never said you were. But Nina! How could she?'

'So now what are you going to do?'

'I'm going to do the shoot. I've never had a magazine cover before.'

'And then what?'

'Kill everyone for lying to me. And if that perverted weirdo with the eyes and the scar that he likes to use as tools of seduction thinks I'm about to fall at his feet and declare undying filial adoration, he's wrong. Apparently Max is taking this very hard, but–'

'Who cares about him? Honestly,' said Morgan, 'if this situation weren't quite so ridiculous we'd probably be taking it a bit more seriously. But for Nina to decide that what you needed to cheer you up was a magazine cover shoot . . . well, the whole thing's fantastic.'

'But Nina's absolutely right. I do need a shoot to cheer me up. It's the only thing I know I'm really good at, and it's nothing to do with my mother, my father or my brother. The only other photogenic person in my family is

Rory, and he'd look horrible in a couture dress, however much he'd love to wear one.'

'Are you going to change your surname?'

'No.'

'What are you going to call Andreï?'

'Arsehole, probably. What do you call Sam?'

'Sam. I can't call him Dad – he's not my dad, is he? The word implies someone who's been around all your life, you know, who's had something to do with you, not some stranger you meet at a party.'

Pandora lay back on the sofa, felt for the reassuring points of her hip bones and sighed.

'I have to say, I am glad you're here. Everyone else is walking about with faces long enough for a funeral. I can get things in proportion with you.'

'You mean, turn it into a joke!'

'Well, you have to laugh, don't you? Otherwise we'd all go mad.'

'Maybe.' Morgan pushed herself out of her armchair. 'I'm going to bed. I'm exhausted. And I'm going to need to look beautiful for tomorrow. I can't believe I'm doing this, Pandora. You must realise how fond of you I must be to allow myself to be photographed.'

'Don't be so prissy. You'll love it, it's a riot. Besides, Saul is the best photographer in the world. You might never get another chance.'

'You're right. How can I be so disapproving till I've tried it?'

'Precisely. So go and get your beauty sleep, darling.' Pandora kissed Morgan. 'And Morgan?'

Morgan turned back from the door. 'Yes?'

'Thanks for coming.'

Morgan made a mocking curtsey and laughed. 'The honour is all mine, your royal highness.'

Morgan was lost. She seemed to have covered the same passages a hundred times. The silence of the house forbade her to make a noise and call for help. And then she heard it, a dull thud followed by a groan. She put her ear to the low door set into a carved lintel in a panelled wall. She heard the groan again and then grunting, something being dragged across the floor.

Gingerly she opened the door and poked her head into the room. It was too dark to see anything. She waited, hoping her eyes would get used to the deep black. It didn't work. Morgan felt about just inside the door for a light switch. She couldn't find one.

'Is anyone there?' No one answered. The shunting had stopped. Morgan, blinded by the inky night, began to pick her way across the room. She could hear someone breathing and headed to where she thought she'd heard the noise, swearing when her leg hit the corner of a table, but carrying on regardless.

'Oh my god! Max!' The hair shone white-gold in the darkness. 'Oh, Max. Don't be dead. Please don't be dead.' She tried to feel for a pulse and her hand felt the stickiness of blood. She hoped she wouldn't be sick. She got up and stumbled about until she found a table lamp. She turned the recumbent figure on to its back.

It wasn't Max. Andreï's scar shone red in the low light

thrown from the brass lamp. The side of his head and most of his shirt were covered in blood. He must have fallen against the table; a gash across his forehead was bleeding profusely. He was going to need stitches to avoid a scar at least as big as the first one. Morgan tried again to feel for a pulse. Faint, but there. She found a cushion and put it under his head. Then she noticed the empty vodka bottle, and the pill bottle beside it, empty too. She stroked Andreï's head, mesmerised by the blood, which was slowing now, coagulating all over what had been the good side of his face. She didn't' notice Max appear, framed in the doorway, his white-gold hair reflecting his father's.

'Go away, Morgan,' he said quietly.

Morgan picked up the empty pill bottle and held it up. 'I think we should try and pump his stomach. He's unconscious but still alive.'

'You,' each word was spoken with exaggerated care, 'have nothing to do with this. I'll deal with it. Go away.'

'Max . . .'

'I said set out. He's mind to protect, you understand. He doesn't need you. I don't need anybody.' As she came towards him he shoved past her to kneel and cradle his father's head in his hands. 'All this circus, all these people. It's all ridiculous. None of you have any idea how to deal with him. Go away and let me get on with it. He's my problem, not yours.'

Chapter 14

Saturday 29 July

Nina stretched and smiled. He was still there. He hadn't got up in the night and sneaked off. She breathed in deeply, relishing the smell of him. It was 5.45 a.m. She had a quarter of an hour before the day began. She would think about Sam later, when the shoot was done. Right now she had other fish to fry, cats to whip, and even photos to take.

Below in the courtyard Saul Smytheson was on fine form, noisily waking everybody up by doing a passable impression of a blue-assed fly. Nina got out of bed and went to look out of the window. Oh dear, Saul was in full make-up and a white shirt. She knew it was only going to run, and then he'd be in a bate all day, convinced that someone would have photographed him sweating and greasy with mascara halfway down his face. Never mind, at least the light was exquisite. Saul's boyfriend appeared, sulky as usual, drinking tea while holding his nose. He daren't not, in case the insides fell out, what was left of them after his cocaine habit had dealt with the rest.

Nina brushed her hair, washed her face and drew on a pair of slim-fitting white Armani jeans and a loose pale-blue Equipement linen shirt. She slipped on a turquoise snakeskin version of the Gucci flip-flops and kissed Sam, deep in sleep, before heading off to help set up. Where was everybody? With that amount of noise Nina thought the courtyard would have been full of people telling Saul to shut up.

Morgan had gone for a walk. She made her way down the path between the marijuana terraces. The light was quite different from that of the previous evening, pale, white and filled with birdsong. She stopped above the pool and watched as the sun came over the lip of the mountain behind her and lit the range, landing a shaft of new light on the waterfall below. She sat on the rock bridge and stared into the distance, her mind blank. She didn't hear Max arrive. He didn't notice her. Eventually, disturbed by the light catching his hair, Morgan looked up and saw him. He stood, taller than she remembered. His shoulders seemed wider, his back straighter. He had an air of determination that she had not seen before. The schoolboy slouch was gone.

She watched him crouch down and begin to sketch, short bitty movements on a small pad he had brought with him. His face was screwed up in concentration. Morgan was so overawed by this image she dared not break the silence. It wasn't until he'd finished whatever it was he'd been working on that he looked around him and caught her staring at him. She caught her breath. She could hardly speak, but managed, 'Hello.'

'He smiled. 'You shouldn't be speaking to me after last night.'

She stood up and went over to him. 'I'm thinking about it. After all, a goody-two-shoes like me shouldn't know how to hold a grudge.'

'You're not that perfect, surely? Anyway, take your time. I'm not very good at speech myself at the moment.' She sat on the rock next to him. 'And I wasn't very nice last night, or the last time we met. I'm sorry if I was a bit aggressive.'

How guilty can a man look? she wondered.

'May I see?'

He passed her the pad. It was not a picture of the view, as she'd presumed it would be. It was a sketch of her, her head bent low over Andreï's, hardly lit by the low table lamp. Morgan handed the pad back and felt her eyes brim with tears.

'At first I thought it was you. I was so frightened. Will he be all right?'

'I think so. A little scared, I think. It's been a shit few days, Morgan, but it's OK. I mean, he's OK, I'm OK, Pandora's OK.' He laughed quietly. 'I mean, nobody died, right?'

'Not quite.'

He put his arm around her shoulder and pulled her towards him. 'Friends?'

She reached up and kissed his cheek. 'I'll think about that too.'

'How's Pandora?'

'She'll survive.'

'Is she furious I didn't go and see her yesterday?'

'Glad to see you still care what other people think of you. No, Max, I don't think it's even crossed her mind. She's just bowled over about the fact that she suddenly has a father.'

'You and she both.'

'Yes. Odd, isn't it? Do you mind?'

'Yes. But I'll learn to live with it. I'll have to learn to share him, I suppose. I've spent my life feeling responsible for his behaviour. Maybe Pandora'll feel like assuming a bit of that.'

'I doubt it. From what she was saying last night she might never speak to him again. But then, knowing Pandora, she's just as likely to change her mind, declare undying love for him and show him off all over London.' Morgan laughed.

'Yeah, well. As long as we all just learn to manage the situation so that nobody else gets hurt . . .' Max stood up and shook himself. 'Aren't you supposed to be having your photograph taken?'

'Oh, shit. What's the quickest way back to the house?'

It was Max's turn to laugh. 'Come on. You are useless. At least you've got your glasses on and can see your way.'

'Shut up and show me!'

*

'Emily! Really, can't I even trust you to be awake for your first couture shoot. Please!'

'Nina . . . I'm sorry. I didn't hear the alarm.'

'No, well you wouldn't, would you, with your head hidden somewhere in your boyfriend's armpit.'

Nick blushed. 'Nina, it was my fault . . .'

'Oh, be quiet. I couldn't care less whose fault it was but you'd better get going, Emily. We start shooting in less than an hour and Saul Smytheson's running round the courtyard wearing most of the jewellery you were so worried about guarding, and none of the dresses are steamed yet.'

'Oh, shit.' Emily threw on her clothes during this exchange, poured half the contents of a bottle of Evian over her head in order to calm her sticking-up hair and hurried into the courtyard, forgetting her sunglasses and being blinded by the early-morning light in the process.

'Come on, Emily, get a grip! Look, the coffee's over there. Go and get a cup and then you can steam the black Chanel and the red Lacroix.' Nina softened. 'And don't worry too much about the jewellery. I've got a surprise that we're going to use.'

Nina headed off to the room set aside for hair and make-up. Emily looked at Nick despairingly.

'Why is it I can never get anything right in this job?'

Nick smiled at her. 'If I understood any of what went on I'd probably be able to help. But as I don't, let's get coffee and then you can show me how to steam a dress.'

Pandora sat sulking, having make-up applied in great swathes. There was no one there for her to talk to and

Angelo, the stupid make-up person, didn't seem to understand that her skin was much too perfect and didn't need any of this stuff. Her whole look would be ruined. And where on earth was Morgan? It was bad enough that Nina wanted them to share the cover, but for the girl not to even bother turning up . . . It really wasn't good enough. She smiled with relief as Rory put his head around the door.

'Are you decent, darling?'

'Oh, please, Rory. Since when have I been coy with you?'

'Are you . . . are you all right?'

'Fine. Take that hangdog look off your face. I'm fine. Nobody's hurt. Except maybe Andreï, and frankly, he deserves it. Were you worried?'

'I could hardly sleep.'

'So how many lovers did you take to while away the midnight hours?'

'Pandora, not in front of the help!' Angelo sniffed. Rory perched on the edge of the make-up table and looked at Pandora. 'Well, apart from the fact that this man is putting so much make-up on you you'll resemble Gloria Wharton, you could look worse.' He pushed Angelo out of the way. 'Stop it, stop it now. These girls have perfect skins – we want to show them off, don't we, darling? Everyone knows that our lovely Angelo can do great art, but we don't have to do it today, and not on our precious Pandora. Here.' He grabbed a handful of cotton wool, and dipping it in cream began to take everything off, ready to start again. 'Honestly, you should know better,

Angelo. And with this light too.' He raised his eyes to heaven and Pandora beamed at him. At last, things were getting back to normal.

'Pandora,' Rory gently wiped around her eyes, 'I'm sorry about all this. I know I should have told you. Your mother didn't want you to know.'

'It's OK. I spent all my life thinking up impossibly glamorous heroes to be my father, and it turns out I have this total shit. But I won't tell anyone if you won't. Let's keep up the pretence that we don't know who he is. It'll be much more fun, won't it?'

'And he'll hate it! I shouldn't think anyone's ignored him before in his life. He won't know what to do with himself.' Rory laughed and kissed Pandora's raven head. 'Pandora, I love you. Let's pretend it never happened and we don't know him and we can blank him and his horrid other progeny every time we see them. But first we have to make you so beautiful that your career is no longer ruined and you'll be able to make enough money to keep me once Don's fired me for being rude to him once too often.'

Pandora grinned. 'Deal.'

Morgan arrived, looking sheepish.

'Hi. What do I do now?'

"Darling, you learn never to be late again and sit down and let this charming man play with your hair for a while. Gavin, this is Morgan, Morgan, this is Gavin, and these are his assistants, Jurgen and Jurgen.'

'Hi.'

'You're not going to fight this then?' Pandora raised a quizzical eyebrow. Morgan was much too relaxed.

'Can't be bothered. In for a penny, in for a pound. I may as well just let you all do whatever you like.'

'My, we are relaxed. Any particular reason?'

'Not really.'

Puzzled, Pandora let Angelo start again with her face, a dusting of pale power, a beauty spot to cover the tiny blemish on her chin, dark-red lip-liner and slightly paler lipstick, rich and shiny, and finally liquid eyeliner, black, over her heavy lids, and mascara put on in so many layers that eyelashes she knew to be over a centimetre long grew to at least a centimetre and a half. Pandora was almost in heaven.

But Morgan was just too quiet and Pandora certainly wasn't going to let that lie.

'Sleep well, darling?'

'Not at all.'

'But everyone's all right?'

'Seems so.'

'Especially you, Morgan. You look lit up from the inside.' Rory was hovering like a bee round a honey pot, his eyes glued to the oil which was being used to calm the ends of Morgan's fabulous hair. 'Nina, look at these girls. These will be the photographs of the century.'

Nina gazed at Pandora and Morgan with pride. They were easily as beautiful as any of the top models. 'I know. They are lovely.' But Nina didn't have time to chat. 'Hurry, will you? I want to get the first shot done before this dawn light goes. The dresses are coming. I've finally persuaded Emily to do a little work. Pandora, you will wear the red Lacroix and Morgan, you're in the black Chanel, OK?'

'But I wanted to wear the black, Nina.'

'Don't sound like the spoilt child you are, Pandora, and let the professionals choose. Rory, will you make sure they do what they're supposed to?'

'Of course, my precious. Oh, lay off that oil, man! We don't want her to look as if she's just got out from under the shower, do we?'

Morgan giggled. This was more fun than she's thought it would be.

'What's the joke?' After her coffee Emily was all business, even down to the fact that she'd put on work clothes for the occasion, a black linen A-line wraparound skirt and a Petit Bateau T-shirt which said three to four years on the label. Her hair was gelled away from her face and she was carrying a file. Nick followed her, pulling a clothes rail on which were hung the two dresses they would photograph first. Nobody answered Emily's question.

'Well, whatever it is, hurry up. Nina's getting ants in her pants about the light. Nick, go and do something else. It's going to get indecent in here.'

'Really? Do I have to go?'

'Get out of here,' the three girls shouted in unison.

'All right, all right. I'm off. I'll go and stand with the extras somewhere.'

'Come on. Let's go.' Emily was getting frantic.

'Blimey, Morgan, this one's got the makings of a real fashion editor in her. She's shouting at us already.' Pandora laughed.

'I'm just trying to keep my job.'

'Give us three minutes.' Morgan jumped up, leaving

Gavin Cheveux in mid-tuck of a ringlet, and dragged off her grotty old T-shirt and shorts, almost ruining her hair in the process. The Jurgens screamed, Gavin covered his face in despair and groaned. What had happened to the professional girls they were used to? Morgan had no underwear on, but nobody cared. The only men in the room had never been interested in girls. She dived towards the Chanel dress, but stopped short once she'd got it off the hanger. 'How the hell do I get this on without treading on it? Which side's the front? Come on, Em. Surely it's your job to help here?'

Emily dropped the file and went to help. She couldn't tell one end of the dress from the other either. Pandora joined them.

'Well, I can tell that neither of you has ever played with this kind of dress before.' Expertly she plunged her hands into the garment, undid two buttons, held out the dress as one might a bath towel and turned to Morgan. 'Arms up, please, and step forward. It has to be wrapped round you.'

'Only if everyone promises not to take any pictures until it's on.'

'Come on, Morgan. Stop pissing around. And stop laughing. You'll ruin your make-up.'

The dress was on. A sheath of black cut velvet woven so that the pattern of Chanel camellias in the mousseline grew into a train ten feet long. Two buttons held the whole thing together at the lowest decent point of Morgan's back. It fitted like a glove. Holding on to Emily for balance, Morgan added the black satin Manolo Blahnick sandals which had been provided to go with the dress. She turned to look in the mirror and found someone she'd never seen before looking back at her. Trying not to look too shocked, and not giving herself time to worry about it, she helped Pandora into the floor-length deep-red Lacroix satin ball gown. She had to admit, the duchess satin was like woven sex, it was so beautiful. Shoes on for Pandora, and final powering finished, the girls headed out into the morning light.

The drawing room end of the courtyard had been set up like a latter-day viceroy's throne room. On one side of the shot was the grand piano, and on the other, two Moroccan page boys in starched white robes, red silk sashes and fezzes. In the centre were the thrones, covered in gold velvet. Little gold footstools were ready for the models' feet. The whole scene was shaded by huge potted palms.

Nina hurried forward.

'Sam, where are you?'

'Here. I'm here.'

'And where are the jewels?'

'I've got them. I haven't let them out of my sight since you gave them to me.' He looked at the two beauties before him. 'Wow. Why do we have to ruin this with jewels?'

'Because they'll sparkle and reflect the light.'

'Nothing to do with advertising?'

'Oh, Sam, not now. Now, this one's for you, Morgan.' Nina took from one box a heavy ruby necklace that she tied round Morgan's neck with the dark-red velvet ribbon provided. There was a matching bracelet and huge ruby earrings. Morgan stood stock-still. She didn't dare move in case one of these priceless objects fell off. For Pandora there were diamonds, a necklace set with black pearls and a bracelet and earrings to match. Morgan couldn't decide which was more breathtaking, the jewels the dresses or the setting! She allowed herself to be put on one of the thrones. Pandora, glittering like the queen she'd always fancied herself to be, settled into the other one and out of habit kicked her shoes off and drew her legs up under her. She leant towards Morgan.

'Isn't this a riot?'

'What do we do now?'

'Giggle and gossip and they take photographs until they're bored.'

'Don't we have to pose and sit terribly still?'

'We're not working with Irving Penn. This is Saul Smytheson – sort of joke fashion photography. We can do anything we like. He just snaps the best bits.'

'Thank God for that.' Morgan wanted to draw her legs up and curl them under her too, but the dress was too tight around her hips. She leant back and crossed her legs, gently feeling the egg-sized stones around her throat. She couldn't help laughing. 'I wish my mother was here. She'd have heart failure.'

'She'll probably make you change your name. If anyone finds out you're her daughter, she'll lose all credibility as a feminist.'

'I know, isn't it awful?'

'No. Your mother's never understood the purpose of these magazines. She takes them much too seriously.

Think of yourself as a tonic, a little bit of feel-good factor for the general public. I mean, not only are you setting yourself up as a doll for men to drool over, but you're wearing clothes that only about two thousand women in the world can afford. No one's seriously suggesting that your average Marks and Spencer shopper should try to look like us, or save up to buy these dresses. We're just what people's dreams are made of, that's all, not real life.'

'Precisely. And anyway, my figure was always like this, even before I put the dress on. I can't help it if the dress looks fabulous, can I?'

'Darling, you sound just like me!'

'I've always wanted to be what dreams are made of.'

'Well then, this is your lucky day. And if you like, you can go and be an economics professor afterwards. Then you can have the best of both worlds.'

'Thanks for the advice. I'll remember it.'

The camera shutter whirred. Saul was almost orgasmic with excitement. He hadn't even had to tell the girls what to do and he was getting the shots of the century. Not only were the clothes perfect, but the girls were relaxed, fabulous; if it wasn't for Bobby, he might even have attempted a little experimenting with the opposite sex. Even the stuck-up redhead who he'd been so worried about was doing her stuff like a hardened professional. Something had happened to her, he didn't care what, but it was perfect for his pictures.

Needlessly Nina called out, 'Relax, girls. We're changing to black and white.'

Gavin dived forward with a huge can of hairspray,

poking and prodding the hairdos with the long pointed handle of a tortoiseshell comb. Angelo bustled about applying a new dusting of powder. The heat of the day wasn't far off and it wouldn't do for either of these beauties to glisten in the wrong places. The Jurgens panted in the shadows, wondering if they would ever see anything quite like this again. Rory, already suffering from the heat, wiped his forehead with a lace-edged handkerchief. The black and white film was in.

'We're going again, girls,' shouted Saul from behind his camera. 'Pandora, can you stand up and lean over the back of the chair and talk to Morgan?' Pandora obeyed. 'Come on, darling, you can give us more than that.' Pandora laughed and pulled the corset of her dress down, pushing her not inconsiderable breasts out as far as they would decently go before leaning down and kissing Morgan's forehead.

Max came out of a side door, still dirty in jeans and a T-shirt. He didn't see the shoot was in full swing and headed towards the girls. Laughing, he got down on one knee and kissed Morgan's hand. She looked at the camera through lashes only marginally shorter than Pandora's and raised one eyebrow a quarter of an inch.

'Hello, princess,' Max said.

'Magic,' said Saul.

Andreï was watching too, gauze covering the gash on his forehead. He was drinking tea. Beta-blockers had glazed his panic of the night before and Max had come up trumps. As a Fyodov should, Max had disposed of onlookers and dealt with a crisis with discretion and efficiency.

Andreï watched his son kiss Morgan's hand and silently wished him luck. If he wanted Morgan, he would have her. The fact that Anna had turned Andreï down was no reason to deny his son the pleasure of the daughter. And she was beautiful, there was no denying it. Andreï felt rather than saw Sam come and stand beside him. He smiled at his old friend and pointed at the girls.

'Sheer perfection. My daughter and yours. I suppose you always knew about her?'

'Fraid so.'

'I'll kill you later, then, for not telling me.'

'Can't we all bury the hatchet? They don't need any more hassle, do they?'

'The children?'

'Hm, and they'll make lovely pictures for on top of your piano over there.'

Nina joined them and took a hand of each of her old friends.

'More than that, this is the saving of my career! Gloria, eat your heart out. The boiler room of HMS *Belfast* won't be a patch on this!' She grinned at the two men. Andreï looked at her with affection, and then noticed Sam's expression. Well, thought Andreï, at last!

Then, with sudden violence, the quiet concentration of the shoot was ruined. Rory, with a roar which would have filled any self-respecting fashion house, caught sight of Andreï, grabbed the poker from the fireplace and launched himself towards his old enemy.

'On guard, you bastard!'

Epilogue

MONDAY 31 July, Emily Carlton-Jones, assistant to Nina Charles, editor-in-chief of the biggest fashion magazine in the UK, has a diary that looks like this:

MONDAY 31 JULY

Start getting ready for the ready-to-wear collections – NIGHTMARE

Ask Nina if you can have some holiday – some hope

9 a.m.	Rory and Nina hair and make-up at Nina's house
12.00	Budget meeting – Nina and publisher
1 p.m.	Lunch, Pandora – me – ask Nina if you can go
3 p.m.	Get Frenchy in from Models One and show her the pics of Morgan. Nina wants her to get an agent. It's all right for some.

NickNickNickNickNickNickNickNickNickNickNickNick

*